CHASING VIVI

A. M. HARGROVE

Cover by Sara Eirew
Photography by Wander Aguiar
Model: Andrew Biernat
Editing provided by Emily Lawrence

DEDICATION

This book is dedicated to anyone who was bullied and to those to weren't afraid to stand up for themselves, even when they had to step out of their comfort zones to do it.

"Love all, trust a few, do wrong to none."

—William Shakespeare

ACKNOWLEDGMENTS

First and foremost, thank you to my readers who continue to support and take a chance on me. Without you, I would never be creating these novels from all the ideas that keep popping into my head. I realize you have hundreds of books to choose from and I'm honored you choose mine to read. I appreciate it much more than I can say.

Thank you, Nina Grinstead, at Social Butterfly for all your hard work and planning, the phone calls, messages, emails, texts, and everything else you do. I'm amazed at your effort you put in and I'd be lost without you. I FLOVE you!!! Also thank you Jenn, Sarah, Candi, Shannon, and Chanpreet. You guys totally rock and I love you!

Terri E. Laine—it goes without saying that no book is any book without you. You are my bestie and writing parter, solo or otherwise. Thanks for listening to my rants and raves. You are the BEST!

Thank you Wander and Andrey for coming to my rescue and pulling Andrew in for a photo shoot. And thank you Andrew for looking so damn good. You all are awesome and I love working with you.

Thank you Sara for your patience—God knows you deserve it. Now that we've established Annie does not like green, we shall move forward. LOL. Hugs and kisses to you.

Thank you to my super awesome beta readers—Kat Grimes, Kristie Wittenberg, Heather Carver, and Andrea Stafford. I know you all always have my back, even when I hit you up at the eleventh hour. I have no fucking idea what I'd do without you. You make my books work and find things a damn detective can't. I love you all to Mars and back.

Thank you Emily Lawrence for making this MS super spiffy. You do have some keen eagle eyes, my friend.

And thanks to Rick and Amy Miles at Red Coat for all their hard work and effort. You guys are amazing.

Hargrove's Hangout peeps, thanks for hangin with me. I love chatting with you all. Let's keep up the hot pics and laughs.

If you want to join in on the fun, click here to join.

To keep up to date with the latest from me, sign up for my newsletter here.

OTHER BOOKS BY A.M. HARGROVE

For Other Books by A.M. Hargrove visit www.amhargrove.com

For The Love of English
A Special Obsession
Chasing Vivi
Craving Midnight (November 2017)
For The Love of My Sexy Geek (A Vault Novella
—October 2017)

The Wilde Players Dirty Romance Series:
Sidelined
Fastball
Hooked

A Beautiful Sin

The Cruel and Beautiful Series:
Cruel and Beautiful
A Mess of a Man
One Wrong Choice

The Edge Series:
Edge of Disaster
Shattered Edge
Kissing Fire

The Tragic Series:
Tragically Flawed, Tragic 1
Tragic Desires, Tragic 2

The Hart Brothers Series:
Freeing Her, Book 1
Freeing Him, Book 2
Kestrel, Book 3
The Fall and Rise of Kade Hart

Sabin, A Seven Novel

The Guardians of Vesturon Series

PLAYLIST

Lost In You … Bush
Let's Work It Out … Texas
Hoping … X Ambassadors
Incomplete … James Bay
Wildfire … Seafret
Raw Diamond Ring … Matthew Mayfield
Mess Is Mine … Vance Joy
So Tied Up … Cold War Kids
Bitter Poem … Cold War Kids
Something Just Like This … The Chainsmokers
Goner … Twenty One Pilots
Swallowed Whole … Pearl Jam
Halo … Beyonce
7 Years … Lukas Graham
Unconditionally … The George Twins
Roller Coaster … Bon Jovi
Say You Won't Let Go … James Arthur
I Need My Girl … The National

CHAPTER 1

VIVIENNE

Even though it's only October, the frigid New York air razors straight through my coat, chilling me down to the marrow. No matter how many layers I add, it never keeps the wind and dampness at bay. I'm already sick of this weather and winter hasn't even hit yet. Why the hell did I decide to make a new life here? Why not Texas or South Carolina? Or anywhere with year-round warmth? I walk the rest of the way to work, huddled deep into my coat.

And speaking of work, my job sucks. My boss is a deceitful bastard. When I interviewed for the position, he made it sound as though I'd be in charge of IT and the business was on the cusp of exploding. I foolishly believed him. My lack of research into Java Beans & More, which is nothing more than a glorified coffee house, should've had me tying up my running shoes and hightailing it out faster than a space shuttle at launch, but every ounce of energy had evaporated from me after Mom's death. Cleaning out the house, putting it up for sale, and taking that huge loss, had zapped me. That and the mountain of debt I was currently facing, which was why I snapped up this job, thinking it was a great opportunity.

Breaking away from Virginia, getting a fresh start, and making a new name for myself initially had me pretty damn excited about moving to the Big Apple. It hadn't mattered then that I'd be living in a space not much larger than a closet, cooking on a portable countertop burner and microwave, and using a space heater to keep warm, because my fucking landlord would turn out to be a crook. I also hadn't cared much that there were sketchy people hanging out in the building and on the stairways at all times of day and night, making drug deals or prostituting themselves. Okay, maybe I did care a little. Make that a lot. But I'd hurry past them, telling myself it was fine. Thankfully, they didn't bother me much after I made it plain I wanted nothing to do with them. Now, I wanted to beat myself over the head. I should've been more diligent when the offer came through, instead of leaping at it like a yapping puppy in search of attention.

The bell rings as I push the door open. Vince's cheerful greeting has me waving back, even though I'm still shivering and hunkered down in my jacket.

"You in there, Vivi?" I hear him laughing from behind the counter.

"Y-yeah." My teeth chatter from the cold.

"You need a warmer coat. Like one of those Canada goose coats."

"Ha-ha, aren't y-you th-the f-funny one? Th-they o-only c-cost a w-week's s-salary."

"Not quite, but close. Maybe you need some fat on your bones. That'd warm you up."

If only he knew. I'd spent most of my life trying to get rid of extra fat. Of expunging those nasty *ViviVoom* comments in my head from Crestview Academy. Girls are so fucking mean. No wonder it was always difficult for me to develop deep friendships. Trust didn't come easy because of what I'd been through. Being called "ViviVoom" for six years of my life was the least of it.

"Nah, I just need thicker blood," I call out to Vince.

Rubbing my hands together, I hug myself for a few minutes, trying to warm up. Then I unwrap the scarf from around my neck and face, but refuse to take my coat off. "Was the early morning busy?"

Vince, who is tall and lean with sandy brown hair and hazel eyes, glances at the coffee cup clock on the wall. "Uh-huh. We're in the lull now. But it'll perk back up in about ten minutes or so."

"Good. I'll get to work then."

I'm upgrading the software in all eight shops and integrating everything into one system. Whoever originally set them up was an idiot. Each shop had its own package and nothing synced. It was a nightmare. I designed a new program for the company and am now in the implementation stage. I get seated at the other computer stationed at the counter.

This is a far cry from my days in the Silicon Valley when I worked my dream job. And this was supposed to be its replacement. What a joke. Then I think about Mom and how I spent her final years taking care of her. Yeah, I gave up my career, but I wouldn't have traded that time with her for anything in the world. When her diagnosis of ALS came, it mowed me down like a tank, exactly like Dad's death in the car accident did when I was twelve. After she died, I sold everything and decided to start over. Make a clean slate. That's how I ended up in New York. I'm still facing a mountain of debt, and this job was supposed to be a stepping stone to get rid of it, but I can see now it's not working out that way.

"How do you like working for Joe?" Vince asks out of the blue, breaking the silence.

I hedge, answering, "Why do you want to know?" I can't tell him the truth. Joe is a fucking lying pervert asshole.

"Just wondering. You seem to have your shit together. I'd think someone of your caliber would be working for a bigger company."

Me too, I want to say. But I never talk about my personal life with anyone. Even though Vince is a nice guy, he's young, only twenty-three, and I don't trust him. I remember when I was his age, only a few years ago, but it seems a lifetime ago. He might get drunk and run his mouth to his buddies about how I thought our boss was a dickface. And there's no way I'm going to dump my shitload of issues on his shoulders either.

"Thanks. I do have my shit together. This job presents a challenge, which is why I'm here." It's a bullshit answer, but I go back to working, hoping it suffices. I'm busy, my nose buried in the screen, keyboarding away, when the bell rings at least a dozen times, but I ignore it.

Vince interrupts me, asking if he can log on. Without breaking concentration, I tell him to go ahead and keep working. I'm on the back end of the program, so it won't affect anything he's doing.

Reaching over with my left hand to grab my coffee, I accidentally knock my cup over, creating an epic mess. I scramble to clean it up. When I finally glance up in search of more napkins to mop up the spill, I'm staring into the most gorgeous set of golden eyes, the exact ones I'd always dreamed about, the ones that made me do things at Crestview I told myself I didn't agree with.

Standing before me is Prescott Beckham—the boy of my teenaged fantasies. He sat next to me in a lot of classes. We ended up as lab partners in chemistry and that was when he proposed the deal. Could I please, oh please, with hot fudge on top help him out with his homework? At first, I didn't respond, but then he said he'd pay me. That grabbed my attention. I was desperate, broke, and didn't have an extra penny to spend.

"I know you don't have any cash. I've watched you at lunch. You eat cheap junk. Not even high dollar stuff. You like Oreos, but you eat those shitty fake kind. I'll pay you. I have a lot of money, Vivi. Please?"

And those damn eyes. Oh, God, his gold-hued irises nearly buckled my knees. I caved and said I'd do it. But I made it clear it was only for the money, not because he'd asked nicely or I agreed with it. The truth was, the money was great, but I would've done it for free. He was that kind of guy—so persuasive, so difficult to say no to, so everything. Not to mention I was secretly in love with him.

I often dreamed about how one day he'd announce to the world that he didn't mind that I was fat and unpopular, that he'd fallen for me anyway—me, in my too-tight skirt wrapped around my pudgy thighs, which certainly rubbed together. Why? Why did I torture myself like that? Why did I let myself believe a guy like him could fall for a girl like me?

Now, here he is in the flesh, all six plus feet of tall, dark, and insanely sexy. And it pisses me off that someone can look so damn edible. Dressed to kill, he's wearing a lovely black coat, which I'm sure is toasty warm and probably cashmere. Peeking from beneath it is a crisp white shirt and striped blue tie. He's come a long way from his Crestview uniform.

"Vivi? Vivienne Renard?" He squints. It's the same face he sees but definitely not close to the same body. This is a common reaction with people I run into who only knew me in my school days. I'm sure he still pictures me in that old pleated skirt where I looked like I swallowed a gigantic balloon. I hated those awful uniforms.

My face remains impassive, or I hope it does, as I answer. "Um, yes?"

Maybe if I pretend not to remember him, he'll go away.

"It's me, Vivi. Prescott. Prescott Beckham. From Crestview."

Dammit. Well, it was worth a try.

"Oh, right! Hi! How are you?"

"Fine, but wow. You look … amazing."

And then I really study him for the first time. He doesn't look so good. Okay, that's not quite true. He's gorgeous. He just doesn't look *as* good as he used to. He looks … rough. That's it. Prescott, who was always perfectly put together, is rough and edgy. The years seem to have taken a bit of a toll on him.

"Thanks." I jerk my gaze away from him, because suddenly

I'm uncomfortable. I don't want to talk about anything to do with my personal life and I have a feeling that's what's coming.

"So, you work here?"

"I do."

"Hmm. I'm surprised I haven't run into you then. I'm in here every so often."

"I guess our timing was off," I say. Damn, I wonder how many times he actually comes in here. It's a good thing I'll be rotating to another coffee shop.

"You live here now, too?" he asks.

"It would seem so."

"How about we go out for a drink some night?" He scrapes his hand over his face, which is covered in sexy scruff.

Absolutely not.

"Thanks for the invite, but I don't think so."

He takes a step back, as though I've physically pushed him. My guess is a man like Prescott doesn't get turned down much. Then I wonder if he's still in touch with Felicia Cunningham, a.k.a. Felatio Cuntingham. That girl had more dicks crammed down her throat than even I care to imagine and she made it her mission to make my life miserable. She was the one who coined the term ViviVoom.

"Then how about dinner?"

So, he's still persistent, a trait I recall from our Crestview days.

"No, but I totally appreciate the offer."

Those damn bourbon-hued irises latch onto mine, and my breath hitches, causing me to almost, almost give in. Shaking my head instead, I confirm what he heard, "Honestly, I can't, Prescott."

He opens his mouth, his very sensuous mouth, to speak, then stops, nods once, and says, "I get it. You still think I'm the asshole from Crestview. I'll probably always be that guy to you. But maybe you should go out with me and find out if I really am." He pulls out his wallet and hands me a card. "If you change your mind, I live here in the city."

I say nothing in response. I don't think I could if I tried.

Then Prescott greets Vince and orders a double shot of something or other. Vince fixes his coffee and after Prescott leaves, Vince wants to know the deal.

"The deal?"

"Yeah, how do you know *The* Prescott Beckham, one of the wealthiest dudes in Manhattan?"

Interesting. I knew he had money, but not that kind.

Waving my hand, I say, "Oh, that. We went to high school together."

"And you turned him down for a date? What the hell is wrong with you, Vivi?"

"I don't want to date a guy from high school, Vince, not that it's any of your business."

He stares at me like I'm loony. "But, he wants you. And he's Prescott Beckham."

"I don't give a rat's ass. Now, I have work to do." When I go back to what I was doing before the beautiful Prescott interrupted me, my brain fires in all the wrong directions. It won't process what I need it to do. I'm not sure how many times I almost throw the stupid keyboard across the counter. And then, to add icing on the cake, my asshole boss, Joe, calls and wants to go to lunch. He says he needs to discuss my progress on the upgrade, but that's a lie. There's only one thing he's interested in and it's not going to happen.

"What time?"

"I'll meet you at Nikki's around noon." Nikki's is where he always wants to meet. I don't know why I ask anymore. It's where he conducted our first interview and he told me then it's his favorite place to eat.

That gives me at least a couple of hours to complete what I'm doing and mentally prepare for his attack. Still, the time flies.

When I arrive at lunch, he's seated at his favorite table. I stiffen my spine and put on my boxing gloves. Only how can you ever be truly ready to fend off a barrage of sexual advances by your disgusting boss whom you've already told in no uncertain terms N-O?

The waitress takes our order and he's well-behaved, asking general questions until our food arrives. It's while we're eating that he goes on the offensive and tells me he's prepared to give me a salary increase if I'm willing to do him certain *favors* in return. I know exactly the kind of favors he's referring to. Joe has been less than discreet about their specificity in the past.

"Um, Joe, I thought we discussed this already."

"Yeah, but I've sweetened the pot, Vivienne. I was sure you'd leap at the chance."

Who is he kidding? I would leap off the Brooklyn Bridge before I'd leap into bed with him. "No, I haven't changed my mind and I never will."

His fork becomes a pointer as he aims it at me. "You know, you really ought to consider this. Didn't you tell me during your interview process that you needed this position? That your mother's death had left you in quite a financial bind?"

My jaw falls open. I hadn't expected him to play this dirty. "Y-yes, I did." I lick my lips that have suddenly turned bone dry. My brain scrambles for something to grab onto, any remote thing I can use against him.

"Then, Vivi, I'd think very carefully about your response to me. You see, I'm being quite generous by offering you a raise after such a short time of employment. And you turning down my kind offer is what I'd consider a slap in the face. And slapping your boss in the face could cost you your job. Do you truly want to risk that?"

I could sue his ass if I had the money. My hands fist and I want to punch something, preferably Joe's face. Instead, I shove one into the pocket of my coat, which I never took off, being constantly cold in the city. That's when my fingers brush over it.

The card Prescott passed to me in the coffee shop. And that's when the idea comes to me.

Do I dare?

It could come back to haunt me, but at this point I can't afford to lose my job until I can find another one, and over my dead body am I being blackmailed into sleeping with my boss.

"Joe, do you know who Prescott Beckham is?"

He shrugs a shoulder. "Well, yeah." His expression conveys that I'm a dumbass for asking. "Who doesn't? He's one of the richest guys in New York. Well, probably the country. What does that have to do with anything?"

I lean an elbow on the table and grab a chunk of hair. Twirling it, I say, "He was in the coffee shop this morning. He comes in a lot. Did you know that?"

Joe sits up in his chair. "No shit. Like how much?"

Dropping my hair, I wave my hand. "Eh, it doesn't matter. What does is that Prescott is a very close friend of mine."

He leans back and now he thinks I'm off my rocker. "Yeah, right, Vivi."

"Don't believe me. I honestly don't care. But he is. We went to high school together. Crestview Academy in Virginia. I can call him right now, to prove my point. But whatever."

"So?"

I scoot in a little closer. "So this. What you're doing to me is considered sexual harassment in the workplace, and I'm sure if I called Prescott right now, he could get me one of his high-powered attorney buddies and sue your ass for everything it's worth. So, Joe, I'll happily accept your raise with no strings attached, of course." I wink at him, adding, "Because you know, that little addition of demanding sexual favors is illegal as shit."

And then I pull Prescott's card out and lay it on the table, watching his eyes saucer.

"Any questions?"

CHAPTER 2

PRESCOTT

VIVIENNE RENARD. OF ALL THE PEOPLE TO RUN INTO THIS morning, I never expected her to be one of them. And damn if she wasn't a sight for sore eyes. Hungover ones, too. Talk about changing from an ugly duckling into a blazing smoke show. Jesus, I can't believe how hot she is. There's not a single thing about her that isn't fucking perfection. But it's that mouth of hers that nearly set me off. All I could think of was how it would feel wrapped tightly around my dick, sucking me until ... It's a good thing I was wearing a coat to hide the boner she gave me. But damn if she didn't turn me down for a date. Fuck that. No one ever does that. Game on. She's just made it my mission to change her mind. It's what I'm good at—getting women to do what I want. Besides, I can't get that image of her mouth on me out of my head. Even though her memories of me probably aren't the best, she did make a little bank off me back in the day. Poor girl ran all over the place doing my homework. If it hadn't been for her, I never would've graduated from Crestview. Too bad she hadn't gone to the same college as me. I probably wouldn't have dropped out. It's not like I needed a degree, though. Family money gets you everywhere, as I like to say.

My coffee cup's empty by the time I make it to Whitworth Enterprises. The high-rise looms before me. Dad keeps trying to find ways to cut me out, but it ain't gonna happen ... ever.

I pass the lobby security, giving the guys a wave as they greet me by name and step on the open elevator, reserved for the top floor only. When it reaches the destination, the doors softly whoosh open, and I exit to see Cheryl's smiling face.

"Good morning, Mr. Beckham."

"Morning, Cheryl." I give her my famous, megawatt grin. She's cute and I'd normally fuck someone like her, but I never mix business with pussy. That's one rule I've never broken and I don't ever plan to. I can do some pretty shitty things at times, but that's a line I'll never cross. Suddenly, Vivi's mouth pops into my head again and I have to think of something else. I don't want another boner as I just got my dick to calm down as it is. Then, as I close in on the executive offices, the atmosphere thickens. My skin crawls. All thoughts of Vivi vanish as I arrive at my own expansive haven. My admin sits like a bear directly outside the door.

"Lynn, how are you today?"

"Mr. Beckham, I'm well, and you?" She scrutinizes me and immediately notices I'm hungover. She reaches in her drawer and tosses me a bottle of water. "Do you require any ibuprofen this morning?"

"Three would be nice, along with a bagel, toasted with butter, please. And eggs. I'm hungry."

"Yes, sir. I'll get that right over to you. Your favorite place?"

"Please. You're an angel. Oh, and is my father in?"

"Not yet, sir, but your grandfather is."

"Great. Thanks." I keep moving into my office and collapse into the chair. The computer comes on at the touch of the mouse and I scan all my investments. Before I'm done, Lynn shows up with breakfast, along with more coffee and water.

God, I love this woman. She's the closest thing to a mother

I've ever had, besides my grandparents. "Have I told you I love you lately, Lynn?"

"No, but I love you, too. Also, you look like shit, again. Prescott, you have got to get a hold of yourself."

Behind closed doors, we're on a first name basis, but around everyone else, she refuses to call me anything but Mr. Beckham even though she's in her fifties.

"I know. I'm a fucking mess."

"Why do you let him get to you like this? You're so much better than he is."

I rub a hand over my face and my scruff feels and sounds exactly like sandpaper. Glancing out the window, I can't even appreciate the magnificent view.

"I just do." The words come out with a groan. "He keeps making those humiliating scenes in public and I look like an idiot because of him."

"No, *he* looks like the idiot. But you're a grown man who's acting like a child. Take it like a man, pull up your fucking tighty-whities, and move on."

"Lynn, you sound like my grandfather—and I don't wear tighty-whities. I don't wear any—"

"More than I need to know. TMI, thank you very much. If not tighty-whities then undies. Your grandfather's right. Listen to him."

"What kind of grown man wears undies?" I mumble.

"Maybe you need to start or at least pull the ones up that are binding your ankles."

I let out an aggravated growl. "It just sucks that he wants me out of here."

She rests a hand on her wide hip. "Have you looked at the name on this building? It's your middle name. If anyone doesn't need to be here, it's your father, not you, you big moron." With a huge huff and some mumbling under her breath, she marches out. When she gets to the door, she looks over her shoulder and says, "You need to brush your teeth again, because you smell like bourbon. And use some mouthwash."

Every time I think back to the first time my father's fucking wife made a pass at me I want to put my fist through the wall. It was back when I was still in college. And stupid, naïve me thought it was a joke. Only she got really nasty, because I didn't take her seriously. Paybacks are hell and last Christmas she finally made her play. Smack in the middle of Christmas dinner, she told Dad that *I* was the one who made the pass and she had to fend *me* off. As if. The fucking cunt.

We were all seated at dinner, ready to dig into our traditional meal. My grandparents were there, along with my cousin and her husband. My step-cunt clinked her glass with a fork and I thought she was going to raise it for a lovely toast, as if she'd ever do something as tasteful as that. But no, she grinned evilly at me and said how wonderful it was that we were all together because she wanted to share some news. At first I thought maybe she was pregnant. Then I wondered whose it was. *The pool guy in West Palm?* I'd seen her with him a time or twelve. But silly me, I was completely off base. Instead, she announced to the family that I had done something so awful, so heinous she couldn't bear to hold it inside anymore. With a shudder of fake emotions, she told the entire family that I had attempted—to her utter horror, of course—to fondle and kiss her several times last summer and again at Thanksgiving. Then it happened. I laughed. Red wine shot out of my mouth as I threw back my head and roared a deep belly laugh. Who in their right mind would believe that I'd chase after that plastic-surgeried up bitch, when I had the cream of the pussy crop at my disposal?

Except the joke was on me, seeing as I was the only one laughing. Dad's face was as red as the cranberry sauce on the table, and my grandparents looked as though they were going to kill her. They hate her as much as I do. And the step-cunt? She sat there acting like a queen.

Then Dad said, "Get out of here."

"Dad, you can't possibly believe —"

He stood up, pointed to the door, and repeated, "I said, get out of my house."

"Fine. I'll leave." Before I left, I turned to the lying cunt and said, "You think you may have won, but you haven't. Just remember, karma is a bitch."

Then as I was heading for the door, I heard my grandfather say, "If he goes, so do we. And you may have forgotten something. The Whitworth name is what made you, Jeff. As for you, I don't know what game you're playing at, but I would caution you. My daughter, with our advice, locked up her will as tight as a drum. My grandson's inheritance is unquestionably his, no matter how hard you try to change that."

I was waiting at the front door for them. My grandmother hugged me when she got there.

"Grand, I never touched her, I swear. I may not be the most stand-up guy when it comes to the opposite sex, but I'd *never* do that."

"Let's get out of here, Prescott. That woman is a viper." She took my large hand into her smaller one and we walked down the porch steps. My dad's house is out in Westchester County, and so is my grandparents'. "Come to our place. I think we have some hotdogs in the fridge." The three of us laughed.

However, it wasn't funny and it still isn't. Dad has yet to come around and nothing I say or do will change his mind. He believes that plumped-lipped wife of his. Now he keeps trying to make me look like a fool. Every opportunity he gets, he tries to belittle me in front of business associates or at public functions. It's getting old and grating.

The phone on my desk buzzes and jars me out of the contemplation.

"Beckham."

"Prescott, do you have a minute?"

"Hey, Granddad. I have hours for you."

His warm chuckle makes me smile. "I'll be down there in a few."

My grandfather is in his early seventies, but he acts like he's forty. I adore him. He's the one I look up to as a father, more so than my own. After I lost Mom, he stepped in because Dad was never around. And I didn't blame him for that. Dad was blown away by everything. So was Granddad, but he handled it a lot better. He took me under his wing and guided me. When Dad finally had his fill of that, because he resented the closeness between my grandparents and me, he sent me away to boarding school. That's when I met Harrison Kirkland. The two of us became fast friends and the best troublemakers Crestview Academy had ever seen. That is until Weston Wyndham showed up. It took a while—and some ass kicking—before he joined us and our duo turned into a trio, but we're family now. If not for my grandparents, Harrison's dad, and those two, I'm not sure where I'd be today.

Granddad pokes his head in the door and says, "Knock, knock."

"Get in here. Since when do you knock?"

"Since today. I want you to know that I've run over the final figures of franchising A Special Place. Scotty, I've run them up, down, backward, and sideways, and I believe it's a go. The contracts should be ready to go, as well, so you can call Weston with the news. You, Weston, and Special have a great opportunity here." Special is Weston's wife and the love of his life.

"You honestly think so?"

"No, I'm lying through my teeth." He taps me on the side of the head. "Of course I think so. I've had some of my best people look at it. It's excellent. Any venture capitalist would jump in on this with both feet."

"Carpe opportunitas."

"Yes! Now get the damn contracts signed so you can start seeing the money roll in." He sits on the side of my desk. His white hair gleams with a bluish tint in the morning sun. "I don't tell you this nearly enough, but your mother would be so damn proud of you." He gets up then. "Oh, and brush your teeth. You smell like bourbon." He leaves me with those words, and I wonder if Lynn told him I'm drinking too much. I go brush my teeth for the second time since coming to work.

Then I call Weston and tell him the news so we can get moving on finalizing the franchise. His parting words are, "I'll pass the news on to Special. She'll be happy because we thought it would take much longer. I know nothing of this stuff. You're the financier; I'm the architectural engineer. Do your magic and shoot the contracts over to me so my attorneys can check everything out."

I get that ball rolling as soon as I hang up. In the meantime, I devise a plan on how to get Vivi to go out with me. She's presented a challenge I can't seem to get off my mind.

It's five after twelve when I grab Lynn to take her to lunch. I let her choose the place and she picks Nikki's. It's close and the food is good, so we walk, though I initially object to that since it's so cold.

"You need the fresh air," she says.

"About that. Did you tell Granddad that I needed to brush my teeth?" I elbow her in the side.

"Absolutely not. The entire building is aware of it."

"That bad, huh?"

"Yeah. Sorry. Honestly, Prescott, if you were the average Joe, no woman would look twice at you."

No wonder Vivi didn't want to go out with me. I probably smell like I cohabitate with Jack Daniel's.

"Message received."

"I'm worried about you. Do you think …"

"What?"

She crams her hands in her pockets and says, "You know … that you may have a drinking problem."

My brows leap toward the sky. "No. Honestly, Lynn, I can stop anytime."

21

With a determined look, she says, "Prove it. Stop coming to work stinking like bourbon. If you don't, you're going to need rehab one day."

"I know. I promise to lay off. Here's the thing. I get to thinking about him and before I know it, I'm grabbing a drink."

"Well, grab something else because he's not worth your time. If you don't slow down, Prescott, I might consider resigning."

"What? You'd quit?"

"Yes, I would. I don't want to stand by and watch you ruin your life over some worthless piece of shit."

"So what you're saying is if I don't straighten up, you'll resign."

"Pretty much. I'll give you a pass here and there, but I'm tired of telling you to brush your teeth every morning. I'm not your mom and you're not five. It's pretty simple. Start behaving and you get to keep me as your admin."

I stop walking. "Oh, come on, Lynn. You can't possibly mean that. Where else can you work that would give you the salary, benefits, extra perks, and hours that you have with me? Besides, I spoil the shit out of you."

"True, but I cover for your drinking way too much lately, and I'm not willing to lie for you anymore." She grabs my arm and we walk again.

By now, we're almost at the restaurant and I have to give some thought to this. "Can we finish this inside?"

"Sure."

We walk through the door and a beautiful sight is moving toward us. It's Vivi, but she's with another man. As she closes in on us, the sun streams through the door, glinting off her honeyed hair. It takes all my self-restraint not to grab her, plow my hands into that damn hair of hers, and taste every bit of her plump mouth.

"Prescott," she calls out to my astonishment and satisfaction. After our earlier meeting, I wasn't sure she'd acknowledge me at all.

"Vivi, this is a nice surprise." I'm even more shocked when she grabs and hugs me. The scent of flowers invades my nostrils, and I don't want to stop inhaling. I return her embrace and am disappointed when it ends. Her reaction to me is a complete one-eighty from this morning, and I can't help but question it. But I'm not going to say something to screw it up either.

Then she introduces the guy she's with as her boss—some dude named Joe. He stumbles over himself to shake my hand like I'm some sort of celebrity. He's a goofy shit with wavy, greased-back hair and way too much cologne.

"Nice to meet you. This is my executive admin, Lynn Cochran. Lynn, this is Vivienne Renard. She and I went to Crestview Academy together. We're old friends."

"Ah, it's so great to meet you. You'll have to tell me some stories about him in his younger days," Lynn says.

"Oh, I'm not sure you want to know," Vivi says, winking.

"Now that's where you're wrong. I can imagine how he worked his way around the ladies."

"Let me say this. He had most of them wrapped around his homework binder, not to mention his letter jacket," Vivi says.

Interesting comment about the homework binder.

"All right, you two, stop telling stories about me. I'm standing right here."

They share a laugh and then Vivi says, "Well, we better be going. Back to work, you know. Don't want my boss to get the wrong impression." She lets out a squeaky laugh.

"Hey, Vivi, give me a call soon, will you?"

"Sure. Nice meeting you, Lynn."

But I get the impression she has no intention of ever calling.

Her boss, what's his name, nearly trips over his feet in his exuberance to say goodbye.

As we're being seated, Lynn says, "Wow. Were those the kind of girls you went to high school with? She's gorgeous."

"Yeah, isn't she, though?" Vivi is stunning. Why hadn't I ever noticed that about her back in the day? Her large silvery gray eyes and that luscious mouth of hers should've told me something, even back then. I was probably too busy being distracted by other girls eager to get their greedy hands on my dick. Vivi wasn't one of them. Too bad. We could've had some fun.

"But that boss of hers is creepy. He looked like he wanted to eat her."

"I hadn't noticed." I was too busy wanting to eat her up myself. Like tongue her pussy until she is dripping wet and screaming my name, and then suck her tits, turning her nipples into rock hard diamonds. I'd give anything to see her stretched out naked on my bed right now …

" … that's what."

"What did you say?"

"Are you even listening to me?"

"Um, yeah." I rub the back of my neck. My dick is painfully stiff from my filthy thoughts. I'm going to have to adjust myself in a minute. My balls feel like they're on fire. "Hey, you're not going to leave me, are you?"

"If you don't start acting right, I will." She stares me down with laser point precision.

The waiter takes our order and brings our beverages.

"Fuck me, Lynn."

"Thanks, but I'll pass. You're a bit young for my taste and besides, I'm happily married. The bottom line is you're a mess, Prescott. If you don't do something about it and turn your life around, you'll end up worse off than that asshole father of yours."

My cheeks rattle as I blow out a breath. "Okay. Message received. Just promise me you won't run off and leave me with some silly temp who doesn't know her ass from a hole in the ground. Please?"

"No promises until you get things under control. That sexy smile of yours might have worked on me thirty years ago, but now you're like a son to me and I'm seriously worried about you. You don't have a spare ounce of fat on you, you work like a group of demons are chasing you, and every day you smell like the bottom of the barrel you swam in the night before. Clean it up—and fast." Her stern, no nonsense voice lets me know this is not a test.

"It's a deal." I hold out my hand for her to shake. And she does. I hope like fuck I can keep the damn promise. If I lose Lynn, my ass is fucking toast, without the butter and jelly.

CHAPTER 3

VIVI

OVER TWO WEEKS PASS AND I DON'T CALL PRESCOTT. Weirdly enough, I'm a bit surprised he never contacts me. The way he acted that day in the coffee shop and then when he saw me at lunch, I was pretty confident he'd be back. Even Vince says he usually shows up at least twice a week for coffee. Maybe he decided I'm not up to his usual cream of the crop female standard. He always did go after the finest, like all those rich girls at Crestview. Not that I would've ever agreed to go out with him, but I'd be a big fat liar if I said it hadn't boosted my ego a bit.

This job is so mundane that thinking about Prescott is a nice distraction. The new software program is running, all the glitches are fixed, and I'm wrapping up my work at this particular shop. Vince and I decide to celebrate that night by grabbing a bite to eat at a nearby restaurant. It's a pub he enjoys because it's on the cheap side and they serve great beers.

"They even have daily specials that don't rob you. A lot of NYU students hang out there sometimes."

"Cool, I'm in. Let's go right after we close, if that's okay with you."

The coffee shop closes at seven, although Joe is debating on expanding the hours to ten. He's looking into it, now that the new programming is near completion. Just the other day he mentioned he'd need the extra income to help cover the added costs of it and me.

Vince is talking, but I'm not paying attention. "Hey, you. Did you hear me?"

"Sorry. What did you say?"

"Yeah, I was talking about how starved I am and about Joe and his idea about staying open until ten. I'm not sure about that. He likes us to work these long shifts, but as a part-time student, I couldn't handle staying here that late."

"Hmm. I guess that won't work for a lot of the employees. But we'll see," I absent-mindedly answer.

"So, what's up with you and Joe? Every time he's around you these days, he acts like he's afraid of you."

"What do you mean?"

Vince laughs. "Come on, Vivi. You must've noticed it. He asks your permission to do just about everything."

I'm shoving my laptop into my messenger bag and look up at him when he says that. "He does not."

"He most certainly does. He acts like your personal lap dog."

That cracks me up. Greasy-haired Joe—a lap dog. "So, just for shits and giggles, what breed would you classify him as?"

Vince is wiping down the last table. "When I was a kid, our neighbor had this squatty, mean as hell bulldog. That dog was the worst animal ever. He barked all the time and would drive us crazy. When the guy finally moved away we were so relieved. That's who Joe reminds me of—an annoying-as-fuck bulldog. And the weird thing is I have a bulldog now who is the coolest pet in the world."

"Maybe it was the owner."

"Nah, he was a good guy. He told us the dog had brain damage from birth or something."

The conversation has me picturing Joe with a goofy bulldog head. Only this dog has greasy wavy fur and is constantly barking. I cover my mouth to try and hold back a laugh. It doesn't work. A loud snort bursts out of me, and Vince looks at me as though I'm on drugs.

"What was that all about?"

After I tell him about Bulldog Joe, he cracks up too. "Oh, Vivi, I can picture him barking, nipping your heels, and following you around the coffee shop."

Vince does his best imitation of that then.

"If you don't stop, I'm not going to dinner." My ribs ache from laughing so much.

"He's the biggest loser, though, isn't he?"

I don't immediately respond. I'm still not one hundred percent sure I can trust Vince. What if he goes back to Joe and tells him?

"Oh, he's not that bad." I watch him for any type of sign to see if he's on Team Joe.

"Seriously? He's disgusting. He makes a play for all the female employees and should be sued for sexual harassment. What he does is illegal as hell. Jenny was telling me the other day that he tried to push her into the storeroom and grabbed her breast while he did it. Then he claimed it was an accident."

Jeez. That's not only disgusting, but scary. "I didn't know. Is that why she quit?"

"Yes! She was worried the next time, he'd fully assault her. As if what he did wasn't an assault. You should be careful around him." Vince's narrowed eyes and set jaws tell me he's serious. "Don't trust him at all, especially when you're alone with him and try not to put yourself in a situation where you are."

"I'm not worried about that anymore. Something happened to that end and I put a stop to it. Let's just say he's more than a little afraid of me."

"So that's it. That's why he hangs on every one of your words."

"I suppose."

"What did you say to him?"

I lift a shoulder and scrunch up my mouth. "I sort of name dropped."

Vince stares at me beneath furrowed brows but says nothing. By this time, he's finished cleaning up and puts everything up for the night.

"Hey, let's go eat. I'm starving," I say to change the subject. We grab our things, lock up, and head to the pub.

The place is fairly packed when we arrive, but we luck out and grab an empty booth. The waitress drops off a couple of menus and takes our beverage order. When she brings us our beers, we give her our dinner selections.

"So what's next?" Vince asks.

"Monday I start on the Upper East Side. I'm rotating in all the shops. This one was the main store and now that the program is implemented, I just need to make sure everyone is trained properly."

"Ah, the Upper East Side. You get to mingle with the rich folk."

I shake my head and take a long swallow of the ice-cold beer. It hits the spot. "And what exactly do you call all those suits who come in and frequent this shop? We're not exactly slumming it down here."

"True, but the Upper East Side is the *crème de la crème*."

"Puh-lese."

"No, it's true. Down here, you get more of a blend. You have the wealthy, but you also have the working class, students, artists, etc. It's more of a hodgepodge. Up there, you'll have the mainstream elite."

"You may have a point. I don't know, in fairness, but it doesn't matter either. I have to go up there no matter what. Ditto to all the other shops in Manhattan. I'm kind of excited to get a taste of different neighborhoods in the city. Haven't had much time to explore since I've moved here."

He reaches over, lays his hand on mine, and asks, "Aren't you going to miss me?"

I know he's just playing around. Vince always does stuff like this. But his fake-serious expression is spot-on this time. "Of course I'm going to miss you. You're my favorite—"

A shadow falls over our table and I think it's the waitress. I look up straight into golden irises. If I wasn't already sitting, I think I would've gone weak in the knees.

"Your favorite what?" Prescott asks in that rich voice of his. His tie is loosened and the top button of his collar is undone, but his shirt is crisp white again and his pants look to be expensive and tailored. They hug his hips and muscular thighs, which are mere inches from me. I tip my head back up to his face and see his familiar strong square jaw highlighted by his chiseled cheeks, and lick my lips. He's definitely one hundred percent male.

"Coworker," I finish as I tug my hand from beneath Vince's. For whatever reason, it makes me uncomfortable to leave it there.

Prescott slides into the booth next to me and says in an accusatory tone, "You never called me, Vivi."

Then he impales Vince with his glare. Vince withers under the intensity of it.

"Uh, look, Mr. Beckham, Vivi, I can leave."

"No!" I quickly jump in.

"That would be a good idea, Vince," Prescott says, overriding me.

"Our food hasn't arrived yet." But my protest falls on deaf ears.

Prescott reaches into his wallet and pulls out a thick wad of bills. He slides them across the table to Vince. I watch as Vince's eyes nearly tumble out of their sockets.

"It's all yours, Vince, if you leave right now."

"Yes, sir." Vince shoots me an apologetic glance, but he eagerly scoops up the money and bolts out of the booth. I can't blame him. He's a struggling part-time student who works a couple of jobs to support himself. Prescott just handed him God knows how much for vacating his seat. "See ya, Vivi. Let me know how the new shop is."

I wiggle my fingers at him as he disappears. "Is it your usual MO to bribe people to do things for you?"

"Only when it achieves a certain goal." Then he cocks a brow and continues. "Though where you're concerned, it always seems there's an exchange of funds, doesn't it? But he certainly seemed amenable to it."

The heat of Prescott's leg burns against my own, nearly singeing me. A shiver ripples through me.

"Cold?"

"This city is a block of ice." Only that's not why I shivered.

He leans back a bit and scrutinizes me. "Maybe you ought to dress warmer. Your clothes are inappropriate."

"Really? I hadn't noticed." My sarcasm isn't lost on him.

"You don't have to be so snarky."

I massage my forehead using two fingers and a thumb. "Honestly, Prescott, the world isn't at everyone's fingertips like it is yours. Your comment didn't clue me into the fact that my clothes aren't suitable. I moved here from the coast of southern Virginia where the weather was milder and I didn't have to walk everywhere in the bitter cold. This has been an unusually freezing October. Winter hit early, though you probably didn't notice since you conveniently ride around in a fancy car, I presume."

"Take a cab then, if you don't want to freeze—or buy warmer clothes."

"Has it ever occurred to you that perhaps not everyone has your level of financial resources?"

The waitress delivers our food and acts confused by the change of people at the booth.

"Just leave them both here. We'll figure it out," Prescott says. He stares at the food for a second then asks me which one is mine.

"This one." I point to the large burger.

He slides my plate over to me and I prepare to eat my meal.

32

I'm starving, having not eaten all day. My stomach rumbles on cue as I take several bites of my cheeseburger. I close my eyes as I chew the delicious food. Prescott is forgotten while I savor the meal.

"Do you always eat like that?" His husky voice pulls me back to reality.

"Eat like what?"

"Like you're worshipping the fucking thing with your mouth and tongue." The comment nails me like a blast of icy air.

I'm suddenly self-conscious of how I must appear to him. Was I gobbling down the food so fast I looked like a glutton? Was he reminded of that fat girl from Crestview? Is that why he said that? The burger that was so delicious a few seconds ago leaves a rancid taste in my mouth. I force the last bit down my throat and wash it down with a gulp of my beer.

"No, I was, er, hungry." My voice sounds small to my ears as I sit here feeling like a scolded child.

His irises are pinned on me as he finishes the remainder of his drink. I'm not sure what it is, but the color matches his eyes. Warm, golden brown.

"By all means, eat away, little wolf." His tongue slowly slides over his bottom lip, and a smile plays at one corner of his mouth.

Glancing back at my plate, the sight of the burger makes me feel ill. "I'm not hungry anymore." I push the plate away from me.

He laughs. "You can't be serious. You were inhaling the thing a second ago and now you're not hungry anymore?"

"Yeah. I think I need to leave."

"Not gonna happen. Unless, of course, you climb over me." His head drops to my legs and a cocky grin emerges on his sexy mouth. Then he redirects his gaze back to my eyes and waggles his brows.

Asshole. He knows damn well I can't climb over him because I'm wearing a skirt.

"So, Vivi, why didn't you ever call me?"

Pivoting in the booth so I can look at him better, I say, "Why would I? You and I never were friends at Crestview. We never hung out. You just used me to do your homework." *And I caved every fucking time.* "Besides, I hated it there. People were rude to me and I don't like being reminded of it. So what would be the purpose of calling you?"

"Whoa," he says, pausing for a breath, "Can't we start from scratch? Let bygones be bygones and all that? We were both young and silly."

I press my lips together, trying to come up with a pleasant response. "Your memory is different from mine. I never had the chance to be silly and young and carefree. You were the popular kid. I was the fat ugly one. The girls were cruel and did terrible things to me. I'm sure *you* had a great time because they all adored you. You can't possibly know what it was like to go through school having every day of your life suck. If you did, you wouldn't be so casual about it."

His eyes shutter to half-mast and he tilts his head. "You don't know that … you don't know anything about me. You presume a whole lot, Vivienne Renard, yet you know very little."

"Ooh. What does that mean? Do you have some deep dark secret hiding beneath the surface you've never shared with anyone? Are you really a broken man and in need of some woman to come and rescue you from self-destruction? Do you loathe the man you've become and are afraid of that person?" I chuckle at my own joke, but then I notice he's not laughing. His eyes are pained as two long creases appear in the small space between them.

In a low voice, he says, "Never presume anything, Vivi. Haven't you learned that yet?" He empties his glass in one long swallow and stares straight ahead.

Remorse flows through me. It was a bit harsh, I suppose. "Sorry. You were one of *them*, you know. I never belonged in that school. I hated every minute of it." I think back to all the memorabilia I trashed—the things Mom saved for me—when I cleaned out the house. All those ugly uniforms she'd kept and scrapbooks she'd made for me, thinking I'd treasure them. The idea of them makes me shudder.

"Why did you go then?" he asks without looking at me.

"My mom wanted me to. After Dad died, I didn't want to rock her flimsy boat." I wish she'd explained to me back then how much it was costing her and how much debt she was throwing herself into. It would've made our lives easier because I would've told her how much I hated that place.

The waitress pops over and we both order another round of drinks. Bourbon is his choice—Weller to be precise. I order another beer. When she delivers them, I watch him swirl it around in his glass a few times before he takes a hearty gulp.

"So, Vivi, why's a smart girl like you working in a coffee shop? You had all the brains. I thought by now you'd be working your way up a serious career ladder in some rocket science capacity."

A rueful laugh leaks out of me. "Yeah, those were my thoughts too. Funny how life never seems to fall in line with what you want."

He rubs his chin and it reminds me of the sound I hear when I file my nails. I peek down at them and they look awful—ragged edges with cuticles crying out for attention.

"So what stopped you?" he asks.

"Life."

"Where did you end up in college?"

"I graduated from MIT."

"No shit." He nods appreciatively. "I always knew you were a damn brain."

"And look where it got me."

"Why not go somewhere else if you're so down on this place?"

I rub my arms. A wicked chill penetrates my bones. The whole job thing sucks. More specifically, it angers me. "I'm on the hunt now and have been for a few months."

"What's your degree in?"

"Computer science and engineering."

"From MIT." He appears pensive.

"Yeah."

"Holy shit. And you're working in a fucking coffee shop for a greasy-headed twat?"

That makes me laugh. "That's about right."

"What the hell?"

"Prescott, it's a long story."

"I'm not in a hurry. Do you see me leaving? Am I trying to dash out that door over there?" He points to the exit.

"No," I say, shaking my head and laughing.

"Tell me. And this better be good because my guess is you graduated with a 4.0 and all kinds of honors. Am I right?"

I shrug.

"Come on, Vivi."

I'm still resisting, but then he smirks. Nothing is sexier than Prescott Beckham smirking. Okay, maybe his ass. But whatever. Then he suddenly says, "Hey, let's play my favorite game."

"No way. I'm not playing Truth or Dare with you."

"Why not? You used to at Crestview."

"Because you always figured out a way to persuade me to do it. Don't you think twenty-seven is a little old for that?"

"Not at all. You're never too old for Truth or Dare. Come on. Don't be such a chicken. If you don't want to tell me something, take the dare." He grins and sticks the tip of his tongue between his top and bottom teeth.

Jerk.

I check the time and see it's almost eight-thirty. "One hour. That's it. I leave at nine-thirty."

"Why then? I didn't think Cinderella turned into a pumpkin until midnight."

"Ha-ha. I have to go to Brooklyn and it's freezing out." I leave out the bit about how scared I am going home so late by myself. "And you have to answer, too."

"I was planning on it. But I get to go first."

"Fair enough."

"All righty then. Truth or dare, Vivi?" He's lowered his voice into that raspy-sexy tone.

My palms are already sweating. "Truth."

"When I saw you at lunch, what did you mean by me 'having the girls wrapped around my homework binder,' or whatever it was you said?"

Well, fuck me. Why'd he have to start with that?

CHAPTER 4

PRESCOTT

VIVI RUBS HER HANDS ON HER THIGHS. SHE'S NERVOUS AND has been ever since I stood over the table. She seems to have more confidence in herself now than she had when I knew her but that doesn't account for her skittishness. Back at Crestview, she had been overweight—I knew that—only I didn't know, or maybe I didn't pay attention, to the other girls giving her a hard time. And why should I have? I had so much going on in my head I could barely keep my own shit together.

"So?" I prod. "Homework binder?"

"You did a pretty good job with me. I only figured you put the other girls in the same boat. You know, with the homework stuff and all."

"I had you wrapped around my homework binder at Crestview. That's your metaphor for finger."

It's not a question. I'm baffled because I had no idea. Yeah, I was a flirt, but I flirted with everyone to get what was necessary. It was the only way I knew how to accomplish my goals. She needed the money and always acted like she had no interest in me whatsoever.

"Of course. You had everyone wrapped around your finger.

Well, maybe more of them were wrapped around your, um." She points in the direction of my dick.

Sexy little Vivi can't say dick out loud. Isn't that the cutest thing in the world?

"Say it, Vivi."

"Say what?"

"You know what." I lean into her and get close to her lips. "Say it."

Her chest puffs out as she says, "Dick." Her lovely neck flushes pink and two bright spots of fuchsia dot her cheeks. This is sweet innocence at its utmost.

"Excellent. Now say cock." I put a great deal of emphasis on the "c" and "k" at the end of the word. Silver gray irises turn stormy and deep creases form on her forehead.

"Why would you want me to say that word?"

"Because it makes you uncomfortable as hell and I'm an asshole. I like to see you squirm, Vivi."

"I won't say that. It has nothing to do with truth or dare. And besides, it's my turn."

I take a couple of good slugs of my drink, sit back, and cross my arms. "Do your worst."

She puts an elbow on the table and rests her cheek on her hand. "Truth or dare?"

"Dare." It's impossible not to laugh at her comical expression. I curtailed her plans.

"You can't do that!"

"Do what?"

"Pick dare."

"I most certainly can."

Her head tilts back, and I can only imagine what she's thinking. A chuckle escapes.

"You're a jerk," she says.

"So I've been told."

"Okay, then. I dare you to tell me why you loathe the man you've become." She gloats at the clever way she's twisted the game. And stupid me should've figured out she'd come up with something like this. Vivi was always brilliant.

"Loathe is extreme. Let's say I'm not particularly fond of who I am right now."

"Fine. Go on."

Now I'm the one who's squirming. Where do I even begin? Vivi is almost a stranger to me. There's no way I can bare my pathetic soul to her.

"I have daddy issues."

"Really?" Her question is one of disbelief and she appears to be holding back a laugh.

"Hard to believe, isn't it?"

"Um, yeah. Prescott Beckham, the guy with the world at his fingertips, has daddy issues? I think not. I Googled you after I ran into you that day. From all accounts I read there were no daddy issues to be found. *Nada*. Try again."

"I have a team that keeps my secrets out of the media. You wouldn't find anything on me. But it's true. I grew up without a mom and my father was not much of one. So, there you have it." I give her one of my best smirks. It usually does the trick on most women.

She leans back and tucks her chin closer to her body. "That's it? And I'm supposed to buy that?"

"That's all I have for sale, Little Wolf. Sorry."

"You're not a very fair player."

"My turn."

"Nope. I'm done." She drinks another swig of her beer.

"No, you aren't. I'm picking for you. Truth. How many men have you fucked, Vivi? And what exactly have they done to you?"

She shoves her arms into her coat and pushes at me to get out of the booth. But I have zero intentions of going anywhere. "Let me out, Prescott."

"Not until you answer me."

"That's none of your business. How many women have you been with?"

"Too many to count."

Her jaw flops open and I close her mouth with a finger under her chin.

"You asked, Little Wolf."

"Don't call me that."

"How many, Vivi? Tell me and I'll let you go."

"Why do you want to know?"

She's so delicious sitting here, her mouth only inches from mine, it's all I can do not to lean forward and close the distance between us. I want to feel those plump lips against me, wrapped around my cock as I push deep into her throat. I ache to hear her moan as I tongue her tight little pussy. I want to bind her in silk and fuck her until she begs me to stop. I know Vivi is inexperienced as shit—I can sense it—and I want to introduce her to sex, to raw, lusty, satisfying sex.

"So I know exactly how far I can take you."

"How far you can take me … with what?"

"How many, Vivi?"

"Two. Now let me out."

"Only if you promise to go out with me."

"Fuck you, Prescott."

"That's precisely the idea." Before she can think of anything else to say, I grab her chin in a firm grip and kiss her. At first, she kisses like a block of ice. Then she warms up, melts, and leans into me as she fists the sides of my jacket. There's a whole lot more to Vivi Renard than she wants to admit and I plan to find out what lies beneath the surface.

When I set her free, her chest rises and falls with exertion. "I dare you to tell me you're not wet. I dare you to tell me that tight little pussy of yours wouldn't love for my cock to slide inside it right now. And I would go so far as to say that when you get home, your fingers will be doing that very thing, won't they, Vivi?" I pause a moment to savor her shocked expression. "I was

right about you, Little Wolf. You live up to your name I gave
you. Except you're not hungry for food. You're starving for
something much wilder, much more wicked than that."

Standing, I allow her to get out of the booth. She's trembling
as she stands. "Vivi?"

"W-what?" she stutters.

"This time I'll expect a call from you. Tomorrow to be exact."

Her head bobs as she hurries out of the bar. When she's gone,
I call the head of security at Whitworth Enterprises.

"Jack, I need to get an address on Vivienne Renard." I let
him know she lives somewhere in Brooklyn and where she
works. I also give him her mobile number. I'm confident I'll have
her address in a day or so.

I call the waitress over for the tab so I can get the fuck out of
this place. My dick is so damn hard that if I don't bust a nut
soon, I'm going to go crazy. Rubbing one off to the fantasy of
Vivi blowing me is going to have to tide me over until I get the
real thing. I hope she doesn't keep me waiting too damn long.

The next morning, when I arrive at work, Lynn inspects me.
Then she follows me into my office.

"You look good this morning," she says.

"Thank you. So do you."

"No. I mean, you look really good. No bender last night?"

I inwardly laugh at the term *bender*. "I don't overindulge
every night, Lynn."

"You have lately."

"I promised I'd do better and I am."

"Thank you. And I'm happy to say you don't need to brush
your teeth."

She doesn't wait for a smartass reply before she leaves. I
avoid mentioning to her that I smoked enough weed to get all of
SoHo stoned out of their minds last night.

My ass barely hits the seat when the phone buzzes.

"Mr. Beckham, Jack from security is on the line."

Hmm. That was quick. "Thanks, Lynn."

I click over to Jack and he gives me Vivi's address. He also tells me it's in the Bushwick area of Brooklyn, where the crime rate is extremely high. After thanking him, I wonder why the hell she chose to live there.

My phone buzzes again and Lynn tells me Harrison is on the line.

"Dude, what's up?"

"Don't you ever answer your own phone?" he asks.

"Not here. Why don't you ever call my cell?"

"I do. You never answer."

I check my phone and there aren't any missed calls from him, so I relay that bit of news.

"I called you a couple of minutes ago."

"Check the damn number you called. It's not showing up on here."

We get that issue sorted out—he had the wrong number under his contacts for me—and then he tells me he's in town. "Got in early this morning."

"Why don't you stay with me?"

"I don't want to bother you. Besides, I have some of my staff with me. We're at The Plaza for a few days."

I push my chair back to put my feet on my desk. "Who fucked up this time?"

"Midnight Drake. I had to get out here and clean up a mess."

"What happened to her? Men? Women? Or both?"

"Both and drugs."

"Ouch." Harrison's a fixer for Hollywood's finest. He makes the worst look their best.

"Yeah, she's going to make a statement tomorrow about how she has an addiction issue and will be entering rehab for an undetermined length of time. I'll be tied up with her agent and producer. She just signed a fucking contract for a multimillion-dollar movie deal. I swear this has been a shit show."

The doodles on the paper get darker and darker as I replicate the circles I draw. "So what exactly happened?"

"She was caught in bed with one other woman and two men. There was bondage, lots of … gadgets shall we say. You know, whips, gags, floggers, toys, that sort of thing."

"Sounds like she had her kink on."

"Oh, her kink was strapped on all right. That along with some heroin."

"She's fucked, man."

"No, she *was* simul-fucked. Heartily. Straight in the ass and pussy. And she was fucked up. Bad thing was she woke up and didn't remember a thing. Says she was drugged and raped. It's a damn mess. You should've seen the pics and videos. Anyway, I'm here to pick up the pieces and reassemble, as usual."

And that's what Harrison does best. I don't know how, but I swear the man could cover up a murder if he tried.

"Did you say video?" I ask.

"Uh, three to be exact. And the shit hit the net. Already got it pulled, though."

"So, dinner tonight?"

"Sure thing. What time?" he asks.

"You tell me. You've got the mess on your grubby paws to straighten up."

"Seven. And let's go to that place you took me to last time — you know, the one the TV chef owns."

"I'll make some calls and see what I can do. Expect a text with a confirmation. And make sure you change my goddamn number in your contacts, you moron."

He's still laughing when he hangs up. Out of the three of us, Harrison was the most put together at Crestview. Weston and I came from fucked up families, whereas Harrison had a decent home life. His dad is the best. Weston and I envied the fuck out of him. I still do. Maybe that's why he's always trying to put people's lives back together and is the damn best at it.

As excited as I am to see him, I can't deny I'm a bit disappointed. A part of me wanted to go and check out Vivi's place, find out more about where she lives. My intentions were to go to her apartment and wait for her to come home from work. But that will have to wait until tomorrow.

At seven, I enter Le Table. The hostess does everything but dry hump me as she seats me. Usually I'm interested in this sort of thing, and maybe would even give her my number, but not tonight. She can't hold a candle to Vivi. Her lips aren't as full, her eyes aren't as gray, and her lashes aren't nearly as long and lush. I'd also bet her pussy has been used and abused by a lot more than two men, and the thought of breaking that tight little thing in is worth the damn wait.

The waiter comes by and I order a Pappy Van Winkle as I wait for Harrison's ass to arrive. He's ten minutes late and I'm already on my second drink. They say you're supposed to savor bourbon that can run upward of two grand a bottle, but I don't. If I like the taste, I'll down it however I damn want to.

"How's the clean-up guy?" I say as I man-hug him.

"Good as ever."

"Hey, golden boy, you look very California-ish with that tan. You've been hanging out in a tanning bed or something?" I like to give him shit.

"Oh, yeah. My favorite thing to do. If you dragged your ass away from this cold piece of granite, I'd show you some sun on the beach."

He's always giving me hell about New York. "And check out those tats peeking out on your neck. Rocking new ink, huh?"

"Yeah, and I'll take that as a compliment."

"You should."

"I'm into skin art these days."

The waiter shows up and he orders some kind of single malt scotch shit. I hate that crap. Reminds me of my dad. After his drink is delivered we toast to our friendship and a great dinner.

He cocks his head and stares. "What's up with you?"

"What do you mean?"

"You don't look like you're on your usual Scotty game."

"Bullshit."

"No, man, I'm serious."

"Come on, Harry. Have you been talking to Westie?"

He holds both hands in the air. "No. I swear. I just know you like a brother. So what's the deal?"

"Family shit. What else? And Weston didn't fill you in?"

"Nah, you know how he is. He's tight as a drum."

I roll the tension out of my shoulders and proceed with, "You remember what happened last Christmas, right?"

"You mean the step-cunt fucktastrophe."

"We had another run-in. Only this time is was at a huge benefit that Whitworth sponsored. Dad called me out in front of a bunch of clients and it got pretty nasty."

"You're joking," he says, leaning on the table.

"Do I look like I am?"

"So what happened?"

"Granddad stepped in and he has so much clout that he diffused the situation. Dad left afterward. It was extremely awkward. Work has been a bitch since. Not that it's been great since Christmas, I'll admit."

"Your old man is a douche. Why don't you divorce him?"

"I wish he'd divorce the cunt he married, except they're the perfect couple."

"Dude, you should come to LA for a visit. Get away from here. Tap into some fresh, you know?"

The waiter shows up and hands us our menus. Harrison can't decide what to get for his entrée, so we just order appetizers and tell him to come back in a few minutes.

"It's a damn meal. If you can't decide, order two."

"Do you ever do that?" he asks.

"No, but you're whining like a girl, so I figured it would shut you up."

He laughs. "You're an asshole."

"It's my middle name."

Someone plunks a basket of bread on the table and Harrison grabs a slice, then slathers it with butter.

"Have you eaten today?"

"Yeah, why?" he says around the bread.

"Just curious."

We talk about more shit and I toy with the idea of telling him about running into Vivi, but I decide to keep her to myself. There's some strange reason I don't want to share her with anyone. I feel strangely possessive of her. And the problem is, after I've thoroughly fucked her, I'll want to own her, too.

"… the franchise?"

Harrison looks at me expectantly.

"Well?" he prods.

"What did you just ask me?" I down the rest of my drink and flag the waiter over to order another and while he's here, we give him our dinner order.

After he's gone, Harrison aims his finger at me. "See, I was right. *You're* not right. Something is fucking with you. Prescott Beckham is all about money and finance—except when he's got his dick buried balls deep in some woman's pussy. And right now, as far as I can tell"—he bends down and looks under the table—"there's not a woman giving you head, nor are you fucking one under the table. But I ask you about the franchise and financials with A Special Place, and you're a damn blank."

I wear a sheepish expression since he caught me in the act of thinking about Vivi. "Sorry. Guess my mind wandered."

"I'll say. Who is she? And the reason I ask is you're not wearing a pissed off as hell look that you'd normally reserve for your father. This is an altogether different look, more introspective I'd have to say."

"Is that so?"

"Yes, that's so. Give it up, Scott."

"Okay, you'll never guess who I ran into."

Our extremely efficient waiter—whom I'm going to heavily tip—delivers my drink.

"Jesus, tell me already. I hate when people fucking do this. Only girls do this shit."

"Vivi Renard."

"Who the fuck is that?"

He doesn't even remember her. "Yeah, you wouldn't recall. She went to Crestview with us."

He laughs. "Did you fuck her, like all the other girls there?"

"No, I didn't fuck her. Christ. I didn't fuck every single girl in school."

One brow nearly jumps off his head. "I'm not buying the Brooklyn Bridge, asshat."

"She did my homework."

The same brow sinks low, joining the other as he thinks hard. Those cogwheels of his analytical brain are spinning, but nothing is catching. "I only remember that fat chick you used to pay, but her name doesn't come to mind."

"That's the one."

"You ran into her? The brainiac? What is she? A nuclear physicist or something?"

"Not even close. She works in a coffee shop."

He leans back in his chair and blinks about forty times. "You're fucking with me. Not that girl. She's the one everyone made fun of. It was bad, man. The girls pretended they were elephants around her. They'd do this funny thing with their arms, swinging them like trunks." He does this half-ass imitation of it as he sits in his chair.

"That's pathetic. I never saw that." Suddenly, I feel pained for Vivi and how awful it must've made her feel. Am I developing a conscience?

He shrugs. "I don't know how you missed it. It was actually

pretty hilarious at the time. Except now when I think about it, it wasn't really. It was quite terrible."

We're both silent for a while.

Then anger hits me. "Why didn't you say something? Call those bitches out?" My tone is harsh as I glare at him.

"Dude, everyone did it. Why would I have said something? She was a townie and all the kids made fun of her."

"Oh, I don't know. Because it was wrong, perhaps?"

"We were all assholes back then. And since when did you grow a conscience and become so worried about other people's feelings?"

I choose to ignore his question because it *is* unlike me. Thankfully, the waiter delivers our plates of steaming food. I've ordered a thick juicy bone-in rib eye and Harrison ordered some froufrou dish that I give him a hard time about.

"I watch what I eat, man, unlike you."

"Just like you gobbled down all that butter? And hey, I watch what I eat. I watch it go straight from my fork into my mouth." I chew my bite with gusto.

"I don't know how you stay so lean. So, tell me about Vivi Renard. Other than she works at a coffee shop."

After I swallow my tasty bite, I say, "I think she does something with their IT. But she's not fat anymore."

"No? What does she look like? I hate to say it, but I don't remember her face."

"Sort of average," I say in a nonchalant manner. But he doesn't buy it.

"Bull-fucking-shit. That's why you're off your usual Scotty game. It's Vivi, isn't it?"

"I don't know what you're talking about. I ran into her. That's all. But I didn't come here to discuss Vivi. I'm more interested in hearing about Midnight Drake and her kink."

He wipes his mouth with the napkin. "Why? So you can pick up a few pointers?"

"Maybe."

He pulls out his phone, but before he passes it to me, he says, "Your eyes only, Scotty. And you never saw this shit. Am I clear?"

"It's on your phone, not mine. Besides, I don't gossip."

"I know. But it had to be said. This shit was all over the place anyway. We were lucky to get it pulled as fast as we did."

I take the phone and watch some of the videos. I'm no prude by any means and have even been to a couple of BDSM clubs in the city, but this chick definitely got caught doing the wrong things with the wrong people.

"I have photos, too, which are just as bad as these. The bondage, spreader bars, labia clamps, the list is endless."

"From these, it looks like it." I hand him his phone. "How're you going to fix it?"

"It's fixed. Tomorrow, she makes a statement, then we check her into rehab. They delay filming for a while. She takes a huge hit on her fees, but it saves her career. We've built a story about how she was abused as a teenager and never told anyone."

"Is it true?"

"Yeah, but she's reluctant to talk about it. It happened in foster care. I had to wheedle it out of her, but I'm the fixer. It's what I do."

Our plates are both polished, so the waiter swoops in to clear them away.

"Harrison, what happens to the people she was with?"

"We're working on that."

"Like what are you going to do?"

His expression loses every sign of friendliness. "I'm not at liberty to discuss it." He won't bend on this.

"Fair enough. I don't want to know anyway."

"No, you don't."

"So let's blow this place and head to mine. I have some great weed at home."

"Actually, I need to get back. We have an early morning call to run through how her statement is going to go and then the cleanup. You know?"

I don't, but I act like I do.

"Hey, come out to the west coast. It would be a good trip for you."

"Yeah, I might do that." It's one more thing I have no intention of doing anytime soon. Not that I don't love Harrison as a brother, because I do. But right now I need to fix my own shit before I can take off and enjoy myself, and part of my shit is finding Vivi and fucking the pleasure out of her. I want to hear her begging for more and screaming my name as if I were the only man on Earth who could give her what she needs. At the moment, that's all I can think about.

CHAPTER 5

VIVI

Prescott was right. I did use my fingers. Not once, but three times. And every time, it was his face I saw when I came.

This morning, I ache. For him. What the hell has he done to me? Every time I think of those wicked words he spoke to me, wetness pools between my thighs. My legs clench together more times today than I care to count. To my horror, I even find myself in the bathroom on a break, frantically rubbing myself, just to relieve the pressure that's built up there.

Why did he have to come into the coffee shop that day?

Today is endless. Then, of all days for him to drop by, Joe prances in and pesters me about some inane issue that isn't an issue at all. He only wants to check on whether or not I'm still doing my job. My brain is everywhere but on work and I'm clearly not on my game.

"Vivi, I was wondering when you'll be finished here," he says.

"Joe, as I explained to you earlier, on Monday. Then I'll be rotating to each of the stores next week."

"Then this is perfect timing."

"For what?"

"I'm having some problems implementing your program."

He's not that stupid. "I believe you need one of the employees to teach you how to use it. It really is quite simple and streamlined."

Then I sense it. He leers at me. Shit. Man, did I walk into his trap.

"I think I'm looking at the perfect person for that. Why don't you come to my office on Monday? I think you'll be the perfect instructor for me."

"Um, actually, as I mentioned, I'll be visiting the other shops to get a feel from the employees what they need from me. You know, a sort of best practices thing."

"You get one week, Vivi. Then I'll consider you all mine." Our stares connect and I nod briefly.

I have one week to find another job.

When I get home, I don't bother with dinner. I get online and immediately apply for jobs again. My résumé is in so many places, I'm not sure where else I can post it. My hand itches to call Prescott. I know he's expecting me to, but finding another job is more important right now. The frustrating part of job hunting is the wait. However, I'm resourceful and willing to do menial work until something better opens up. I'll scrub floors or be some kid's nanny if I have to just get away from the scumbag. Joe makes my skin prick when he ogles me.

By the time I turn off the lamp, which sits on the floor next to the air mattress I sleep on, it's close to 2:00 a.m. I see it then. A text that nearly burns a hole in my phone glares at me accusingly. I can almost hear his voice, saying those dirty things to me all over again. And worse, I can hear him scolding me for not calling.

Vivi, it's after midnight, which means today is FRIDAY. You were supposed to call me YESTERDAY. I meant what I said. You owe me a phone call. And I expect to get one. CALL ME! I don't like being ignored.

Shoving the phone under my pillow just to get the damn thing out of my sight doesn't help a bit. It actually makes it worse. I imagine the damn text attacking my phone, infecting it like a virus, sending all sorts of malware throughout it. Oh my God, this is ridiculous. I have to be up in four hours, and Prescott Beckham is fucking with my head. If I didn't live in such a dangerous area of Brooklyn, I'd put on some running shoes and work out my frustrations pounding the streets. But the way my luck runs, I'd get kidnapped, fall into the hands of human traffickers, and no one would ever hear from me again. The thing is, who would give a flying fuck? I have no family, expect for one distant aunt who I rarely speak to. I could be shipped off to some remote corner of the world and that would be it for Vivienne Renard.

When my phone beeps, I'm still wide ass awake. This is going to be the day from hell. By the time I get to work, my stomach is a raw bundle of nerves. Vince is off this morning and won't be in until one. Jackie is here and greets me as I enter.

"Good morning, Vivi."

"Morning, Jackie."

As I get behind the counter, she asks me if I'm okay. "Yeah, why?"

"You're as pale as a ghost. Are you coming down with something? The flu is going around, you know."

"Yeah, I know. I'm fine, though."

Her hand snakes out to land on my forehead. "You don't feel feverish."

"Like I said, I'm fine. I didn't sleep well, is all."

She launches into a long drawn out explanation of why I should take melatonin and how it would benefit me in getting a better night's sleep. All I want to do is yell at her to shut up because what I need is a better job that doesn't require me to work for pervy Joe. But I bite my tongue and smile because she's only trying to help.

"I'll give it a try." Then the issue of Prescott nags at me, but I sweep it under the old rug again.

"How 'bout a cup?"

"Make that a jug," I say.

Jackie laughs. "Latte sound good?"

"Please. Would you mind if I pick your brain?"

"Sure."

Between customers, I question her about the new system — specifically her likes and dislikes. Most of what she doesn't like has to do with her unfamiliarity with certain aspects of it. After I explain things and walk her through everything, she has better opinion of the system.

"Joe should've hired you a long time ago."

"He couldn't have afforded me back then," I mutter.

"What's that?"

"Nothing. So what are you studying? You're at NYU, aren't you?"

"That's right. I'm in the creative writing program. I want to work for one of the Big Five one day as an editor."

"The big five?" I ask.

"You know, one of the big trade publishing houses."

"Right." I take a huge sip of my coffee to cover my idiocy. I hate looking stupid. I should've known what the Big Five were given how much I devour books, or used to anyway.

As I'm sitting here jotting down everything she told me, the bell over the door rings, indicating another customer has entered. It's close to noon, which means the soup crowd will be in. The "More" in Java Beans & More is the soup, bread, and other lunch items the shop serves. It's not the traditional fare, like sandwiches and salads. Joe got it right when he negotiated with one of the local Italian restaurants to sell their soups and bread.

He also contracted with one of the local bagel companies. That's what makes us a hit for the breakfast crowd. If you don't get here early, you're out of luck.

"Can I help you?" Jackie asks.

"I'd like Vivi to wait on me." He pronounces every single letter of my name with precision.

Fuck me sideways. *Prescott.*

Glancing up, I look directly into a pair of angry golden eyes. The pen in my hand shakes, so I set it on the counter to hide my fear.

"Um, hey there." Maybe if I act jovial, he'll get over his anger. "How're you today?"

"You were supposed to call me. Did you forget? Or … wait. How could you? I texted you, let's see"—he pulls out his phone and silently ticks off the number of messages he sent—"six times, Vivi. I texted you *six* times."

Out of the corner of my eye, I see Jackie observing this exchange with her mouth agape.

"About that. I was busy."

"At"—he checks his phone again—"twelve-thirty in the morning? Were you entertaining someone, Vivi?" He leans on the counter, caging me with his arms. "Are you in the habit of receiving guests at such an hour because as I was led to believe you only had two—"

"That's enough, Prescott."

"Oh, Vivi, it's not even close to being enough." His lips are a hair away from mine and for a moment I'm sure he's going to kiss me, or maybe even bite me. Then he surprises me by stepping back and aiming his finger at me. "You owe me a call. I expect it today."

He walks out as though he owns the world, and in many ways, he does. The next hour and a half are so busy, my hands are full helping Jackie fill orders. But my mind is glued to Prescott Beckham. What would it be like to go out with him? To sleep with him?

But I know the answer to that. I'd be ruined for anyone else forever. There's absolutely no way I can do it.

When the crowd finally thins, Jackie leans on one of the stools we have in the back and asks, "Who was the god?"

"What?"

"Come on, Vivi. Don't play dumb."

"Nobody, really."

"You expect me to believe that?"

"I'm starved." I walk over to one of the soup pots and ladle up a cup. It's minestrone and delicious. "Mmm. I love this stuff."

"Almost as good at Prescott looks," she says.

Her grin has me smiling back.

"Shut up," I say. "And how do you know his name?"

"That's what you called him. That man is totally off the hot charts. Is he an ex or something? The heat rolling off you two was enough to cause the soup pot to boil over."

"No, he's not an ex," I huff.

"I sure wish he looked at me the way he looked at you. I'd nibble on his baguette any day of the week."

"Jackie! Jeez, you don't even know him."

"So? With eyes and an ass like his, who needs to know more than that?"

Leaning away from my tasty cup of soup, I say, "Come on. That can't be all it takes."

"Hmm. Sometimes." We're interrupted by a group of customers but when they leave, I prod her to continue.

"It depends on the guy. The one who was after you reeks of money."

"How do you know that?" I'm truly curious to see what she says.

"His clothes. He was wearing a Burberry coat, those fucking awesome Louis Vuitton high tops that I'd give my pinky toes for, and—wait a sec. Don't you pay attention to this shit?"

I'm tying a chunk of my hair into a knot, untying it and retying it. "Actually, no. What's the point?"

She smacks me on the shoulder. "The point, my friend, is you can learn a lot about a person by what they wear."

"That's ridiculous."

Jackie tilts her head, then bites the corner of her lip. "Let me see. While your coat isn't cheap, you'd totally love a thick warm coat, but can't afford it." She pinches my sweater between her thumb and forefinger. "This sweater isn't heavy enough for you either, is it? You're freezing all the time, and from the looks of your wardrobe, my guess is you're on a super tight budget. Every time I see you, you're dressed in clothes that are suitable for a warmer climate. Your boots are several years old, and not something you'd wear when it's freezing in New York. That tells me you're not from here and haven't spent much time in these parts. Oh, and one other thing. Your messenger bag is quite worn and looks like it's seen better days. It doesn't really match the rest of your stuff. Wanna know what that says to me? If I were to bet, I'd say you used to have a better one, maybe even a much more expensive one, but maybe sold it in a consignment shop for some extra cash."

"What are you? A detective or something?"

"Nope, just very observant. I take a lot of creative writing classes. And I take my studies very seriously. See, clothes say a shit-ton about someone."

I don't respond, though I know she's waiting for me to.

"What happened, Vivi?"

"What do you mean?"

The bell rings again and she's torn away by a customer, thank God. The last thing I need is her snooping into my life. Unfortunately, the customer only orders a regular coffee and a cookie.

Instantly, she's back to her probing questions. Only this time, her eyes are soft and sympathetic. "You can tell me. I know what it's like to need a friend. You and Vince are close, I know. I also know it's nice to have a girlfriend, too. Not that I'm trying to push Vince out of the way or anything."

I bat my hand, saying, "No, it's not like that at all. It's just, well, my mom died and things got a little rough with the medical bills."

Suddenly, I'm unexpectedly being hugged. It's weird as hell because I can't remember the last time I was hugged by anyone. The time I saw Prescott in the restaurant, I hugged him to make a point to Joe and that was weird as shit, too.

The thing is, while my mom was ill, she couldn't put her arms around me. I held her many times, but there were never any warm embraces returned. My eyes fill with water and that familiar knot, the one that used to live in my throat, reappears. There's no way in hell I can break down in here. There are people twenty feet from us.

"Um"—I clear my throat—"Jackie, you've got to let me go." When she does, I dart into the bathroom to regain control. I'm a trembling mess. Leaning on the sink, I splash water on my face. As I stand there, my phone buzzes. Why am I not surprised to see who it is?

I'm still waiting for a call.

I want to yell, "Yeah? You're going to be waiting for quite a while, dude!"

Jackie's waiting for me with an apologetic frown. "I'm sorry, Vivi. I didn't mean—"

"It wasn't your fault. You were trying to be nice. To be honest, it felt good to be hugged and it sort of threw me."

"I meant what I said about being your friend. That is, if you're ever in need of another."

The rest of the afternoon goes by smoothly, except for the damn texts I keep getting. Then around five, a man shows up with a gigantic box. It's wrapped in beautiful paper and tied in a pretty bow.

"I have a delivery for Vivienne Renard."

"I'm Vivienne."

"Sign here." He hands me a computer pad and I put my signature on it. The box sits on the counter and he leaves me staring at the monstrosity.

"Aren't you going to open it?" Jackie asks.

"I guess." I tear the paper off and the box is from Saks.

"Oooh, pricey."

When I lift off the lid, I forget how to breathe. Inside is a gorgeous, tweed winter coat. I pull it out as Jackie gushes over it.

"Jesus, Vivi, it's a Chanel. That must've cost at least a few grand."

"What! Who pays that much for a coat?"

"You know who."

When I go to stuff it back in the box because there's no way I can accept anything like this, I notice there's something else inside. It's not exactly little either. I push the tissue paper out of the way, reach in, and pull out a Canada goose down coat.

"Somebody really likes you, girl."

My brain fires in all the wrong places.

"At least you won't be cold anymore." She giggles.

"It's not funny."

"Oh, come on. By the way, who's Mr. Prescott Moneybags?"

"Prescott Beckham."

"Say what?"

"Prescott Beckham."

"You mean the rich dude?"

I gesture toward the coats. "Do you really have to ask me that?"

"You need to chase him down."

I stare at the box and only then do I notice the card and underneath something red peeking out. When I pick up the card a satin thong sits there.

Of all the …

Jackie looks over my shoulder and snickers. "Seems to me he has plans for you."

Opening the card, I shiver at the words that blare at me. "Will you please call me now?"

"I'd be dialing that man's number, if I were you."

"Yeah, but you're not me, are you, Jackie?"

A week passes with no sign of another job. I resign myself to the fact that I'm going to have to quit and take a waitressing job or two until I can land something permanent. My funds aren't exactly plentiful.

There's another option. Pulling out my phone, I check out the pictures there. The diamond ring and bracelet are the last things I have left of my mom's. They should bring in a hefty price because the ring is over two carats and has plenty of smaller diamonds around it. The bracelet is loaded with diamonds and sapphires. The jewelry is all that's left from what Dad gave her during our better days, when money was no object. I had hoped I could keep them as a reminder of those times, but that's not going to be an option. The thought makes my stomach churn with acid.

If I could sell at least the bracelet, the money could pay my mortgage for six months. The problem might be finding a buyer who is willing to pay the asking price. I do have the option of going to a pawnshop, but they don't always give the best price.

Turning on my computer, I run a search for websites that will allow me to sell it online. It doesn't take long to locate one, but I must send them appraisal documents to prove the value of the bracelet. Luckily, I was forward thinking and did that before leaving Virginia. They are scanned into my computer. I email the company and send them the appraisal, along with a photo of the bracelet. Then I go to the closet and check the bin where the stuffed animals are kept. Inside each one is where the jewelry is hidden. I didn't know what else to do. Knowing where I was moving, and that there might not be a safe place to keep them, I figured it would be best to keep them here. It was a smart move, considering how dangerous this area is.

Next, I start a job search for any kind of work that can keep food in my fridge and the electric bill paid. If I can sell the bracelet and work a couple of jobs until I land a real job, perhaps I can make it here. If not, plan B will be instituted. The problem is, I don't have a plan B.

Gotta get working on that.

On Monday morning, I meet Joe at his office to offer him a deal. If he doesn't stop harassing me, I slap him with a lawsuit.

"You're funny, Vivi. How exactly have I been harassing you?"

"Come on, Joe, you know exactly what I'm talking about. You want one thing from me and it isn't training on the new system I installed. So tell me, do you want me to continue my rotation in the shops or do I resign now?"

He pushes his large leather chair back and stands.

"Vivi, you'd really resign?"

"Yes, I'm prepared to do that."

He takes my hand and I shudder, jerking it out of his grasp.

"What, you don't like to hold my hand?"

His slimy voice sends a chill down my spine.

"No, I don't like to hold your hand. I don't want you to touch me."

"But we could have such fun together."

"Joe, you are my boss and this is inappropriate."

"Only if you don't want it."

I flash him a scathing look. "What makes you think I want this? I've told you no on how many occasions? I can't even count them anymore."

He runs his hand over his greasy hair and I want to gag. "I promise, one night with me and you'll change your mind."

"Enough." I reach into my pocket and pull out my phone. "I have enough here to prove sexual harassment. This has been going on since the beginning of our work relationship and I'm taking this to an attorney. Consider this my resignation."

I'm marching to the door on my way out of his office, when he slams me against the wall. Air gushes from my lungs in a whoosh as my chest is crushed into the hard surface. It happens so fast I can't process. As awareness hits, I realize I've underestimated Joe and that I'm in real danger.

He whispers against my cheek and his steamy rank breath fans across my face. My body vibrates in terror. "You think you're pretty fucking smart, don't you, Vivi? With that degree from MIT and your little nasty trick? You also thought I bought into that Prescott Beckham bullshit too, didn't you? Well, I followed you for weeks and never saw any interaction with him." He grabs my phone and even though I can't see what he's doing, I'm sure he's erasing the conversation I recorded.

"Now try to see what your little attorney or your so-called friend can do with that." I hear my phone drop to the floor. Then he unbuttons my coat and says, "You've teased me long enough, you little whore, and I'm finally going to get what I deserve."

Think fast!

My back is toward him, so I can't knee him in the groin, but I can struggle and scream. A screech unlike any I've ever let loose before belts out of me and goes on and on. I squirm enough so he can't get his hand clamped over my mouth. Somehow he loses his grip and I wiggle enough to elbow him in the solar plexus. It's not sufficient to do any damage, but it allows me room to turn and knee the hell out his balls. Now I make a break for it and run like my ass is on fire, screaming for help.

By this time, people are gathering about. Maybe they heard my scream. I'm not sure. But I keep yelling, "He tried to attack me. He tried to rape me." And I keep repeating myself.

Some kind woman takes me in her arms and someone else calls the police. Joe stumbles through the door and claims I'm a lunatic who attacked him. The police arrive and take us both in for questioning.

A female officer asks if I want to go to the hospital, but I decline. I explain everything that happened, starting from when I was hired. I don't leave out any detail, including what Vince told me about Jenny, the girl who resigned. My chest and the front of my shoulders are sore where Joe slammed me into the wall and I keep rubbing them, trying to relieve the ache.

"Are you okay?" the officer asks.

"It's just bruised, I'm sure."

"May I?"

I take off my coat, but my sweater covers up everything.

"Would you mind slipping your sweater off your shoulder a bit?" When I do, I'm shocked to see the purple already showing up.

"Yeah, that's going to be a lot worse by tomorrow. You should get that checked out by the hospital. You might have a fractured collar bone or something."

"I don't have any insurance."

She pats my hand. "If he caused this, you may not need it. It's also another way to add evidence."

Maybe she's right. I don't know anymore. Why did Joe have to go and do this? Now I won't be able to look for another job. Dammit.

"Come on. I'll drive you over."

"Thanks."

As it turns out, I have a cracked rib. The doctor says there's nothing they can do but treat the pain. The police officer has them take pictures to submit as evidence of the attack.

On the way back to the station, she says, "I don't suppose you threw yourself into that wall, did you?"

"What?"

"He's claiming you attacked him."

"Yeah, I usually like to break my own ribs."

She chuckles. "That's what I thought. I think this will work out for you."

"I was going in there to resign. I recorded his conversation. It wasn't the first time, like I said. All I wanted was to get out and find another job. Now I've got a broken rib to deal with and most likely a court date."

She casts me a sympathetic glance. "Hey, one good thing came out of this. He won't be doing this anymore."

"Don't count on it. I wouldn't put anything past that slime ball."

CHAPTER 6

PRESCOTT

WHY THE HELL WON'T SHE CALL ME?

After I sent the coats, I thought I'd immediately hear back from her, but nothing. She didn't even send me an acknowledgement. Then almost a week later, the box was sitting on my desk when I arrived at work with a note inside. She'd written: "Thanks, but no thanks."

The Little Wolf struck back.

She's devouring up my days, not by the hour, but by the second. I wanted to possess her. Well, that joke is on me. Vivienne Renard fucking owns my ass, balls, and dick. I have to figure out a way to get all of them back, because I'm a worthless piece of shit without them.

"Mr. Beckham, your father would like to see you in his office," Lynn says through the phone. Then she whispers, "Tell the bastard to fuck off, and you'll see him in yours."

"Lynnie, I'd never put you in that position. Let him know I'm on my way."

"Chicken shit."

She's right. For the life of me, I don't know why I let the son of a bitch get to me. Maybe it's because I still want his praise. *And why the hell is that?*

When I get to his door, the one thing I don't do is knock. This is more my business than his. Granddad is right. I have more of a right to the Whitworth name than he does. And now with him siding with the step-cunt, he doesn't deserve much respect at all. My grandfather barely acknowledges him anymore.

"You wanted to see me." It's not a question. I'm brusque and to the point.

"Sit."

"I'd rather not."

"Fine. You need to straighten your ass up."

"You're not in a position to tell me how to run my life. You lost that ability at Christmas."

He winces. That's a surprise.

"Your stepmoth — "

"She's nothing to me."

"Prescott, please."

"No. In fact, I'd rather you never speak of her in my presence. I've made that perfectly clear."

He offers me a slight nod.

"Is there something else you wanted to discuss, perhaps about business? If not, I have things to do."

"No."

I walk out. I have no idea what he wanted to tell me about my life and don't care. Whatever that bitch did to make him wince doesn't concern me. He can deal with her shit.

When I pass Lynn, I motion her into my office.

"Well?" she asks.

"He started talking about me straightening up, but I cut him off, reminding him he lost that right. Then he tried to bring up the step-cunt, but I cut him off again and that was it."

"Hmm. That's a curiosity, isn't it?"

"Not for me. I don't want to know anything about her, but that's all he wanted."

"Next time he calls, I'm going to tell him to come to your office instead."

"That's fine, but don't feel the need to put yourself in a tough position on my behalf."

"What? You don't think I can handle it?"

Lynn is a master at handling people. She could tame a damn lion if it came to that and I tell her so. But I'll never ask her to do my dirty work, especially where my father is concerned.

She waves a hand. "That's not dirty work. I think it would be fun to put the bastard in his place. You're like my son and he's shit on you."

"Dammit, why couldn't he have married you?" I hold out my arms to hug her.

"Because I would've beat his ass to a pulp. Besides, I kinda like my husband."

"Oh, yeah. I forgot about him."

She punches me in the arm. "You're a fucking mess. Now get back to work. Jack from security called. He said it was urgent."

"Thanks, Lynn." And then an idea strikes me. "Hey, where do you and Larry like to eat?"

"Larry likes to eat at home. He hates getting dressed up. You know that."

"I didn't ask where you liked to go … I asked where you liked to eat. There's a difference."

She gives me the name of a restaurant.

"Don't plan on cooking tonight. Expect a delivery around seven. Just let me know what you want."

"Thanks, boss."

She deserves much more than a fucking dinner. I remind myself to make sure she gets a huge quarterly bonus. Lynn keeps the office running for me and I wouldn't know what to do without her.

I immediately call Jack and his news sets me on edge.

"What do you mean she came home in a police car?"

"Mr. Beckham, all I can tell you is the guy we had watching

69

her place reported back to me that she came home in a police car."

"Then I want you to find out exactly why that is. And don't call me back until you know the answer." He doesn't have an opportunity to respond before I end the call.

What the goddamn fuck! Vivi comes home in a police car and they don't even think to question why? Was she injured? Or in trouble? I'm on the verge of going over there myself when Weston calls. What the hell is going on today?

"Dude, what's up?"

"Nothing," I practically yell at him.

"Whoa, is someone having a rough morning?"

"Shit. Sorry." I scrub my face and sigh. "Had a meeting with my dad," I semi-lie. I've never lied to Weston before and it doesn't sit well with me. It actually disturbs me more than I care to admit.

"Sorry, man. You want me to call back at a better time?"

"Nah. Let's talk now." This may be exactly what I need to get my mind off Vivi.

I have the financials back for A Special Place and I explain it all to him. A couple of investors have suggested we set up a few more restaurants in other locations to see how they go. I told them there were already restaurants located in emerging markets in the southeast such as Charlotte, Charleston, and Birmingham and they were doing extremely well. "After I told them that, they were all in."

"Did they give you a time frame?" he asks.

"I'm thinking we'll have contracts to sign by Christmas. It's time to buy some property, dude."

Weston laughs. "Like I have time for that, but I'll manage."

"You can't put Special on it?"

"Not for this. This is my area of expertise. She'll come in for the outfitting."

"Sounds like a plan."

"When you coming back to Atlanta?" he asks.

"When we have the final contracts all ready to go. Why?"

"Just asking."

"I'll let you know when I hear definites."

"Okay. We'll make it happen. There may be land buying trips in our future."

I wonder if Vivi would get along with Special. What the hell am I thinking? Vivi doesn't even get along with me! It would be a cold day in hell before I got her to agree to go on a trip with me. I can't even get the woman to fucking call me. It would be fun, though, if I could.

After we end the call, my momentary distraction is gone and I'm back to wondering what the hell happened to Vivi. I wish Jack would call. It's not even ten and I'm acting like a caged bull.

Lynn walks in and hands over some papers for me to sign and I jump when she slaps them on my desk. She notices how edgy I am.

"What's wrong now? You were fine a few minutes ago."

"It's nothing."

By the look she gives me, I know she doesn't believe me.

"Oh, here's my order for our dinner, and thanks again."

She leaves, glancing over her shoulder one last time before she walks out.

The thing with Vivi is driving me nuts. If someone hurt her, they're dead. Maybe it's that fucking building she lives in. She needs to move, but dammit, she won't fucking talk to me. I can't even help her and I'm fully capable of it. I sent her those damn coats to keep her from shivering in this freezing weather, but she wouldn't have anything to do with them. What the fuck am I supposed to do?

By lunch, I've worked myself up to the point I have to go home to smoke a blunt and calm my ass down. It's after two when I return. Lynn examines me with lifted brows. I shrug, choosing to ignore her.

Finally, Jack calls.

"She was taken to the police department because she was attacked."

"What?" I shout.

"Calm down, Mr. Beckham. She's fine, as far as we can tell."

"As far as you can tell? Please elaborate on that."

"Our informant tells us she went to work in midtown …"

"Wait. Did you say midtown?"

"Yes, sir. It's the office of Joe Delvecchio, the owner of Java Beans & More."

"Yes, yes, I know. Go on."

"Apparently, they had an altercation whereby Vivi accused him of attacking her and attempted rape, but he claims she attacked him. She was then taken to the hospital and was discovered to have suffered a broken rib," Jack explains to me. By now I'm ready to climb out of my skin.

"Fuck, fucker." The motherfucker *hurt* her. He's going to pay.

"She is fine and the police have filed charges against Mr. Delvecchio."

"Jack, I want her tailed at all times. Don't let anything like this happen again. You understand?"

"Yes, sir."

"One more thing. I need the address of Mr. Delvecchio."

I hang up the phone and notice my fist is clenching and unclenching. I suppose it's in anticipation of what I'm going to do to Joe Delvecchio when I see him. That greasy motherfucker has it coming. Vivi will be the last woman he tries to assault.

There's one thing I hate and that's a bully. But a man who bullies a woman for sexual favors, a man who tries to force her, is lower than dog shit in my book.

When I'm done with him, Joe Delvecchio is going to wish he'd never met Vivi Renard.

CHAPTER 7

VIVI

IT TAKES ABOUT A WEEK BEFORE I CAN INHALE WITHOUT piercing pain shooting into my chest. Vince called when he heard what happened. Of course, it was because the police stopped by the shop and wanted to talk to him and Jackie, along with all the other employees. They even called Jenny. Everyone corroborated my story, putting Joe up a shit creek without a paddle. Vince checks up on me quite a bit now.

"I told you the man was dangerous. Thank God he didn't rape you," Vince says.

A violent shudder rips through me. "Don't remind me. I've never been so scared before."

"I'm so sorry that happened to you. But at least you're safe now."

Looking around my apartment, I'm not so sure about that. "Yeah," I say, though my voice is weak.

"You okay?"

"I'll be fine. I just need to get another job." Too bad my rib is still pretty sore.

"Well, take care of yourself. Don't forget, if you need anything, give me a call."

"Thanks, Vince. Hey, is the coffee shop still open?"

"Nah, they all closed. I think he's going to sell them."

"Damn. I wish I could buy them."

Vince laughs. "Me too. See ya, Vivi."

After I hang up, I check my emails again to see if there are any hits for jobs. Excitement strikes when I notice a new unread email, but it turns to sadness when it's from the website I listed the bracelet on. There is an offer for it very close to my asking price and I'm blown away. The email gives me all the pertinent information to contact the potential buyer. Before I lose my nerve, I quickly shoot off an email to him. I need the money and am out of options, I remind myself.

It's almost lunch, so I root around in the fridge for something to eat, but it's pretty bare. I grab the last apple and after it's gone, I take a hot shower. When I'm dressed and my hair is dried, I count the cash on hand and what's left in my checking account. It's pitiful. There's a total of one hundred twenty-seven dollars. Joe was supposed to pay me the day after he attacked me, which means that's not going to happen. If a job doesn't open up fast, I may be on the streets.

I check all the job sites again, hoping something magically appears and then apply for waitress openings. There are lots of those. The high-end restaurants won't consider me, but the other places might. I jot down the addresses of a couple of dozen places. Then I head to Manhattan for the afternoon. My best hopes are to get hired by a couple of restaurant/bars where I can work and earn good tips. If that doesn't work, maybe I can file for unemployment.

Thankfully, at one restaurant, I am in luck. The owner, Diana, is in and she has been looking to hire someone. My interview goes well, although she is curious why someone like me wants to be a waitress. When I explain the truth, she says she'll hire me under two conditions: first, I have to give two weeks' notice before I quit; and second, I have to let her know my schedule for my other jobs, when I get them. That's certainly fair, so I agree. I'm hired me on the spot and have to report in at eleven in the morning for training. I visit a few more places with the hopes of finding an additional job, but come up empty-handed. It's about six when I head back to Brooklyn, stopping at the grocery to pick up some items before going home.

My apartment building is fairly quiet at this time of day, mostly because the action doesn't begin until later at night. I jog up the stairs and my key is already out as I approach the door.

I bolt the door behind me when I'm inside. As if the lock was a cue, my stomach growls loudly. I rush to the fridge to empty my load. It's not much, but will get me by. Then I turn on my makeshift stove to heat up some water for the Ramen noodles. When college was over, I figured the days of eating these were gone. Guess I was wrong.

After dinner, I check my messages. There's a response from the email regarding the bracelet saying he definitely wants it. He'll be available to meet me tomorrow night. That means I'll have to do it after work. That poses a problem. I don't want to walk around town, carrying a bracelet worth that much money. Wearing it isn't an option either. If someone were to see it, I'd get mugged in an instant. I get off at seven, so I can be back here afterward and meet him someplace. But there's nowhere to meet him around here. At least, nowhere safe.

As I see it, the only choice I have is for him to meet me down-stairs. He can call when he gets here. As soon as he does, I can run down, and we can make the exchange. He left me a phone number in his message, so I decide to call him.

When I give him the details, he doesn't balk.

"My neighborhood isn't the safest," I add, "so it would be wise to bring a bodyguard or a really bulky friend, if you have one. I'm not exactly comfortable carrying the bracelet around, which is the reason I want you to meet me here."

"I'll be outside tomorrow at nine. Will that work?" he asks.

"Yes. Can you call when you get here?"

He agrees.

The next morning, I'm a bit anxious to begin my new job. When I arrive, the manager introduces me and everyone is very helpful. In no time, I pick up the best sellers on the menu, but it takes a little while to learn the program on the computer. The system seems antiquated, and in need of an update. My brain tells me there's a better way to do this, but I keep my mouth shut. That isn't my job description any longer. Waiting tables is.

I'm working with one of the waiters, a guy around my age named Eric Thompson, who's showing me the ropes and giving me great pointers. There's a lot more to remember than I anticipated. He's patient with my errors and reminds me somewhat of Vince.

"Your first job waiting tables, huh?"

"Yeah, and it's nerve-wracking. I'm afraid I'll spill something on the customer," I say.

"You will, eventually. It happens to everyone. When it does, do some major sucking up. And pray it happens to a guy and not a woman. They're always worse than men."

"Really?"

"Yeah. They hate to get their clothes messed up. Men don't love it, but aren't pussies about it."

The way he says it makes me laugh. I'm carrying a tray loaded with drinks, so I tell him to stop. "Watch me dump this on someone." I'm glancing at him and round a corner. Just as I spot another waiter coming toward me, I hear Eric's alarmed, "Careful!"

Only it's too late. The tray comes straight up onto my chest as six glasses of ice water and soft drinks spill down my front. I'm soaked through to my skin. I can either laugh or cry, so I choose to do the first. Eric looks on and then a huge burst of laughter roars out of the both of us.

"What the hell am I going to do?"

He's bent down, wiping up the mess. At least I didn't dump the drinks I'm holding on the other waiter.

"You're going to dry off and find something to change into while I refill this order. Come on." He grabs my dripping wet wrist and pulls me in the back. When he yells out what happened, one of the other girls says she has a shirt I can wear. My bra is so wet it's a sponge. I head to the bathroom to do my best in drying off. Then I put the shirt on and go find Eric.

"How can I help?"

"We're good. Follow me." The rest of the afternoon runs pretty well. At the end of my shift, Eric says in a couple more days I should be good to work on my own. This is good news, because I can use the tips.

The train takes forever and is unusually crowded that night. I'm stressed out by the time I get home, anxious about how everything will go. The first thing I do is take a quick shower to rinse off the stickiness that's coated my skin all afternoon. I wiped off as best I could, but there was still a residue left behind. The hot shower helps to relax me. As I'm drying off, I notice the bruises and how the purple is fading from my skin. The discoloration reminds me how lucky I am that's all I ended up with. Once I'm dressed, I'm glad my jeans and sweatshirt cover up all what's left of the bruises.

About a quarter before nine, I go to my closet, pull out the stuffed bear, and carefully undo the seam. I poke around in the white fluffy stuffing until I find the bracelet. Releasing the breath I was holding, I pull the thing out and inspect it, making sure all the remnants of stuffing are removed. It'd been inside the bear a long while. Then I wrap it in the velvet sleeve my mom kept it in and put it in an envelope, along with the appraisal papers. Right as I finish, my phone rings. It's him. I wish my apartment faced the street so I could look out and see him, but it doesn't.

"I'll be right down," I tell him. I throw on my coat, put the envelope in the pocket, and leave. I make quick time on the stairs and push my way out of the door to see a fancy black limo double-parked on the street. Standing next to my building is a man in a dark suit. He's much younger than I thought he'd be and much more attractive.

"Miss Renard?"

"Yes, are you Mr. Acosta?"

He smiles and his teeth gleam under the streetlight. "Yes, I am. You have something for me?"

"Only if you have something for me in return."

His deep chuckle makes me smile. "Would you mind very much if I see it?"

"Right here?" I look around and check our surroundings.

"It's fine, Miss Renard. You don't have to worry."

"Mr. Acosta, have you noticed where we are?" He must be crazy not to be alarmed.

"Miss Renard, I have … people that won't let any harm come to me. As I've said, it's fine."

"People?"

"You told me to bring a bodyguard."

"I don't see one."

"That doesn't mean one isn't here," he says.

Even though I'm leery, I slip my hand into the pocket and pull out the envelope. I open it so he can look inside. I also show him the papers.

"Very good. I know you don't trust me, so here is the certified check you requested. I'll let you look it over."

It's in an envelope and I don't want to pull it out, so I scan it through the opening to make sure it's legit. It seems to be in order.

"Are you satisfied? I can assure you it's good and if you have any problems with your bank, call this man." He scribbles a name down on the back of a card and hands it to me. "He's with the bank from where the check is drawn. He'll be happy to help you."

"Thank you." I hand him the envelope.

"Miss Renard, if you have any other jewelry you wish to

dispose of, please call me directly. And might I suggest choosing another place to live?" With a slight dip of his head, he turns and walks to the waiting limo. A huge dude appears to open the door for him. He gets in and they drive off. When I go to head inside, someone grabs me from behind and drags me to the side of the building. As soon as I start to scream, a hand clamps over my mouth, cutting off my cry for help.

CHAPTER 8

PRESCOTT

JOE DELVECCHIO NEVER KNEW WHAT OR WHO NAILED HIM. I waited until he made bail. When he exited the jail, I watched the little fucker prance around as though he didn't have a care in the world. Little did he know. Later that night, I gave him a broken nose and a few broken ribs. Figured what goes around …

He fought like a girl, trying to scratch me, and whined like a fucking baby, too. The pussy. Too bad he didn't grow up learning how to properly fight, like I did. I wouldn't have minded a challenge. It would've been an excuse to do more damage. One punch and he sagged, and when the second came, he dropped like the dead. I left him lying there, crying like a little girl, the greasy-headed douche.

I'd made sure it was dark, so he couldn't see my face. Kept my mouth shut the whole time, too, though I didn't want to. I wanted to tell him it was all for Vivi, but I didn't. If he ever so much as tries to get near her again, I'll castrate the little prick.

She didn't leave her place for days, but when she finally did she went job searching. This woman. I was a little stunned by her.

The guys keep a close watch on her while I work. I can't

slack off in that regard. But tonight, I decided to drop by and see what she's up to. I come up to her apartment building and that's when I spot her.

She's talking to some guy with a damn limo, who clearly doesn't belong in this neighborhood. Then I see her exchanging —what is that? Drugs?—for an envelope. There can only be money inside.

Holy fuck it all. This woman is going to be the death of me.

So I do something kinda stupid. I grab her. Scare the shit out of her, too, which I hate.

She sinks her teeth into my finger and now it's me who wants to scream.

Putting my mouth next to her ear, I say, "Hush, Vivi. It's me, Prescott. I'll let you go if you promise not to yell." I shift her body so she can see my face. Large, frightened eyes stare back at mine. "Okay?"

She gives her assent with a slight bob.

The demure, terror-stricken doe quickly morphs into the growling little wolf cub. "What the hell do you think you're doing? You scared me to death."

"Me? What the hell are you doing? Selling drugs now?"

"What are you talking about?"

Her heaving chest distracts me momentarily and I don't answer.

"Are you going to stand and stare or will you answer me?"

Grabbing her arm, I pull her inside the building.

"What are you doing?" she asks.

"Going inside. We're not going to discuss this on the street."

"I didn't invite you in." She tries to snatch her arm away, but I don't let go.

I decided to check on her tonight, because I was concerned about the recent accounts I've been receiving since the near rape. She is jobless, close to being penniless, and seeking employment. She's never called, of course, and her activity outside the apartment has been minimal until yesterday. Then I show up to see this interaction with some high-class dude and all I can think of to explain it is that she's gotten so desperate, she's resorted to selling drugs.

We get to her apartment door and I say, "You can unlock it, or I can break it down. Your choice."

"What's wrong with you?"

"Not a damn thing. Your choice, Vivi."

She takes out a key and turns the lock. When we walk inside, I'm utterly appalled she lives in a place like this. I knew it would be bad, given the location, but I never expected it to be this bad.

"You live here?"

Her eyes narrow. "What kind of a stupid question is that?"

A quick scan of the tiny apartment tells me everything I need to know. She needs to get the hell out of here. "Pack your things. You're moving."

"Oh? And exactly where would I be moving to?"

"I own a building. You can rent one of the units in it."

"I can barely afford this one."

"You won't have to pay me until you find a job." I dare her to say she can't afford it now.

"I have a job. I still can't afford it. Besides, what makes you think you can push me around?"

"I'm not. I'm trying to help, to make your life better."

She laughs. "Right." She drags the word out. "Then you'd have me exactly where you'd want me. I'd owe you, Prescott, and I refuse to be dangling from your hook."

Pointing to the only piece of furniture in the room, which is an old shabby chair, I say, "Sit."

"I'm not your damn dog, either."

"Please."

We fight a battle through our glares. She's tough. Most people would shrivel beneath my unrelenting gaze, but not Vivi Renard. She's grown quite a pair since Crestview. She has somehow managed to fill her spine with steel.

"Fine, don't sit. Would you please tell me what I witnessed on the street tonight?"

"Not until you tell me why the fuck you're stalking me. It's pretty creepy, Prescott."

She has me cornered. Vivi must be one hell of a chess player. Scraping my teeth over my lower lip, I think over how I'm going to handle this. "You'll probably find this hard to believe, but I've been worried about you."

There, that is part of the truth, after all.

Her eyes widen ever so slightly, just long enough for me to catch it. "Why would you, of all people, be worried about me?"

"You're my friend. I worry about my friends," I answer with a shrug.

"Prescott, we are not friends. You used me. Yeah, you compensated me nicely, but nevertheless, if I hadn't been smart, you would've never spoken to me at Crestview. That wasn't a friendship. So for the life of me, I can't understand why you want anything to do with me now."

I run a hand through my hair, because she's right. Yeah, I sort of had a soft spot for her, but if her brains hadn't been a part of the picture back then, I would've never noticed her to begin with. Her brilliance isn't what interests me now. She's fucking gorgeous and I want her. But it's become more than that. I've become obsessed with Vivi Renard. My desire for her has surpassed the level of fanatical … it's damned obscene.

"You haven't answered my question. Were you selling drugs to that guy?"

She puffs out a breath. "Do you honestly think I'd do something like that?"

Flinging my arm out, I say, "Look at this place. I wouldn't blame you. I'm pretty fucking sure you'd do anything to get out of here. You don't even have a stove. Or a proper bed to sleep on. It's only November and it's fucking freezing in here. Does your landlord even turn on the heat? What's it going to be like in the dead of winter when it's really cold outside?"

Her lips press together in a hard line. Man, have I hit a nerve.

"You know what? You're right. I don't have the luxury of living in a fancy place, which I'm sure you do. I wasn't lucky like you are. The reason I was meeting that guy tonight was to sell a piece of jewelry I inherited from my mom. I was hoping it wouldn't come to that. Unfortunately, it didn't work out that way. The check I received will enable me to keep this lowdown apartment and will save me from financial ruin until I can find another job—not that it's any of your damn business."

Jesus. The fuck. Now I feel like the world's biggest douche. I hold out my hand to her ... for what? So she can tell me to stick it up my ass, where it belongs?

Deciding to switch tactics, I ask, "Have you eaten yet?"

"No. I was going to make some Ramen noodles after my transaction. I don't suppose you'd want some?" she asks sarcastically.

"I actually love Ramen. How about we go find the real thing?"

Vivi cocks her head and drills me with her gaze. "On one condition."

"What's that?"

"You don't go batshit possessive on me."

"Deal."

We head out of her apartment, she locks up behind her, and we go to the car that awaits me.

"You have a car? You're so spoiled."

"I have no comment for that." I check my phone for the closest restaurant that sells the best Ramen and locate a place in Manhattan. Then I instruct the driver to take us there.

"Manhattan?" Vivi asks. "There isn't one in Brooklyn?"

"Not the best. I want the best."

After another huff from her, she settles into the seat.

"Tell me why you had to sell that piece of jewelry." I want the specifics.

"I already told you."

"I mean, why are you in such financial straits? You weren't that way at Crestview. Well, I knew you needed money, but I thought it was for spending, you know, fun."

"How would you know?" She sits up and angles her body toward me. "You never paid attention to me."

"Nobody went to Crestview who had serious financial issues. Crestview gave very little aid and never gave scholarships."

"Why are you so nosy?"

"I'm not. I'm trying to figure you out. You came from a well-to-do family, went to an upper crust school, graduated from MIT, for fuck's sake, and now you're practically slumming. No, you *are* slumming by anyone's definition, even yours. What gives, Vivi?"

"It's none of your damn business, Prescott."

"I'm making it my business. Your family obviously doesn't give a fuck. Somebody has to."

Her hand snakes out to slap me, but I catch her wrist before she has a chance. "What the hell?"

"Leave my family out of this," she says through clenched teeth as her body trembles.

"You can either tell me or I'll find out on my own."

She instantly sags against the seat and her balled up hands rub at her eyes. After a long pause, she begins. "My dad died in a car wreck while I was at Crestview. I was only twelve."

"I don't remember that."

"You probably weren't there then," she says.

"Yeah, I was. I started Crestview when I was eleven."

"Well, Dad was killed in a car accident and left behind a ton of debt. Mom sold the big house, moved us to a smaller one, and we managed. Or I thought we did. I wanted to transfer to the public school, but she preferred I stay at Crestview. I did it to make her happy. It was stupid, because it added to her mounting debt. She mortgaged the house to the hilt. She hid it from me and I had no idea how bad it was. Then came MIT. Even then she never let on." She pauses, shaking her head to herself, even as her hands clench.

"After I graduated, I landed a job in California. I was doing well and could've helped, but she pretended everything was great ... until she got sick. It was ALS. She was ill for almost three years, which was why I moved back to Virginia—to care for her. The bills were enormous still. I gave up my job and didn't have any income to cover everything, even after selling the house."

She goes into detail of how she stayed with her mother until the end. Vivi gave up an exploding career to care for her dying mother. But the two plus years she spent in Virginia were the nail on the coffin of Vivi's career and her rise up the ladder to success. Now no one wants to hire her, and I get that. It's hard to bring someone back into the fold after they've lost the momentum of growth and been away from the industry for that length of time. It's not impossible, but it's especially true of the tech industry where things change at the speed of light. If you have a huge gap and you're behind the eight ball, oftentimes you need a door opener. And Vivi doesn't have one. Or she didn't —until me.

"So that's why I was selling one of Mom's bracelets. It was one of two pieces I have left."

"Why didn't you come to me?" It bothers me she didn't.

She glares at me. "I don't want to owe you anything, because then you can show up and collect any time you want."

"No. That's not ... I'd never do that." It's disappointing she thinks of me that way.

The car comes to a stop and I see we've arrived at our destination. "Let's talk about this over dinner."

They're crowded, so I use my persuasive skills—also known as bribery—and score us a table. After we're seated, Vivi shoots me a pointed stare and asks, "Do you always do this?"

"Do what?"

"Hand out money like candy?"

"Like I told you before, only when it achieves the desired outcome. We were in need of a table and a couple of c-notes did the trick."

"A couple of c-notes. What about all those people who were here before us?"

I shrug. "They were welcome to pass the host a few bucks, too."

She glares at me in disgust. It's obvious she has a disdain for the way I throw money around. "Maybe they didn't have a few bucks."

"The host had the option of saying no, too, you know. He's the one who should carry the blame. After all, he knew there were people waiting longer than us."

This hits home and it's an inarguable point. She sits back and sips her water.

"I know you have a great disdain for my money, but I don't understand why. Help me get there."

"It's not the money. It's how you use it."

"Vivi, I'm willing to help you, no strings attached. I'm serious."

The waiter comes by and takes our order. Vivi gawks as I order enough food for ten. She's hungry and what we don't eat, she can take home.

"Do you actually plan to eat everything you ordered?" she asks.

"I have a large appetite and wanted to sample a few things. We can share. You can take home the rest."

She nods, but the skepticism stays in her eyes.

"So, can we come to some sort of agreement, Vivi?"

"What kind of agreement?"

"You'll let me help you without any conditions whatsoever, and as friends only." I nearly groan when the words come out of my mouth. How did I all of a sudden turn into a fucking boy scout?

Realistically, there is no way in hell I plan on hanging around

Vivi Renard without trying to get her into my bed. But I'd never blackmail her into it. I fully plan on using other ways to convince her. Plain and simple, I have one goal and that is to fuck Vivi until she begs for mercy, or better yet, for more. And when she does, she'll do it willingly.

CHAPTER 9

VIVI

WHY IS HE BEING SO DAMNED CONSIDERATE ALL OF A sudden? My last couple of encounters with him weren't like this at all. What happened to asshole Prescott—the guy who thinks he owns everyone? Asshole Prescott is self-serving and domineering. Which makes me wonder what happened to the guy I remember from high school. Sure, he was sort of full of himself back then, but in his own way, he was always decent to me. Yeah, he needed me and used me, but still. This sudden consideration for my well-being reminds me of that kid, just a little. At least more than asshole Prescott, anyway. In any case, I have to respond to his proposal.

"Don't take this the wrong way, but I don't think that's possible."

His eyes bore a hole into me. The urge to flinch is as strong as if I'd suddenly been stung by a wasp. By sheer force of will, I stand firm. Actually, I have to press my legs together and remind myself that running out of here like my hair's on fire will accomplish nothing. Folding my hands, I place them in my lap and clench them tightly together.

His unrelenting glare doesn't cease. Neither does mine. I

won't back down and lose this game he likes to play. I won't allow him to make me the weaker one at this table. My hands turn numb from the pressure, but I don't care.

Finally, his lids shutter his gaze and I relax a bit.

"You surprise me, Vivi."

"Me? Why?"

"You're different."

"How?" I ask. I'm curious to hear his reply.

There are a few things about me that have changed since he knew me. My physical appearance for one, but I'm also no longer the demure girl he once knew.

When I got to MIT, I recognized in order to get ahead in the world, I needed to be more assertive. That's when I grew a backbone. It wasn't easy by any means. At first, it was a stretch to sit in front of the class instead of the back where I was most comfortable. I nearly had anxiety attacks over taking the lead on class projects. Yet, in continually forcing myself to become the person I wanted to be, it became easier to be that person over time.

That's also when the pounds dropped off. I worried less over what I was putting in my mouth and more about what was important to me. The weight came off gradually and by the time two years passed, I was down six sizes.

"Your appearance, for one. But you're … stronger, too."

"I should hope so. That girl you knew in high school was bullied, and let herself continually be." I shake my head in disgust. "It probably didn't matter to you then. It makes sense. You were so caught up in your own popularity. The wonderful Prescott Beckham. All you had to do was smile and it set all the girls' panties on fire. One click of your fingers and off they'd run."

I don't mean to sound so bitter, but every time I think of those nasty bitches and how awful they made me feel, the emotions roll out of me uncontrollably.

"You act like it's my fault. I never did anything they didn't want."

I blow out a long breath. "No, you didn't. And to be fair, you were never mean to me. But you lived in your own cushy little world, Prescott. I'm sorry. My memories of Crestview aren't exactly as warm and fuzzy as yours."

His unyielding stare is back. "What makes you think my years there were warm and fuzzy?"

"Are you kidding me? You were the guy every girl wanted. Why wouldn't they have been?"

He leans forward, resting his elbows on the table. "So just because all the girls wanted me means I was happy?"

"Well, you always looked happy."

His eyes narrow. "You never looked *un*happy. And just so you know, I never saw those girls bully you. I wasn't just ignoring it. I was *unaware* of it. If I had seen it, I would've done something about it."

Is he fucking kidding me?

The whole school knew about it. Even the administration was aware of it, only they never did anything because of how much money those girls' parents funneled into Crestview. My locker had shit covering it every day and on more than one occasion I saw the principal silently watch those girls do their elephant imitation of me.

"I'm not going to get into a debate over this, but you must've been blind not to have seen their elephant imitation of me. And don't tell me you don't remember how fat I was."

"Come on, Vivi. Don't talk about yourself like that."

"Admit it, Prescott. If it hadn't been for you needing my brain, you would've never spoken a word to me."

His eyes shift, as does his body. Ah, so I've made the big guy uncomfortable. Good. I've lived most of my life in a state of discomfort. Do I feel badly about it? A little. It's not in my nature to be this way, but dammit, he's pushing me.

"I'm sorry. High school guys are idiots. And I fell into that category."

"Fell or fall?" I ask pointedly.

I hear him blow out a heavy breath. Maybe I've hit a nerve. Who knows? I don't even know why I care. It's not like anything's going to come of this. He's not the kind of guy I want to get involved with. My heart could never handle a guy like Prescott Beckham. He'd take what he wants and casually discard me like a used up piece of trash. And I don't play that game when it comes to my heart.

"You seem to have an extremely low opinion of me."

I ponder his statement, but don't speak.

"What did I ever do to you, besides pay you, and rather nicely I might add, to do my homework? I wasn't mean. I never joined in on the bullying, which, for the second time, I was not aware was happening. Now I'm honestly trying to help you, but you keep slapping me in the face."

Assessing the situation, I notice I'm still sitting here with my hands folded in my lap like a prim little miss. I unfold them and lean forward. "Let's be honest here. You're not helping me for altruistic reasons. There's something you want from me and we both know what it is."

He slowly runs his tongue over his bottom lip. On any other man, it would look creepy. On Prescott, it looks downright delicious. And he fucking knows it. I clench my thighs together, because damn if it doesn't get me wet.

"Is there anything wrong with that, Vivi?" His hooded expression, coupled with his sinful lips, has me rethinking my stance for a moment. I straighten my spine.

"Not if we're both in, but I'm not in, Prescott." Even if I'd like to be, just to ease the itch between my thighs. Like I'm going to mention that to him, though.

Thankfully, the waiter shows up then with a tray covered in so many dishes I almost laugh out loud.

"This is going to be a challenge," I say, in reference to the food.

"I'm up to any challenge you throw at me. And just so you know, I'm a tough competitor." By the smirk on his face, he's definitely not talking about the massive quantity of food that sits in front of us.

Why does he have to exude such potent sexuality? And why does he have to be the best looking guy I've ever known?

"Good to know. But I doubt I can eat as much as you can."

"Oh, I don't know. I think with a little practice you could learn to take in quite a bit."

The fork in my hand clatters onto the table. Damn his innuendo. I swallow nervously, involuntarily picturing what he suggested. How would it feel to have him sliding in and out of me?

I look up at him. His triumphant grin displays his arrogance, but leaves me floundering for a response. When nothing clever comes to mind, I snatch up my fork and dig in. His raspy chuckle sets my nerves on edge and raises goosebumps over my flesh, turning my nipples into rocks.

"What's the matter, Vivi? Do you have doubts about what I say? Because we can put it to the test if you'd like."

I glance up again, which is something I don't want to do, and say, "No, I don't want to put it to the test."

"Are you afraid you'll like it?"

"Do you ever take no for an answer?" Exasperation laces my tone.

"I don't get no for an answer very often. Come to think of it, I don't think I've ever been turned down."

"Yes, you have. From me. Just now. Now stop pestering me about it."

He chuckles, low and deep. God help me. My traitorous nipples are about to pierce holes in my bra. It's uncomfortable sitting here.

Then he dips his head and in a quieter voice, he says, "Vivi, how would you like it if I ate out your pussy? Licked and sucked your clit till you screamed?"

I gasp. Oh, *God*.

"Don't flatter yourself, Prescott," I practically pant out. My body is humming and I'm sweating. I want to fan myself, but that will only prove to him what he already knows. And no fucking way to that.

"Truth or dare," he says.

"Not this again."

"Why not? I thought it was kind of fun the last time we played."

"I'm trying to eat the exorbitant amount of food you ordered, which you don't seem to have the slightest interest in."

He shrugs a shoulder. "What can I say? I came here for the company. Back to our little game. Truth or dare?"

Deciding to be brave for a change, I say, "Dare."

His eyes widen and he gets a wicked gleam in his eyes.

Fuck me upside down. I take that back. Fuck me in circles. I'm so screwed.

"I dare you to spend one night with me."

"Not gonna happen. Not ever."

"That's not how the game is played," he says as he sits there wearing a smug expression.

My fork swings through the space between us. "I have the option of not taking the dare."

"No, you had the option of choosing truth over dare. You chose dare and you know what my dare is."

"I can't possibly spend the night with you."

"You don't have a choice, Vivi, because I won't allow you to return to that slum you call a home."

The set of his jaw and the tiny muscle twitching on his cheek tells me I'm at the business end of this declaration.

Leaning back, I make my own announcement. "You don't own me and have no right to decide that."

"I'm making it my right," he says, his tone clipped. "Until you understand that I won't let you put yourself at risk for nothing more than pride—and don't try to fool yourself into believing that place is safe—you won't be going back there."

I fold my arms across my chest. He thinks he can order me around like one of his employees. Well, he can't.

"You can't do this."

"I can and will, even if I have to carry you out of here kicking and screaming."

"You wouldn't."

The stony glare clues me in to his answer. He absolutely will. This is a man who always gets what he wants. Then a weird thing happens. His eyes soften around the edges and the hard set of his mouth eases.

"Let me help you. Please." This time it's more of a plea than a demand.

"I ... I can't."

The meal is forgotten and all I know is I need to get the hell away from this man. He does things to me, things I don't even want to contemplate. I have too much crap on my plate to add Prescott Beckham to the heap.

"I have to go."

"No, Vivi, don't—"

Before he has a chance to say anything more, I leap to my feet and shoot for the door.

CHAPTER 10

PRESCOTT

VIVI IS EVERY BIT AS STUBBORN AS ME, BUT THERE'S ONE thing she hasn't considered. I have more connections than she does. I grab my phone and hit a number. "She's out the door." That's all I have to say. My driver will intercept her.

The waiter stops by and I ask him to box up our dinner. He brings it to me along with the check. I leave him a sizable tip for his trouble.

When I get outside, the car—and Vivi—are waiting. She's acting like a pouty ten-year-old. I can't blame her. I'd be pissed off, too.

"Take me home," she says through gritted teeth.

"We're going home."

"My home, not yours."

"Answer me something. Be truthful, please. Do you like living there?"

"No!"

"All I needed to hear."

We drive the rest of the way in silence. When we arrive at my place, she stubbornly refuses to get out of the car.

"You can either get out on your own, or I'll carry you. You choose. But dammit, Vivi, I'm not playing games."

With a growl, she gets out and stomps toward the door. I want to laugh at her because she has no idea where she's going. I grab the large bag filled with our food boxes and follow her. The doormen wave at me and call me by name. I briefly introduce them to Vivi, explaining to them she is to be allowed up whenever she wants. Her angry expression makes me want to laugh, but I don't.

Then I usher her toward the elevator and up to the top floor. The building only has eight stories, and I have the entire eighth one and the level above it. It's really too much for me, but it was a great buy when they were redoing it, so I grabbed it.

When the doors open, we walk out into a small foyer, and I unlock my door with an electronic keypad.

"I can create a code for you, if you'd like."

"Don't bother. I won't be coming back," she says sourly.

"We'll see."

When we enter, I can hear her intake of breath. She doesn't speak, but her expression tells me more than words. Her eyes widen into circles and lines form on her forehead. She's impressed.

"Walk around. Check it out. The stairway leads to all the guest rooms, of which you're more than welcome to stake your claim. My room is on the main level. You can check that out, too."

I head to the kitchen to put away the food. "I'm not sure if you ate enough. I can keep this out if you want," I call out.

"That's okay." She walks around slowly until I lose sight of her. I let her explore where she wants. If she feels comfortable here, maybe she'll want to stay. Grabbing a bottle of merlot, I uncork it to allow it to breathe. Then I wait.

A few minutes pass and she returns. "You live here alone?"

"Yeah."

She eyes me skeptically. "Why do you have such a large place?"

"I found it during the pre-construction phase and it was a great deal."

"I'm pretty sure your idea of a great deal and mine are radically different."

I won't gratify her with an answer.

"Besides fucking me, what is it you really want, Prescott?"

"I want to help you. I don't want you living in that slum. It's highly unsafe." Vivi's not stupid, though. She'll see through any excuse I offer. So I decide to be straightforward. "And I do want to fuck you."

"Why?"

"What do you mean why?"

"I don't think it was a difficult question. Why do you want to fuck me when you can have any woman in Manhattan? Let's be honest. I don't have a penny to my name, which doesn't exactly put me on your level. So why me?"

Isn't that the same thing I've been asking myself lately?

"You intrigue me."

"So you want to fuck every woman who intrigues you?"

"No. I only want to fuck you."

She steps into my space, which actually shocks me. "Guess what? You're not going to get the chance." Then she walks over to one of the sofas and sits down, crossing her legs and arms. That tells me something. She's not game for letting me in.

"Would you care for some wine?"

"No, thanks. I have to work tomorrow, and I need to get going."

"You can't leave."

"This is the way I see it. Either you let me go tonight, or I leave tomorrow when I go to work. One way or another, I'm gone. You don't own me, Prescott. I realize you have money, and from the looks of this place, you must have a lot. But you can't kidnap me and keep me prisoner."

"You sure about that?"

Her eyes dart about the room as her face pales. I didn't mean to frighten her. I wouldn't force her into anything, even the silly dare I proposed.

"No, Vivi, don't be afraid. I was only joking."

"I don't believe you." She stands and heads to the door. "I'm leaving now and don't try to stop me, because I'll scream."

"Look, I swear to you I'd never keep you here against your will. I just hate to see you go back to that awful apartment. Let me put you up in a hotel if you're not comfortable staying here."

"I can't accept that from you. My debt is—"

"I don't give a goddamn shit about your debt!" I yell. "It's your safety I care about. If you go back there and something happens, I'll feel responsible. Just one night, that's all, until we can make other arrangements. I promise not to do anything inappropriate."

"This is awkward," she says.

"Only because you're making it that way."

"I don't want your charity."

I'm about to strangle her. "It's not charity. It's one fucking night, Vivi. We'll find you an alternative place to live. I own rental property. It won't be charity, because I'll charge you rent. I'll fucking charge you what your current rent is. Then when you get a job, I'll raise it. Does that satisfy you?"

Her lips purse as she thinks. This is a damn good offer and I'm not sure how she can refuse it. She'd be crazy to.

Then I add, "Why don't we do this. Let me check you into a hotel and that way you can sleep on it."

"Yeah. Okay. No pressure, though?"

"No pressure." At least not until she's moved in and things have settled down a bit. Then I'll try again. Maybe she'll be softened up toward me by then.

Then I stop and think. *Since when did I become Mr. Considerate?*

CHAPTER 11

VIVI

PRESCOTT TAKES ME TO THE JAMES. IT'S NOT VERY FAR FROM his place. I've never stayed in such a luxurious hotel. He books me a room for three nights. When I try to object, he says it may take me that long to make a decision.

"Vivi, it's nothing. Don't worry about it."

"I don't have any clothes."

"Give me the key to your apartment. I'll send my driver over and he can pack a bag for you."

"No, that's too much."

"Vivi." He uses that warning tone of his. Then somehow, I'm rummaging through my bag and handing him the key.

He smiles then and suddenly I'm grateful for what he's doing. I have that check for the bracelet tucked inside my bag and it's a relief to know I don't have to go back to that horrid place tonight.

"Thank you."

"You're welcome. And order room service or whatever you want. Charge it to the room. Money is no object, Vivi."

I don't know how to respond to that. When you dig through

the bottom of your handbag, searching for loose change so you can buy a meal, it goes against the grain to live like this.

He must read my mind because he says, "I can't begin to understand what it's like to be poor. I won't pretend either. But I've never thought less of people who didn't have money, if that's what's running through your mind."

"No. That's not it at all. I was just thinking how … oh, forget it. Promise me something."

"What?"

"Don't ever take having all that money for granted."

He gives me a quick smile in response and leaves.

The desk clerk asks if I'd like assistance in checking into my room. Since I have no luggage, I decline and take hesitant steps toward the elevator, observing the clean lines of the decor on the way. It's modern but inviting.

Although no one gives me a second glance, I still feel uncomfortable in my casual clothes here. I know it's my imagination, because there are other people hanging out in jeans and not dressed up at all.

I walk into the elevator and then notice my room is one of only two rooms on the top floor, or a penthouse. He's booked me the best in the house. When I enter, I can't keep the smile off my face. I've never stayed in anything so grand. There are magnificent views of Manhattan from both the bedroom and living room. The bathroom is amazing, with every amenity imaginable. The shower is decadent, having two rainfall showerheads and two handhelds. There's also a gigantic bathtub on top of that. I'm in heaven and never want to leave.

There are robes in the bathroom and I contemplate taking a shower, but decide against it in case the man shows up with my clothes. I may as well enjoy this place, though, so I flop out on the couch and turn the TV on. I'm just getting into an episode of one of my favorite shows when there's a knock on the door. I open it to find Prescott standing there.

"Can I come in?"

"Sure."

He's carrying a duffle bag from my closet. "Here." He hands it to me.

"Thanks. That was fast."

"Mason doesn't waste time."

"Mason?"

"He's my driver."

I peek inside the bag to see an array of things. Not that I own much but this will get me by for the next couple of days.

"Hey, thanks for setting me up in here. This place is awesome. I've never seen a bathroom like the one in here."

"That nice, huh?"

"Yeah." I laugh. "I can't wait to take a shower."

His chest rumbles with laughter. "I can help you with that if you'd like."

"Funny guy."

"I try."

"So, Prescott, where do we go from here?"

"I'll show you a few properties tomorrow and you tell me what you think."

I rub my forehead. "Um, I have to work from eleven until seven."

"We can do it after."

"Okay."

He gets ready to walk away, then turns at the last minute. "Vivi, you think the worst of me. But we used to be friends—or sort of anyway. At least I thought we were." Without another word, he leaves.

I suppose it makes sense that he did think we were friends. In some ways, I guess we were. Only I dreamed of more, which was a problem.

Now he wants more, too, but only in the way of fucking. I know if I give him what he wants, I'll end up with a broken heart. And that's the last thing I need right now.

~

The next morning, I stop at the bank to deposit the check and end up arriving at work a little early. Eric's already there, prepping tables. He gives me a full-on smile and I shake my head, remembering the drink catastrophe from yesterday.

"Did you get cleaned up when you got home last night?" he asks.

"I was so sticky. I swear my bra was glued to my skin. Ugh."

"You're not the first person that's happened to and you won't be the last."

"Well, I'd prefer not to go through that again. So I'm still shadowing you today, right?"

"Yep. Today and tomorrow. After that, you're on your own."

Our lunch crowd is thick, and things run smoothly until I screw up an order for a customer. The woman is a bitch about it, and while I do everything I know to make it right, she still insists on seeing the manager. We call him over and he does a song and dance, smoothing things over. Afterward, he pulls me aside and lets me have it.

"We can't afford these types of errors. It's a simple matter of entering the item into the computer." His snappy retort surprises me because up to this point, he's been so even-tempered.

"It's not simple and the system is antiquated," I say, which isn't the wisest reply.

"Excuse me?" His head tips forward as he looks down his nose at me. I've done it this time.

"Honestly, this system is confusing and makes it difficult for the wait staff. There are much better software options out there."

"Vivi, that's not the point. The point is you are responsible for getting the correct order to your customers. Can you or can you not accomplish that?"

"Yes, but I thought I had."

"You obviously hadn't or she wouldn't have made such a stink. I'm willing to let it go this time, since you're in training, but the next time, it comes out of your paycheck. Understand?"

"Yes." Jeez. After he leaves, Eric approaches.

"Sorry. We won't let that happen again. I should be checking your orders."

"It's not your fault, Eric. The program here is awful. It should be categorized or at least alphabetized. But anyway, onward we go."

We finish up the lunch crowd and during a lull Eric asks if I want to join him and a few others after work for some drinks.

"Aw, I wish. I have plans tonight to hunt down another place to live."

"Oh? You in the market for a roommate?"

I lean my hip on the counter and say, "I may be. Why? Do you know of someone?"

"Yeah. Me. My roommate just moved to the west coast. So I'm frantic." He places his hands in the prayer pose. "I've been asking God to send me an angel to help and look what happened."

"Where do you live?"

"The East Village. It's a very—and I mean very—small two-bedroom. If you don't mind living in cramped quarters, I'm neat and like things organized. So if you're a slob, speak up now. It would never work for me."

"No, I'm not a slob at all. I like things orderly, too. How much is rent?"

He tells me and it's a very fair price.

"I'd want to see it first. And my friend has offered me an exceptional deal, too, that I need to check out."

"Your friend?"

Shrugging, I say, "Yeah. He has some rentals he's willing to let me have at a steal."

"Hmm. He must be some friend to have rentals as in plural."

"You might say that."

"Who's this friend?"

"Just a guy."

"Yeah," he says with a knowing grin. "Just a guy."

"He is. We went to high school together."

"And you're still dating him?"

"Eric, he's a friend. We're not dating."

He holds his hands up. "Hey, just asking. So when do you think you'll know? I have to tell my landlord something soon. He's waiting on a lease renewal and is eager to get rid of my ass so he can hike up the rent."

"Two days at the most. Is that okay?"

"That'll work. When do you want to see the place?"

"How about tomorrow? Maybe before work? Then we can come in together."

"Sounds great." He finds a piece of paper to write down his address and hands it to me. "Okay, I'm stoked. I've wanted a girl for a roommate forever. By the way, you know I'm gay, right?"

"I didn't, but thanks for clarifying," I say with a little laugh.

"Does it matter to you?"

"Not at all. Why would it?"

"Just checking. I didn't want it to be an issue later. So just for clarity, you wouldn't mind if I had guys over or anything?"

"Nope, not a problem."

He hugs me. "I see the beginnings of a great friendship here, Vivi. Even if we don't move in together."

"Yeah, same here. By the way, what do you do when you're not working here?"

He steps back. "I haven't told you? I'm in the process of building my interior design business."

"That's great. I've always wanted to learn a bit about that. I'm digging this roommate situation more and more."

"Oooh. Maybe I can find more ways to entice you then … like I have all kinds of connections with my buyer's card. I can take you places you've never been before."

"Really? Like where?" Now, I'm intrigued.

"For starters, the D&D Building."

"What's that?"

His hands fly to his face and he acts as though he's having a heart attack. "My God, Vivi. You just killed me." His expression is so comical; it beats anything I've ever seen. I crack up.

Then he leans in close and says, "Can I share something with you?"

"Sure."

"Imagine this. A building, eighteen stories tall, filled with every gorgeous piece of lingerie you can imagine, and I'm talking La Perla, darling. Add to that, the hottest men you've ever laid your eyes on. Then layer it with oodles and oodles of sex toys and I mean the fancy brands. Lelos or whatever the hell they're called. That's the D&D building for me. It's eighteen floors of designer heaven. Nothing but fabrics, carpets, flooring, furniture, design concepts, you name it." When he finishes, I think he may climax. He fans himself for a minute. "Whew, too much fantasizing for me."

"It sounds amazing."

"I'll take you one day and you'll see for yourself."

One of the other waiters calls out to us. "The crowd is thickening. Better get a move on, you two, or you'll be in the weeds."

"Come on, Viv. Let's go." He grabs my hand and I realize he just gave me a new nickname. I smile. Eric is fun and exactly what I need in my life.

We work our asses off until the next shift arrives to take our places. I'm happy to call it a day and head home.

As we walk out the door, Eric asks, "You headed back to Brooklyn?"

"No. I'm actually staying in SoHo tonight."

"Oh?"

"Yeah." I give an awkward shrug. "My friend."

"So you're at your friend's tonight?"

"Not exactly."

Eric stares and waits for an answer.

"I'm at The James." I'm hoping he'll let it pass. He doesn't.

"Say what?"

"I'm in a hotel for the next few days. It's kind of a long story."

His mouth curves into a conspiratorial grin. "I imagine it is. This friend seems like someone you need to hang on to if he's putting you up in The James, girl." Then he taps my elbow.

"It's not like that."

"Well, whatever it is, I'd try to sweeten the pot, if you know what I mean."

"Stop. It's not going in that direction. It's … complicated."

"Oh, I sense a juicy story somewhere in there."

"For God's sake, don't tell me you're a gossip."

His mouth falls open as he takes a step back. "Me? A gossip? Never. I was only thinking that if this person, an old high school friend, put you up in such a classy place, then you must mean more than you think to him. So I thought … oh, forget it. It's not my business, is it?"

"Nope. But I appreciate it a lot." I pat his arm so he knows I'm not angry. "Come on. Let's go home. We can take the train together."

"Good idea."

We link arms and are headed toward the subway entrance when I hear my name.

"Vivi."

Standing next to his car is Prescott.

"Oh, hey. I didn't know you'd be here," I say.

"I came to pick you up so we could check out the apartments like we planned."

"Is that your friend?" Eric asks. He sounds as though he might faint.

"Uh, yeah."

"Whoa. No wonder you're staying at The James. He probably could've bought the place for you."

"Vivi? Are you coming?" Prescott calls.

"Yeah, hang on," I answer. Turning back to Eric, I say, "I'll see you in the morning. I'll text you when I'm on the way."

110

"Sure thing, but I have a feeling I just lost my potential room-mate. I can't compete with that, but I'd happily trade places with you if you'd like." Eric saunters off then, laughing. I have to chuckle. He's crushing on Prescott.

I turn toward the object of Eric's lust and notice his tightened expression. His narrowed gaze following Eric tells me all I need to know. If only he knew.

"Who's your friend?" His tone is cool.

"He's the one who's training me at work."

"I didn't know someone with a degree from MIT would need much training to be a waitress."

"That's not fair. Everyone needs to be trained in a new work environment. How did you even know where I worked? I never told you."

"I have my sources."

"Stop spying on me. It's creepy, Prescott."

He doesn't bother to comment but only says, "Get in," as he holds the door open.

With his shitty attitude, I'm not sure I want to anymore. "I don't think so."

"We have a deal, Vivi."

"Yeah, we did. But I found a roommate, so I no longer need a place to live."

"What the hell do you mean you found a roommate?" His voice booms.

"I'm not sure how much plainer I can be."

He runs a hand through his too sexy hair. "Who is it?"

"Why is that important?"

"Just answer the fucking question."

"Lower your voice and it's none of your business."

"Yesterday, you were living in a fucking nightmare of a place in Brooklyn and last night you agreed to our deal. I set you up in The James. Today you went to work, and now you suddenly have a roommate? I want to know who it is. Is this person trust-worthy or will they steal you blind?"

The idea of that has me laughing. "Seriously? Have you bothered to notice my stuff? Who in the hell would want to steal it?"

His jaws clamp together so hard his teeth click. The tic on his cheek picks up speed, telling me exactly how much I've pissed him off.

"The truth is, I've been looking for a roommate to share bills and the cost of rent, but I haven't met anyone until now. My new job led me to that person."

"Oh, and who might that be?"

"Eric. The guy who just left."

His hand suddenly snakes out and clasps my wrist, pulling me into the steel wall of his chest. "Like hell. He's the last person you'll be living with, if I have anything to say about it."

His mouth crashes onto mine, cutting off any chance of a reply, along with all coherent thoughts in my head. I'll say this for him. Prescott Beckham is one sinfully sexy kisser, but not in the way I imagined. The kiss is savage, vicious, and yet sensual. While it lacks tenderness, it's filled with everything a kiss should be—lust, passion, and fire. Every nerve in my body hums, sending my pulse racing. I know one thing. If I'm not careful, my heart will most certainly be in this game, whether I want it to or not.

CHAPTER 12

PRESCOTT

Vivi live with another man? Over my dead body.

I'll just have to show her a thing or two about who's the boss in this little thing that's going on between us. And fuck whatever plans I had on being nice. When she went behind my back and arranged to move in with someone else, she just sealed her own fate.

However, there's one tiny problem. Make that a big problem.

Vivi and her sexy as fuck mouth.

One taste, one lousy little taste, and now I want all of her. When our mouths connect the chemistry erupts. I used to think that was some kind of cosmic bullshit, but there's this invisible line between us, this flow where she's reaching into my soul that I can't explain. If I thought the first time I kissed her set me off, I was badly mistaken. This time all bets are off. Now I know I was right. Vivi will be mine and nothing will stop me.

I place my hands on either side of her head and tilt it just so, allowing me full access. Then I take her mouth exactly like I want to. I dominate her until she moans and her fingers dig into my arms. But even then, I don't stop. I want her lips bruised and swollen, so that when she sees her little friend, he'll know. He'll know exactly who owns her. Me, not him.

One hand slides down to her ass and cups it as I kiss her. I squeeze that soft round globe of flesh until she squirms against me. It doesn't take long before she straddles my thigh and grinds herself against it. People move about us on the sidewalk. I hear a stray laugh as they go by, but I don't give a damn. The world could destruct, go up in flames around us, and I wouldn't blink an eye. We're two sexually charged people caught up in the moment. The hand on her ass pushes her into me, harder, eliciting a groan from deep within her. Damn, do I want this woman. My dick is hard, harder than I can remember it being in a long time.

I sink my teeth into her lower lip, not hard enough to break the skin, yet enough to let her know I'm in control. She whimpers, but I quickly soothe it with my tongue. Then I do it again. Her hands slide up to my neck and pull me closer. I've won.

When I detach myself from her, I'm satisfied by her look of confusion. I nudge her into the car and have the driver take us to the first apartment on the list.

Her heavy breathing gives me great pleasure. Leaning toward her, I ask, "How wet are you?"

"What?"

"Do you want me to repeat the question?"

"No, I heard you. I don't care to answer."

"My guess is you're soaked between those thighs of yours."

Her intake of air is exactly what I was going for.

"I bet if I were to slip my hand down your pants I'd —"

"That's quite enough."

"I disagree, Vivi. We haven't even begun. The way you responded to my kiss told me a lot more than you think."

She crosses her arms and stares directly ahead of her. "Why do you have to be such an ass?"

"I'm not. I'm merely being honest, which is more than you are."

She frowns, then tugs at the bottom of her jacket. For a moment I think she's going to come back at me with a sassy reply, but she doesn't. Her rigid posture indicates her annoyance with me. That's okay. I'll get her to relax soon enough—when her legs are spread and my tongue is lapping her pussy, making her scream out an orgasm.

"Stop it," she says.

"What did I do now?"

"You're sitting there, acting so smug and arrogant."

A hoarse laugh echoes through the car. "I am not."

"Yes, you are."

"Fine. I'll sit here and act super serious. How's this?" I try to look solemn. I'm damn sure I fail because I just want to laugh.

"You think you're funny, don't you?"

"Not at all." She's fuming and the fact that she loved every second of my kiss makes it even better. "Better stop frowning or it might stick forever."

We arrive at our first stop and I open the door. Then I hold out my hand for her.

"Now he suddenly develops manners," she mumbles.

The building is a high-rise on the Lower East Side and the doorman waves us through. After an elevator ride to the tenth floor, I lead her to the vacant apartment. It's a nice one-bedroom that would suit her needs well … and mine, too.

She does a walk-through and announces it's lovely.

"I thought you'd like it. It's also a great location."

She murmurs her agreement, but that's it.

So we move on to the next, where her reaction is much the same. We get into the car and drive to the last rental. When we arrive, she takes note of where we are.

"Don't you live here?"

"I do. Come."

"I thought we were looking at places for me," she says.

"We are." I usher her into the building and then to the elevator.

When the doors close, she folds her arms over her chest. "I won't live with you."

"Did I ask you to?"

She clears her throat, then fidgets with her coat sleeve. I watch her out of the corner of my eye and see her stiff posture relax when I press the button for a floor other than my own. She follows me out of the elevator to the vacant apartment. She's not very good at hiding her love for this one. Her gray irises gleam and those still puffy lips curve up in a smile she tries to hide.

"You like?"

"Yeah," she breathes. "It's lovely. It really is. Did you furnish it?"

Nodding, I say, "I offer it sometimes as a corporate rental. But it's yours for the taking."

Her soft eyes turn to mine as she says, "I can't. This room-mate situation is too good to pass up."

Anger clouds my vision. "How can you think about that other man when I'm offering you this?" I jab my arm out in front of me for emphasis.

She laughs. A good solid belly laugh.

"What the fuck is so funny?" I ask.

She's doubled over and can't speak. This is not cool. Her finger comes up in the air. At last, she stands, and for the first time in my life, I get a look at Vivi in a state where she's having fun. And she's fucking perfection. A brilliant smile graces her face. She's relaxed, which has erased the constant lines that reside on her forehead and in the corners of her eyes.

Damn if I don't want to wrap her in my arms and kiss her. Softly, passionately, and even sweetly.

"Eric, my soon to be roommate, is gay. He thinks *you're* hot. Not me." And she erupts into another fit of snorting laughter. Oddly enough, I laugh along with her.

"Oh my God, this is so hysterical. I can't wait to tell him you were jealous of him."

"You will do no such thing." I laugh out my response.

"Yeah, I will. This is too good to pass up. My God, he practically tripped over his tongue when he saw you. And you were jealous of him." She lets out another snort-giggle. Until now, I never considered her the giggling type. But for whatever reason, it doesn't annoy me. In fact, it's charming.

"It's not that funny." But it really is. I think about what Weston and Harrison would say and I laugh right along with her some more. When the funny passes, we stand and stare at each other awkwardly.

"Well, I think I should be going," she says.

"Yes. We're going to dinner. Come on."

She stops and looks me square in the eyes. "You don't give up easily, do you?"

"Never."

"It's Friday night. You don't have plans?"

"Yes, dinner. With you. Come on."

We get on the elevator and when it goes up, she asks, "What tricks are you playing?"

"No tricks, just dinner. I promise."

We get to my place, where my cook has prepared us a meal. It's nothing fancy, just simple Italian fare.

"It smells delicious in here."

"I have a great cook. His name is Gerard and he spoils me. He's been here all day cooking things for the weekend. We're in luck. Can I get you a glass of wine?"

"Wine would be nice."

I bring her a glass of one of my favorite Tuscan chardonnays. "Have a seat."

We sit in the living room and I ask her about her new job. She explains it's a means to an end. "I'm still looking, but I hope to find something soon."

I want to tell her I can help, but if I do, I know she'll refuse the offer, just like she's refused everything else from me. When her stomach lets out a huge gurgle, I ask her if she's hungry with a smile.

"Starved."

"Vivi, do you ever eat?"

"What do you mean?"

"Every time I see you, you're starving."

She tucks her chin in. "Well, that's because you catch me when I've been super busy. Like today, I didn't have time to eat because I was working all day."

"Every time I've seen you, you've been too busy."

"I appreciate you're concerned over whether I get nutritious meals every day."

I want to smack that rear end of hers for being so damn sassy. Instead, I reach for her hand and pull her to her feet. Then we head into the kitchen where I take the dinner Gerard prepared out of the oven. It's some kind of a chicken dish. There are salads in the refrigerator too. I set up places at the counter and we dig in. By the sounds Vivi makes, she loves it. I'd rather hear her making those little mmms with my dick between her legs, but I'll take what I can get … for now.

"You have it made with your own personal cook. This is amazing."

I stare at her mouth as she speaks. One day, that mouth is going to be mine, and no one else's.

My gaze is riveted on her lips as I answer. "I know. He cooks a bunch of stuff ahead of time, so all I have to do is heat it up."

"You're so spoiled. Who has their own personal chef?"

I eventually look back at my plate in order to eat unless I want food all over me. When we finish, she tries to clean up, but I don't let her. "You wait tables, right?"

"Well, yeah."

"My turn to wait on you. Go." I point to the living room. Much to my surprise, she doesn't sass back, but goes and takes a seat. Then she fumbles with the remote control, trying to turn on the TV.

"How d'ya turn this thing on?" she calls out.

"Hang on." When I get in there, she's eyeing the remotes with confusion. "Let me get that."

"Why are there so many?"

"Ah, the curse of too many devices." I hit the right buttons and we have action on the big screen.

"Way too complicated."

"You're IT. You would've had it figured out eventually."

"Ha-ha."

I stare at her as she flips the channels. After about an hour of watching some show where I have no idea what's going on, she announces she has to leave.

"I have to work tomorrow and I'm going to move tomorrow night. I need to get my stuff out of that apartment in Brooklyn."

This grabs my attention and my possessiveness flares. "I'll help you."

She shifts her body to face me. "Why are you doing this, Prescott? Is it just for the sex? I need you to come clean with me."

"I thought we've been through this already."

"We have, but all I get from you is the old 'we're friends' thing. But see, this is what bothers me—I'm not *that* different from the girl who did your homework at Crestview Academy. Some things have changed, sure, but not all of them. I wasn't good enough for you then, but now I am all of a sudden. The only real difference is that I've shed some pounds. From my perspective, though, the inside of me—my heart and my mind— are the same. I'm much stronger and assertive, yes, but my emotions still run deep. So you can't possibly understand how that makes me feel to think you only want me now because I'm no longer fat."

"Vivi, I—"

"Let me finish. I've moved past how shitty I was made to feel at that school. I forced myself to rise above it and crawl out of my shell at MIT. I knew if I didn't, I had no chance of ever landing in a career. It wasn't easy, but in the long run, it made me a better person. And maybe that's what you see, maybe that's what you want, but underneath my tougher exterior, the same Vivi you knew is still in here." She pats her chest with an open palm.

"Vivi, what happened in the past is done and there's nothing I can do about it now. I was a sex-crazed teenager who went for the girl who was throwing herself at me that week. I can't change what I did a decade ago. I know you're the same person. Actually, the truth is, you've impressed me with the way you've changed. The old Vivi would've never stood up to anyone. But I liked you then as I do now. I just have my head out of my ass now to see it—to see you."

"But you really didn't like me. I was your means to an end. And I have to be honest with you. You're not looking so good these days. I'm not sure what happened between then and now, but it must not have been good. I'm sorry for that. I am. It still doesn't change things. I really don't want to get involved with you. I think we need to go our separate ways. You have your life and I'll have mine."

"Fine—if that's how you want it. But if you believe the lie you're telling yourself, Vivi, the one that has to do with not wanting anything to do with me, then you have changed. You've changed a lot since I knew you. The Vivi I used to know wouldn't have lied."

I leave her sitting on the couch and make a call to my driver. "A car will be waiting for you downstairs. You can let yourself out." Then I walk toward my bedroom without another glance at her.

She's made up her mind, so I'll let her go ... for the time being. She can lie to herself until she's blue in the face, but I know want and desire when I see them, and Vivi Renard wants me. One day soon, I plan to give her exactly what she craves.

CHAPTER 13

VIVI

PRESCOTT'S SURRENDER HITS ME OUT OF NOWHERE. UP UNTIL this point, he's been so persistent, I wasn't expecting this reaction at all. I watch his back, or his ass to be precise, as he retreats. It is a very fine one, too. Then I put my coat on and leave. The driver stands by the car, but I tell him no thanks. It's not too cold tonight and The James is close enough to walk. On the way there, I call Eric.

"Hey, I thought you'd be tied up." He laughs at his little joke.

"Ha-ha. I'm headed back to the hotel. Do you want to help me move out of my crappy apartment tomorrow?"

"Um, we have to work. Have you forgotten?"

"Nope. I meant after. I don't have much and I'm checking out of The James in the morning. I'll drop off my bag at your place when I stop by to look at it, but I've already made up my mind. The rest of my things can fit in a couple of suitcases."

"Wait. You don't have any furniture? Not even a bed?"

"I have an air mattress."

He doesn't say anything for so long I think the call dropped. "Eric?"

"I'm here. You just shocked the shit out of me."

I'll have to explain everything to Eric later even though it's not something I look forward to. But I need to know if he can help, because if he can't, I'll have to figure something else out. I don't really want to do it alone.

"What about your rich boyfriend?"

"He's not my boyfriend."

"Is he available? As in, would he be —"

"No. He's not your type." Then I laugh because I'm reminded of my conversation with Prescott.

After I explain about how jealous Prescott was over Eric initially, we both crack up. That story will always make me laugh.

"Anyway, will you answer my question about tomorrow night? Jeez," I huff.

"Oh, of course I'll help. We can go straight there after work. An air mattress. We need to get you a real bed, Viv. That's crazy as shit."

"Don't knock it. It's actually pretty comfy."

"Uh-huh." He doesn't buy it. "You can sleep with me until you get a decent bed if you want. And you don't have to worry about me trying anything. I'm totally not interested in anything you have below the waist. Or above it for that matter. No offense."

"None taken. But my air mattress isn't bad. Really."

"Yeah. Whatever. I'll see you in the morning. Shout at me on the way."

We tell each other goodbye and I'm across from The James already. When I get to my room, I quickly change and crawl into bed. This is a far cry from my air mattress. Large and soft, with expensive sheets I couldn't dream of affording, I decide to enjoy my last night in it.

It's a crazy notion to think of how much money Prescott must have. Those apartments we visited were all very nice — in high-end buildings with rent I could never afford on my own. Then I get to thinking about what kind of business he's in. Pulling my laptop out, I look up his name again. The screen lights up. When I first looked him up, I was more curious about his general financial status. I'd had no idea he was so prominent in society. One of Manhattan's wealthiest, like Vince or was it Joe said—I can't remember which. I learned from my previous Google search that he's the grandson of Samuel Whitworth, one of the founders of Whitworth Enterprises. But I didn't go much deeper then, but now, that's exactly what I want to explore.

Dozens of pictures fill the screen of Prescott with beautiful women on his arm. He certainly doesn't experience a shortage of dates and he looks like he owns the world. Every one of the women clings to him possessively, too. Interesting. They all appear to be from the higher echelons of society, wearing designer clothing. Doesn't this make me feel more confident? I should've stuck to the business section of his life. Moving on.

Whitworth Enterprises has its hands in all kinds of business holdings—real estate, hotels, restaurants, resorts, and they even own a film production company. One of their fortes is mergers and acquisitions, where they buy up or merge floundering companies and turn them into income-producing businesses.

Damn, no wonder Prescott has all that money at his disposal.

Apparently Samuel Whitworth is a gem, too. There isn't a bad thing anywhere to be found about him. Prescott's father, Jeff, is a different story. He's been around the block with a few wives and, though Prescott is right that there's nothing particularly bad out there about their relationship, I noticed the absence of one. Especially in the recent articles, they aren't ever in the same picture. Not like Prescott and his grandfather, who always seem to be together. Credit, that could mean nothing, but coupled with his "daddy issues" comment, it makes me wonder. Hmm. Maybe Prescott does have a turbulent relationship with his father. If that's true, that could be the reason for him looking rough and haggard these days.

Digging a little deeper, there's nothing on Prescott's mother. Where is she? Why isn't she in any of the pictures? Was it a nasty divorce? And how old was he when it all happened? My hand rubs a circle over my heart as it's prodded by a sudden burst of emotion. I can certainly understand the loss of a loved one. Shutting my computer down, I try to sleep but a troubled man with golden eyes keeps me awake for a very long time.

In the morning, Eric meets me at the entrance to his building. "You look hellish."

"Yeah, I didn't sleep so well."

"Hate when that happens. Well, come on up to the casbah."

Eric wasn't exaggerating when he said the space was small. It looks like a one-bedroom they threw up a wall in the middle of to make it a two-bedroom.

"Don't say I didn't warn you. That's why I require you to be neat. This place would be out of control if I had a slob for a roommate."

Holding up my hand, I say, "No, I get it. The place I'm in now is a slum. And super tiny. This is definitely an upgrade."

"Not compared to what fancy pants showed you last night, though."

"Fancy pants. I don't think he'd appreciate you calling him that."

"With the way he looked at you, he'd probably kill me for it." Then Eric laughs. "He's a serious dude, isn't he?"

That doesn't even come close. "Yeah, I guess so. This is a recent thing, though. Or at least since Crestview."

"Crestview?"

"That's where we went to school together. He was carefree back then—or he acted like it anyway."

"Hm. What's his name anyway?"

"Prescott Beckham."

"Wait, wait, wait. *The* Prescott Beckham—like the billionaire?"

I sigh. "Yup, that's the one."

Eric leans back and grins. "So you went to high school with the famous Prescott Beckham."

"I just said that, didn't I? And junior high, too. It was a boarding school."

"Whoa, girl, you're secretly a fancy britches bitch yourself, aren't you?"

Choosing to ignore his comment, I move past him into the tiny living room and inspect the place closely. Then I walk over the where the bedrooms are. They are of equal size and each have a tiny closet. Across the hall from them is a bathroom that has a shower stall only.

"Sorry, no big spa tub for you to take your long soaks in."

"I'm lucky to have hot water where I live now, so as long as you have that, I'm happy."

"I'm a little scared to see where you live, Viv."

"Yeah, you should be. Just wait."

"Why'd you move there?"

I explain my lack of funds and how I rented it online.

"Ew. Never ever do that again. Very unwise. And you're so smart."

"Hey, we need to get going."

On the way in to work, we talk about sharing expenses. Then Eric lets me know what his pet peeves are. It's been quite a while since I've had a roommate, since college to be precise.

"It annoys the hell out of me when I grocery shop and go to the refrigerator to find all my shit is gone. If you ever do that I'll beat your ass."

"Duly noted, but I wouldn't be that inconsiderate. On that note, do you want to do completely separate groceries or joint dinners? I realize you have your life and I have mine."

"Separate. If we decide to cook one night, we can just grab what we need then," he says.

"What about stuff like coffee, tea, and other staples?"

"We can buy those jointly. And cleaning supplies," he suggests.

I click my fingers. "Is there a laundry room in the building?"

"Yeah, on the third floor. It's really nice, too."

"Oh, that's awesome. There's one in my building, but I'm afraid to use it."

We get all our details ironed out by the time we make it to work. Before we walk in, Eric stops me. "This is your final training day and then you're on your own. You good?"

"Yeah. I need another job, though."

"A friend of mine works at this super cool club in SoHo. He said they were looking for a bartender. You interested?"

"Until I can find the real thing, I'll take any job."

"Any job?" He slaps my ass, then laughs.

"You're not funny, Eric."

"Yeah, but think of the money you could be pulling in."

The restaurant is already humming when we get inside. We don't open for another thirty minutes, but we get to work preparing the tables. Eric lets me know on Saturday the busy times can vary some. He's right. Today is like a never-ending revolving door, with people coming and going. There is barely time to breathe. When our shift finally ends, my butt is dragging.

"You ready to go?" Eric asks, his voice all cheery.

"Are you not dead?"

"No, why?"

"That about killed me."

"Aw, you'll get used to it. So what … a train or an Uber to Brooklyn?" he asks.

"The train. It's faster."

He grabs my arm and off we go. When we get to my neighborhood, he says, "Fuck me, Viv, why didn't you tell me to bring a gun?"

"Because someone would steal it from you and use it to shoot you."

"Okay, then pepper spray."

"Pepper spray doesn't work for gangs. Just shut up and hurry." We make it upstairs and he sags against the wall in relief.

"I'm having a heart attack. I don't think I can go back out there. This place is awful. How could you sleep here?"

"I got used to it."

He shudders and I laugh. "Stop it, you nerd. It's not that bad. There could be rats and stuff."

"Ack." He lets out a screech and I crack up.

"Come on." I open the closet door and pull out two suitcases, handing him one. "Fill it up."

"I didn't believe you, but you were right."

"Yeah, the only things I bought after I moved were a couple of lamps, the electric burner, and I think that's it. Living with you will be like living in the Taj Mahal."

"Good thing these suitcases are huge."

We cram them full, placing the entire contents of the apartment inside, which are mainly clothes and shoes. I have a few towels, some sheets, dishes, and glass items that we wrap the towels around, and some pictures. A couple hours later, we're dragging the suitcases downstairs, along with the lamps, into the waiting Uber. I left the old TV and space heater behind to the next poor sucker who rents this miserable shithole.

On the way to my new home, Eric says, "Glad we made it out of there alive."

"Who the hell would want my shit? It's not worth a dime."

"They wouldn't know that until after they killed us."

I chuckle. "Can you imagine their disappointment? Killing us over a pile of worthless crap."

"Hey, Viv, this stuff means something to you, though."

With a slight shrug I say, "I suppose."

"How'd you end up at an expensive boarding school? I know it had to cost a shit-ton, if Beckham went there."

"It's a long story. Maybe I'll tell you over a glass of wine. No, make that a bottle or two."

"That bad, huh?"

"I don't know. Maybe. Maybe not."

"I have a good shoulder if you ever need one."

When I turn to look him in the eye, I notice through the streetlights illuminating the interior of the car, the kindness radiating from his face. He pats my leg and pulls me against his side. "If you ever want to talk, I'm here, just so you know."

"Thanks, Eric. I appreciate that."

We unload my stuff and tote it upstairs. Eric laughs at me when I attach the little motor to my mattress and blow it up. "You'll see. This thing is really great."

After it's blown up, I put on the sheets that I located in one of the bags. Eric walks back in and hands me a few blankets. "Here. I noticed you only had one. Just in case you get cold."

I jump up and hug him. "Thank you." I don't tell him how I slept in front of the space heater to stay warm at night. It might freak him out.

"Okay, give it a test and tell me what you think."

He lies down on it and grins. "Not too bad really."

"See. Told ya."

"Since we don't have any shifts tomorrow and it's still early for a Saturday night, do you want to go and grab a pizza? I know this great place and I'm starved. And it's only a couple of blocks from the club I was telling you about. We can stop there afterward and I'll introduce you if you'd like."

"Yes! I'm hungry, too, and that sounds great."

We throw our coats on and go. The restaurant is busy but not extremely so. We place our order and grab a booth as we drink our beers.

Eric likes to chat and tells me he's from a small town outside of the city. He has a brother and sister, and his dad is an attorney. "Mom stayed at home while we were growing up, but when we got to high school, she pursued her passion for interior design. That's how I became interested in it. She'd bring home fabric and paint samples and I went crazy. I begged her to bring me along on jobs. So I studied it in college."

"That's pretty cool. Why didn't you go to work with her?"

"Because she's in the burbs and I want to be here. I want to make a name for myself—you know, on the commercial side of it with real estate developers."

"I guess this is the place to be then."

They call out our order number and Eric goes to grab it. The pizza is delicious and we practically inhale it. When we finish, we walk over to the club.

It's a really cool place with a mixed crowd of twenty and thirty somethings. Eric takes me to the bar and introduces me to Lucas. He's tall, blond, and totally hot. Blue eyes the color of the sea draw me in and I feel my mouth curving into a huge smile.

"Hi, I'm Vivienne."

"Nice to meet you. How much experience do you have?"

"Absolutely none."

His mouth drops open a bit. Clearly he wasn't expecting that response. "We get super busy in here late and I need someone who can keep up."

I jump in and say, "I can learn. Fast. Ask Eric. He just trained me."

"She's right. She mastered the art of waiting tables in four days. You know how busy we get."

He taps his fingers on the bar. "You probably waited tables in college or something. Everybody's done that before, at least once."

"I never had."

"Never?" His eyes narrow as he assesses me.

"Not once. The truth is I'm looking for a job in IT. My degree's in Computer Science and Engineering and I'm trying to get back into my field. Until then, I need the money."

"You really are a quick study then?" he asks. His skepticism appears to be fading.

"Eric can attest to it."

"I'll give you a trial run for a few days. If you can't pick it up, I'll have to let you go. We'll do some week nights when we're not as busy."

"Perfect. When can I start?"

"We're closed on Sunday. Is Monday good?"

"Monday's perfect." Lucas and I shake hands and that's that.

129

I have job number two. And then I think of something. "Hey, Lucas, if I find my real job, I'll give you fair warning, too."

"Thanks, Vivienne."

"Call me Vivi."

Eric and I order a drink to toast my second job. "Thank you. You've been such a big help to me already."

"You're welcome. Here's to a long and fruitful friendship."

We clink our glasses together and drink. As Eric swallows, his eyes bulge. At first I think he's choking, but when I go to slap his back, he waves me off.

"You okay? I thought you were choking. I was getting ready to administer the Heimlich."

He doesn't answer, only stares. And then I know why. The heat warms me from behind and I know exactly who's standing there.

Without turning, I say, "Hello, Prescott. Care to join us?"

CHAPTER 14

PRESCOTT

I WALK INTO MY FAVORITE CLUB, AND WHO SHOULD I FIND sitting at the bar but Vivi and her new little pal. It seems everything in my life is centering around her these days. Not only is she fucking taking over my thoughts, but now she's also invading my hangouts. She's probably going to be using my personal stylist, massage therapist, and shopping in the same stores I frequent before I even know it. Fuck, how will I cope? Isn't that the question of the year?

Her little friend stares at me like he either wants to run or fuck me. No, wait, that's not it … he's not sure how to tell her I'm here. It makes me curious as to what she's told him about me. Probably that I'm a giant prick, which would be accurate. Let's see if I can live up to my description.

"I'd love to join you two, Vivi. Is this your new roommate? Eric, isn't it?"

"Yes. Eric, this is Prescott. Prescott, meet Eric." We shake hands and I give him the death grip. He winces. Vivi kicks me. I give her my most charming grin.

"So, how was the move from your elegant apartment, Vivi?"

"No need to be nasty. It was fine." Her lower lip sticks out a bit and I want to bite it.

"Are you nice and settled? All homey-like?" I wiggle my brows.

"What's up with you? Why are you being such a jerk?" she asks.

"Just living up to your opinion of me, I suppose. Eric, what type of business are you in? Besides the waiting tables thing. Or is that your lifelong ambition?"

"Prescott," she huffs.

"It's fine, Vivi. Actually, no. I'm an interior designer trying to get my business going."

"Ah, I see. Like that's a unique field."

"All right. I think we'd better leave, Eric. This place has become a little too nasty for my taste."

As she stands, I grab her wrist. "Eric, why don't you run along like a good little boy and let Vivi stay."

"Let's get something straight, Prescott. Nobody makes decisions for me. Now let go."

I unclamp my fingers and she straightens. "Come on, Eric."

I watch as they walk to the opposite end of the bar and speak with the blond bartender who's in here all the time. Eric pays for the drinks and they leave. I really was a bastard, but this is my hangout and maybe they'll think twice about coming back in. I've also successfully burned all my bridges with her. It's probably for the best. No use in keeping any hopes open. I've thought about it since last night and realized that Vivienne Renard will never give me a chance no matter what I do. So I may as well let her see the man she thinks I am.

I sit at the table, crushed by my own actions. Eric is a nice guy, no doubt. Vivi wouldn't be hanging out with him if he weren't. I reminded myself of my father then, and it's a bitter pill to swallow. Anything remotely similar to him makes me cringe.

"Hey, mind if I join you?" Glancing up, a redhead with big tits leans toward me. She wears a low cut shirt that exposes even more of her ample cleavage. They're globe-shaped and shoved high toward her chin, an indication that her boobs are artificial. High-profile is the term I've heard used to describe them and these definitely fit the bill. If they were any higher, they'd bump her in the nose.

She doesn't wait for an answer before sitting down and moving into my space, a space I hadn't intended on sharing.

"Actually, I sort of wanted to be alone."

"Oh. Rough night, huh."

"Something like that."

"Maybe I can take the edge off for you." She offers me a knowing smile, but I'm not in the mood. Funny thing, I haven't been in the mood ever since I saw Vivi in that fucking coffee shop.

"I'm sure you could," I say noncommittally.

"And I'm damn good. You'd be a happy man for a long time." She licks her lips.

Nodding, I say, "Yeah, I bet. But not tonight, sweetheart. It's not in the cards for me."

"No? Why?"

"It just isn't."

She scoots her chair close and before I know it her hand is on my dick, but it's as limp as a sock. She paws it a little until I move her hand away.

"Like I said, not happening."

"Too bad. We could've made some beautiful memories."

I almost laugh at her line. Maybe she should come up with something original.

When she's gone, I move to a different seat, one where there isn't a vacant chair next to me, so I don't have to deal with that shit anymore. If I want to fuck someone, it's going to be on my terms no matter how hot the woman is. A few hours later and who knows how many drinks, I close my tab and leave.

"Thanks, Mr. Beckham," the bartender says.

"You bet."

The chilly air slaps a little sobriety back into me and along with it comes a lot of regret over the way I acted toward Vivi and Eric. He's just a nice guy trying to make it in this world, which I know nothing about, and I was a royal shithead to him. I was born into wealth and have no idea what it's like to struggle financially, like Vivi does. What would it be like not to know where your next meal comes from? Or how you were going to pay your rent? The thought is even more sobering than the cold air around me. Now I'm kicking myself in my own stupid ass for not getting Eric's full name. I could've gotten to be friends with him and found a way to help Vivi through him. Maybe it's not too late. I do know which restaurant they work in and I have a top-notch security team that can find out anything. I file that away for Monday morning.

When I get home, I pull out my bowl and pack it with a bud. The alcohol wasn't exactly my tonic, so I need a little extra to take off the edge. All I can see are Vivi's mouth and eyes. Her lips were as red and plump as a summer strawberry and her irises reminded me of a storm filled sky. I fill my lungs with smoke and hope the weed will ease my tension.

I stare at the skyline, but her image doesn't go away. She's hot as fuck—the sexiest woman I've laid my eyes on in months, maybe ever. And every time I close them, an image of her pops into view.

I want to punch the wall because no matter what I try, she'll have nothing to do with me. This is the first time in my life I'm at a loss where a woman is concerned. Usually they fall at my feet. Not her. She doesn't give a shit about anything I have to offer her. And the craziest thing of all is she needs it the most.

Even in my fucked-up stoned mind, the clarity of her face is so damn vivid I can almost feel her smooth skin beneath my palms. But it's only a fantasy and will remain one unless I come up with some ingenious plan that will win her over. The only thing I can think of is to get her friend Eric on my side and after tonight that's going to be as difficult as winning Vivi over. I laugh at the joke of my life. Here I sit, king of Manhattan. And yet the only thing I want is as far from my reach as the fucking moon.

In the morning, I wake up with my face smashed into the cushion of the couch. Seems the weed must've taken effect after all and conked me out before I could make it to bed. Pain radiating down my neck and into my back tells me exactly how I slept—completely scrunched up and contorted in a bad way.

My first stop is the fridge for a bottle of Gatorade. I'd like to hit the shower to loosen up the kinks in my muscles, but I'll save that for later. Next on the list is a monster workout. My home gym is equipped with everything I need. I hit the treadmill for an hour and sweat out the alcohol. Next I lift weights until my muscles are fatigued and lose their proper form. Now I make a giant protein shake and hit the shower. I'm beginning to feel like a human again. It's a good thing because I'm supposed to be at my grandparents' for dinner in an hour and it takes about that long to get there. I get dressed and leave.

Traffic is light and my grandmother is waiting for me when I pull up. There's no woman on Earth I adore more than her. Small in stature, she barely reaches my chest as her arms wrap around me in a fierce hug. She's strong for being so slight in physique. Her silver gray hair gleams in the sunlight and every time I see her I'm reminded of how much she's done for me, always going out of her way to help me, especially after everything with Mom.

"How's my boy doing?" Her question interrupts my rambling thoughts.

"I'm fine, thank you."

She inspects me. "You're not taking care of yourself, Scotty. Are you eating?"

"Yes, ma'am, I am."

"And sleep?"

"I'm sleeping fine, Grand." I take her hand as we walk inside.

"Why don't I believe you?" Doubt crinkles the corners of her eyes.

"Probably because you're perceptive and know me better

than anyone."

"What's wrong then, honey? Please don't tell me it's your father."

"Partly." And then I decide to seek her opinion. "You know what, maybe you can help. There's this girl."

Her eyes shine like the stars and maybe this wasn't such a good idea to bring her into this. "There is?"

"Yes, but that's the problem. She doesn't want anything to do with me."

"Not you?"

"Yeah, Grand, me."

My grandmother thinks the sun rises and sets with me. She has no idea what a douche I am.

"What's wrong with her?"

"I've been wondering the same thing." I chuckle.

"You're a little shit, Scotty." She squeezes the hand she still holds.

"I know. And that's the problem. She sees right through me."

"Let's sit down and talk this one out, shall we?" We take a seat in her favorite room, the sun porch. It overlooks the back of their property and offers quite a view of rolling hills with a creek running through. Grand loves to garden, so in the spring and summer there are lots of flowers everywhere. "Who is she?"

"Someone I used to know from Crestview."

"Really?"

"But we never hung out or anything. You might say she was the ugly duckling that turned into the gorgeous swan."

"Prescott, did you treat her badly when you were in school?"

"Not that I recall. I sort of liked her, as friends, you know?"

And that's the truth. Vivi was shy, kept to herself, but there was something about her that appealed to me, other than the homework deal we had. She was kind. Maybe that was it. She always listened to what I had to say, even if it was stupid bullshit.

"And?"

"I ran into her, oh, I don't know, a while ago. She's fallen on hard times lately. It's a long story."

Grand pats my leg. "Do you see me running off anywhere?"

I can see by the look Grand gives me, she is in for the long haul, so I tell her what I know about Vivi and how her mom passed.

"Oh, dear, how tragic. How isolated she must've felt afterward. You should invite her out here sometime."

"I'd love to if she'd give me the time of day."

"You haven't charmed her with that handsome smile of yours?"

"I've tried everything, even sent her gifts."

She scrutinizes me and asks suspiciously, "What types of gifts?"

"A winter coat for one. She moved here from Virginia and didn't have a decent one. I also tried to get her to move into one of my rentals. You should see where she was living. There were prostitutes and drug dealers hanging out everywhere."

"Scotty, you were trying to buy her, like a mistress," she accuses.

"No, Grand, I was just—"

"Let me finish. She's an independent woman who's used to caring for herself. You show up and want to take over her life. You have a very strong personality. I can only imagine what you said to her." She sits there shaking her head.

How does she know all this?

"I was only trying to help." I sound like a petulant child.

"Sweetheart, you don't have to explain that to me. I'm only showing you how it must've looked from her point of view. Women see things differently from men. You roar into her life like a March wind and in your mind, send her lavish gifts. She would have probably liked it better had you sent her a Starbucks Gift Certificate."

Chuckling, I say, "Um, probably not. She worked at a competing coffee shop."

"Hush. You get my meaning. You can't give women extravagant gifts, especially someone like her. Start small. Send dinner to her home. Or maybe even something smaller such as a box of chocolates. Women do love their chocolate."

"But that's so mundane."

Grand scowls. "You're missing the point. This woman needs a few raindrops and you're deluging her with a flood. And for the love of God, Scotty, don't offer to set her up in an apartment. That only tells her you're interested in one thing. Women know men only think with that appendage in their pants at first. Set yourself apart from the rest, if you truly want to impress her, that is."

And that's the real question, isn't it? Do I want to impress Vivi, or do I want her only for her pussy? With the way things are going, she's not giving that up very easily, so it looks like I have my work cut out for me. And the more she holds out, the more I want it.

Throughout dinner, I think of ways to win her back, using my grandmother's approach. Delivering dinner, sending chocolates and flowers, all those simple things that seem so boring to me, but maybe to her they don't.

I'll know soon because starting Monday, I'm going to find out where she lives. That's step number one. After she moved out of that shithole in Brooklyn, I pulled my security team off of her since she'd be safe living with Eric. Once I locate her again, I'll move on to getting to know her roommate. If he's a loser, I'll do my best to like the guy, even if I have to suck it up every day. I have an edge, which is getting Eric's foot in the door of his interior design career. We have an entire decorating division at Whitworth. I could bring him in for interviews, but only if he agrees to help me win Vivi over. If he does, and is hired, he could gain invaluable experience with us and later move on to open up his own business. This could help him launch a very successful company and he'd be a fool to pass up this opportunity.

The larger piece of this, I realize, is I'd be a bigger fool to let Vivi slip through my fingers.

CHAPTER 15

VIVI

A FEW WEEKS LATER, AND I'M IN FULL BARTENDING MOTION AT
The Meeting Place. It's actually a blast mixing drinks and my
chaotic brain is pretty damn good at it. Even Lucas is impressed
with my mad skills. After the third day of training, he'd asked me
for the hundredth time if I hadn't bartended before.

"Never," I told him.

"Not even at weddings or for a catering company?"

"Nope."

"You're damn good at this."

"Why, thank you, kind sir," I joked.

Lucas and I make a pretty good team behind the bar. So good
that Lucas has me to work on Saturday nights, the busiest of the
week. The first time he asked I was shocked. I double-checked
with him to make sure I heard right and he only laughed.

When I got home that night and told Eric, he was excited. "I
smell money for you. You should pull in some big tips. Guys love
girl bartenders."

"I hope."

"You'll see."

I discover Eric was right. I make a shit-ton of money at this.

Well, a shit-ton compared to just waiting tables. Lucas and I split the take because we cross over so much and that's the fairest way to do it. As we're cleaning up one Saturday, and doing the tally, Lucas says he'd like me in there every weekend just for the money.

"Yeah, it's a lot, right?"

"More than usual, for sure. Hey, why don't you call it a night? You worked your ass off, Vivi. Thanks."

"Oh, it was fun, actually." And it was. I enjoyed being around all the people who were having a great time. "Enjoy your Sunday," I say on my way to the door.

"Hey! Don't walk home alone. One of the guys can take you. Someone should be heading out in a minute or two."

"I'm only a few blocks from here. It's fine."

"You sure? I don't want anything to happen to you."

"It's SoHo. This is a safe area."

"Yeah, but you never know."

"I'll run. Promise." I leave before he can stop me. The streets are empty save for a car or taxi here or there, but I make it home without incident. Eric is in bed, so I creep around like a burglar. Then my phone beeps. It's probably Lucas, checking on me. But when I see the text, I nearly drop my phone.

You shouldn't be out walking alone at this hour. It's dangerous.

It's from Prescott. Is he still stalking me after I've made it perfectly clear I want nothing to do with him? And how does he know where I live? I never told him.

Oh, right. He's the mighty Prescott Beckham with all kinds of information at his disposal. He probably hired a private investigator and had me followed. Well, that's just too bad. I'm not going to give him the satisfaction of answering his text.

Unfortunately, the doucheface has now planted his mug into

my mind and by the time I crawl into bed, he's all I can see. I want to punch the shit out of my pillows because of him. Why does he have to be so damn sexy and why did he have to tell me there's more to him than I'm aware? Why do I believe him now about his daddy issues?

I was better off thinking he was an ass for the sake of being an ass. Now that I think he has some sort of a troubled past, I have this ridiculous urge to fix him, which is the stupidest thing ever. I'm the one who needs fixing, not him. I'm the one who's at bankruptcy's door. All he has to do is snap his fingers and everyone, including their mothers, come running. Even Eric mentioned him the other day. I almost choked on my chicken noodle soup. He thinks I should reconsider seeing him.

Everyone that touches or gets close to Prescott Beckham must go slap-ass-crazy as fuck. He was rude as hell to Eric and now Eric feels sorry for the man.

"He might need your help, Viv. Maybe something went wrong in his past. People don't act like that without a good reason."

"What are you? Dear Abby or whatever the hell her name is?"

"Oh, come on. When you told me your story I nearly cried. You don't open up to every single person you meet. Maybe he's the same. Do you know what his home life was like? Maybe he was abused. It happens all the time."

Oh, God. I hadn't thought of that. "Shit, Eric. Do you know something I don't?"

"No. I'm just saying. Think about it."

"Not until he learns some manners."

And that was the end of that conversation.

But the truth is I can't stop thinking about him. And why? There are a gazillion sexy guys out there. Take Lucas for example, but I don't think about him. Groaning, I roll over for the tenth time and slam my fists on the bed. Why am I such a sucker? *You know why, Vivi. You've always had a mad crush on the man.*

Why did he have to be such an ass just because I moved in with Eric? Why can't I just move on and forget him? *You know the answer to that, too. Because he wants you.*

When my room gets a little less dark and a lot more gray, I drag my tired-as-hell body out of bed. What's the use in lying here when sleep is as evasive as my chance at winning the lottery? I sneak into the tiny kitchen and put a pot of coffee on to brew. While I wait, I stare out our window that overlooks East Third. Ironically, Prescott only lives a couple of blocks away. I'm sure he's found out I work at The Meeting Place already.

After I grab a mug of coffee, I open my laptop and, for the third time, start searching for everything I can find on Prescott Beckham. There's a ton of information about Whitworth Enterprises, his grandparents, cousin, and father, but again, nothing comes up on his mother. This is so weird. Not even a first name pops up, though obviously her maiden name would have been Whitworth. I could pay to have her searched for, but I can't afford to spend the money and am I really that nosy?

The sun is glaring. I'm still staring at my laptop, which has long since gone to sleep, when Eric pads into the room. "How long have you been up?"

"Since dawn."

"Why?"

"Couldn't sleep. You know who texted me when I got home last night? Told me I shouldn't walk home alone that late."

"He's right, you know."

"Not you, too? I didn't want to bother anyone or wait for them to finish up. And really? It's not but a few blocks."

Eric shrugs. "All I'm saying is he was worried, maybe. And he was right. Don't get angry with me."

Then my eyes zero on him and I smirk. "So, what did you end up doing last night?"

"I went out to a club. Why?"

"Looks like someone had a good time."

"What … why do you say that?"

"You need to look in the mirror and maybe put a shirt on."
Then I spit out a hearty laugh. Eric is covered in purple love
bites, from his neck to the waistband of his pajamas. "Someone
must've been trashed last night."

He looks down and actually turns bright pink. "Oh, God.
This is awful. You must think I'm —"

"A guy who had a great time last night. No need to be embar-
rassed about that. Was he cute?"

"Shut up, bitch," he says over his shoulder. He returns
wearing a shirt, along with a sheepish grin. "Yes, he
was. Very."

I clap my hands and ask, "Oooh, are you going to see him
again?"

"Yeah, we're going to dinner tonight."

"That's awesome." We fist bump.

"Enough about me. Let's talk about you and Mr. Fancy
Pants."

"There's nothing to talk about. I'm making breakfast.
Want some?"

"As long as you make pancakes."

I whip up a huge batch, because even though Eric is tall and
lean, he's a bottomless pit.

He cleans his plate, mopping up the last bit of syrup and
asks, "What're you up to today?"

"I don't know."

"Let's go for a run after the pancakes settle."

"Sounds good." I watch him clean up and think about what a
hot catch he'll be for whomever gets him. Dark hair with dark
eyes to match, Eric is as kind as he's good-looking.

"What are you staring at?" he asks, catching me.

"You. Too bad you bat for the other team."

"Oh, no. Don't tell me you're crushing on me."

Snorting, I say, "Don't flatter yourself. I'm just thinking
you're one of the sweetest, kindest people I've ever met, and
you're pretty damn fine, too."

"Well, I'll take the compliment. Just so you know, the feeling is mutual."

"It's great to have a true friend here. I'm glad we met, Eric."

"Aw. Come give old Eric a hug."

As we're hugging I ask him when he got so old.

"I was born old, darling."

And I suppose that's true about some. Eric seems to be an old soul. He sees inside of people and doesn't judge, which is what I love about him. As we're hugging, my phone buzzes with a text.

"Hmm, who could that be?" I ask.

"Won't know until you check your phone."

I look and see it's Vince. I tell Eric how I know Vince, and that he wants to meet for lunch today.

"You should go. You haven't seen him in a while."

"Yeah, and he lives so close."

I text him back and we make plans. Later that morning, Eric and I go for our run, and I swear I see Prescott.

"Hey, is that Prescott over there?"

"Where?"

"On the other side of the street."

"I don't see him," Eric says.

"I must be getting paranoid." Maybe I'm the one who needs help if I'm seeing things.

"Eh, it was probably someone who looked like him."

Except Prescott is unmistakable. Tall, dark, and ruggedly handsome, he's a standout in any crowd. That's why women fall at his feet, no questions asked. His eyes are unforgettable. Once you stare into them, there's never going back. Deep golden, they're compelling, nearly hypnotic, and one of a kind. And his mouth … I have to get my mind off him or I could trip and break an ankle.

Eric is a few feet ahead of me and we turn the corner when I crash into a solid object and bounce backward, falling flat on my ass. Damn, it hurts like hell because I fell squarely on my tailbone. I'm sitting, collecting myself, when two hands lift me up.

"Thanks, Eric, I don't know—"

"Not Eric. Are you okay?"

I'm staring into the object of my earlier daydreams. "Prescott? Wh-what are you doing here?"

"Running. Same as you. Are you okay, Vivi? You crashed into me pretty hard."

"Uh." I rub my throbbing ass. "I'll be fine."

He drops to a knee and ties one of my shoes that became undone somehow.

"I can call my driver to take you home, if necessary."

"No, I'll shake it off. Come on, Eric." I start to run, but my tailbone really hurts. I must've bruised it pretty good. There's not a thing in the world that can be done for it, though, so no sense in stopping.

"Mind if I join you?" Prescott asks.

What the hell can I say to that? It's not like we own the damn sidewalks. "Sure, come on, though I'll probably slow you down, especially now."

"It's fine. I was going long and slow this morning."

"Oh, how many miles?" I ask.

"Around fifteen," he says.

"Crap. You training for something?" Eric asks.

"No, I just like to run."

"Holy shitballs. That's a lot of running," I say.

"I run daily, but Sundays are my long runs."

"How long are your daily runs?" Eric asks.

"It depends on my time, but usually six to eight miles."

"You're a beast," I say.

Prescott laughs. "So I've been told. And an asshole. And often a jerk."

He's using the names I've called him.

"That I will agree with."

He stops and for some reason so do I.

"What?"

Out of the blue, he asks, "Can we be friends? I know I was a major ass to you and Eric. For that I apologize. But can we try, Vivi? I'll behave. I promise." He stands much taller than me and the sun is shining directly in his eyes. His hand comes up to shade them as he squints.

"I know, I just know I'm going to regret this, but okay. Only I'm warning you. This is your last chance."

What the hell have I just done?

Jesus, God, help me. He smiles and if it weren't bright enough already, the light just intensified. Prescott Beckham has hands down the most perfect smile God ever bestowed on a human being. My hand covers my chest to still the out of control pumping of my heart. If the stupid thing doesn't slow down, it might jump right out my ribcage and land in his hand.

"You won't regret it. I swear." Then he picks up his running pace again, and I join in. Only this time I lag behind so I can enjoy the view of his lovely butt. "Get up here, Renard, and stop checking out my ass."

What the hell? Does he have eyes in the back of his head? "I wasn't checking out your ass."

I'm still eyeballing it when he turns and catches me.

"Uh-huh. Just as I suspected. Get a move on or you'll never finish at that pace."

"Asshole," I mutter.

"I heard that. I have very acute hearing."

"Along with three hundred and sixty degree vision, too. For your information, I was admiring your shoes. What other tricks do you have up your sleeve?"

"I can't discuss them with you."

"Why not?"

"Because I promised to behave. That's why."

"Oh." That shuts me up, but I kind of like our banter. Eric is up ahead, by almost a block. "Should we catch up with Eric?"

"He's a big boy. I think he can handle it on his own. Are you a fan of chocolate?"

"Yeah, who isn't?"

"I don't know. Just curious."

We run back to my place, him in the lead. *Lucky for me*, I snicker quietly. "Hey, how did you know where I live?"

He doesn't answer immediately, but then says, "I have a security team at work. They can find out just about anything, Vivi."

"If you want to walk me home from work, just show up next time. It's a little disturbing having you stalk me."

A smile twitches at the corners of his mouth. "I might do that. Will you consider giving me your work schedule?"

"Maybe. But it'll cost you."

"How much?" he asks.

"One piece of chocolate," I say and then turn around and run through the door. I don't have much time before I have to meet Vince, so I strip off my clothes and hop in the shower. Eric comes into the bathroom while I'm showering.

"That was pretty cozy," he says.

"He was actually fun, although my tailbone hurts like a mofo."

"So? I want details."

"I caved, Eric. We're going to try the friend thing. I don't know if that was the smartest thing to do, but I couldn't resist. Why does he have to be so fucking hot?"

"That he is. I had to move on or my running shorts would've looked a little awkward there."

"Lusting after Beckham, are you?"

"What hot-blooded gay man wouldn't? If it makes you feel better, I think you did the right thing."

"I hope so." I rinse off my hair and put conditioner in. "I'm going to be late and Vince will kill me."

"He'll survive. Just text him."

"I will. Scram. I have to dry off."

The door opens and closes and I rush through the rest of my routine. My hair is still damp as I dash out of the apartment.

When I show up a few minutes late, Vince is waiting on me.

"Hey." He waves me over. "You look a little flustered."

Filling him in on most of the details of my life, leaving out the Prescott bits, he says, "Damn, I'm exhausted just listening."

He gives me the skinny on what's been happening with everyone. School's good; he's working in another coffee shop; and he'll hopefully graduate in two semesters. He's semi-dating someone he's super excited about. Or at least that's my impression.

"What's her name?"

"Milli. She's from Oklahoma of all places, studying music at Juilliard."

"That's awesome. Good for you, Vince."

"Yeah. She's way more talented than me."

"What does she play?"

"The violin. She's unbelievable. I've never heard anything like it."

"Wow. I always wanted to play an instrument. My mom enrolled me in piano and then flute, but it was a huge fail. I sucked."

He laughs, saying, "Same. I was awful at music."

"So, do you ever talk to Jenny? Or Jackie?" I ask.

"Jenny called a few weeks ago. She dropped out of school and decided to move back to Florida. This semester took it out of her, I guess. Jackie found a job at another coffee shop. She's doing well."

"Aw, I should call both of them to wish them the best."

Afterward, Vince and I promise to stay in touch. He also says he'll stop by The Meeting Place for a drink one weekend and bring Milli.

Eric is waiting for me when I get home. "How was your friend?"

"Fine." I take off my jacket and just as I'm getting ready to put my feet up and relax, a packet that sits on the small dining table catches my attention.

"What's that?"

"No idea. It's for you."

"Hmm." I grab it and unwrap it. Inside are two items—a gourmet chocolate bar and another smaller box. Inside the other box sits a large strawberry dipped in chocolate.

"Gee, I wonder who sent you that," Eric says, joking.

Opening the card that accompanies it, a flush heats my face as I read it.

"My, oh my. Must be something sexy," Eric says.

"Uh, a little."

"What happened to 'we're going to be friends'?"

"He acknowledges that in here."

"Please share," he begs.

Holding the note to my chest, I say, "I can't." Then I inspect my little gifts. Prescott's sense of humor is contagious and I laugh out loud.

"You can't do this to me."

"Okay. I told him not to stalk me after work, because it creeped me out. So he asked if I'd share my work schedule. I said it would cost him a piece of chocolate."

"That's not even funny."

"Yes, it is."

Pulling out my phone, I text Prescott the following:

The Meeting Place, Friday, 7 to 1:30 a.m. Thx :)

Eric stares at me. Then he says, "Wanna make a bet?"

"What kind?"

"Do you or don't you?"

"Depends on how much."

"Five bucks," he says.

"Okie dokes."

"You're going to fuck his balls off within a month."

CHAPTER 16

PRESCOTT

GRAND WAS RIGHT. THE CHOCOLATES WERE A SCORE. I WAS A little worried the strawberry and note went too far, but when I got her text, everything was cool.

Yeah, the note must've scored some points. I hesitated a few times on it.

Vivi,

We said friends and I promise it'll be that. You wanted a piece of chocolate in return for your schedule, so here you go. But dammit, I had to get you the strawberry too. Do you want to know why? Of course you do. And don't say I'm breaking my promise because I'm not. This is only Prescott paying Vivi the sincerest compliment.

I bought the strawberry because when I saw them all lined up in a row, they reminded me of your lips—perfectly shaped, red, plump, and the sweetest things I've ever tasted in my life.

So now you know. And you'll also know that as long as I live, whenever I see strawberries, I'll always think of you.

Your dear friend,

Prescott Whitworth Beckham

How the hell did I become such a romantic? I have no idea, but I admit the note was genuine and I sent it in the hopes she wouldn't run away screaming like her ass was on fire. She didn't.

I'm going to listen to Grand from now on.

Next, flowers, or dinner or something similar—but I won't overwhelm her now. *Baby steps, Beckham. Baby steps.*

This shit is hard. It's not in my nature to do things this way, but this fucking horse is going to learn to do pony tricks if it kills him.

When I get to work, Lynn is waiting on me.

"Hey, Lynn, I hope you had a nice weekend."

"I did. Have you forgotten your meeting this morning?"

"No, I haven't. I'm prepared. I had a productive weekend."

"Well, this is a change." She hands me a bottle of water and a coffee. I smile my thanks.

"You have thirty minutes."

"Thank you."

We're making an offer on a piece of property in lower Manhattan that my grandfather and I think would be a great turnaround for a hotel. When I enter the conference room, I'm the first one there. Soon, Granddad joins me, and then later Dad follows. He glowers when he sees me.

"Hey," I say.

He nods slightly but offers no other greeting.

The agents for the sellers of the building arrive, along with the owners, and Lynn comes in to provide coffee and refreshments. When everyone is comfortable and we exchange greetings, the meeting begins. Everything is running smoothly. The owners are happy with the fair price we've offered. We're about to get signatures on paper, when Dad decides to fuck it up.

"I'm not sure if I'm comfortable with this price. I think it's too high, Prescott. I don't think you are capable of handling this transaction."

"Excuse me?" I say. This is so completely wrong. You don't conduct business like this with customers sitting here.

"You heard me."

"Jeff," Granddad says. "What is this? We've done the comps and you've had the figures for over a week."

"I did some research of my own," Dad says.

Our clients watch this unprofessional display progress until I finally say to them, "Excuse us all a minute. We need to discuss this outside."

"No, we don't. We can talk right here," Dad says.

"Jeff," Granddad says, his tone menacing. "Enough already."

"The price is too generous. I don't think we should go forward with this."

Granddad leans forward. "You're forgetting something. You're not in a position to make that decision and your approval isn't necessary or required in order for this transaction to go through. If you can't stop interrupting us, I will ask you to leave this room." Then he looks at the clients, who are clearly uncomfortable by this exchange, and says, "I apologize for my son-in-law's lack of manners. Shall we proceed?"

Damn. Granddad put him in his place. He sits there, pouting like a scolded kid, and I guess he is that, but why did he act like such an ass in front of clients?

The rest of the meeting runs without a snag and we close the deal with everyone happy, except Dad. After everyone files out, my grandfather asks us to remain behind.

"Jeff, what was the meaning of that?" he asks.

"I think you made a huge error and I tried to warn you."

"That's not what you did. You tried to make Prescott look like a fool and you failed. My question is why?"

"I didn't do that. I was trying to save this company from foolishly spending money." Dad's face is mottled.

"That's ridiculous. Prescott has an astute business mind,

much better than yours. He never would've gone after that building in the first place if it hadn't been a viable option. And let's talk about foolish spending. How many times have I had to bail you out of your awful business proceedings? Don't bother answering that. It was more than I care to count. I'm beginning to think it's time to sever your ties with Whitworth. As it stands, you're not even a shareholder. I've only allowed you to remain here because of my daughter and Prescott, but I have no idea why I didn't boot you out after the shit you pulled last Christmas. I'm giving you one week to get your business dealings in order, Jeff. After that, you no longer have a role here."

Holy fucking shit. Granddad did it! I never thought he would. Dad's jaw sags open as the words penetrate.

"Close your damn mouth, Jeff. You brought this on yourself. You and that liar you're married to. And don't worry—you'll be compensated. Maybe not as well as you are now, but I'll work something out so you won't be living on the street. But tell that wife of yours she might have to cut back on the number of plastic surgeries she gets every month."

I bite my cheek to keep from laughing. I wish Grand were here. Would she ever be proud of her husband.

Dad storms out the door without uttering a word.

Granddad says, "I'm sorry you had to be a witness to that."

"I'm not. It's been brewing for a while. Thank you for supporting me."

"Prescott, I meant every word. You have a keen sense about you and I trust your judgment. Your father never did have that, no matter how much I worked with him."

I'm proud to hear those words from the man I respect most in the world.

"Thank you, Granddad. That means a lot to me. Can I say I loved the plastic surgery comment?"

"Your grandmother would've loved that one, too."

"I thought of her when you said it."

"Honestly, if that woman's lips get any more inflated, they're going to explode."

"That image is a little disturbing."

"As it is to me," he says.

"Hey, we got a great deal on that building. Now it's time to get it refitted."

"Son, you have your work cut out for you," he says, chuckling.

"Nah, I love this part. The change is what I like best."

"You do have the best eye for it."

"Nope. Weston does. I'll send him the floor plans as soon as we get them. He'll come up with something amazing. Then we go to work."

"You're lucky you met him at Crestview, coming from a long line of architects," he says.

"Yeah, and his own firm has really taken off."

"That doesn't surprise me. Weston Wyndham is a talented young man."

On my way back to my office, I pass Dad's and see him cleaning out his desk. Why does he have to be such an ass? It's obvious where I inherited that trait from—a chip off the old block. Right at that moment, he glances up. A look of utter contempt comes over him as he barrels toward me.

"This is all your fault. You planned this. You set out to ruin me, didn't you? Made my life miserable all those years, getting into fights and never doing what you were told. And now *this*. You think you're clever, worming your way into the old man's business. And all because you can't have what's mine."

The venom that spews from him shocks me. I step backward as he jams his face into mine.

"That's right. You. Can't. Have. Her. No matter how hard you try. She'll never be yours."

What the fuck? Then it hits me. He still thinks I'm after the step-cunt. Shoving him off me, I growl in his face, "I don't want her. I never have. And she's playing *you* for a fool." Removing myself from his presence, I walk to my office, head held high, and notice how everyone on the floor is staring. "Sorry for the disruption, everyone."

Lynn follows me inside and closes the door. "Jesus, this place is a soap opera today."

"Tell me something I don't know."

"I can't because you know everything."

Falling back into my chair, I say, "And I thought today was starting out great." I lean my head back and groan.

"It's not all bad. You closed the deal. And your dad won't be here to make you feel like shit anymore."

"You're right about that. But he has it in his head that I'm after his stupid wife. And she's fucking around on him only he doesn't see it."

"He will when she dumps him. As soon as she finds out about today, she'll move on to greener pastures."

"You think?" I ask.

"Hell, yes. Jeff is what, fifty?"

"He's forty-nine."

"Okay, and she's what, in her thirties?" Lynn asks.

"Maybe late thirties."

"Prescott, she'll want a younger, richer version of him, which was why she was hitting on you."

I shudder at the thought. "That's sick."

"Just saying. Anyway, I hate to break up your self-pity party, but while you were in the meeting, five calls came in that you need to handle right away. All of them are urgent and have to do with the merger you're working on."

"On it. And FYI, it was not a self-pity party. I'm just blown away by everything."

She pats me on the back. "I know you are." Lynn gets the whole situation as she's been with me throughout the entire mess.

"Hey, Lynn, thank you."

She gives me a thumbs-up on her way out the door.

I take care of the phone calls and Granddad comes in. He wants to discuss the house.

"The house?"

"The house you grew up in."

"Oh, you mean Dad's."

"No, son, it's not your dad's. It's yours."

"Mine?"

Granddad explains that my grandparents bought the house for my parents to live in when they got married, but the deed is still in their names, which makes them the current owners. They've only allowed Dad to stay there because of me, but under the circumstances, they don't feel comfortable with that anymore. They're signing the deed over to me because they believe my mother would've wanted it this way.

I start to laugh, a little at first, but then I'm bent over at the waist. "Oh, God, that bitch will die when she finds out. And thanks, Granddad, for making me do the dirty work."

He laughs right along with me. "Hey, Scotty, do you think her lips will be able to handle the shock?"

We're both snorting so loud that Lynn comes in to check on us. "Are you two up to no good?"

"You might say that," I answer her.

"I'm glad to see your spirits have lifted."

"Oh, they have."

Lynn leaves, and suddenly I rethink things. "Granddad, would you mind if I sit on this for a bit?"

"What do you mean?"

When I stop to think about it, I don't want to stoop to his level. My grandparents had a better influence on me than that. Even though it may sound crazy after all the shit he's put me through the last few years, I don't feel good about evicting him from the house. Her, I wouldn't mind. But he's my father and even though he may not have much integrity, I do.

Granddad beams. "I've said it before, but I don't say it nearly enough. Your mother would be so proud of the man you've

157

become. Take all the time you want, son." He leaves before I can respond.

Those words always stagger me. I've never thought of myself as someone who'd make my mom proud. To hear him say that means more than I can say. As I analyze it, a question arises. When did I become so caring? For whatever reason, I attribute this change in me in part to Vivi. A mere few days ago, I would've told my dad to kiss my ass. Now, I'm making a conscious effort to become a better person. I know I treat my employees well, but I do have a nasty streak that sneaks out from time to time. But if I can behave exactly like I did about the house, maybe I'll become my grandfather instead of my father. It's Granddad I've always admired.

Maybe if I can let go all of the issues I have with Dad and focus on the future, I can become a better man—a man I'd be proud to be.

When I get home that night, I text Vivi, but then I remember she's probably still at work. So I'm surprised when I get a response.

The restaurant. 7:30

I text her back.

Dogs or cats?

She hits me with: ***Neither. Fox.***

Isn't she something? Maybe I should just call her Foxy. But that won't work since she's already my Little Wolf. It's almost six. I better get a move on if I'm going to find a stuffed fox before I pick her up. I have to drive uptown to make the purchase and bribe them to stay open, too. But I make it worth their while.

When I get to the restaurant, I'm early, so I leave my little surprise in the backseat, get out of the car, and wait a few doors down. She comes out and sees the waiting vehicle, with the driver standing next to the door. She greets him as he opens the door for her, but when she gets a look at what's sitting on the seat, she throws her head back and lets out a loud belly laugh that can be heard all the way down the street.

I jog over to the car. "You like?"

"Oh my God. This is too funny! Where did you get it?"

"Uptown. Do you like his hat?"

She tries to grab the thing out of the car, but it's too large. It's a giant stuffed wolf, with a cowboy hat that rests on its head at a jaunty angle. The thing is ridiculously funny because it has a stupid little grin. What makes it even better is that on its lap is a baby fox, also wearing a hat.

"The hat's the best. Maybe I can borrow it sometime."

"Nah, your ears won't fit through."

"What do you mean?"

"Hers are stuffed through the little holes on top."

"Ahh. I see. This is perfect. Thank you for Mr. Wolf." She leans up and kisses my cheek.

"Anything for you, Little Wolf. And it's Ms. Wolf. Couldn't you tell by her skirt?"

She tries to hold in a laugh, but isn't successful. "I forgot about Little Wolf."

"I didn't."

"You don't seem the type who forgets about anything." She raises a brow.

"Mmm. You're probably right. Come on. Let's get out of here. Have you eaten?"

"Actually, no."

"Good. Neither have I. What would you like?"

"You choose," she says.

We end up at a small bistro near our homes and order dinner. She asks me about my day and I end up telling her what happened with Dad. She actively listens and is compassionate about the incident.

"Oh, Prescott, you must've been devastated by his behavior. I'm so sorry you had to experience that." She grabs my hand and I want to fold. This is different from my grandmother offering me sympathy, or my grandfather understanding that my dad is a complete dick and idiot. This is Vivi, who is an outsider to this situation, but she's empathetic and kind. It makes me uncomfortable. I don't want her to see this vulnerability.

Clearing my throat, I straighten in my seat. "It's fine. I'm used to it by now." A weird chuckle leaks out of me. *Jesus, get a hold of yourself, dude. You sound like a girl.* Then a tingling sensation sweeps up the back of my neck and over my face. I swear to God, if I'm blushing, I'll die.

"Excuse me a second." I tear out of my seat like a firecracker exploded in my pants. When I get to the bathroom sink, I look in the mirror and my skin is the color of a summertime tomato. What the fuck will she think of me? That I'm the biggest pussy on the damn Earth, that's what. I have just emasculated myself.

The door opens and some dude walks in. I need to pull it together and get out of here. After I splash cold water on my cheeks, I return to a waiting and concerned Vivi.

"Are you feeling okay?"

"Yeah. For a minute there …"

"Do you want to leave?"

"We haven't gotten our food yet," I say.

"We can get it to go. It's fine."

I can't believe my own ears when I say, "You wouldn't mind?"

"Not at all. You might be coming down with something."

"Maybe." A big fat case of pussyitis. I signal to our waiter and instruct him to make our dinner to go. He brings it a few moments later, boxed up and labeled. When I drop Vivi off, I have to help her inside because of the huge stuffed critter. She laughs all the way upstairs as I struggle with the ridiculous gift. But I'm happy she likes it. When I say good night, I thank her for listening.

"Anytime you want to talk, Prescott, call me. I'm a good listener."

"Thanks. Good night, Vivi."

My exterior cracked and I allowed her to see much more than I ever intended. This causes a huge problem, because now I appear weak and defenseless to her. It's the exact thing that occurred with my dad. The singular time I opened up, took a chance, and laid everything on the table with him, it backfired — and our relationship never was the same. It deteriorated bit by bit, until I don't even have any type of connection with him anymore. Now what the hell do I do?

There's one person who can calm me down.

The phone rings twice before he answers, "Prescott. What's going on?"

"Weston, I need to talk. And I may need for you to put Special on if she's there."

"What's going on?"

"Woman problems."

"You?" And then the fucker starts laughing.

"This isn't funny. Not in the least."

"Calm down and tell me what's happened."

"Before I do, get Special on. She won't give me shit like you do."

"You sure about that?"

The way he says it makes me speculate, but I need another woman's opinion. My gut tightens, but damn, I know their history and it's not that different from mine.

"No, but do it."

I hear him yell, "Spike, come here for a sec. Prescott's on the phone and needs our advice." That crazy ass nickname of his brings a brief smile to my face.

When all three of us are on the phone, I tell my Vivi story, the condensed version, leaving out as much Prescott-assholery as possible. There are parts where it's impossible not to. Besides, Special knows me. She's heard all the stories from her husband and me.

"First off, I can't believe you did some of that shit to her," Special says.

"You don't have to go there. I already know how bad that is. What I need to know is ..." What exactly do I need?

"Yes?" They're waiting.

"Right. So my relationship with my dad sucks. It's the worst. The last time I opened up to anyone, other than Westie or Harry, it was with him and backfired so bad that—"

"Stop. You can't compare everyone to your dad. He's a jerk," Weston says.

"Not only that, if you go around acting like a d-bag, she's going to put up her walls and refuse to ever have anything to do with you," Special says. "What exactly do you want with her? Just another notch in your belt?"

"What?"

Weston cracks up. "Yeah, she used that term with me, too. It's from Mimi. Her grandmother."

"Yeah, sorry. I'm old-fashioned. What can I say? So, back to the point, do you just want to fuck her?" Special asks.

"Is that important?" I ask.

"Yes, you idiot. If you only want that, why does any of it matter? Do what you have to do to accomplish your goal, fuck her, then move on. But—and this is a gigantic but—if you want more, doing it that way could destroy a potential relationship. See, to me, it sounds like Vivi wants to see more of what's inside of Prescott. And maybe by opening up to her you really haven't fucked up. It could be the best thing you've ever done. Stop worrying about it and move forward. She seems really cool."

It all sounds so goddamn easy, but … "Yes, but now I'm weak."

"Weak? How are you weak?" Special asks.

"Because she could use what I told her against me. When someone knows these kinds of things, it's easy for them to destroy you with that knowledge. That's what happened to me with my dad. And being vulnerable isn't something I'm comfortable with."

"Are you deaf? Jesus, you can't compare her to your father," Weston says. "Your father is a narcissist. He's never had your best interests at heart. When did he ever give a shit about you? Don't you remember how we compared notes at Crestview? Our dads sucked. Vivi doesn't sound like the type that would do anything remotely similar to what your dad did. Think about the things she's already done. Her behavior is miles away from his."

"I suppose."

"Relax and put yourself in her shoes. What would Vivi do? Ask yourself those questions," Special says.

"You're right. I knew I needed a woman's perspective. Thank you, Special."

"Just don't fuck her over or I'll come up there and kick your ass for being such a dick."

"Got it, Spike," I say.

After the call, the looming question hanging over me is what exactly do I want with Vivi? The day I saw her in the coffee shop, my first reaction was to fuck her. Then in the next few episodes after that, I was convinced I'd do it. Now, I'm not so sure.

She didn't go for that plan, didn't fall straight into my arms like all the other women I know. Vivi has turned out to be different in every possible way. And it looks like I'm changing a bit myself. No, make that a lot. The old Prescott would've walked away without a second glance. Though, I'm not a hundred percent sure if I like the new one yet.

The fact that I've engaged the help of Eric makes everything even worse. He's the one who told me she was working at The Meeting Place, and when they'd be running that Sunday. I probably should've kept him out of it, but my devious mind wouldn't leave it alone. The amount of guilt I feel over it stuns me. It's a goddamn noose around my neck. I'll make it up to Eric and hold up my end of the bargain. If he's a good interior designer, he'll end up making money and a name for himself because of it. But if Vivi ever finds out he helped me, we're both fucked.

CHAPTER 17

VIVI

It came out of nowhere when Prescott opened up to me. I wasn't expecting him to share such an intimate detail about his life, but it makes him much more … human. The cold exterior he displays is replaced by something less inhibited. He reminded me of the carefree Prescott from Crestview, even though he never shared anything from his personal life back then. The Prescott of today is locked as tight as a vault and withdrawn, but he's also cocky, arrogant, and confrontational. Now I can see why. Or at least I'm beginning to get a little insight into it. If this is *one* situation with his father, I can only imagine what it must've been like growing up with him.

An image of my dad cutting the turkey at Thanksgiving one year pops into my head. He was the worst turkey slicer ever. Mom used to call him the annihilator. He'd run around the dining room table making what he thought were gobbler noises. I'm not sure if they were, but he'd chase me and I'd threaten not to eat a bite of the bird. When he was finished mutilating Mom's masterpiece, she would sigh, and then we'd all crack up before eating. We never did know if he did it on purpose or really couldn't figure out how to cut one properly. He died before telling us. I never appreciated those times … not until after he was gone. Thanksgivings were pretty lonely after that. We tried to make up for it, but eventually gave up and went out to eat. Dad was simply irreplaceable.

"How was dinner?" Eric asks, shattering my reminiscing.

"Oh, it was sort of brief. Prescott got sick and we had to leave. That reminds me." I grab the meal I never ate and plate it up.

"Hmm. Smells awesome."

"Mmm. It is."

"I hope he's not getting that stomach bug."

After swallowing my bite, I say, "Me too. That means I may get it. Ugh."

Then Eric sees Ms. Wolf. "What the hell?"

"Yeah, that was waiting for me in the car when he picked me up." I explain the meaning behind it.

"He doesn't bother with a small intimate gift, does he?"

"Oh, I don't know. The chocolate wasn't extravagant."

"No, I guess not. Hey, I wanted to ask you. What are you doing for Thanksgiving? It's Thursday, you know."

"Yeah." I've been trying not to remind myself, but that memory I just had brought it back full force.

"So?"

"Oh, gee, Eric. I have so many plans." I do an exaggerated sigh.

"Come home with me to my parents'."

"No way."

Eric is very kind and caring and the fact that he asked me is super sweet. However, I don't think I could emotionally handle being thrust into a happy family situation right now. His posture sags and so does his expression right along with it. "Why not?" he asks. "You'd love my family. They're the best. You'd have so much fun."

I jump in saying, "It's not that at all. And I'm sorry you took it that way. Thanksgiving is just a hard time for me." That wasn't the best thing for me to say. So I soften it with, "Besides, I have to work on Wednesday night."

He instantly perks up. "All the more reason for you to come then. Work won't be a problem. I can leave early Thursday morning instead. My sister and brother will be there, and so will my grandparents. You'll fit right in, Viv. In fact, you'll probably think your last name is Thompson and not Renard."

I set my fork down and walk over to him, where I give him the biggest hug I can muster up. "You are the best roommate in the whole wide world and I don't know what I would've done if I hadn't met you. Seriously."

He hugs me back. "Somehow, I have a feeling there's a big but coming."

"Well, yes, yes, there is. Thanksgiving is one of those holidays that was always really special to me. You know how some people love Halloween because they love dressing up? Or Christmas because they love decorating? I'm like that about Thanksgiving. It was my dad's absolute favorite. And because of that, I get the blues every year. Pretty bad, too. That's why I don't want to come. It has nothing to do with your family. I know if they're anything like you, they have to be amazing."

"You can't be alone, Viv. It just wouldn't be right. I'll be thinking of you the whole time and then my Thanksgiving will be ruined."

"Oh, shut up. Besides, I want to be alone. Don't you see? It's kind of my way of having Dad and Mom with me still."

"It's hard for me to see it like that."

"That's because you still have your family. So go and be with them and do me a favor. Never take them for granted." Now it's his turn to hug me.

The next two days go by without a word from Prescott. I stay purposely busy so I don't think too much about it. I text him to check up on him, and he replies with a short message saying he's better, but that work has him in a jam. The text is a bit curt, but I ignore it and go on with my day.

I'm pulling a shift at the restaurant and then going directly to The Meeting Place, so I have a long day ahead of me. When I finish at the restaurant, I'm already tired, so I can't think about how I'll feel at one in the morning. The amount of money I'm bringing drives me through it.

We're fairly busy tonight. I guess it's because tomorrow is Thanksgiving, and most everyone has the day off. It's also why I agreed to work. The restaurant is closed, which means I can sleep late.

Friday morning I have an interview for a position with one of the hedge funds in town. They need a new software system in their firm and are looking for someone to design one specifically for them. I'm considering giving up hope on finding a real job and maybe just doing consulting work or even these short-term projects. Though I'd love the work, it's rather disappointing to kiss the idea of benefits goodbye.

"Hey, Vivi, I need some olives, STAT," Lucas calls out. We keep a backup supply on my side of the bar, but when I go to find some, there aren't any.

"We're out. I'll run to the back and get some."

"Make it quick. I've got a couple of customers waiting on some extra dirties."

I hand him my supply as I pass, saying, "Use these. I'll be right back."

There's a storage room in the rear of the bar, so I thread my way through the room, dodging customers and tables, until I reach the hallway leading to the bathroom and back exit. The door is to my right, so I open it and flip on the light. The small room is neatly organized, so I quickly spot which shelf the olives are on. As I reach for the jar, I hear the door close and suddenly I'm grabbed from behind and shoved into the wall. A body presses up against me as my arm is pulled and twisted backward so hard I scream. But a hand clamps down over my mouth and nose so I can hardly breathe.

"Shut the fuck up, bitch. You thought you had taken care of

me, sent me off for good, didn't you? Surprise. I'm back and it's my turn now."

My mind races as my pulse joins in. I have a single-minded focus and it's to get away from him. One arm is useless but that still leaves me with the other. Taking my elbow, I aim for what I hope is his solar plexus. I miss, skimming his ribcage, but it gives me some wiggle room. My adrenaline surges. The arm he has wrenched behind me should be screaming, but I barely notice it. I open my mouth, making him think I'm going to scream again and his hand slips inside my mouth. Biting down as hard as I can, I taste his blood.

"You fucking bitch. You're gonna pay for that."

He rips my shirt from the back of my neck down and buttons go flying from the force. But I'm not done fighting. I kick back with my foot only to find air. Not stopping, my leg keeps at it like a crazed mule. If he's going to rape me, he'll have to work for it, by God. Fear drives me and I won't stop until I'm either unconscious or dead. My head snaps as he fists a bunch of my hair. In that instant of shock, he spins me around and fires a jab straight to my cheek. The blow jerks my head, knocking it into the wall. I'm momentarily stunned. He's gained an advantage and punches me in the face again and again until I'm the proverbial rag doll in his arms. He must release me, because I slide to the floor as he kicks me in the ribs.

I won't make it out of here alive, will I?

The question scares me, even when I'm in too much pain to make sense of anything. He stops for a second and mumbles something to me, but my mind is clouded, so I don't grasp what he says. Then the door flies open as someone yells out my name. My attacker is suddenly gone and Lucas is here. "Shit, fuck." Then he yells, "Help! Call nine-one-one!"

It never occurred to me that Joe Delvecchio would return to seek his revenge.

The ambulance arrives in minutes while Lucas sits with me, holding my hand.

"Stay and work," I mumble, but the words don't come out exactly like that. My lips won't work. When I touch them, they're fucked up and swollen.

"I called a few people in and we're good. I'm not going to let you ride alone."

The paramedics are loading me onto the gurney when I sense a commotion. Lucas squeezes my hand and says, "I think you'll be in good hands now."

"What the fuck happened? Who did this?" a hoarse voice asks.

I don't have to look to know who it is. Lucas must've called Prescott. How did he know to get in touch with him? And how did he have his number?

The medics start covering me up.

"I'll take it from here, Lucas."

"I know," he says. "All I ask for is an update."

"You'll have it."

Then Prescott asks the medics if he can have a minute. My eyes are so swollen I can barely open them, but he stands next to me.

"Prescott?"

"Yeah."

"I'm really scared." I reach for his hand. "Will you hold my hand?"

"They're injured, Vivi. I don't want to—"

"Please."

A warm hand covers mine and it comforts me. "M-my face. Is it?"

"It's beautiful. Perfect as always."

"That bad, huh?"

"You shouldn't be talking right now."

"Are my teeth knocked out?" I ask.

"What?"

"My teeth. Are they all there?"

He clears his throat. "Yeah, they're still there."

"A jar of olives," I say.

"What?"

"Olives. We keep them in the storage room. I went to get them and he must've followed me in there."

"Fuck. Don't think of that now."

"I have to. I need to tell you in case I forget. You need to remember the details."

"Let me get my phone."

Why would he need his phone? So I ask him.

"To record what you say."

"Okay." I tell him everything I remember. "I figured I was going to die in there." I swallow back the tears.

"It's going to be okay, Vivi. You're going to be fine."

"What if he doesn't stop?"

"Don't worry about that now." He pats my hand gently. "We'll make sure he stops."

The paramedics step in and say it's time to go. Then they roll me out to the waiting ambulance, where a crowd has gathered. Lights are flashing everywhere and I can see two police cars. It's a reminder that Joe Delvecchio is in one of those cars. I try to search for Prescott, but the gurney moves too fast. Then the men lift it up and slide it into the vehicle. It's bright inside and they begin attaching things to me. It stings when they stick a needle into my vein.

Prescott tries to ride in the back, but they don't let him. They explain if he wants to go with me, he has to take a seat in the front. He eventually does and the doors close as we pull away.

We arrive at the hospital and they run all kinds of tests to rule out a serious head injury for one, but my injuries include a fractured arm and rib, a bad concussion, some bruises, and cuts on my face. My hands are cut and bruised, too. The doctors say I'm going to be in pain for a while, but I'll have a full recovery. That's good news. The only time Prescott leaves that night is when they wheel me away for the scans. Other than that, he's there with me constantly.

The next day, he pops in to say he has to go to his grandparents'. I'm so groggy, I sleep most of the day. That night when I wake up, I find him sitting in a chair next to the bed.

"Hey," he says.

"Hey." I open my hand and he places his in it. "Thank you for being here with me yesterday."

"I didn't really do anything."

"Yeah, you did. I was a little freaked and you helped me get through that."

The truth is I'm still freaked out, only I don't mention it to him.

"Vivi." His voice is filled with anguish and I lift my eyes to his. He doesn't say anything else and I'm not sure why. I only know my head is so messed up from the medication that I can barely keep my eyes open.

"You should sleep," I hear him say. I nod, relieved to be closing my eyes.

On Friday morning, I'm released from the hospital. I have to cancel my interview, explaining how I was assaulted and beaten. Not a great story to tell a potential employer.

Prescott picks me up, and as he's bringing me home, he suggests something. "I told my grandparents about you yesterday. They were worried about you staying by yourself, especially since Eric's gone until Sunday. So Grand, that's what I call my grandmother, thought you should stay at my place. I happen to agree with her, and she's always right, so I'm offering."

My first thought was how did he know Eric was gone, but it's immediately replaced by the idea of not wanting to stay alone. I've never been frightened like this and before I can think, I'm agreeing to his suggestion.

CHAPTER 18

PRESCOTT

THE BIT ABOUT WHAT GRAND SAID WASN'T ONE HUNDRED percent true. She did say it probably wasn't wise for Vivi to be alone. I sort of added the other part. The combination of the way Vivi moves, slowly and with obvious pain, and her battered appearance has me convinced she absolutely shouldn't be alone.

When I got to The Meeting Place and saw her, so many emotions plowed into me at once—rage at the one who did this to her; fear for her well-being; worry, anxiety, helplessness—too damn many to name. A tidal wave swept me away, and I had no way of stopping it.

Yet it was the moment outside the ambulance that almost shattered me, and I fucking swear, that's when Vivi Renard truly cracked through my impenetrable exterior and tapped into my heart and soul. I don't know how she fucking did it, but every time I look at her, I hear her ask if I'll hold her hand. How can the smallest gesture bridge the widest gap? Break through the toughest shell?

"I'm ready." Her weak voice interrupts my musings.

"Let me do that for you. You shouldn't be carrying anything."

"Thanks."

As we cross over the threshold of my apartment, she asks, "Are those ice packs from the hospital in the bag?"

"Yeah, and we can get more if you want."

"No, those are enough. I didn't remember bringing them." Her eyes pinch at the corners.

"Hey, the doctor said memory loss for a few days is normal. You've been through a very traumatic event. Forgetting about ice packs isn't a big deal."

She's suddenly crying as she stands there. Fuck.

Dropping the small bag, I rush to her and wrap her in a gentle hug, careful not to hold her too tight. "Go ahead and cry, Vivi. It's okay."

She grabs me with her good arm and hangs on. Sobs wrench her body and I'm powerless to help my wounded Little Wolf. Other than the situation with my dad, this is foreign as fuck to me. I awkwardly pat her hair as I would a puppy. Consoling Vivi throws me out of my comfort zone. I have no problems tying a woman to my bed and fucking her until she screams out several orgasms, but not this. When her sobs ease a bit, I move her to the couch and go in search of some tissues. Handing her some, she thanks me.

"I'm so sorry I—"

"Don't apologize." I take a seat next to her and cover her hand with mine. "You've been so strong, Vivi. After everything you've been through, all the trauma, you need a good cry. Maybe even more than one."

"I hate to cry. I didn't even cry at my mom's funeral."

This conversation is getting too deep for comfort, so I change the subject. "I have an idea. How does a hot bath sound?"

"It sounds nice."

As I reenter the living room from starting the bath, I gather her things and say, "You should stay in my room. And before you object, here's why. There are no stairs to navigate, the big tub is in there, and I can stay in one of the rooms upstairs. There's plenty of room here, so it won't be a problem for me. I have all the bathrooms stocked with my favorite things, so there's nothing to move. I can get dressed in the closet, which is large, so it won't be a bother at all. If you don't believe me, go in and check it out yourself."

Her fucking eyes are so swollen I can't read them. Eventually she nods and I walk her into my room. It's large by any standards. There's a king bed that faces a great view of the city and she'll be able to relax in here if she wants.

"The closet is through here." I show her the way. It's basically another room, outfitted with drawers, shoe racks, and a dressing table for his and hers. "And then through there is the bath." I lead her to it. When we enter, I see the bath is coming along, but not quite there yet.

"When it gets high enough, just push this and it'll turn all the jets on. There's a robe in here if you want and I'll bring your bag and leave it in the room."

"Thank you."

"Just call out if you need me. I'll leave the bedroom door open so I can hear."

"That would be great. With this arm, I might need you."

My Little Wolf looks utterly dejected when I leave. Feeling helpless is miserable. There's one thing I can do, though, while she's bathing.

In a few seconds, I'm tapping in a number on my phone.

"Mr. Beckham. What can I do for you, sir?" a crisp voice answers.

Unclenching my jaw, I say, "Neil, do you remember that incident I had your firm handle a while back regarding a Joe Delvecchio?"

"Yes, I do."

"It seems Mr. Delvecchio was released from jail and on Wednesday night, he brutally assaulted Vivienne Renard." I explain in finite detail everything that happened. "I want this handled properly this time. Put your entire fucking team on it. I don't care how much it costs, how many hours it takes, or how many people you need, but I want the D.A. to have every resource available to help with this case. The bastard could've killed her. Am I clear?" My hand holding the phone trembles.

"Yes, sir. I'll send somebody down to get on it immediately."

"No fuck-ups this time. Oh, and, Neil, if at all possible, I don't want Vivi to have to go to court. If we can do this through affidavits or recorded statements, do it."

"Sir, I'm not sure that will be possible, but I'll do my best. I'll get someone down to talk to the prosecutor and the police right away."

A vein throbs at my temple. Inhaling, I say, "This never should've fucking happened. No bail this time, or if you can't manage that, make it sky high."

"Yes, sir. I'll follow up on that. Have the police interviewed her yet?"

"They were at the hospital, but I don't have all the details on that and I don't want to ask her."

"Where is she now?"

"Here with me. If they interrogate her, I want a member of your team present. Vivi is … distraught and fragile right now to say the least."

"Yes, sir. Mr. Beckham, may I recommend something? In cases such as hers, especially since this is her second attack, it might be a good idea if she sees someone, such as a psychologist."

"I'll mention that to her."

"Victims suffer from PTSD and the sooner she talks about it the better."

"Good idea. You wouldn't happen to know anyone, would you?"

"As you know, my area of expertise is corporate law. My associate who handles criminal law will know. I'll get with her and have her email some recommendations to you."

"Thanks, Neil." Still unsatisfied, my body rumbles with anger. What it needs is two hours in the gym, but I don't want to leave until Vivi is out of the tub. I hover near the door, in case she calls out. My phone rings, and it's Lynn.

"Where are you?"

Fuck. "I'm sorry. I forgot to tell you I wasn't coming in."

"Are you sick?"

"In a manner of speaking."

"Let me call you back." She hangs up and I know she's going into my office where she can speak freely. About a minute later my phone rings again and it's her.

"Hey."

"So?" she asks.

"I'm helping out a friend today."

"Excuse me?"

"Yeah. Something pretty bad happened."

"And you just didn't do your usual of sending someone over?"

"No."

"Are you okay? You sound off. Your dad didn't—"

"No, nothing like that. It's a friend. A female friend."

"Ah, the clouds are parting now."

"Lynn, it's not like that either. The truth is she was assaulted on Wednesday night—literally had the shit beaten out of her—so I'm helping her out."

"Good Lord, Prescott. I'm sorry."

"Yeah, me too."

"Is there anything I can do?"

"Fuck yes. Why didn't I think of you before? How fast can you get to my place?"

"Ten minutes?"

"Transfer your calls to your cell and come on."

"I'll be there as soon as I can."

I'm hovering by the door when the buzzer goes off. I let Lynn in and she says, "You look like shit."

"Yeah, and it's not the alcohol."

She takes off her coat as she says, "That didn't even cross my mind. You look like you haven't slept in a week."

"It's more like two days."

She rubs the chill off her hands. "So what can I do?"

"Follow me." I lead her into my bedroom until we get right outside the bathroom door. "Vivi? Is everything okay in there?"

Her small voice comes back to us. "Yeah, I'm good."

Through the door, I explain that Lynn, my admin from work who she met that day at the restaurant, has come in, just in case she needs some help. "She's like my mom, so if you need a hand getting out of the tub, give us a shout, okay?"

"Thank you. I think I will. This arm is useless."

"Are you ready now?"

"Yes, please."

"She's bruised up something terrible, so be prepared," I whisper to Lynn.

Lynn nods as she walks into the bathroom and I hear her introducing herself. I hear them chatting as I leave the bedroom, closing the door behind me.

Maybe it's time to put the coffee on or order in some food. I'd better make the coffee and wait until they show up. When they do, Lynn's brows are drawn together and she's biting her lip. Vivi shuffles around like she's older than Grand. She grimaces with each step and her eyes crimp at the corners. Clearly she's in pain.

"Vivi, when did you last take your pain medication?" I ask.

"Before I left the hospital. I don't like the way it makes me feel."

Vivi twists her fingers, and Lynn gains my attention over her head.

"I understand, but you need to keep the pain under control. Let me get you some water and one of your pills. Are you hungry? Can I get you some coffee?"

"I'm hungry, but my stomach feels off."

"Probably because you haven't eaten much. I can order in."

Lynn huffs out a response. "Don't you have anything here?"

"Well, yeah, but I don't cook and Gerard has the week off."

"Didn't I tell you he was a spoiled brat, Vivi?" she said, as she prances off into the kitchen. The sounds of cabinet doors opening and pots banging come to us and I smile. Leave it to Lynn to take over.

"I like her," Vivi says.

"So do I. She's my lifesaver in the office."

"I can tell."

"I'll be right back." Her pain pills are on the nightstand, where I left them, so I dump one out of the bottle and bring it to her. "Would you like water? Juice? You name it."

"Water, please."

I get into the kitchen to see Lynn cooking an old-fashioned breakfast.

"I thought this would do her some good."

"I agree. What did you want?"

"She's in terrible shape, Prescott," she whispers. "I've never seen anything like it."

Rubbing my face, I agree with her. "I wasn't there when it happened and it was a good thing. I probably would've killed the motherfucker."

"You've known her awhile. Why the sudden interest now?"

"She moved here recently. I haven't seen her in years."

Lynn sees more in me than I'm willing to share. "Do you mind if I go hit the treadmill while you cook. I'm—"

"Go. I'll hold down the fort."

After making sure Vivi takes her pill I change and run a very hard thirty minutes. When I'm done, I'm actually slightly calmer. Grabbing a towel as I leave the room, I rejoin the ladies. Lynn is about finished cooking and Vivi appears more relaxed.

"Has the medicine kicked in yet?"

"Some. I'm better."

"Good." I tell Lynn not to wait on me. I head to the shower first and when I notice some of Vivi's things in the bathroom, a sense of uncertainty slides over me. I want her here, yes, and I want to help her, but how far do I want to take this? Will she expect more from me and if so how much?

Am I jumping to conclusions? I'm confused because I don't even know what exactly it is I want with her. I need to stop repeating this ridiculous conversation in my head and just move forward already.

Water streams down my back and washes the remainder of my frustrations away. By the time I get dressed, the tightening in my chest has eased.

"It smells really good in here," I say. "Bacon, one of the best aromas ever."

Vivi sits at the counter and I ask her if she's comfortable there.

"Yeah, it's fine."

"Are you right-handed?"

"No, left," she says.

"Shall I feed you, then?" It's her left arm that's broken.

"No, I may need you to wipe my face, though, if I make a mess of myself."

"I can do that."

Vivi says to Lynn, "Thank you for cooking this. It looks and smells so delicious. I can't remember the last full meal I've had."

Lynn cooked pancakes, eggs, bacon, and hash browns. Damn, I had no idea I had potatoes here.

We eat in silence. My plate shines after I'm done. "I was starved. That was excellent, Lynn. Thank you." When I get up to clean, Lynn starts to protest, but I shut her down. "You cooked, I clean. My house, my rules."

It doesn't take long because Lynn is a neat cook and cleaned up as she went. Vivi droops in her chair. "Vivi. How about a nap?"

"Can I sleep here? I'm too tired to move. All that food, you know."

"I have a better idea." Before she can object, I pick her up and carry her into the bedroom. "Let me get a blanket." There's a throw on the couch, so I grab it and cover her. "Now sleep." Her eyes are already closed.

Lynn and I work while she naps. She wants to know all about Vivi and I tell her a little bit, filling her in about the attack.

"That shit needs to go to prison forever."

"I wish. But if I have anything to do with it, he'll serve time now. I have Neil's firm on it."

"Neil? Isn't he corporate law?"

"Neil is, but there's a criminal division in his firm that will handle it."

"What about her family? Where are they? Has she called them?"

"She doesn't have anyone. Her parents are deceased and she's alone."

Lynn throws her hands up in the air. "That's it. I'm adopting her. The poor child."

"I know."

"Why, Prescott Beckham, you've more than a soft spot for this girl, don't you?"

"Not up for discussion."

"Remember when I asked you to ease up on the drinking?"

"Yeah?"

Her hand wraps around my forearm. "I never mentioned another word to you about that, but I know you did. You never came into work again stinking like a distillery. If I were a betting woman, I'd say Vivi had something to do with it."

"Your point?"

"My point is this. That is an extremely fragile woman in there. I love you like a son. But you are as stubborn as a mule and you grew up the hard way, Prescott. I was at Whitworth when it was all unfolding. I witnessed the arguments between your grandfather and your father. You have a backbone forged of steel. I'm not sure if she does. She may. All I'm saying is be gentle with her. She's not your run of the mill girl you're used to dating."

"You don't have to tell me that."

"She's just so … broken at the moment."

"So, what you're saying is I'm not the guy to put her back together?"

"I'm not sure anyone can right now."

CHAPTER 19

PRESCOTT

Lynn and I are standing near the kitchen counter when a piercing scream jars us both out of the conversation.

Fuck, Vivi!

When I get to the bedroom, Vivi is thrashing on the bed, trapped in the coverlet. She's fighting it as though her life depends on it.

"Vivi, it's me, Prescott. Wake up." Touching her face, her puffy eyes twitch open and focus. Then those same eyes dart about the room, until they settle back on me. "Everything's fine. You're safe."

"I was dreaming. I was back in that room and I couldn't move."

"It was a nightmare. But I'm here now. He can't hurt you and I'm going to do everything in my power to make it impossible for him to ever touch you again."

She leans into my chest and I feel her trembling. "I don't want to sleep, because I relive it all over again. I can smell him, taste his blood when I bit him, feel his breath against my skin, hear the hatred in his voice." She shudders violently.

What the fuck do I say to that? I want to find the fucker and shove his dick so far up his ass he'll spit the damn thing out his mouth.

"I'm sorry. But I'm here for as long as you need me and I swear I'll do everything I know to protect you. I don't know much about what to say to make you feel better. Quite honestly, I'm at a loss. But whatever you want from me, just ask. I'll fucking give it to you, I promise."

"Does Eric know I'm here? And Lucas? I don't want them to worry."

"Yes, Eric and Lucas are aware."

"I don't want you to leave. I'm afraid, Prescott. And I feel like such a big dork for saying that."

"Don't be ridiculous. We're going to find someone for you to talk to about this. You're suffering from PTSD and you can't fix this by yourself, you know?"

"I can't afford to seek help."

"Shut up. And if you argue about this I'll … well, I'll find some way to persuade you to my side."

She's quiet and then says, "You're right. I'm freaked out and every little noise makes me jump out of my skin."

"We'll sort it out. Do you think you can sleep some more?"

"Oh, God, no."

She decides to get up and Lynn goes back to the office. There are a few things she needs to handle for me. I'm going to spend the day with Vivi.

As Lynn is leaving, she hands Vivi a scrap of paper. "This is my cell if you need anything. And I mean it. Call me. I'll gladly help."

"Thank you for being so kind."

After she's gone, I say, "I believe you've made a friend."

"Lynn's great."

"I'd be so lost without her. She's my right hand. And I mean that."

We watch movies and TV as I wait on her the rest of the day. It's been ages since I've spent a day doing nothing and it's weird.

Vivi dozes a lot, which is what she needs. I make sure she takes her pain pills every four to six hours. Though they make her pretty dopey, they at least help her rest.

When it's time to go to bed, she asks me to sleep with her. "I know you probably don't want to. You probably regret asking me to stay here. But I'm frightened and I'm usually not that kind of person."

"You lived in the scariest place ever and didn't bat an eye. So you don't have to convince me. I don't mind sleeping with you, Vivi." Then I laugh. "Hell, I've been trying to get you into my bed for how long now?"

She tries to muster up a laugh, but it quickly fades. "And look what you ended up with. Something from a freak show."

"Oh, come on. You're not something from a freak show. And this is temporary. It'll fade away. One day, you won't even remember how you looked."

"You're wrong. From now on, this will always be the face I'll see in the mirror. That man has shattered every image I had of myself. He stole my happiness and replaced it with fear."

I hate the agony I hear in her voice.

"We'll get it back, Vivi. I promise."

"Don't make promises you can't keep, Prescott."

CHAPTER 20

VIVI

Everything terrifies me. Prescott is the only thing that stabilizes me. He wraps me in his arms and makes everything better again.

But isn't that messed up? I can't go through life running to him every time I get frightened. I lie in bed thinking about this as his larger than life body cocoons me.

In the morning, I tell him I need to get help. "I thought about it during the night. I have to gain my independence again."

He smiles. "Vivi, I'm glad to hear that. But this happened on Wednesday. It's Saturday. You're still recovering. It's not like you've waited three or four months."

"No, I just want to get a jump on it. I can't stand feeling terrified all the time and the thought of stepping foot outside this apartment freaks the hell out of me. Like really bad." My voice rises involuntarily on the last sentence.

He gestures with his hands as if he's pushing down the air. "Okay, I get it. The attorneys I've hired to handle this case are supposed to send over a list of recommended therapists. As soon as they do, we'll make the calls until we find someone you gel with. Sound good to you?"

"Attorneys you hired?"

"Yeah, we are going to get this guy. And if you try to argue with me, I can assure you it will fall on deaf ears."

"Well, then. I guess I won't argue then. But I was going to thank you and also add that I don't know how I can repay you."

"There will be no repayment."

When I go to speak, his hand flies up. "Stop. We'll be using a firm the company keeps on retainer. They have an entire department that handles criminal cases and will do the prosecuting."

"Won't the state do that? Since I was a victim?"

"Yes, but we're going to do everything we can to make sure he goes to prison. The district attorney will have some assistance from us, you might say."

"Oh, I didn't know you could do that."

"Technically, you usually don't. My firm has connections. The DA is close to one of the partners, so information will be shared."

"Is that legal?"

"Yes, because it's evidence. We're not doing anything illegal. Not to change the subject, but would you feel comfortable staying here alone? I was going to run out and pick up something for breakfast."

"Yeah, I'm fine. Just make sure you lock the door."

"I will. Don't forget, there's security in the lobby too."

After he leaves, the mirror beckons me. Ever since I woke up in the hospital and peeked at myself, I've avoided looking again. But an urge strikes and I have to see what the damage is. I want to do it while Prescott's not here.

His bathroom is massive and the mirrors over the sinks are too. They were hard to avoid when I was in here bathing, but I kept my head averted. Now, I lift it and stare. The image is every bit as ugly as it was in the hospital. I thought maybe the swelling had gotten better, but I've turned a hideous shade of purple, and my cheeks are still distorted even though some of the swelling has gone down. Reminding myself it could've been worse, like my skull could've been smashed in or I might have died, I steel myself and leave. I'm not sure when I want to see this face again.

This is only part of my worries. What the hell am I going to do about work? I can't possibly wait tables with a broken arm. Or tend bar, for that matter. Fuck my life. But I learned long ago that self-pity only makes it worse. Focusing on the bright side is what I need to do.

Positive thought number one: I survived the attack.

Grabbing the remote, I search for something to watch on TV. Prescott has been more than generous to me and I must find a way to thank him, only I'm afraid it will have to wait a while. I'm basically helpless at the moment.

I'm dozing off when the noise of the door opening wakes me.

"It's only me," Prescott's calls out. He walks in with his arms full, followed by one of the bellmen from the lobby. "Vivi, this is Kaz. He's usually on duty during the weekends. I told him if you needed anything he should help."

"Oh, thank you and nice to meet you, Kaz." Kaz is an older gentleman, perhaps in his late fifties, with wiry gray hair. His kind smile puts me at ease.

"A pleasure, miss." He gives a slight bow of his head and then says, "Will there be anything else, Mr. Beckham?"

"No, let's unload the cart and you can take it back down with you."

"Yes, sir."

Cart? Sitting up, I crane my neck and see they brought a cart up with a bunch of bags on it, but before I can see exactly what it holds, Prescott blocks my view. Then he reaches in his pocket and pulls out his wallet to tip Kaz.

After Kaz leaves, Prescott hands me something he's holding behind his back. "I brought you a surprise."

"Please don't. You've done so much already."

"Not really." He moves one arm so I can see what he has and I laugh. He holds a stuffed wolf with a makeshift sling on its front leg. He has it rigged so it looks like the wolf is sitting with his front leg folded over.

"He's so cute."

"It's a she. Her name is Vivacious. After you. When you get your arm out of that cast, you can take Vivacious's off."

"Vivacious. Clever."

"I'm going to call her Viv. Oh, here." He hands me one long-stemmed red rose. "There is perfection in a rose. The petals are velvet and delicate, yet made to weather any storm—and the scent can't be imitated. Even though the best perfumeries have tried, none can quite get it right. You are a rose, Vivi."

Tapping a loose fist against my heart, I try to hold it together. *I will not cry. I will not cry.*

"Hey, it's all cool, Vivi."

That does it. Tears tumble freely. This big lug, this asshole, just turned me into mush. Again.

Strong arms support me as I sag against him. And he smells so fucking good. How can I even notice this through snot, tears, and a swollen face?

"Thank you. A million times over," I mumble into his neck. "You're so kind."

He rumbles with a laugh. "Not many people would agree. And I can remember a time …" his voice trails off.

"Yahhhh, I was wrong, okay?" I pull away and spear him with my gaze. "You … I don't know what I'd do without your help. Prescott, thank you." I reach for his cheek, but he moves away and takes my hand instead.

"Vivi." The emotion in his voice is punctuated by his raw gaze. "I, uh, I'm not very good at this, so bear with me. I'm here for you as long as you need me. And I meant every word. You have strength in you that I don't think you understand. Your backbone is filled with titanium. After everything you've been through, most women—hell, most men—would've curled up and crawled into a hole, but not you. You're still here, fighting. And no, you're not at your best right now, but you will be. One day, you'll look back on this day and remember what I said."

"Now can I touch your cheek?"

"Oh, is there something special about my cheek?"

"Not just your cheek."

"My ass, then? I've been told—"

"Shut up, Prescott, you're ruining it for me."

The mirth disappears from him and strips me of my defenses. My heart flutters wildly, because he can't possibly do what I think he might.

But he does. His head inches closer and so do his lips, the ones I've always dreamed of for years, the ones I've fantasized about until I climaxed. When they touch mine, they are as light as butterflies dancing across my flesh. I imagine it's because he doesn't want to hurt my already misshapen lips. I open my mouth to sigh and his tongue pushes through. I fist his shirt with my hand and pull him to me, but he holds firm, keeps it gentle. It's all I can do not to crush myself against him.

When he breaks the kiss, my body aches for more and I moan.

"Vivi, I don't want to hurt you. Your face and arm need to heal." Is this the same man who, at one time, could only talk about fucking me?

"Who are you and what have you done to Prescott Beckham?"

"I think maybe Vivienne Renard is turning him into a better man."

Prescott isn't a very easy man to read, unless he's angry, but this time I look into golden eyes that are open, honest, and caring.

CHAPTER 21

PRESCOTT

Talk about baring one's soul. The greatest thing of all, though, is the vulnerability didn't come as I thought it would. Why is that? Maybe it was the kiss that accompanied it—and the fact that she wanted it to go on and I had to stop makes me feel like a fucking king sitting on top of the world.

If she wasn't in such bad shape, I would've let it continue—but her face wasn't exactly in ready-for-kissing condition. One thing stopping did, though, was gain her respect. Or I think it did. She gazed at me warmly as I tucked her into bed last night anyway.

We spend a quiet, lazy Sunday morning together, before discussing hiring someone to stay with her while I'm at work. Eric comes to visit in the afternoon and at one point makes such a fuss, I have to steer him aside and tell him to pull his shit together.

"She's been through it, man. Don't let her see you react like this. She needs your strength, not some pussy shit. Got it? If you can't handle it, you gotta leave."

He runs his hands through his hair over and over. "Lucas

said it was bad, really bad. But I, shit, yeah, okay. You're right. All I want to do is hug her."

"Hug her, but do it like a man. And don't squeeze her. She's broken, Eric. She needs you. She needs us all."

"Okay, got it."

I have to hand it to him. He squares his shoulders and heads straight for Vivi with no hesitation in his steps.

"Vivi, tell me what you need from me. I can do whatever. Sit with you, help you when I don't have to work, just say the word. I've got your back."

"Thanks, Eric. Do you know anyone who does hair? I need this mop washed."

I perk up at that. I want to be the one who washes that mane of hers. "Uh, Vivi, I can help you with that."

"You wouldn't mind?"

My sour look conveys my answer and I instantly regret it as she shrivels. I soften my tone, saying, "Of course not. I'd love to help."

That's the honest truth. The idea of sinking my hands into her lustrous hair, of feeling my fingers running through the thick, wet strands makes my dick perk up. I'd better stop thinking about this.

"See, Prescott will help you." Eric smiles warmly and pats her good arm. "Oh, I almost forgot. I'm such a loser." He reaches for the bag he carried inside and pulls out several items, one being a paperback, some gossip magazines, a book of crossword puzzles, and a box of chocolates.

"This is so sweet. Thank you, Eric."

"I thought you'd need something to occupy your mind, other than the TV. That book is supposed to be really good. The girl at the bookstore said it was the latest in hot romance."

Vivi likes hot romances?

"Just what I need," she says. Vivi eyes me shyly, and it's pretty damn cute. I wonder if she's blushing. It's impossible to tell because of the bruising on her face. "The crossword puzzles are sure to keep me busy for days."

Eric makes a comment about how smart she is and that she'll have them all completed within a week, but I'm still thinking about the romance novel and her little remark. After a few more minutes, I excuse myself and leave the two of them alone to chat —most likely about me. The last thing I want to do is crowd her. Giving her space and allowing her to feel at ease will hopefully allow her to relax here faster.

Heading to my home office, I call Grand to check in. She was concerned about Vivi and I want to find out if she may know of someone who could possibly come in and sit with her while I'm at work.

"How's your friend, Prescott?"

"She's settled in here, for the time being." And I bring her up to speed on things.

"Let me make a call and I'll get back to you."

I thank her and try to get a little work done while I wait. When I turn on my computer, there's an email waiting from the law firm with a list of recommendations for Vivi. It includes the names of ten psychiatrists who deal in PTSD. I print the list. Starting with the first name, I begin my research and take notes. After the tenth one, I'm satisfied with all of them. Vivi can decide who she wants to see.

Moving on to my calendar for tomorrow, I get things lined up. I have a busy day since I haven't been in the office since Wednesday. When I check the week, I've forgotten that I'm supposed to go to Atlanta Wednesday night and meet with Weston and Special. We're signing the final contracts for the franchising of A Special Place on Thursday. That means I'll need to have someone here with Vivi, or Eric will have to stay here. I also make a note to schedule an interview with him and our interior design team. The rest of my week looks pretty set. When I check the clock, I realize how much time has passed. Just as I'm about to leave my office, my phone rings.

"Hi, Grand."

"I may have the perfect person for you. She lives in Brooklyn and is looking for part-time work."

"That's great. Did you tell her this would be only only for a few weeks at the most?"

"Yes, and she was fine with that. Here's her number."

After thanking Grand, I call her. Her name is Regina and she sounds great. She is ready to come in tomorrow at seven-thirty and will bring a list of references with her. She gives me a detailed report of how many people she's worked for and the reason she's not working is her current employer is recovering from a fall and is in restorative care. She'll be out for another four to six weeks. This is ideal—not for her employer, of course, but for Vivi. I finish up in here and head back into the living room.

Eric and Vivi are laughing. Her laugh reminds me of champagne bubbles as they float to the top of a glass. And it makes me happy to hear that sound.

When she sees me, she says, "Prescott, Eric was telling me about the restaurant. This woman came in a few weeks ago and was a real jerk to me. The manager sided with her and it pretty much pissed me off. Apparently, she came back yesterday and he had to wait on her. Even he got her order wrong and got so flustered he had to have another waiter step in and handle things."

"Served him right, too, for the way he treated you, Viv," Eric says.

"She must've been a bitch," I say.

Eric laughs. "Or worse. Personally, I think she needed to get laid. But then again, don't we all."

A hush settles over the room and Vivi clears her throat.

Eric doesn't let it go. "Oh, I didn't mean … what I meant was—"

"We get it, Eric." I save the poor guy from him cramming his entire leg down his throat. "I came in here to ask if you'd like to join us for dinner. I was going to order something in."

"Yasss. Come on, Eric."

When Vivi says that, it's hard to say no. Eric ends up eating with us as I order in Italian from a great little restaurant around the corner from here. During dinner, I let Vivi know about Regina's interview tomorrow morning.

"I can't let you do that. You've done too much already."

"You can't stay alone. Besides, it's done already."

"It costs too much," she insists.

Eric blinks and stares, like he's watching a tennis match. Normally, I'd want this to be private, but he's as concerned about Vivi as I am.

"Vivi, be serious. Do you honestly think I can't afford it?"

She squirms. "It's not that. Of course you can afford it. I can't and I'd want to pay you back."

"I wouldn't think of it." I stand firm.

"Prescott, I'm racking up all kinds of debt with you."

"Um, in my book, the definition of debt is something that is owed. You don't owe me a thing, hence no debt."

Her arms fold over her body and she doesn't exactly appear thrilled. This isn't what I want. It's not about the money and she needs to understand that. Before I can explain that, Eric comes to the rescue.

He grabs her hand. "Look, sweetheart, excuse me for barging into the convo, but this is Mr. Moneybags here. He's not exactly hurting for pennies, if you know what I mean. Let the man help you out, Viv. My God. He's doing everything he can to make this awful situation better for you and you're throwing one roadblock after another at him. Not to mention, he's right. You can't stay by yourself yet. I can't be here with you when I work and neither can he, which puts you in a bind."

She sucks on her puffy lip, exhales, long and slow, and then nods. "Fine. I'll accept your charity, Prescott. And thank you."

Eric throws his arms up in the air and yells, "Hallelujah."

She slaps his arm. "Shut up."

After he leaves, I want to say more to her. I don't like that she's thinking of it as charity, but I'm afraid of opening up that can of worms again. We sort of closed it when she accepted my offer and I don't want to drive it into the ground.

"So, would you like for me to wash your hair?"

"I'd love a shower, but I don't know what to do with this arm."

"We can figure this out."

After wrapping it in plastic wrap, taping it, and then sticking it in a couple of garbage bags and duct taping it again, she's ready to get wet.

"I hope this works."

"Worst-case scenario, we send you off to get a new cast."

She asks if I'll stay in the bedroom in case she needs my help. We set everything out she could possibly need, and I sit on the bed, impatient for her to finish. It takes forever. I pace, then sit, then pace. Did she fall and hit her head? Should I call out to check? I don't want to sound like an overprotective mother. Twenty minutes pass, then twenty-five. When it gets to thirty, I'm ready to storm the door down. Finally, I hear my name.

"Yes," I practically shout.

"Can you help?"

I almost take the door off the hinges and yell, "You okay?" I must've scared the poor woman to death because she shrinks from my thunderous arrival. "Shit. Sorry. I thought you might've fallen or something."

The fright vanishes from her face. "No. I need help in wrapping my hair in the towel." She stands with the other towel haphazardly wound around her and any movement whatsoever will have the thing unwinding. I brush the hand holding it together aside and tighten it, tucking the ends in. Then I wrap her hair up in the other, trying to create a turban like women do. I fail. "Sorry. I'm not very good at this."

"No, it's good. Thank you." Her gracious smile speaks volumes.

"Let's see how the plastic worked." I unwrap her arm and

we're happy to note it was a success.

Then I think of something. "Give me a minute." I sprint out and run upstairs. All the guest rooms have terry robes. One of them might fit her a little better. Grabbing one, I run back down to the bathroom.

"Here, you might like to put this on. I have them upstairs in the extra rooms."

"Oh. Thanks. Can you …?" She aims her gaze at the door.

I leave to let her exchange the towel for the robe. When she calls out, I return.

"This is great. I had to shimmy my arm a bit, but it worked."

She hands me a brush and asks me if I would mind. As I get rid of the tangles, she lets me know how much she enjoyed the shower.

"The hot water felt so good. And that shower is amazing."

"Yeah, it's pretty good."

She lets her hair air-dry and changes into her athleisure clothes, as Eric called them. I wait for her in the living room.

"I want to tell you something, Vivi. Hear me out. I know you worry about the money I spend on you, but if the situation were reversed, I'd like to think there would be someone out there who'd do the same for me. I'm not selfish with my money. I don't try to buy people." Then I remember how I bribed the host at the restaurant that night and I add, "Well, there are times I use it to attain certain goals. But not in a particularly bad way. The coats I sent you a while ago, I sent those because I knew you needed them. You were struggling to get through this freezing weather. It looked bad on my part. I see that now. But I really did want you to be warm."

A slow smile builds on her face. "Why have you turned into this nice guy? It was so much easier to hate you when you were an ass."

"Hmm. Hate is such a strong word. I never wanted you to hate me"—I rub the back of my neck, trying to figure out what to say—"and maybe I grew tired of being that asshole."

CHAPTER 22

VIVI

I'M STILL SMILING AT THE IDEA THAT PRESCOTT BECKHAM just admitted he was tired of being an asshole, when he leans close and kisses me. He's still an asshole. Except, not really. Somehow the tables have turned. Now I'm the asshole who can't stop thinking about fucking *him*.

"Prescott." I don't think about what I'm doing. If I did, I would second-guess myself. I crawl on his lap and take his face between my palms. Then it's my turn to kiss him. Softy. Slowly. I run my tongue across his upper, then lower lip.

"Vivi," he warns. "You're playing with fire."

"You've already lit a fire in me, so what does it matter?"

"Fire sometimes burns out of control, and even the most diligent can't contain it."

"We won't know until we test it, though, will we?"

"You're bruised, and your arm is broken."

"I've been bruised and broken since I was twelve. Nothing new here."

"I can't fix you," he says as he slides his hands into my wet hair.

"Never asked you to."

"Do you know the first thing I thought when I saw you in that coffee shop? You were sitting there, looking flustered as hell, with a bunch of napkins in your hand. I couldn't believe it was you at first. But there was no mistaking your eyes. I always thought you had great eyes. So damn expressive. They gave you away every time. As I watched you, I told myself I was going to fuck you. I'd do whatever it took, but eventually I'd be between your thighs and you'd be mine, every single inch of you. And here we are, Vivi. That opportunity sits in front of me like a piece of fruit hanging from the vine, begging to be picked, and suddenly, I've developed a conscience. The weirdest thing of all is I'm not even sure if it's because you're injured."

He moves me off his lap and stands. After shoving his hands in his pockets, he says, "I have to admit, this is a first for me. You've changed the rules, and I thought I was the play maker."

His hands fly up and rake through his hair, making a mess of it. I've never seen him look sexier than this moment, where he stands before me, frustrated as hell. The humanity of this situation creates a larger space in my heart, but I also recognize the danger it places me in.

"Why do you have to be so controlling?"

His head snaps in my direction, away from his feet, which he'd been staring at for some reason. He raises a hand, and then lowers it as he shakes his head. "Old habits, I suppose."

"That's not an answer. Before, when you were pursuing me, you were so hardened. It wasn't like you were even nice."

"That's not exactly true. I was nice when I first saw you, but you didn't give me the time of day. I'm not used to being brushed off."

I guess he isn't. When you're gifted with the looks of a god, why would he be?

"You know an awful lot about my past, Prescott, but I know very little about yours, other than you went to Crestview. Why is that?"

"What do you want to know?" The question seems innocent

enough, but the edginess rolling off him tells me he's not willing to open up quite yet. I push anyway.

"Tell me about your family."

The stiffening in his posture indicates I'm right. He definitely doesn't like this line of questioning.

"My family." A humorless laugh escapes him, but then his eyes light up. "Well, my grandparents are two of the most amazing people in the world."

"Tell me more."

"Granddad and his father started Whitworth. I never knew my great grandfather because he passed before I was born. But Granddad is more my father, really. And Grand is special. They raised me, if you want the truth. My dad didn't. When I was young, I was a handful. So my grandparents took me under their wing and then Dad got fed up with me anyway and sent me off to Crestview."

"What about your mother?"

His expression turns into a blank slate. "I never speak of her."

"Oh?"

"It's not up for discussion." And bam, just like that, he completely shuts down.

"O-okay." I'm shocked by his reaction. "So does your dad get along with your grandparents?"

"Hell to the fucking no on that. He's so far removed from them in every way, and hopefully I'm equally as distanced from him." He tells me about his dad's marriages and briefly of his current wife. The hard edge to his voice is a clear indication of how much he dislikes the woman. "She's a liar and, well, I've run my mouth enough already." His jaws clamp together and that tiny muscle on his cheek twitches. Jeez, the woman must be a total bitch.

"I envy your relationship with your grandparents."

His expression immediately softens. "They're amazing. I only wish I had lived with them for longer than I did." Then he clams up again.

"College?"

A raspy chuckle comes from him. "You weren't there to do my homework. Take a guess at how long I lasted?"

"A year?"

"I'm not that much of an idiot."

I wince. That wasn't very nice. Scooting back, I pull my knees to my chest. "Oops. Sorry," I murmur.

"You shouldn't be. It wasn't that smart of a move to have you constantly do my homework in high school."

"But I didn't do all of it." Why am I coming to his defense?

"You did most of it. Well, in the classes we shared anyway. I could've never passed physics or calculus. Or those other classes for the super brilliant kids you were in."

"Oh, shut up. You were just intellectually lazy."

He barks out a laugh. "Intellectually lazy. That's a good way to put it. The truth is I hated school. I couldn't stand those asshole teachers telling me what to do. And by the way, I'm no longer intellectually lazy, for your information."

He's right about the teachers. Many, though not all, of them had a superior attitude. "Good to know. But if you think the teachers were assholes to you, you should've walked in my shoes. That's why I studied so hard."

"What do you mean?"

"They looked down their noses at me, because I didn't have money like the rest of you did. I had to prove my worth through my brains. At least you had the proper financial means." If I had known how much money Prescott actually had back then, I would have never associated myself with him. "Me, I was on the level of the maintenance man. God, I hated that place."

"Was it really that bad?" Disbelief coats his tone.

"Every teacher, even the principal, knew those girls bullied me, and not a single one of them did anything about it. My locker was vandalized every single day. It got so bad I started carrying around all my books with me so I wouldn't have to go there anymore. How could they not notice the nasty words, day after day, written across my locker? No one else's had awful things on them." Then I explain something else. "And here's another little tidbit of information. I should've been named vale-dictorian. My grades were higher every semester than Evan Chandler's. But when I questioned the administration about it, asked for proof, they said I was wrong. This isn't me being petty. I know it for a fact because Evan and I were in almost every class together and the ones we weren't, I aced. So how did he magically come up with a higher GPA?"

"Jesus. Those bastards went that far?"

There's no reason to answer, so I shrug. "Turns out we both hated it there and didn't know it."

"I didn't hate all of it. I met my two best friends there and am still closer to them than anyone. Well, except my grandparents."

"Who?"

"Do you remember Weston Wyndham and Harrison Kirkland?"

"Oh, yeah." Fuck, how could I have forgotten that? The three of them were inseparable. And the hottest guys anywhere. No wonder they got away with everything.

"What's that look?" he asks. "You're scowling."

"No, I'm not."

"Vivi, I know a scowl when I see one."

I tuck my hair behind my ear and paste on a smile.

"I'm not."

"Okay, you're not anymore. But you were. Don't you like either of them?"

"No, it's not that. I don't really know them."

"So?"

"Nothing." He is not going to wheedle a thing out of me, including my thoughts that they were just a bunch of spoiled rich kids, too.

"Let me just say this, and we'll drop it. Weston and Harrison are both stand-up guys. They would have my back in any situation—any kind at all. And whatever it is you heard about them, if it was bad, it was most likely false."

The strength of his tone and his adamancy has me believing him. I nod. "Fine, but I really don't have a problem with them."

"Did they make fun of you at Crestview?"

Sighing, I say, "I don't remember. The girls were the ones who were the meanest. Can we drop this? It doesn't matter anymore. All this happened years ago. I hated it there, but it's over. I have no intention of ever going back for a reunion or anything, so what's the purpose?"

He lifts and lowers one shoulder. "I don't know. Maybe I want to make sure my best friends didn't harass you."

"You'll have to ask them. When you're overweight in junior high and high school, everyone makes fun of you, so it all sort of blends together." It's strange that he's suddenly become so concerned about this.

His brows bunch at the bridge of his nose. He gives me a slight nod, but the creases remain. Then he blurts, "I … I need some space."

He jogs up the flight of stairs and disappears from view. I sit and wait, thinking he'll reappear. But I'm wrong. An hour passes and he never returns. Eventually, I go to the huge empty bedroom, alone, and wonder how I'll sleep in there without him to comfort me.

CHAPTER 23

PRESCOTT

A FISSURE HAS FORMED WITHIN ME AND IT'S RIPPING ME IN half. One side wants to reveal every tiny detail about myself to Vivi, but the other wants to punt and run like the wind. And isn't that exactly what I just did? Now I'm wearing out a path in the carpet, because I can't relax enough to get into bed. Guilt practically has me running back down those steps, because I know she's afraid to sleep alone, but I can't find it in myself to do so.

Why don't I just tell her about me? It's not that big of a deal. Only the voice inside me screams out that it is. It will show her just how weak of a man I am.

I cram my hands into my pockets to stop them from shaking. What the hell was I thinking when I brought her here? I should've known this would happen. Vivi is astute, much more than most. She'll see right through me.

There's not a chance in hell I'll be able to sleep being this tense. The best thing I can do now is hit the treadmill. My problem is I don't have any running clothes up here. Maybe I have something in the gym. I head in there to check and find a pair of shoes and some shorts hanging on a hook, so I don't waste time in stripping.

Sticking in my earbuds, I crank up the volume to drown out any remote possibility of thinking, and set the machine at a grueling six-and-a-half-minute mile pace. Fifty minutes later, I'm calm and levelheaded. Or at least I think I am, until the music stops playing. Vivi's face instantly pops into my mind the moment it does and dammit if I'm not back to square one.

A hot shower might calm me down, so I head there. Maybe if I rub a quick one off, that will help too. God knows she's all I think about anyway. Ever since I entered that coffee shop, things south of the Mason Dixon line have been in a constant state of inflexibility.

Stepping into the warm spray, it cascades over my skin, rinsing the sweat of my workout off. After I soap up and rinse off, my cock screams for attention. The ache in my balls has been there for at least a solid month now. Any time I've thought of easing it with another woman, a sour taste spreads in my mouth. I've never been one to feel particularly faithful toward anyone, likely because I've never been committed to a woman. But somehow Vivienne Renard has fucked up my life and ruined it for any other piece of ass. No more pussy-whoring for this man, unless I can get her out of my system, and the only way I see doing that is to fuck her. She seems in, but if I do, she'll want more than just a quick fuck. And I have a real bad feeling I might, too.

My hand squeezes tightly over my dick, pumping up and down, imagining how it would feel if this were Vivi's pussy. Warm and wet, tight and slick. I imagine her moaning as I thrust harder and harder, hitting her in the spots that set her off. Jizz shoots up and covers my fist just as the hot water rinses it away. Oddly, I'm not satisfied. The ache in my balls has only eased temporarily. It still lurks in the depths of me, seeking a permanent release, and my hand isn't the answer it's looking for. The solution lies in my bed, downstairs, where I left her. And aren't I the brave guy, standing here, naked in the shower, with my dick in hand?

Disgust coats me as I turn off the water. Every possible solution I come up with is shot down by my logic. After I dry off, I climb into bed, frustrated as ever, and know that sleep will be as attainable as going to the moon.

The room eventually turns gray, then brightens, and I climb out of the bed that should've brought me comfort. Instead, all it held for me was a night of sheer annoyance. And I only have myself to blame.

After another quick shower, I run down the steps and tiptoe into the bedroom, hoping not to disturb Vivi. At least one of us should be able to sleep. But when I walk into the room, my beeline for the closet is halted by her voice.

"Where did you disappear to last night?"

I turn toward her. "I, ah, slept upstairs."

"I see."

No, she doesn't. Slipping into the closet, I quickly dress. All my clothes are perfectly organized. Shirts by color, then suits. Ties are arranged in drawers, nicely laid out and also by color. I'm picky about this because it makes getting dressed so much easier.

I finish tying my tie and walk back out to face her.

"Prescott, if I make you uncomfortable, I can leave."

"No, it's not—"

"Please don't lie to me. I don't want to stay where I'm not wanted. Put yourself in my shoes for a minute."

She's right. I must've made her feel awful. But, shit, I feel awful too, and I don't know how to respond to her.

"Look, I'm running late this morning. Regina should be here any minute and will take care of you. If she doesn't suit your needs, you can fire her. But I have to go." And then I do the chicken shit move and leave.

"Prescott," she calls out behind me, but I don't stop. My feet are on a mission, straight to the door and they keep right on going.

"Prescott, wait," I hear as the door closes. *Come on, elevator.*

The doors open, I step in, and down we go, before she has a chance to stop me. When I get outside, a driver is already waiting for me. The ride to work is tense. I hated doing what I did to her.

Then my phone dings.

Nice move, Ace. What's up with you? Tell me what's going on. I need to know. You won't even speak to me.

My finger taps the phone. What do I text back?

We'll talk tonight. Just a lot on my mind. Big meeting today and I have to go to Atlanta on Wednesday. Let me know about Regina.

Suddenly, I feel like the proverbial married couple that has issues and doesn't talk them out, instead talking around them. Here I am telling her I have to go to Atlanta on Wednesday like it's something I should naturally report to her. How weird is that?

Lynn is already at her desk when I arrive and she lets me know in plain words I look like crap.

"Is everything okay?"

She's fishing for information on Vivi. Should I bring her into the fold? I'm so fucking confused, I don't know what the hell to do. I'm the twelve-year-old who just saw a girl he likes for the first time. Fuck me. That has to be it.

I've never done this—had a relationship with girls, that is—so I didn't get the chance to go through the growing pains of relationship building. I'm so ill at ease I don't even know how it's supposed to work. All I know is to find pussy, fuck it, and leave the minute I tire of it. I don't know what to do when I actually *like* a woman, and not just for the sex.

"No, nothing is okay, if you want the truth."

She follows me into my office.

"What's wrong? Is Vivi okay?"

How do I answer this loaded question? Lynn stares, and if she does it long enough, she'll puzzle me out in no time.

"Talk to me, Prescott. You look like you don't know what's up or down. And if you don't stop with the hair thing and rubbing your chin, you'll have a bald spot and a chafed face."

"You certainly pick up on cues, don't you?"

"My husband says I should've been a detective."

"I don't know what to do with her."

"Vivi?"

"No. Queen Elizabeth."

"Smart-ass. What do you mean?"

I can't bring myself to speak.

"Does she want to take walks or something?"

"Oh, Jesus, you are so far off base, it's not funny. And of all people, I thought you'd jump on this train and figure me out."

She laughs. Totally cracks up. What the hell?

"Prescott is at a loss. I love it. You of all people, who always have women falling at your feet."

"I do not," I huff.

"You don't think I notice all the girls in the admin pool who practically throw themselves at you? But you're smart as a whip and know better not to tangle yourself with them. However, they still do it. You could have any woman in this town. All you'd have to do is snap your fingers. And you, my dear boy, are at a complete loss as to how to handle Miss Vivi Renard. Do you know why?"

"No! Isn't that the point of this conversation?"

"You are falling for the poor girl."

"Poor girl? So you feel sorry for her?"

"Yes, because I'm afraid you're going to allow her to open one of your many doors—and you don't think I know that you have more than one, but I do—and when she gets one foot in, you'll slam the thing on it and break it into a million pieces in the process. And stop scrunching up your brow so much. I'm going to have to send you to my plastic surgeon for some Botox if you don't quit."

"Can we please stay on topic for a second? Why do you think I'll break her foot?"

"It's her heart, you big dummy. I was using the door and foot image as a metaphor."

"Whatever. Why do you think I'll do it?"

"Because you're scared. Look at you. Have you looked in the mirror? Mr. Confidence has morphed into Mr. Confused."

"You're not helping." And she's not. I'm looking for advice, not criticism. Then again, I'm not giving her much to go on.

"What exactly is it I'm supposed to help with? I just gave you my opinion. What more do you want? You're afraid to let yourself go. Do you want to know what I think you should do? Is that what you're asking?"

I rub my chin and scratch my head. She grabs both hands and pulls them down. "Stop it already. You're acting like you have fleas or something."

"I give up. What do you think I should do?"

"Court the woman."

"Court?"

"Date her. Don't try to screw her brains out like I know you usually do."

"I do not."

She huffs, "Oh, come on. I've smelled you reeking of sex after some of your little lunch trysts."

I take a step back. "Why didn't you say something?"

She shrugs. "Anyway, back to Vivi. She has something that most women don't. Do you want to know what it is?"

"Yes. And just say what's on your mind and stop dragging me along like this."

"Okay. She has integrity, brains, and she doesn't give a damn about who you are, how much money you have in the bank, or what you do for a living. In other words, Prescott Whitworth Beckham, if that woman ends up falling in love with you, she'll fall for *you* and not your name, connections, or how much you're worth. And that's exactly why you should go after her with everything you've got. Woo her, but gently. And bare your fucking soul to her. Get rid of your demons. She won't hold anything against you. Vivi has a pure heart. Don't you see it?"

"I don't know if I can do it."

"Then it will be the gravest mistake of your life and the greatest loss you ever sustained."

She turns away and leaves, closing the door softly behind her.

Maybe she's right. What if I dove in head first? The worst thing that could happen is she'd look at me differently and then what? She'd leave and I'd never see her again. We run in different circles so not a problem, right? Except, it's a huge problem, because I want her.

Bad enough to change my entire life, though?

Taking a risk for Vivi shouldn't be this difficult, but it is. How will I ever shed my cowardly skin and get brave enough to do it? The only way I know is to try. Only I don't know if I have the balls to do it.

Grow some, motherfucker, grow some.

CHAPTER 24

VIVI

PRESCOTT LEAVES AND THE PLACE IS EERILY QUIET. MY BRAIN scrambles for answers, but finds none. Whatever I did, it'll have to wait until I can question him again. And who knows if he'll give me an answer.

Shoving those thoughts away, I get up and brush my teeth. The doorbell rings in the bathroom. Leave it to Prescott to think of everything. I shrug the robe on, look out, and press the intercom.

"Yes?"

"It's Regina."

"Hang on."

Opening the door, I greet her and introduce myself, telling her how happy I am she's here. She's perhaps in her late forties, early fifties, and reminds me of my mom. Her hair is graying, and she doesn't bother with coloring it. It's cut short and nicely styled. She's dressed in casual navy pants and a nice white shirt.

"Mr. Beckham told me about your injuries. I'm terribly sorry and I hope you're feeling better."

"I am, thank you. I would love a shower. Except, I need my

215

arm wrapped. Can you help?" I explained how Prescott did it, so she follows my instructions.

Regina laughs and is engaging to talk to as she tells me about herself. Both of her two children have graduated from college. She beams with pride as she says they are the first ones in both her and her husband's family to have done so.

"That is wonderful," I comment.

By the time she finishes helping me with my arm, I feel like she's my friend. When I'm done, she helps me with my hair and getting dressed.

"Would you like to go outside today?" she asks. "You know, to get some fresh air?"

The idea sounds very appealing and I wonder if I'll be frightened. "I think I would. I may move a little slow, however."

Her hand waves through the air. "Oh, I'm used to it. Mrs. Simpkins is nearly eighty, and I take her for walks every day. But I've got to say, she's spry as an elf the way she moves around."

"I can promise I won't be moving like Tinkerbell. I also have to warn you I may be more than a little skittish because of the attack."

"I can understand that. Maybe if you go and see that things are fine, it will help you some," she says.

I agree.

Regina fixes me a huge breakfast. I can't imagine the elfin Mrs. Simpkins eats this much. I leave half on my plate.

"You eat like a sparrow. No wonder you're so skinny and I'm so fat."

"One, you're not fat, and two, I wasn't always skinny."

Regina cleans up the kitchen while I check my email, hoping there's a response from one of the jobs I posted. But then again, what if there is? An interview looking like I've been cage fighting probably wouldn't go over too well. From the looks of my empty inbox, I don't have to worry about it. As Regina is just about finished with the cleanup, the doorbell rings.

"Are you expecting anyone?" she asks.

"No."

She answers the door and an attractive, elderly woman walks into the living area. She stands there, scrutinizing me.

It takes me a few seconds to rise out of my seat, but I do. "Hello, I'm—"

"I know who you are. You're Vivienne Renard, my grandson's friend."

Whoa! This is the grandmother Prescott adores.

"Yes, ma'am, I am. And you're his grandmother. He speaks of you often."

A smile flirts with the corners of her mouth. "He does, does he?"

"Yes, ma'am."

"Hmm. You were raised to have manners, unlike most youth today."

"Ma'am?"

"And I detect an accent."

"Oh, yes, ma'am. I'm from Virginia."

"Prescott mentioned he went to Crestview with you."

"Yes, ma'am, he did."

"Please, sit. I understand you've been through quite an ordeal. I'm sorry for that."

"Thank you." I sit and so does she. "I didn't know you were coming. Would you care for some coffee or tea?"

"No, thank you. I came to meet the woman my grandson has suddenly taken a keen interest in."

This woman, though somewhat smaller than me, has a huge presence as she sits here. She sets my nerves on edge. There's quite a fierce quality about her and I'm pretty sure I know why she's come.

"Tell me about yourself."

"What would you like to know?" I ask.

"Everything."

There's no subtlety to her, so I spill it all, leaving out nothing.

I'm bold and don't act as though I require pity, telling it as it is. When I get to the part about the attack, I'm gracious where Prescott is concerned. And in telling it, I recall exactly how much he's helped me. My eyes tear up at remembering, but I refuse to show any weakness and let them push past my lids.

She pats my hand a few times, but then she moves on to why she's here. And she's blunt.

"I'm glad you're feeling gracious toward my grandson, but if you hurt one hair on his head, I will personally run you out of this city so fast, you won't know what hit you."

"Ex-excuse me?" I'm not sure I heard her correctly.

"I don't have to repeat myself. I love that boy with every heartbeat in my body. He's been through just as much trauma to the heart as you have, if not more. I don't know what he's told you about his past, so I won't say more since it's his story to share, not mine. But, I won't have him hurt. Ever."

"What makes you think I can hurt him?"

She smiles. "Vivienne, either you are extremely naive, blind, or perhaps you simply don't know my grandson very well now that I think on it. In all the years I've known him, he has never mentioned a woman to me by name, had one stay in this home, or worried about what one thought of him. I know you're thinking—how does she know he's never had a woman stay here? Trust me, I know. The company has several corporate apartments he uses for his dalliances. But he doesn't use his personal residence." Then she leans forward and says, "He even asked me for advice regarding you. He told me about the coats you returned and how he wanted to set you up in an apartment. Do you know what I told him?"

I'm staring at her like the proverbial deer in the headlights.

"Of course you don't know. I told him he was treating you like his mistress."

I'm incredulous that he asked his grandmother for advice on how to date me.

"You see, in reality I know my grandson is not perfect, but in my eyes he will always be. I love him more than anything, and will protect him at all costs. So, Vivienne, don't you dare hurt him."

"Ma'am, please call me Vivi." It's all I can think to say.

"Never. A woman with a face such as yours deserves a grand name. Vivienne suits you perfectly. And you may call me Sara. I have a feeling we'll be seeing each other again." She pats my hand again. "Well, I'll be on my way. Oh, and, Vivienne, I would prefer it if you keep our little visit to yourself."

"Yes, ma'am, I will." I can't begin to imagine what would happen to me if I told Prescott about it. "Thank you for stopping by."

She lets out a hearty chuckle. "I'm not sure if you really feel that way or not, but I appreciate the comment. Good day, Vivienne." And she leaves, telling Regina goodbye on her way out.

I don't know how to feel about her visit. She's enlightened me about something. Prescott wants me enough that he went to his grandmother for advice. That's like a son going to his mother, which is a huge deal. At least I think it is. But then when she said that bit about Prescott's heart being traumatized, my imagination spins on what might have happened to him. He never discusses his mother and she's off-limits, so I'm positive it has to do with her. Sara indicated there was a story in his past, but it was his to share. This frustrates me even more because I want to help but am useless unless he opens up to me.

"Are you ready, Vivi?" Regina's voice breaks through my tumbling thoughts.

"Oh, sure."

We end up walking around the block and going to a nearby park. It's chilly out, but not unbearable for a December day. Afterward, we stop for mochas at a local coffee shop. It reminds me of Java Beans & More, and I think about my friends from there as I watch the barista making our mochas.

A wave of homesickness hit me, not for the home in Virginia, but for the one I left behind in California. The friends I made during my few years out there have all fallen off my radar, one by one. As I sit here and remember that life, I realize it was the one I had dreamed of and worked so hard to build. I don't regret a moment of taking care of my mom, but I wish there was a way to get back on track. What the hell happened to me, really? How did I fall down this rabbit hole to Hell?

"Where have you gone?" Regina asks.

"Sorry. I was only thinking about better times."

Regina grabs my hand. "Listen to me. You're young and have a long life ahead of you. Once this passes, you get out there and grab it with both hands, sweetie. Don't let a minute pass you by."

"You're right. I was only thinking of my former life in California." I explain what happened and she tears up. "I didn't intend to burden you with this. I'm sorry."

"Don't apologize. Things will turn around soon. Christmas isn't the best time to be searching for jobs. My kids tell me that the best time is in the spring."

"Hmm. You may be right."

"Keep that pretty chin of yours up."

I chuckle at her comment. "You mean this purple chin."

"No, your chin isn't purple. The upper half of your face is, but not your chin."

"Well, I have that going for me then." We laugh together.

We finish our mochas and I feel a little better.

"Vivi, you do have something going for you."

"What's that?"

"A man named Prescott Beckham. I would say that's a lot going for you."

My cheeks spike in temperature and I'm grateful the purple disguises it. "True, but I don't want to depend on him. I'm used to being on my own, relying on my own skills, you know?"

"I admire that. I was only saying if you're going to date someone, you picked a winner."

My mouth curves upward, but what exactly are Prescott and I doing together? Seems to me we're dancing around every issue out there. Maybe I need to grow some balls and come right out and ask him. It's either going to be that, or I'll move back in with Eric. Come to think of it, that thought sort of fires me up. I miss Eric's cheerfulness. Even his visit yesterday perked me up. If I'm well enough to move around like this, there's really no reason for me not to move back with him.

When we get back to Prescott's, I call Eric, but he doesn't answer. I text him and ask him what he thinks. Again, he doesn't respond, so I wait. There's no use making plans unless I get his commitment and agreement to help me.

It's late afternoon when I hear from him.

"Sorry, Viv, I was swamped today. I had work and some other things. But I think you need to stay put. At least for another day or two. You have help there."

"It's weird here. He's weird, Eric."

"What do you mean?" I explain what happened.

"Hmm. Maybe he had a lot on his mind."

"Then why didn't he just say 'Vivi, I have a lot on my mind'?"

"You know how strange men get sometimes. Another day, two at the most. I'd feel better with you having someone there during the day."

Releasing the pent-up air in my lungs, I say, "All right." Maybe Prescott just is overwhelmed with things and doesn't know how to handle me.

Regina leaves around five and she's left dinner in the oven. I told her not to cook, because Prescott still has food from his chef, but she insisted.

"You have a good rest of the night. Dinner will be ready in an hour. All you need to do is pull it out. It's not heavy, so you should be fine. If Mr. Beckham's not home, that is."

I thank her and she leaves. Being injured isn't for sissies. This is so boring I could punch a hole in the TV. Even though I'm still sore, sitting here is driving me crazy. I'd rather be busy, doing something. There has to be a dozen or more books on my Kindle, so that's what I decide to do. About two chapters later, restlessness takes over. Why am I so fidgety? Is it because I'm expecting him to walk through the door any minute?

I give Vince a call to pass the time and he's so shocked at what happened, he hardly carries on much of a conversation. After a few minutes, he promises to call in a couple of days. He's studying for exams and when he's through he wants to meet for lunch.

An hour passes and dinner is done, so I take it out of the oven with my good arm. It's slightly tricky, but I manage. Another thirty minutes pass, and no Prescott. I decide to text him. The dinner is only lukewarm now.

Regina made dinner and it's getting cold. Are you coming home soon?

Finally, I get his response.

Tied up here. Don't wait on me.

First surprise and then disappointment cause my heart to shrink incrementally. I berate myself for waiting at all and expecting him to eat dinner with me. He does, after all, run a multibillion-dollar company and I should expect for him to have duties that extend beyond regular work hours.

Picking my sappy-assed self up, I fill a plate with the chicken dish Regina made and try to find something else to watch on TV. The food is delicious and I eat every bite. I clean up and get ready for bed. Nothing on TV interests me, so I decide to read in bed. This lying around crap is ridiculous.

The book I'm reading is a sexy one, which isn't exactly what

I need right now. All it makes me want to do is hunt down my vibrator, which is impossible because it's at home.

I'm so done with this. Tomorrow I'm going home. When Regina arrives, I'll have her help me move my stuff, and that'll be the end of this.

After punching my pillow a few hundred times, sleep eventually claims me even if a sexy dark-haired god with eyes of gold haunts my dreams.

CHAPTER 25

PRESCOTT

After arranging for Eric's interview, which will be this afternoon, I call to let him know.

"This afternoon!" he cries. "I'm headed to work!"

"What time does your shift end?"

"Seven," he says, panic gushing out of him.

Thrumming my fingers on the desk, I tell him to expect a call from me around one-thirty. He is to say he has a family emergency.

"I can't do that. It'll leave them shorthanded."

"I can push your interview back until five. Will that help?"

"Some. And call me at three. We'll be over the lunchtime crush. That'll give them time to get one of the night staff to come in early."

"Fine."

"Oh, and how's Viv?"

"Fine. I have to go." There will be zero discussion between Eric and me regarding that subject. I have to figure out how I'm going to explain myself to her tonight. Why did I have to promise a conversation so soon?

Lynn orders in lunch for me and after I finish, I have a call from Weston. We firm up our details for the trip on Wednesday. Then my phone rings.

"Mr. Beckham, your grandfather has asked you to step down to his office when you get a minute."

"Thank you, Lynn." Her formality always makes me chuckle.

After logging off the computer, I head to Granddad's office. People greet me as I pass, especially the women. The suggestive grins they offer make me wonder about what Lynn said earlier. I used to imagine what they wore beneath their skirts, but not anymore. The bruised-up woman who's sleeping in my bed takes up most of my thoughts about lingerie these days.

When I round the corner and open the door, I'm surprised to see Grand here.

"Prescott." She leans in and kisses my cheek as she says my name.

"Son, have a seat."

Granddad's expression is full of uncertainty. Eyes that are usually bright and cheerful are now cloudy as the corners seem to tug downward.

Grand gives his hand a squeeze. "Go on, Samuel, best to get this over with."

"What's going on?" I ask as my chest suddenly fills with lead.

"There's no use beating around the bush, so I'll get right to it. Your grandmother and I received a letter from an old friend of your mother's."

Now the weight in my chest becomes heavier and it's difficult to breathe. Anytime my mother is brought up, the desire to cover my ears is almost unbearable.

"I know this is a tough subject, but what we have to tell you is, well, shocking to say the least." Granddad stops, takes his glasses off, and pinches the bridge of his nose.

"What did the letter say?"

He begins with how Grand opened the mail this morning to find it and called Granddad. They both read it several times. Their slow, gentle way of building up to it makes me want to scream, because all I want to know is what the goddamn letter says. I bite my tongue.

"Then she went on to talk about your mother's death."

"Stop. Can you please fast forward to the pertinent part or tell me however this all pertains to me? I don't want to discuss Mom."

"Son, this will come as a complete shock to you, but I want to tell you first that we have asked her to give us proof that she has it. We have already contacted her."

"Proof about what?" I ask, my voice rising.

Granddad comes around. "Prescott, sit down."

"Just tell me."

"Not until you sit."

What the fuck is going on? My brain spins as my ass hits the chair.

"As difficult as this is for me to say, you have to know. The man you know as your father isn't your biological father. At least that's what this letter tells us."

"What?" Did he just say what I think he said? "Are you saying that Dad isn't my father?"

"Here." He hands the damn letter to me.

I practically tear it out of his hand in my eagerness to see what's in it. The more I read, the more my hand trembles. When I'm finished, the paper slides through my fingers.

"We're sorry, son. We don't know what else to say," Granddad says.

"Why didn't she just say something?" My heart bleeds for my mother. Or does it bleed for me and all the years I haven't had her here with me?

"We can't answer that," Grand says. Her face seems to have aged a hundred years in the last few minutes. "The last thing we want is … don't let this impact you, Prescott."

"Grand, how can it not? The man I've known all my life as my father, isn't. Does he know?"

"According to the letter, he does," Granddad says.

"I must've breezed over that part. So he let me believe the lie, too." I pause. "Now the million-dollar question is: Who exactly is my daddy?" Sarcasm bleeds from every pore when I ask the question.

Grand takes my hand. "We think this woman knows. Hopefully she'll provide us with more details when we meet."

"So, we're going to meet?" I ask.

"Your grandfather and I thought it best. You never know with these things whether people are after something. You're not exactly low profile, sweetheart."

I bury my hands in my hair. Why now, of all times? I don't need any more confusion added to my already fucked-up head.

"When will this meeting occur?"

"We are waiting for her to get back to us. She left us all her information and hasn't asked for a thing in return," Granddad says.

In other words, they believe she's legit. While we sit here, Granddad's phone rings. His admin tells him she's on the line.

How convenient.

"Best to get on with this." He takes her call, but I find my thoughts going straight to Vivi and wondering how she'd handle this. Granddad hangs up and says, "I hope that was okay."

"I'm sorry, I zoned out."

He smiles kindly. "We're meeting here at five-fifteen. She works in the city, so it was convenient for her."

"Fine."

Grand squeezes my hand again. "Prescott, are you all right?"

"No, Grand, I'm not. My entire name is a charade."

Grand says, "Look me in the eye, young man."

I do as she commands. Grand can be sweet, but she has a steely side to her too.

"Don't you *ever* say that again. You carry the Whitworth genes. Your mother was a Whitworth, and the last time I checked, your middle name is Whitworth. Your name will never be a charade to your grandfather or me. Do you understand?"

"Yes, ma'am, I do."

"And let's get one more thing straight. The charade is the man you called your father. You never acted like him or took after him. Now we all know why."

She's right about that, although I thought I inherited his asshole gene. Now I wonder who I got that from.

"Go and get some work accomplished and we'll talk again later," Granddad says.

"Yes, sir, I will."

When I get back to my office, Lynn wants to know why I'm so glum. I can't share this news with anyone yet, at least not until I have all the details. "Nothing. Or rather I can't disclose it yet."

"Okay. You had some calls come in." She hands me the paper with them listed.

Now I have to get my work done and push this to the back of my mind. Like that's gonna happen.

The afternoon drags. Eric shows up at a quarter till five. I want to escort him up to the interview myself. He's so damn twitchy you'd think he had fleas.

"Calm down or they'll think you've never been on an interview."

"Honey, I can't help it. I'm about to have an ex-orgasm."

"A what?"

"You know. I'm excited, exasperated, exhausted, exploding …"

"I get the idea." I've never seen Eric act so fluttery before. "Do you need a drink? You know, to calm your ass down?"

"Shit. Am I that bad?"

"Yes."

He raises his hands. "Okay, okay. Pulling my shit together now. I won't let you down. I swear." Then he gives me the Boy Scout salute.

"Oh, for fuck's sake. You were not a Boy Scout."

He's insulted. His mouth presses into a thin line. "Yes, I was. What? Just because I'm gay I couldn't be one?"

"No, I didn't say or mean to infer that. You don't appear to be the type who likes to camp and hike."

"Oh, but I do. I love that stuff. I've hiked a bunch of the Appalachian Trail."

I'm so shocked by his statement, he could push me over with his pinky. Eric, hiking on the Appalachian Trail just does not seem to fit in my mind.

"Yeah, I just demolished your image of me, didn't I? We'll go camping sometime, Fancy Pants. You'll see."

A hearty laugh rips out of me and he joins in. "I'll take you up on that. Come on, let's go. Oh, and don't call me honey in front of anyone."

"Why. Will they think we're lovers?"

I grumble out an unrecognizable response as I escort him down to the floor where our design team is located. Eyeballs pop when it's me who makes the introductions. Then I ask if someone would call me when they're finished. "Never mind. Eric, text me. I'll be in a meeting and won't be taking calls."

"No problem."

I leave the room and the air is thick with questions everyone is dying to ask him. I would love to be a fly on the wall, but I have to be downstairs for the big meeting, which I'm not looking forward to.

When I notice the time, I see I'm five minutes away from kickoff. My gut twists in knots and I'm not sure if I want to hear what this woman has to say.

My grandparents are waiting for me and the three of us look more than a bit apprehensive.

Granddad's phone finally rings, alerting us to her arrival. When she walks in, she looks familiar. Her face tugs at my memory, but when she smiles, it hits me. She's one of my mother's friends who used to visit her.

"Hello, Prescott, Mrs. Whitworth, Mr. Whitworth," she says, greeting us warmly.

"Laura, thank you for coming," Grand says.

We sit and Laura launches into the most disturbing story I've ever heard. She explains how she and my mom, Simone, were great friends. She adored my mom and they'd been close since they were children. After I was born, Mom suspected Dad wasn't my father, but wasn't certain until I grew older. Then she had me tested. My dad didn't want to do it, but agreed—as long as it would be kept a secret. He didn't care to lose his place in the family business, I suppose. Mom begged Laura never to speak the truth to anyone. After Mom died, Laura received a letter from her. I guess she mailed it the morning of her death. In the letter she told Laura never to tell anyone her secret. But then Mom went on to say if she did, to wait until I was an adult and could handle it. Laura kept the secret until now. She says it just felt like Mom wanted me to know. She stares at me when she says this.

It doesn't feel like I'm exactly handling it very well. At one point in her story, Laura started crying, and admittedly, so did I. Even Grand dabbed at her eyes, and Granddad cleared his throat.

Essentially, we are all a mess.

Dammit, Mom. Why'd you have to do this?

"Why didn't you come to us sooner?" I ask, my tone accusatory.

"I know you must think I'm awful. I didn't know what to do, actually. At first I thought, what they didn't know can't hurt them and all that, but then it kept eating away at me." She rubs her throat for a minute.

"So my father knows. Or rather, Jeff knows."

"Yes."

"So who is my biological father?"

A look of sympathy passes over Laura's face. "Simone never shared his name with me. All I know is she met him up at Lake George. You had a home up there at one point, didn't you?"

Grand nods.

"She went up there alone, sometime after she and Jeff were

231

married. I do know that. I also know he passed, because she told me as much. It was around the time when you were five or six."

So my biological father is deceased. There's an element to me that's not exactly sad, but regretful over the fact I never knew him.

"Your mother was never happily married, Prescott. I may be overstepping my bounds here, but I think you should know she wasn't the type to go off with different men. The fact that she did it with one at all was shocking to even her. And she had a great deal of remorse over it. It stayed with her for … well, I think you know."

"Why the hell didn't she just get divorced?"

"Jeff threatened her."

All three of us, Grand, Granddad, and me, all simultaneously say, "He *what*?"

Laura's head drops and she stares at the floor. Then she speaks. "He wasn't very kind to her. Maybe you all saw a different side to him, but she said he stayed with her for the money and position. Without her, he was nothing."

A spark ignites in my gut and turns into a raging fire. My grandfather and I glance at each other. If what she says is true, I will toss that ass out on the street and not have an ounce of regret.

"I want more information on this, Laura."

She perks up. I imagine it's because my entire demeanor has changed. I've gone from sad and pathetic, poor Prescott, to a man out for revenge.

"He was verbally abusive."

"You're sure about this?" I ask.

She sneers. "Oh, I'm sure. I witnessed his outbursts many times. He was quite offensive, even when I was around. I can only imagine what he was like when they were alone. I used to beg her to leave, but she wouldn't. I guess he had some kind of a hold on her."

"Can you be more specific?" I ask, glancing again at my grandparents.

"I can try. Once I was over there, you were away, and I can't remember where. But the two of us were outside, talking and laughing, when he stormed out and yelled at us both. Told us we were nothing but worthless whores and that I needed to go home. I was married, still am, and was insulted. When I went to give it back to him, Simone grabbed my arm and shook her head in a silent warning. I shut my mouth, got up, and left. She was afraid of him; I have no doubt. There was fear in her eyes. But this happened a lot when I was there."

My jaws clench. He never laid a hand on me, but then again, I probably would've run to Grand or Granddad and his ass would've been toast. "Do you have any evidence that he hit her?"

She shakes her head. "No, and if he did, she hid it from me. Again, that wasn't the only time he did that. He would say awful things about her, too. Tell her she was good for nothing, lazy, and worthless. I don't think he liked for her to have friends around much."

Grand adds, "Maybe he felt threatened."

"I think she was deeply depressed, but hid it from everyone. She always put on a happy face."

And that's exactly how I remember my mother … always smiling and telling me how much she loved me. She never spared her hugs and love, that's for sure.

Grand asks her some more questions and I can't imagine how this must make her feel—the man their daughter married and the same man they've financially backed for all these years, is now uncovered as being not only an asshole, but a verbally abusive one. And he may be the one who contributed to her suicide.

Suicide. The word makes me nauseous.

As I sit here, my phone pings. It's a text from Eric.

I give everyone an apologetic look. "Would you excuse me? I have someone in my office I need to see."

My knees even shake as I walk. *Get a hold of yourself, Prescott.*

Eric is standing at the windows, looking out at the skyline. It's dark now and all the buildings are lit up, making the scene look like a postcard.

"How did it go?"

"Dude, this view. Better at night than during the day."

"Yeah, I know. So, the interview?"

He gives me two thumbs up. "I rocked it. But hey, you didn't tell them they had to hire me or anything, did you?"

"Nope. I told them you were a friend, but if you weren't a fit, that was their business."

"Okay, cool. I want this job really bad, but I also want it on my talent and merits, you know?"

"I do. So it went well, though?"

His grin pretty much is my answer. "Yeah, really well. They're supposed to call tomorrow." Eric is pumped as hell. It makes me feel good that I can help him.

"Great."

"Did someone shit on your parade today?"

A bitter laugh escapes from me before I can stop it. "You don't know the half of it."

"Damn, I'm sorry, man. Anything I can do to help?"

I slide my thumb across my lower lip. "It's a family matter, really. There's nothing you can do, but thanks for the offer."

"Hey, I also wanted to let you know Vivi called me earlier. She left a message and texted. Is everything okay over there?"

I wish I knew. "I'll find out when I get home. So, I have some family stuff going on that I have to get back to."

"Oh, not a problem. I don't know how to thank you, even if I don't get the job. And, Prescott, please don't tell Vivi I helped you. I don't want her to know. But just so you know, I hope you two work it out."

"Thanks, man." I slap him on the back and lead him toward the elevators. When we get in sight of them, I head back to the family gathering.

Right before I walk in, I hear Grand say, "So you think it was mostly her volatile relationship with Jeff that led to her suicide?"

"That and the idea she was never able to cultivate the relationship with Prescott's true father. I think it weighed heavily on her. In all the years I knew Simone, she was never happy with Jeff. The one thing I know for sure was she loved you with her whole heart, Prescott."

And doesn't that make me want to go and kill that motherfucker?

Laura leaves and promises to call if she remembers anything else, although I'm not sure what good it will do.

When it's just the three of us again, Granddad says, "Son, I know you want to go and take your revenge out on him for what he did, but keep a level head. We only know what Laura said, and time can distort the truth."

"Do you really believe that, Granddad?"

"I don't know what to believe right now."

"I do. Mom committed suicide. You all thought she was fine and she wasn't, so she must've been hiding something."

Grand is shaken. Her skin is ghostly pale and I reach to hug her. "I'm sorry, Grand. I don't know what to say."

"Nor do I, Scotty. I'm so sad she felt she couldn't reach out to us. All these years we've wondered."

We decide to go for drinks and dinner. Before we leave the offices, I see a text from Vivi and let her know not to wait for me. I can't focus on that at the moment. Grand is hanging on to the both of us like lifelines.

During dinner, they both get me to promise I won't do anything stupid. But it's Grand's voice that gets me to agree.

"I've lost one child. I couldn't bear it if something happened to you."

"Don't worry. When I go to evict him, I'll be well represented. I'm not going to do it alone, but now I don't feel bad about it either."

They both are in agreement.

It's after nine by the time we leave the restaurant. My head throbs, and my heart aches. I don't really want to go home and face Vivi. She'll want an explanation, for which I'll have none. I won't open this part of my life up to her. Maybe one day, but not tonight.

One of my corporate apartments is close, so I go there instead. It's actually one I showed Vivi. There's a locked closet where I keep some suits and things, toiletries, and other items on hand if I decide to stay there for the night. It's empty and lonely after being with Vivi for the last couple of days, but I need space to think about what happened earlier.

Maybe after my head clears a bit, I'll be able to look at this more calmly. The fact is I've heard of these situations but never thought it would happen to me. Then again, who does? I'm not close to my dad nor have I ever been. What I'm feeling is more of a betrayal than anything. And anger that Mom couldn't tell anyone, or find a way to get help.

Pouring a glass of bourbon I keep on hand here, I gaze out at the view as I sip it. Memories of Mom begin to crash into me, and then they're replaced by Vivi's face. I'm either losing my mind or this is a clear indication I need to get my shit straight and decide what to do with the gorgeous piece of ass who's waiting for me at home.

Wait, that's so fucking wrong. Vivi is not a piece of ass. She never was and never will be. And that's the problem, isn't it?

This whole thing has spiraled out of control and now I'm at a loss on how to deal with it. I knew what kind of life to live before I walked into that coffee shop and saw her sitting there. I would've kept living it, unencumbered. But fate had different plans for me, it seems. And now it makes me wonder what the hell it has in store for me next.

CHAPTER 26

VIVI

THE LIGHT CREEPING INTO THE ROOM IS A SURPRISE. WHEN I went to bed last night, I never thought I'd be able to sleep. Here it is, morning, and when I check the clock, I realize it's time to get up. Regina will be here very shortly. It's shocking that I never heard Prescott come in last night. Or even this morning to change. Weird.

After I brush my teeth and wash my face, I drag my sluggish feet into the kitchen and notice the food from last night is still out. Why didn't he put it away? But the place is eerie, so quiet. And he should be up and showered by now. I walk up the steps slowly, calling his name as I go, but he doesn't answer. I'm not sure which of the rooms he's using, so I check the first and it's unused. I go on to the next and it's the same. The last bedroom is the one, but it's empty. The bed is made and when I check the bathroom, it's obvious the shower hasn't been used. He didn't come home last night.

But why? Did something happen, maybe to one of his grand-parents? If that were the case, he would've reached out and called. I'm suddenly pissed. Really, really pissed. That's the only reasonable explanation for him not getting in touch. *Like he's going to call to tell you he's spending the night with another woman? Get the fuck real.*

Marching back down the steps, I go straight to the shower and bathe. This is it. I've had enough of this mercurial living situation. I don't know what's up or down anymore and I have enough shit to deal with—like how the heck I'm going to pay my medical bills, or bills in general for that matter. I can't work for how long with this stupid broken arm? I wish I could get my hands on Joe Delvecchio's balls right now. I'd smash the hell out of them until they resembled pancakes.

When I'm done showering, I dress and hear Regina in the other room. I go to greet her.

"Good morning, Vivi." Her cheery voice greets me.

"Regina, I don't know how to tell you this, so I'll just say it straight up. I'm moving back to my apartment as soon as my hair is dry."

"But Mr. Beckham wants me for two weeks."

"I'm so sorry. You'll have to speak to him about that."

"Does he know about this?" she asks skeptically.

"He didn't come home last night, so I couldn't tell him," I say sourly.

"Oh, dear."

"It's best if I'm in my own place. I think you understand."

"Sure I do, sweetheart." Then she asks, "Do you need help with your hair?"

"Of course I do, but I won't let you. I'm doing this on my own. Just like I showered and taped my arm up on my own. It's not too bad. Not as good as you doing it, but I did fine. Oh and dinner was delicious. I left it out for Prescott but since he never came home, I'm afraid it's ruined. Sorry."

"No need to apologize. You fix your hair and I'll make you breakfast."

"That's a deal."

I fume the entire time I'm tearing the brush through my tangles, sure I'm ripping half my hair out. Right now, that's not important to me. Vacating this apartment is. I gather my things and stuff them into my bag. When I'm ready, I join Regina in the kitchen.

"I'm worried you won't be able to cook for yourself."

I wave my hand. "No worries there. I have a roommate and he likes to cook."

"Your roommate is a man?"

"Yeah, but he's gay."

"Will he take care of you then?" Her expression is hopeful.

I nod my reply. Who the hell knows? I've always taken care of myself, and will now. I eat as much as I can, not wanting to hurt Regina's feelings, but my stomach is hive full of buzzing bees. I'm so disappointed in Prescott I can't think straight. The minute I cracked the door open to let him in, he pulls a manwhore move.

"Are you ready?" I ask.

"If you are."

I order an Uber, which I can't really afford, and we go downstairs. It's already waiting when we get there. I live close, so it's only a short ride. Once we get inside, Regina leaves my bag in the living room.

"Please come in."

"Vivi, what are you doing here?" Eric asks, walking out from his bedroom.

"I'm home."

"I can see that, but I thought we decided you were going to stay another day or two. I didn't think you'd be back so soon."

"Well, here I am."

After I introduce Regina to Eric, I explain that Prescott shut down and then didn't come home. I tell him how I can't handle feeling like he doesn't want me there and his manwhoring just confirmed that.

Eric looks like he wants to say something, but I cut him off.

"So what's up with you?" I ask.

"I had an interview yesterday and then I sort of partied after."

"Oh? Where did you interview?"

Now his face flushes a bright shade of crimson.

"Oh, God, I should've told you, but I had an interview at Whitworth. Prescott got me in the door."

I disguise my super hurt feelings and plaster on a smile. "Eric, that's wonderful. This could be your big break you've been waiting for."

"You're not mad?"

"Of course not. You have to seize the opportunity when it hits."

He almost knocks me down to hug me.

"Whoa, boy, hold it back a bit."

"Sorry. I was freaked that you'd hate my guts."

"Okay, pump the brakes on that thought. My feelings might be a little hurt that you didn't tell me, but hate you? Isn't that a bit extreme?"

I catch a glimpse of Regina over his shoulder and it registers she must feel like the third wheel in the conversation. "Hey, let's talk about this later."

Then I go to Regina and say, "I don't know how to thank you. You've been more than kind."

Her warm smile lets me know she feels the same. "I wish you all the best and if you ever need a helping hand, please call me." She presses a sticky note into my palm and then leaves.

"She seemed nice."

"She is. But I couldn't stay there another minute."

Eric puts his arms around me. "I'm sorry for everything you've been through. It's going to get better, Viv. I have a good feeling about things."

"I wish I did."

I lug my bag into my room with Eric protesting. "I have to do these things for myself. Besides, I feel much better." Physically, anyway.

"Want some coffee? There's still some left."

I accept his offer to make me a cup. We sit and talk over things that have happened. His excitement over his interview is contagious. He gives me hope at finding a position.

"Why don't you do consulting in the interim?"

"I might have to. But I'm going to talk to Lucas about coming back to work."

"You can't be serious. You only have one arm."

"I have two, but only one works." I hold them up for emphasis. "I can still mix drinks one-handed. Besides, I go to the doctor next week and find out what my restrictions will be."

Eric's brows slant in question.

"Really. I think I can do it."

"We'll see. The other hurdle is making Lucas believe you."

Shrugging, I add, "I'll just have to prove it to him."

The following Tuesday, I go for my check-up. My physician is pleased with my progress and says the X-rays look good. He's not exactly keen on the bartending idea, but agrees to let me do it as long as I promise not to lift anything heavier than a glass. But the best news is he's going to switch my cast to a splint next week. That means showering will be easier and I'll be able to scratch my arm without using a coat hanger.

The little things in life.

Prescott never called nor did I really expect him to. I'm sure he came home to an empty house and assumed things were over. If so, he'd be right. I won't allow my heart to be involved with someone who thinks he can treat me like his own personal doormat. I'm still pissed, though, not gonna lie. But I'm more pissed at myself than anything. I let him in. Okay, not all the way. We didn't have sex or anything. Yet, I would've ripped my pants off that one night if I hadn't been so banged up. And this is all that damn Joe Delvecchio's fault. Everything goes back to that little greasy-headed fucker.

I even have to go to court for that sleazy bastard's trial. I only hope I can sit there without trying to scratch his eyeballs out. The attorneys that Prescott hired called, but I told them not to bother. The idea of being tied to him in any way leaves a bitter taste in my mouth. I'll let the prosecutors do their jobs and hopefully, he'll go to prison, as he deserves. Lots of pictures were taken of me when I was in the hospital, swollen and bruised, and that has to help the case. I'm still purple in some areas and turning green in others—an attractive sight for sure.

I delay my visit to The Meeting Place until after my cast has been changed to a splint. Lucas warmly embraces me. He's called a few times, but it was early on. Now over two weeks have passed and my face isn't swollen anymore. He tells me how good I look.

"Oh, come on, Lucas. I look like a moldy grape."

He laughs. "Now that's a unique description."

"Well, I'm purple turning green. You can't argue with that."

"You look awesome. I don't care what you say."

"And you're full of it. But, I'll take the compliment."

It's late afternoon, so the place isn't crowded yet.

"How's business?" I ask.

"Great. But I miss you back here with me."

I scrunch up my face. "That's why I'm here. I want to return to work."

"Viv—"

"Before you say anything, hear me out. My doctor cleared it. He said it's okay as long as I don't do any heavy lifting with my arm. Mixing cocktails is fine. I can do most of it one-handed. Lucas, you have to let me come back. I'm going out of my mind. Please." I fold my hands in a prayer pose, but it's awkward since the one is in a splint and kind of angled funny.

"Oh, man, Vivi. What if that crazy ass possessive boyfriend

of yours comes in here? If he sees you working, he'll kick my ass from here to California."

The blank look on my face must clue Lucas into the fact that I don't know what he's talking about.

"Prescott Beckham. Your filthy rich boyfriend who will destroy me if I do this."

I take a giant step backward and hold up both arms like I'm under arrest. "Whoa, whoa, whoa." Then my index finger shoots up. "One, he is not my boyfriend and I don't care what anyone has told you." My second finger joins the first. "Two, he doesn't have even the tiniest say in what I do." The third finger pops up. "And three, I really don't care what Prescott Beckham does. He can jump off the Empire State Building as far as I'm concerned."

"Wow, you two must've had one helluva fight."

I give a noncommittal shrug, not wanting to give him details. This is too personal and Lucas is a work friend.

"All I can say is the night you were injured—"

"Can we not rehash that? It's a little raw for me."

"Yeah, sorry. So, you really think you can handle it?"

I perk up. "I'd like to start on a slow day or night. Definitely not a weekend."

"Okay, Vivi, we can do that. I've missed you, like I said. You're a great worker."

"Eeeep!" I hop a little and then hug him. "Thank you. I promise it'll be fine."

That's my mantra and I'm sticking with it.

When I get home to tell Eric, he looks like someone threw him in the spin cycle. "What's wrong with you?" I ask.

"I'll tell you what's wrong. Whitworth Enterprises, that's what. Those people are crazy over there. I had no idea accepting that position would require me to be doing all this stuff before I actually started it."

"What are you talking about?"

"Oh my God, Vivi." He fans himself dramatically. "I have to take a drug test, then they do a background check on me. I guess they want to make sure I'm not doing heroin on the side or I'm a Russian spy or something. Then I have to get them copies of my certifications so they can get me ID cards for all the markets we'll be going to."

"Seems to me that's sort of the usual for any large corporation."

"I know, but I have to maintain my other job and it's hard to find the time to get it all done."

Poor Eric. But I can't really feel sorry for him because he's getting ready to step into the job of a lifetime.

"Quit the restaurant, Eric. You're too nice. Just tell them what's going on and you can't do it all."

"I can't. They've been too good to me."

He's loyal, I'll give him that.

"Then, power through it and look on the bright side. Think of how exciting your new job will be."

He nods slowly and I laugh at his lack of energy.

"It's not funny."

"If you could see your face, you'd laugh too."

"When I went for the interview, Prescott died when I called him honey."

That actually makes me laugh. "Did you do it in front of anyone?"

"No. I'm not that stupid."

"Too bad. I would've loved that."

"Yeah, you would've." He smiles. "But that would've spelled disaster for me. He was a little crazy looking as it was, given his day."

Holding up my hand, I say, "Stop. I don't want any more information on him. But, hey, why don't I cook us dinner tonight?"

He sighs. "That would be so nice."

I look in the fridge and decide a quick trip to the corner market is in store. I run out and pick up a few items, and while

I'm headed in, I notice a dark sedan parked nearby. I don't bother looking in to see who owns it, because I know.

The stalker has returned, but too damn bad. I pick up my pace and as I reach the door, I hear him call out my name, but *too fucking bad*. Maybe he should've thought about that before he stayed out all night with some skanky ho. I raise my hand in the middle-fingered salute and keep moving.

When I open the door to our apartment, that hand is shaking. Dropping the bags on the counter, I lean back and take long deep breaths. It pisses me off that he still has this effect on me. *Traitor body*.

He never bothered to call or text, but yet he shows up like I'm supposed to what exactly? "Oh, hi, buddy. It's great to see you." Excuse me, but hell to the fucking no on that.

Eric walks into the tiny kitchen. "Are you okay? You look like you've seen a ghost."

"I'm fine."

"Vivi. I'm not stupid."

"He was outside."

Eric chuckles. "I wondered how long it would take. A man who stared at you like he did wouldn't stay away forever."

"Too bad for him."

"Why don't you give him a chance?"

Turning to face him, I plant my hand on my hip. "Whose side are you on anyway?"

"No side. I'm just—"

"I vividly recall you telling me to give him a chance before. I did and look where it landed me. Eric, I adore you, but stay out of this. Prescott has earned his one and only chance with me. He fucked it up good."

I go back to fixing dinner.

"I won't say another word except have you ever thought that maybe something happened?"

"Yeah? Well, that's what phones are for."

He grumbles something and walks away. The truth is I'm

weak where Prescott is concerned and I don't need to be around someone like him. Maybe he does have his own issues, but I don't need to add them to mine. I need someone who'll build me up and not crack me into tiny pieces and then watch them scatter into the wind. And he's proven, again, what type of man he is.

CHAPTER 27

PRESCOTT

It's been over two weeks since I've seen Vivi. The apartment was empty when I got home and all that remained was a note from Regina along with Vivi's scent.

Inhaling, I let the fragrance coat my senses. Her image was vivid and sharp, almost as though she stood in front of me in reproach. I could hear her asking why I hadn't called and where I'd been. I could see doubt cloud her gorgeous eyes and her uncertainty over my flimsy explanation of where I'd spent the night. My gut burned with the acid of how I'd raised her suspicion in me. Why hadn't I texted or called her? What the hell had I been thinking?

How can I fix this? *I'm* the problem. Not her. I've probably destroyed what I'd built and her distrust in me will never allow her to believe what I tell her. Everything is ruined and I only have myself to blame. All because I was stupid and fearful of revealing the truth of my past.

Except, I don't even know my past anymore. I'm currently a man without a name. I'm not even Prescott Beckham. I don't know who the fuck I am. The irony of it all smacks me in the face.

Regina said if I needed anything to contact her. I arranged for her to be paid the entire sum for the two weeks. It wasn't her fault this happened. The blame falls on my shoulders.

My trip to Atlanta was pretty fucking miserable. Weston and Special tried to talk it out of me, but I didn't even tell them about my father. I didn't have it in me to bring the whole mess up. We took care of business and when I was leaving, Weston told me the door is always open. I knew that already, but it was good to hear the words.

Lynn is on my ass once more because every morning I smell like a bottle of bourbon again. She doesn't even tell me but hands me a toothbrush, toothpaste, and then says I need to chew some gum.

"Get some help, Prescott. I don't know what happened, but I know it has to do with Vivi. I hope you didn't hurt her."

"Lynn, I wish it were that simple."

"It's not that father of yours, because he's not here anymore."

I nod in silence.

"So?"

"I don't want to discuss it."

"Okay, boss, but I don't want to work for you if you're going to be like this."

She backs out of the office without another word. Who can blame her? No one wants an alcoholic for a boss.

We're in meetings all morning and afterward, Granddad stops by. He makes a suggestion that floors me.

"I think you should relocate, son. As much as this pains me to say, I think it's time for you to get out of here. You're a wreck and it's not doing our business any favors. Leaving here and running our ops in Denver might be the answer."

"Denver, huh?" I almost stagger to my chair and this time it's not because I'm hungover.

"Yes. It's a good fit, Prescott. They need your brilliant mind to pull in some deals over there. That group is performing, but not like I think it should. You could change that."

Moving to Denver. I love the city. It would be close to our resort in the high country where I could get a lot of skiing and snowboarding in during the winter months.

"Granddad, it sounds appealing, but I need to iron out some issues before I go."

"Prescott, I was thinking the first of the year. And I'll be truthful with you. I'm worried you're headed down a slippery slope. Your grandmother and I don't want to see you end up depressed like your mother or in need of rehab either."

I plunge my hands through my hair. Lynn better not have put this bug in his ear. "Has Lynn talked to you?"

"About what?"

Granddad is an open book with me. If she had, he'd say so.

"Never mind. I'm sorry you're so worried. I promise to do better. All that stuff about not knowing who my father is has gotten to me."

"I wish I had answers for you, I really do."

"I know. But thanks, as always, for your support."

That night when I go home, I make a decision to try to contact Vivi. Since I haven't called, there's no use starting there. Maybe if I try to see her, she'll listen to what I have to say. As I'm getting out of the car, there she is, walking home with a couple of bags from the local market.

When I call her name, she shoots me the middle finger and sprints inside. That tells me how much work I have in store just to get her to talk to me.

I wait a couple of hours and call. Of course she doesn't answer. Then I text about thirty minutes later. No response. Vivi is really going to make me work for it. Can I blame her? Hell no.

That night when I fall into bed, the sheets still smell like her. I refuse to let the housekeeper change them, who probably thinks I've gone mad, which I'm close to being. I count the number of texts I sent to Vivi and there are fourteen. She's most likely enjoying this. I can see the smart look on her face when she notices it's my number. Maybe I should call her from the office tomorrow. She doesn't know that number and maybe I'll luck out and she'll answer.

Then a thought hits me. I wonder if she's spending Christmas with anyone. It's creeping up on us. Eric is probably taking her home with him. Good for her and him. The holidays snuck up on me with everything going on and I haven't gone to any of the parties I usually attend. Our company Christmas party is this Saturday and I was sort of hoping I could talk her into going with me. Doesn't look like that's going to happen. Maybe I need to start from the beginning and send her cute things again.

In the morning, the first thing I do is call her from my office phone.

"Hello?" she answers curiously.

"Please don't hang up. I need to know if you're okay and I'd like to explain things." The words rush out of me.

"You should've thought of that before you spent the night with some skanky woman. Don't call me again." The line goes dead.

She thinks I was with another woman? *Of course she does.* How could I have been so fucking stupid? Wouldn't I have jumped to the same conclusion if I were her? I said I needed space, left her alone, ran out of the apartment, and then instead of coming home to talk, I just never showed up at all—and I didn't text or call her either. Not only do I need to find a way to explain to her about *me* and what's really going on, I need major damage control. Fuck me upside down.

I run out to Lynn's desk. "Come in here, quick. I need you."

She runs in behind me. "What is it?"

"I need help impressing a certain woman. Like really impress but not make her think I'm trying to buy her or anything."

"Prescott, what did you do now?"

"No time to explain. Just come up with some things. You know, cute things women love to get. I got her this giant stuffed wolf that she loved. Just to get you started."

She stares at me like I'm the devil. I am. "Can you ice skate?"

"Yeah, but she has that cast on her arm, so nothing like that."

Lynn huffs. "How much money?"

"No object."

She leaves and comes back in thirty minutes with a list. She slaps it on my desk. "So help me God, if you've done anything to Vivi, I'll personally kick your ass. *This* is why you've been pining and you're back into that bourbon." Then she sails out like the biggest cruise ship known to man.

When I look at the list, I know why Lynn works for me. The first thing I do is call Eric.

"I need your help."

"With what?"

First I tell him I wasn't with any woman. Then I tell him about my plans. The first one will be implemented on Thursday —with Eric's help.

Eric is supposed to call Vivi and ask her to meet him somewhere. He's going to tell her he has a surprise for her.

"She's going to hate me forever."

"No, she won't. I'll make it up to her. I'll do everything possible for that not to happen, but I need to see her and she won't talk to me."

"Okay."

Eric will get Vivi to meet him at a café and then we have arranged for a car to drive them to another high-rise where the company helicopter will be waiting. He's going to say he wants to show her a project he's working on, but in fact I'll be waiting in the helicopter. Only at the last minute, Eric will duck out, leaving her climbing in with me in the back.

"Promise me one thing. If she sees you and doesn't want to go, don't force her."

I laugh. "I'm not going to kidnap the woman. I only want to talk to her."

"Yeah, okay."

The two days crawl by and when I get to the waiting helicopter, I'm sweating like I just ran six miles. I hope I don't smell like it. The last thing I need is for her to climb inside here and wonder what the stank is all about. They should be here in twenty minutes, so I pour a drink to loosen up. About five minutes before they're due, I tell the pilot to start her up. Even if she refuses to go with me, the helicopter still needs to return to the airport in White Plains.

I'm waiting there, almost holding my breath, when the door opens, and the security guard escorts them out. Jesus, Eric has her blindfolded of all things. What the hell is he thinking? Now she's really going to hate me. He gingerly escorts her to the waiting helicopter and when the door opens, he says, "Okay, Viv, big step up."

"I can't believe you're doing this," she says.

"Believe it," he says. "Now sit so I can buckle you in." This is my cue to take over. He shuts the door and runs like hell.

"We're a go," I tell the pilot. And we lift off. But as soon as she hears my voice, she rips off the blindfold and her eyes are two orbs of ice.

"What the hell are you doing?" she asks, acid dripping from her tongue.

"The blindfold wasn't my idea. In fact, I had no idea he'd do that. But I wanted to show you the city from the sky." I give her my best smile, while I sweat buckets. This woman is reducing me to a puddle of water.

"I don't want to see the city from the sky. Or at least I don't with you."

"It was the only way I could get you to talk to me." I hand her a headset and put one on myself. She flings it away.

"Okay, we can yell and let the pilot hear us."

She grimaces and picks it up.

After she plunks it on her head, I say, "I wasn't with a woman that night. I spent the night alone because I found out earlier in the day that the man I've known all my life as my father is not my biological father. My mother had a fling with someone and I was the by-product."

Her face contorts into a multitude of expressions. But I don't wait for her to respond. I keep going before I lose my nerve.

"I don't expect your sympathy. That's not why I'm telling you. I just wanted you to know that I didn't sleep around on you. The truth is I haven't been with another woman since I saw you, Vivi Renard, sitting in that damn coffee shop." I hope she believes what I'm about to share with her because it's damn real and this part is killing me to tell her. "I have a lot of issues that surround my parents. My dad, or the man I thought was my dad, is a class A jerk. I don't have much of a relationship with him. Let me amend that. Make that zero relationship with him. Last Christmas his current wife pulled one hell of a stunt at our family dinner." I tell her the story and how she'd hit on me before. "Consequently, my relationship with him, which was awful to begin with, deteriorated even further. Now I'm left with having to evict him from the house I grew up in, the one he thinks is his. It's a fucked-up mess, if you want the truth. And I haven't even gotten to my mother yet."

Vivi's eyes no longer resemble a stormy sea. At least I've gotten through to her on some level. But I also don't want this entire trip to be about my problems.

"Would you care for a drink?" I ask her, lifting mine to show her.

"Is there wine?" she asks, her voice small.

"Yes, and, Vivi, I really do want you to enjoy Manhattan from the sky. Look out there. Isn't it something?"

I hand her the glass of wine and notice a hint of a smile tugging at the corners of her mouth.

She cranes her neck, not wanting to miss anything. "Look! The Statue of Liberty."

"Yeah. All lit up too. I love the view at night. The views from here are ... well, you can see for yourself."

She's gawking all over the place and I want to laugh, but I press my lips together. She's so fucking adorable. She licks her lips and I groan.

"Are you okay?"

"Fine."

"This is so amazing," she breathes. And she's quiet then as she enjoys the sights. I point things out to her here and there, just so she doesn't miss an important landmark.

Then, out of the blue, she asks, "Why didn't you share this with me before?"

I expected this. "Good question. It's a part of my life I don't share with anyone. Only a half a dozen people know. And I've never told a woman before. You're the first." I slide my hand down my face. "I don't share things like this 'cause it opens me up to vulnerability and that scares the shit out of me, Vivi."

The dim lighting of the interior casts a shadow over her face, causing the creases in her brow to be more pronounced than they are. "But I told you about my mother being sick and all my problems. I would've thought that put us on even ground."

"To you. But telling you, strips me of my—and I know it sounds ridiculous—strips me of my strength. It weakens me."

"Yeah, must be a man thing. To me it makes you more human. Humility isn't a bad thing, Prescott."

One thing I am not is humble. I may exhibit some of those qualities at work, such as complimenting my employees over a job well done, or doing jobs no one else wants to. Under ordinary circumstances, I'd consider myself arrogant. I could use a lesson from Vivi on this. She's unpretentious and modest and doesn't like drawing attention to herself.

"You should teach me humility, Vivi. I need a good lesson in it."

"No, you don't. When I was hurt, you came in flying, ready to fight off anyone who could harm me."

"I'm pretty sure that was behavior more typical of a Doberman than someone with humility."

She lets out a warm laugh. "True. But there's humility inside of you. The way you describe your grandparents, for one. It's written all over your face, and in your voice. I've said this before. You're too hard on yourself."

"I need to ask you something, not to change the subject, but have you seen that psychiatrist yet?"

She glances away quickly. "Uh, I went once but then cancelled my follow-up."

"Why?"

She chews her bottom lip for a second. "The truth is I can't afford it. The visits are way out of my price range."

"Goddammit, why didn't you call me?" I yell. My voice booms through the headset and she jumps in her seat. "Shit, I'm sorry," I say, seeing her reaction. "I prearranged with the doctor that your sessions would be paid for. I knew you didn't have the money for them."

Our eyes connect. Proud gray ones challenge equally as proud gold ones. But this is important and I won't back down. "Vivi, this is vital to your mental health and well-being. I don't care if you and I never see each other again. You must get help and you have to let me cover the expenses. One day, when you have a job and are out of debt, pay me back. I don't care. I have more money than I'll ever need or spend in my life. Just let me do this for you," I plead.

"Okay. But pinky promise you'll accept the money when the time comes."

"Yes! Even though I don't know what the hell a pinky promise is."

"This." And she sticks out her pinky finger and tells me what to do. It's kind of cute, so I go with it. It must be a girl thing.

The pilot comes over the headset and asks if we want to circle the city again.

"Vivi?"

"No, I'm good."

"Take us in to Whitworth, please."

"Yes, sir."

When we land, I escort her off the helicopter and into the building. "I don't suppose you'd care to see my office, would you?"

"Sure, why not."

The building is vacant now. We take the stairs down one flight, since my office is on the top floor. It's silent since everyone has gone home. I point to Granddad's office and keep walking until I get to the next corner one, which is mine. Then I open the door, using the electronic key card. When the lock clicks, I push the door open, and Vivi's inhaled breath lets me know she loves the view from the dual glass windows.

"Wow. This is what you look at every day?"

"During the day it isn't nearly as spectacular." I don't add that the view is much better with her in here.

"This is unreal. I wish I worked here."

"Say the word and that can be arranged." I'm not joking. My face is as serious as it's ever been and she knows it.

"I couldn't."

"Why not?"

"It would be bad for work. And us."

"I don't see how. You'd be in IT. I'm not there. Our paths would never cross."

For a moment I believe she considers it. The back of her hand presses over her mouth and she looks hopeful, but then she lowers her head and sighs. "It wouldn't work."

"How about I see if we could use you as a consultant until you find something permanent?"

"I have to think about it."

I move in front of her and take her hand. "Let's go and eat dinner. You must be starved."

"I can't. The helicopter was wonderful and I loved it, but maybe some other time. Thank you, though."

"Okay." I hide the letdown behind a smile. She's not ready

for me. For us, I should say. At least she didn't scream the entire ride. That's a plus. *Baby steps, Prescott.*

Escorting her out of the building, I help her into the waiting car and instruct the driver to take her wherever she wants to go. She thanks me and I watch the car drive away. Then I call Eric.

"Thanks, man. I owe you."

"Is she going to chop off my balls?"

"I don't think so. But tell me if she had a nice time, will you? I don't want to know the details, just text me *yes* or *no.*"

"I will. And for whatever it's worth, I'm on Team Prescott. And don't ask me why, because I have no idea."

I laugh and thank him. Eric is one of the good guys. I hope the job works out for him.

Thirty minutes later, I smile as I read his text.

Yes.

On to my next plan.

CHAPTER 28

VIVI

"AT LEAST IT WAS AWESOME," ERIC SAYS.

"Awesome, stupendous, amazing, the greatest experience of my life. Are you kidding? But I still want to kill you for not warning me."

"Sorry, not sorry. You never would've gone. And damn, Viv, the guy is desperate for you. If you ask me—"

"Did I ask you?"

"No, but I'm telling you anyway. He's in love with you."

"Are you nuts?"

Eric takes my hand and drags me to the couch. "Sit."

So I do.

"Listen up. Men and women are different. Just because I'm gay doesn't mean I don't think like a man. He has issues. Everyone does, including you." He points his index finger at me and wiggles it. "His may actually be bigger than yours. Give the guy a chance."

I cross my arms and harrumph. "I told him about mine."

"Apparently he told you about his. And from the sound of it, you are now in his inner circle. I don't know, nor do I care to know, what those issues are. The fact he bared his soul to you tells me he trusts you and has extremely strong feelings for you. Why else would he do that?" I can't answer that and Eric takes my silence as permission to continue. "So stop hedging and just date the guy. Frankly, I'm tired of all your whining and the back and forth between you two."

"What?"

"You heard me."

"But I thought he spent the night with someone."

"Fine. But did you even ask him or give him a chance to explain?"

I sit here like a sullen child. And maybe that's how I'm acting. I haven't really been acting like a grown up at all, have I? What was he supposed to do when I wouldn't even talk to him or take his calls?

"He offered me a job."

"And?"

"I refused."

Eric throws his hands up in the air. "You are the dumbest, most idiotic woman on the face of the Earth. How the hell did you graduate from MIT?" Then he stomps out of the room.

I chase after him. "Eric, stop."

He turns and taps his foot, waiting for me to speak.

"You really think I should take the job?"

"No, Vivi, I think you should be a bartender for the rest of your life."

I groan and grab my head.

"Would you stop all this angst and think for a minute. God opened a window for you and you're sitting here, like a dumbass, staring at the thing. You have to know that Prescott called me by now to enlist my aid in getting the two of you together. You have that degree from MIT. You're supposedly brilliant, though I'm beginning to question that. I would think you had deduced that by now."

"I figured as much. I just didn't want to ask you."

"He did and I did, so now you know the truth. He did it with the promise of an interview for me at Whitworth. At first I told him no. But then the more I thought about it the dumber it was of me not to take him up on it. My business wasn't taking off and I didn't want to wait tables forever. So call me an asshole and self-serving, but I did it. Besides, I had a feeling that the two of you should be together anyway. Now he's offering something similar to you and you're acting like a moron about it. Take the fucking job! Run with it and show that company how amazing you are. Build your reputation back up. Then if you don't like the damn job, you have a résumé again. And the same if you and Prescott don't work out. Just don't be stupid, Vivi."

Eric's right. I really can't pass this opportunity up.

"Have I been that much of a whiny ass over him?"

"Whiny ass doesn't begin to cover it. Wimpy, whiny, grumbly, you name it. The man has bent over backward to help you. Has opened up his fucking bank account to you and you keep kicking him in the balls. If it were me, I would've already tossed you into the river and never looked back. Personally, I don't know what your problem is. Yes, you've been through a lot. Way more than I ever want to handle and I get that you don't want to put your heart out there, but *damn*. This whiplash thing is too much for a roommate to take."

Jumping up, I dig through my handbag, searching for my phone. Then I send Prescott a text.

Thank you for the ride tonight. It was amazing. V

He hits me back with a quick, *Glad you liked it. I have some more tricks up my sleeve. Are you interested?*

I send him a laughing emoji because I can only imagine what kinds of tricks he has in mind. Then I send him this:

I've been thinking about your job offer. I'd like to talk about it some more.

He is fast with: *Lunch tomorrow?*

Sounds great. Where?

My office. Noon.

Okay, will this be an interview or lunch, I wonder. I'd better scrape up a résumé. I have one already, so I'll bring it with me just in case.

In the morning, a major case of nerves attacks me and I wish Eric were here to calm me down. It's been a long time since I had a real job interview and I'm not even sure if this is one. What the hell should I wear?

I comb through my closet and decide to play it safe, opting for a pair of black pants that could be either for work or just going out to lunch, and a nice black sweater that lands in the middle of work and business casual. It's something I'd definitely wear to work, but not interview worthy. If I were interviewing, I'd wear a suit, but if it turns out to be an interview, I can say I thought it was only lunch. As for my résumé, I can say I was bringing it to him so he could pass it along. That covers my bases pretty well.

About eleven-thirty, my phone goes off and it's a text from Prescott telling me to expect a car in fifteen minutes. I thank him and go down to the waiting vehicle at eleven forty-five. My stomach is so knotted up, I don't know if I can eat.

The security desk asks for my name and when I tell them, a guard escorts me to a special set of elevators designated for the executive floors. It requires a key to get in. The guard slides in his card and when I'm inside, he presses the appropriate floor and tells me Mr. Beckham will be waiting. I thank him as the doors are closing.

When the elevator stops and the doors quietly whoosh open, Prescott stands there with a smile, offering me his hand.

"Vivi, how are you?"

"I'm fine. You?"

"Better, now that you're here."

People are everywhere, but I can't help notice how every eye in the place is focused on us.

"Is it my imagination or are we the center of attention?"

"You're perceptive. I've never brought a woman up here before, so they're curious and I'm sure the break room will be buzzing with rumors in about two seconds."

When he says that, I almost trip over my feet. I'm the first for a lot of things, it seems.

"Can I ask you something?"

"Anything."

"How many women have you taken for helicopter rides?"

"One."

I stop walking. A dozen or more people are watching us, but I don't give a damn. "The first here, the first in the helicopter, the first in your home. Is this a pattern?"

He slides his teeth across his lower lip. "I'd say it is."

Now I know without a doubt that Prescott Beckham has pulled out all the stops for me, far more than I could've ever imagined. But it's not just that. It's that I realize exactly how much he's truly opened up for me. I thought he was a vault, and partly, he was, but there's a change in him and it's a wonderful one. Whatever code he lived by with other women he hasn't applied it to me. In other words, he's more than trying. He's doing whatever it takes. Eric's words come back to me then, *bent over backward*. He has, hasn't he? It's not everything; it doesn't mean he'll never hurt me again, but it's a start.

"One more question. How many women from here have you dated?"

"From Whitworth?" he asks.

"Yeah."

"None."

I grab his hand and hold it. This is a monumental moment for me, hearing these things. I don't know why I asked him in a room full of people, but I did. We've only just resumed walking when he suddenly stops. I turn to face him this time. "Now that you understand this about me, does this mean you'll date me?"

"Yeah," I say, grinning broadly.

"Good." Then he pulls me close and kisses me. And I'm not talking about a peck on the lips. This is an all-out, toe-curling, belly-clenching kiss where his arms curl around me and my knees lose their bones.

When he lets me go, he says, "It's about damn time." Then continues walking us toward his office. I'm dazed. Trying to pull myself together, I let him drag me along for a moment.

We get to a desk where a familiar face sits. "Vivi, it's great to see you. And you're looking so much better these days."

"Thank you, Lynn. It's great to see you, too."

She hugs me and we chat while Prescott walks through a door, which I assume is his office. When he's gone, Lynn says, "Boy, I'm really glad to see you. He hasn't been worth a damn since … well, since whenever you two had your disagreement or whatever it was. Don't do that to me again."

I laugh at her comical expression. "I won't. Promise." Then I wiggle my fingers in a wave and follow Prescott.

"I hope you don't mind, but I've had lunch delivered here." It's spread out on a table in here and it looks delicious.

"This is wonderful. Thank you. Lunch with a view."

"And afterward I want you to meet my grandfather."

"Oh, maybe some other time."

"No, today. Then I'm taking you over to the IT department so you can meet everyone. I've arranged for you to interview with the department head this afternoon."

"Oookayy. A little warning would've been nice."

He waves me off as though it's nothing and we sit down to eat.

I pick at my food because my stomach is filled with marching ants on their way to fight a battle. I'm thinking ahead to not only the interview, but the meeting with his grandfather. WTF! I already met the matriarch and I have to wonder if Sara mentioned anything to her husband about that.

Prescott stops eating. "Is something wrong with your meal?"

"No, it's great."

"Then?"

"Gee, I don't know. Maybe it's because in a few minutes I'm going to meet your grandfather. Or could it be that I'm interviewing with the department head of IT and I'm not the least bit prepared? Although, I was forward thinking enough to bring a résumé for you to pass along."

Prescott laughs. "You're the smartest, most brilliant woman I've ever met. Use that gray matter of yours and you'll be fine."

Maybe I should tell him that Eric thinks I'm a dumbass.

"Can I clue you into something? You haven't been around me long enough since Crestview to discern whether I'm brilliant or not. And exactly how much do you know about IT?"

He takes his napkin off his lap and wipes his mouth. Then he says with a sexy smirk, "Vivi, can I clue *you* into something? You seem to have forgotten that I own this company. Well, my grandfather and I do. And we don't have shareholders we have to please. This interview is a courtesy only. I can demand they hire you. I, however, choose never to do that. But I, unlike you, have a shit-ton of faith in you. Once you meet Dan Stevenson, who heads our IT, he'll put you at ease, and you'll impress the shit out of him." Then he leans back and adds in that overconfident manner of his, "And if you don't, I'll fire the dumbass."

I almost swallow my tongue. "You'll do no such thing."

"Of course I won't, but you have nothing to worry about."

His plate is polished while mine looks like a bird picked at it. "Why don't I set your lunch aside and let's go meet Granddad and then after your interview, when your appetite has returned, you can finish it?" he asks.

"Fine. But this is a little weird, meeting your grandfather."

"Why? He already knows you're going to work here."

"Oh, God," I groan.

He helps me to my feet, straightens my sweater, and then combs his fingers through my hair. "Perfect." Then he kisses me. "Now you're ready."

"Wait." I run some gloss over my lips. "Now."

When we walk out, Lynn says, "Oh, good. Mr. Whitworth just called asking when you were coming."

Prescott holds my hand as we walk.

"Sorry if my hand is sweaty. I'm a little nervous."

His only response is to pull me closer to him. I'm acutely aware of all the eyes on us as we walk.

I lean into him. "Do you always command this much attention here?"

"No. I never walk around holding a gorgeous woman's hand. They're curious about you."

"Oh, great. When they find out I'm interviewing, everyone will hate me."

"Are you really worried about that?"

"Not really."

We stop and Prescott speaks to an admin, who tells us Mr. Whitworth is waiting on us. When we walk in the expansive office, which is almost exactly like Prescott's, my knees are shaking.

"Granddad, this is Vivi Renard. Vivi, meet Samuel Whitworth, my amazing grandfather."

The older gentleman immediately stands, walks over to us, and takes my hand in both of his. "It's so wonderful to meet you, Vivi. My grandson speaks very highly of you."

"And he does the same of you, sir."

"Please call me Sam, or Samuel." His silvery white hair gleams, but his bright blue eyes are kind and welcoming. He puts me at ease immediately.

"Okay, Sam."

We chat about my interview. He asks me some pointed questions about my education at MIT and my previous experience at my former job in California.

"Prescott, I believe she's going to fit right in here."

"Granddad, I've been doing my best to convince her of that."

"I'm a bit nervous because Prescott sprang this on me when I got here."

Sam laughs. "Sounds like something he'd do. Don't waste a minute of your time being nervous. You and Dan will get along perfectly."

Prescott wears a satisfied smile that screams *I told you so*. I elbow him in the ribs. We chat a few more minutes when Prescott announces he'd better get me down to IT.

"Yes, we don't want her to be tardy," Sam says. "Why don't you bring her out to Westchester for Christmas, son?"

Holy shit. What the never-ending fuck?

"I'd love to, that is if she doesn't have plans."

They both stare at me, waiting for an answer.

"Uh, no. I'm actually open that day." An awkward sounding laugh sneaks out of me and my cheeks heat.

"Great. I'll let your grandmother know. The more the merrier. And it will be loads better than last year, won't it?"

"You did have to bring that up, didn't you?" Prescott asks.

"Oh, we'll make a toast to old Puffy Lips herself."

I'm lost in the Puffy Lips comment and I watch Prescott shake his head.

"We'll see. I'll talk to you later about the Grandview account."

"Right. And let me know how Vivi's interview goes. Vivi, it was great meeting you and I look forward to seeing you soon."

"Thank you and same here, sir."

We leave and Prescott walks me to the elevator. "Told you he was awesome."

My brain reels. "Yeah. But Christmas?"

"It'll be fun."

Okay, Viv, slow down. Focus on computer science for now.

The elevator drops two floors and we exit to our next destination. Prescott leads me straight to the boss's office. His admin drips honey as she ogles him.

"Dan should be expecting me. And this is Vivienne Renard."

"Hello." She doesn't even look at me as she speaks. "Mr. Stevenson is waiting."

Prescott turns to me. "I'll introduce you, then I'm out to a meeting. When you're finished, just come back to my office, okay?"

"Sure." And then he plants a kiss on me.

He certainly hasn't been short on public displays of affection since I said I'd date him. As I turn, I notice the admin glaring at me, but I shrug it off. I can't worry about her.

Dan is gracious and after Prescott leaves, we settle into business. I make it perfectly clear to him I want this job on the basis of my merits, and not because of my relationship with Prescott.

"Funny you should say that, because he told me the exact same thing."

That's good news. Dan asks me about everything from my education to my first position and how I ended up in New York. I hold nothing back, but I don't throw down the sympathy card either. The truth is I've been out of the market and I'm the salmon swimming upstream. I promise if he hires me, he won't regret it, because I won't be outworked or outsmarted.

We talk about my skill set, some of the projects I worked on for my former employer, and at the end of the interview he says, "Quite frankly, I'm surprised you haven't been hired by at least a dozen companies by now."

"It's the gap on my résumé. Anytime someone sees that, they go on to the next one without stopping to ask questions. I never get a chance to explain."

"So true. How about starting the first of the year?"

"I'd love to." I want to jump out of my chair, do the happy dance, and yell WOOHOO, but I don't.

"This is what we can start you at." He tells me the number and I really want to do a cartwheel and a backflip. Too bad I'd break my other arm if I tried.

"Sounds excellent. Thank you, Dan. This is going to be the beginning of a great working relationship. I can already see it."

"Same here, Vivi." We both stand and he walks me to the door. "I'll get the ball rolling on your employment contracts and paperwork."

"Great. And, Dan, have a great Christmas."

"Same to you."

Oh my effing G. I cannot *believe* this! I'm getting a visual of my mountain of debt shrinking into a mound.

I practically skip my way back to Prescott's office and when Lynn sees me, she says, "Someone looks mighty happy."

"I got the job!" I whisper-yell.

"Job?"

"I interviewed with IT."

"That's so great. I didn't know. He never told me."

"Probably because I didn't even know I had an interview until I got here."

Her head swings back and forth. "That boy." Then she motions me to come closer. "Can I share something with you?"

My head bobs up and down.

"He doesn't think things through sometimes, but he truly has a heart of gold." Her face tells me how much she adores him.

Why does everyone seem to be on Team Prescott lately? Then again, it seems I've jumped on the bandwagon myself.

"I'm beginning to see that."

She gestures with her head. "Go on in. He's probably on the phone, but it's fine."

"You sure?"

"If he knows you're here and I told you to wait, he'd fire me."

My eyes must look like golf balls or something because she quickly says, "I'm only kidding. That man couldn't fire anyone. Now go on."

When I walk in, he's leaning back in his chair, phone in hand, feet propped up on his desk and crossed at the ankles. His tiger eyes zero in on me, and he keeps on talking. I hear him say, "Let's wrap this up before the new year. I don't care how much. It'll be worth it. We can talk next week. Fine." He hangs up the phone and asks me, "Has your appetite returned?"

It has, but not the one he's referring to. He looks like a billion-dollar sex machine, sitting there, owning the world. And I'd like to climb on top of him and go for the ride of a lifetime.

"Vivi, what wicked thoughts are running through that pristine mind of yours?"

"Wicked thoughts? What makes you think …?" My voice trails off as I watch him rise and stalk over to where I'm standing.

"You can't possibly hide sexual desire from me. I can practically smell it."

Good Lord, it must be a thousand degrees in here. Sweat beads on my forehead and I don't even dare think of what's happening between my thighs. The ache grows and my belly tightens at the mere thought.

"You dirty little girl." He takes his thumb and rubs his lower lip.

No, don't do that.

"The Little Wolf may yet live up to her name after all."

Then he kisses me—a dirty, hungry kiss. He devours my

mouth, nipping my lips, sinking his teeth into them, tugging, and teasing, until the ache between my legs grows unbearable.

When he releases me, my chest is heaving in sync with my racing heart.

"One thing hasn't changed. I still want to fuck the innocence out of you."

"What makes you think I'm innocent?"

"Everything about you is innocent, pure."

"I've been with men before," I say.

A throaty chuckle rumbles from him. "Just because you've been with men doesn't mean you're not innocent."

Those words make me heat even more from within. "I'm not sure what you mean."

He runs a finger from my chin to the top of my sweater. "You'll find out. I'm going to do some very filthy things to you soon, and when I do, you'll not only love them, you'll be begging me to never stop."

CHAPTER 29

PRESCOTT

AT FIRST I WAS AFRAID I WENT TOO FAR WITH MY DIRTY TALK. History had shown that it didn't always successfully mix with Vivi. But when those deep cherry spots appear on her cheeks and her hand reaches for her neck, I know I'm on the right track. I think Vivi secretly loves it. Just wait until I have her stripped bare, her pink pussy exposed. But that's not all I'm going to take care of. That little ass she's been parading around will get some attention, too.

Baby steps, I remind myself.

So I switch gears on her and totally throw her. "Tell me about your interview."

"Interview?"

"Your job interview. Remember? The one you were so nervous about?"

Her hand flutters through the air. "Oh, yes, the interview." A breathy laugh, one that makes me want to kiss her again, rushes out of her. "I start after the first of the year."

"I suppose a celebratory dinner is in order then."

"Tonight?"

"Why not?"

"I have to work at The Meeting Place. I promised to fill in for one of the bartenders. Lucas is shorthanded."

Dammit. I don't want her tending bar anymore. It makes my fucking skin crawl knowing there are men out there checking her out. But, *fine*.

"How about I meet you there and take you home? No stalking."

"Sweet." She stands on her toes and kisses my cheek.

"That's it? The cheek?" Then I point to my mouth and she grins. She places her lips on mine like a two-year-old would, making a loud smacking noise.

"Better?"

"Not in the least." Grabbing her by the ass, I pull her against me and kiss her, making her think of what might come later. "Now it's better."

"I'll say."

As I'm releasing her, she grabs my face and plants another kiss on my lips. "Until later."

After she's gone, I realize my plan backfired. I wanted to start a fire in her, but I'm the one left with a boner. All I can think about is the tight pussy that awaits me, if I'm lucky. I wonder if she'll let me slide into it later tonight. Trying to take my mind off it, I pour myself into work that needs to be done.

At around five-thirty, Granddad enters my office and wants to know how Vivi's interview went. When I tell him she's starting after the first of the year, his grin explodes.

"I'm so happy for the two of you. You make a great couple, son. I can't wait for your grandmother to meet her."

"Do you think she'll like her?"

"I do. I really do. Vivi isn't one of those flashy women your grandmother despises. In a way, she reminds me of your mother. You were too young to remember, but she was like her—beautiful in a simple, yet elegant way."

That's a great way of describing Vivi. She's elegant and gorgeous, but not flashy or overly done.

"Prescott, have you told her about your mother?"

"She knows some of it," I answer.

"Son, I know it's difficult, but I can see your heart is involved with this woman. Don't you think it would be wise if you told her the whole story? It may provide her some answers to …"

"Go ahead and say it. I won't be offended, Granddad."

"To how you are, in some respects. If she knows the reason for how you were, too, it will be easier to understand."

"But I'm fine now."

"Yes, you are. I was thinking it would add some insight into why you're the person you are, though."

"I'll tell her someday. But not now."

He pats me on the shoulder. "Your call. See you tomorrow night. Are you bringing Vivi?"

I laugh. "I don't know. I'm going to spring it on her."

Granddad grumbles. "Oh, Prescott. I won't tell your grandmother about that. She'd chase you around with that old wooden spoon of hers."

I'd like to chase Vivi around with a wooden spoon, now that I think of it.

"I can be very persuasive when I want to be, you know."

"I'm sure you can be. I'm old, but I do have my memory."

We both chuckle at that one. I'm sure Granddad was a player until he met Grand. He's still a charmer with the opposite sex.

"And, Granddad, that idea about Denver …" I let my voice trail off.

"I understand. We'll table it. If the need arises over there, we can rethink it at a later date. Just focus on recentering yourself, son."

I work well past ten, catching up on things I've been slack on lately and then go home to change. When I'm there I start thinking about what Granddad said about telling Vivi. I toss a bourbon back, because the thought of it sets me on edge.

Picking up the phone, I call Weston. When he answers, I check to see if he has a minute. Interrupting him on a Friday night isn't something I like to do. He lets me know it's fine, so I call Harrison and loop him into the conversation.

"What's the deal, Scotty? It must be bad to get us all on board," Harrison asks.

"Yeah. It's about Vivi."

"Vivi?"

"Vivi Renard." And I fill Harrison in on what's going on with her since I haven't talked to him about it.

"Holy shit. I remember you mentioning her when we went to dinner that night. So you're banging ViviVoom, then?"

"If you ever call her that again, I'll beat you to a bloody pulp."

"Dude, back it off a little. I didn't mean anything by it, okay?"

"She was bullied by those assholes at Crestview. Were you one of them, Harrison?"

"No! I never did shit like that. It was what the girls called her. Calm it down, man."

"Hey, Scotty, it's cool, okay? He didn't mean anything by it," Weston chimes in.

"Okay, yeah."

"So, brother, what do you need?" Weston asks.

"I have to tell her. The whole fucking story. And you know how I am about that."

"Fuck. Listen, just do it, and get it over with. If she's worth having a relationship with, she'll be cool and levelheaded about it," Harrison says.

"It's me I'm worried about."

"Prescott, I've told you this before. The situation was bad but the perception in your mind is worse."

"Yeah, well, I doubt that."

"Think about Special and me. We had a shit-ton of obstacles to overcome, yet we did it. I know you'll be good, man." Weston wears rose-colored glasses ever since he fell in love. I envy the hell out of him.

Our three-way conversation continues with them eventually convincing me to tell Vivi. They have a point. If she knows, everything about me will be out in the open. So far my opening up has only made her like me more, and I have no reason to believe she'd ever use this information against me in any way. So I agree.

After we're done discussing my shit, I'm on my third bourbon, which is stupid, because I need a clear head, when Harrison mentions something about Midnight Drake being home from rehab. I'm only half paying attention because I'm still trying to figure out what to say to Vivi.

"Good luck with it all," I say.

"Hey, same to you."

We end the call wishing each other a Merry Christmas in case we don't talk again. It's a little after eleven, so I get ready to head to The Meeting Place. Vivi doesn't get off until one, but I can wait for her there. I'm on my fourth drink and feeling the buzz. My alcohol consumption has decreased significantly in the last month or two, so it doesn't take me nearly as much to get drunk. Right before I head out, I decide to hit the pipe. A little herbal encouragement might ease the tension between my shoulder blades, not to mention in my skull.

On the way there, I realize that hit off the bowl wasn't the best idea. I'm completely buzzed. What the fuck was I thinking? Maybe it'll be too dark and crowded in there for her to notice. The last thing I want is for Vivi to see me completely hammered.

When I get out of the car, I stumble onto the sidewalk and nearly fall as I bump into someone. Excusing myself, I head inside. Thank God it's packed. Weaving my way up to the bar, I spy her as she awkwardly makes drinks with the broken arm. I have to hand it to her, though, she doesn't miss a beat. She laughs at something a customer says and keeps on working.

Eventually, I get a seat at the bar, but it takes a lot of

wedging my way in here and there. At last I order my favorite bourbon from my favorite girl.

"I wondered when you'd show up."

"And here I am. You're pretty handy there with that arm."

"Oh, yeah." She offers me a grin as she slides me my drink. "You wouldn't believe what I can do one-handed."

"Is that a fact?"

"Uh-huh." Then she races to the next customer, leaving me to my drink and my whacked thoughts. Jesus, why the hell am I so cracked about this? It's Vivi and she'll be fine. She knows most of it, except for the finer details.

Uh, right. Beckham. You left out that little detail where you didn't speak for a year.

I guzzle my drink and slam my glass on the bar. She hears it and looks at me with a raised brow. I toss her an *I'm sorry* look but raise my glass to let her know I need another.

"Thirsty tonight?" she asks.

"Something like that." My words are slurred. It's loud in here and I hope she doesn't notice. Maybe I should've gotten a table so she can't count the number of drinks I have. "Why don't you get me a couple? Then you won't have to bother with me so much."

"Are you okay?" she asks.

"Sure." I give her my best smile, but my lips feel a little numb.

She's giving me odd looks, but I can't do anything about that. She brings me two bourbons. At this rate, she's going to have to walk me home and not the other way around.

Two hours later, I'm completely shitfaced.

We get ready to leave and the stagger I unsuccessfully try to disguise is an all-out indication of my state of sobriety.

"Prescott, you're tanked."

"Completely. Let's go. There's a car waiting."

"Why did you drink so much?"

"Because I had to."

When we get to the car, I almost face plant on the curb, but somehow, I do a little twirl thing and laugh it off as a dance move. "Weston would be impressed."

"Weston?"

"You wouldn't believe the way the man can dance. He's a regular Justin Timberlake."

"Uh-huh. And you're absolutely gray goosed."

She made a funny. I slap my knee and howl like a wolf. Then I think on that.

"Little Wolf is funny." Then I go, "A-Woo," in my best wolf imitation.

She pats me on the back. I'm not sure if she thinks it's good or not.

The ride home is a blur but when we get to my place, she half drags me to the elevator as I wave to the guys at the desk. When the doors close, it's only the two of us and I know I have to say something.

"I'm sorry. I shouldn't have had so many boo-bons." Jeez, I'm trying not to slur, but it's so hard.

"I can't imagine why you drank so much."

"There's something I have to tell you, and it scares me. I hate to talk about it, so I guess I got drunk." My brain tells me I sound a lot clearer to myself than I'm sure she hears.

We get to my floor and I stumble to the door. When we get inside, she helps me to the bedroom.

"Let me get you some water," she says.

I'm brushing my teeth or trying to anyway when she returns. I have more toothpaste on my face than in my mouth.

"You look like a toddler," she says.

"Ishthatbad?"

She pulls the toothbrush out of my hand and tells me to spit and rinse. Then she wipes my face off.

"Can I kish you, Vivi?"

She gives me a quick kiss. It's not enough, so I pout. Her hand reaches for mine and then she tugs me into the bedroom. "Lie down, mister. I think you need to sleep."

"No, no. I need to tell you something. It's why I drank so much."

Her hand shoves me backward and I plop on the bed. She takes off my shoes and I look up at her sadly.

"I'm such an idiot. I had it all planned. I was going to tell you my stupid secret. And now look at me. I'm so stupid drunk you won't listen to me."

She lies down next to me and takes my hand. "What is so awful that you had to get so hammered to tell me?"

I roll on my side, and a dizzy wave smacks me in the head, but I don't let it deter me. Staring at her, I say, "You're so pretty. Have I ever told you this? I mean absofuckinglutely smack me in the balls beautiful."

She snickers.

"No, no." I reach for her hair and take a piece of it in my fingers. "You probably think I tell all the girls that, but I never do."

"Prescott, I'm glad. And thank you."

"But that's not what I wanted to tell you. Well I did, but I didn't. God, you have the most expressive eyes. I used to envision them as I imagined us fucking. I'd get lost in them." I twirl her hair in my fingers. "I don't suppose that was a particularly romantic thing to say, was it?"

"Actually, it was pretty sexy."

"Yeah?"

"Yeah."

"So what did you want to tell me?"

"Oh, right." Taking a deep breath, I sort out my thoughts for a second because they're pretty fucking scrambled right now. "So, my mom committed suicide when I was a kid. I was eight years old when it happened." I stop for a second as the memory nearly overwhelms me. "When I got home from school that day, the nanny who usually picked me up went to the kitchen to fix me a snack. Mom always met us in there. That day she didn't, so I went looking for her. She wasn't out back in the gardens, where she could be found sometimes. So I checked the other rooms. I remember calling out her name. It was weird because she was always waiting for me to get home and so happy to see me. She would ask me all kinds of questions about school. But not that day. So I went upstairs into Mom and Dad's bedroom. I found her there. In the bathtub. She'd slit her wrists. She must've been there a while because there was blood everywhere. Their bathroom was white and all I can remember was the stark contrast of the red against the white tub and white marble floor, where one of her arms dangled over the edge of the tub. I called out her name and rubbed her hair. Mom had pretty hair. It was dark brown and long. I hugged her face and grabbed her arm. Then I sat down on the floor next to the tub and was there when the nanny found me.

"The nanny called my grandparents and the police. It was obvious my mom was dead. The pool of blood I was sitting in had congealed, but to my eight-year-old eyes, I was unaware. The shock that Mom had even been contemplating suicide threw everyone the biggest curve ball, but most of all me. To me, my mom was the sweetest, happiest, most loving person in the world. I remember her reading me bedtime stories, taking me to the park, playing hide and seek and doing the fun things that moms did with their kids. I don't have those fond memories of my dad. And suddenly, she was gone with the snap of the fingers. And that was the day I stopped talking.

"I didn't speak a word for over a year. My grandparents took me to every specialist, psychologist, and psychiatrist they could find. I was hospitalized for a month. But no one could get me to say a word. Dad yelled at me a lot. But nothing. I lived a mute existence. I wasn't catatonic, which everyone always asks, because I was responsive. I simply wouldn't speak."

I sigh and suddenly in that space, Vivi is talking.

"Oh, God, Prescott. First off, you were traumatized. It must've been so frightening."

My intoxicated self gazes at her eyes—eyes that are glazed and clouded with pain on my behalf. I don't want her to hurt for me. That wasn't my intention. I only wanted her to understand the whole story.

I reach for her cheek and touch her smooth skin. "I don't remember being scared. I only recall not wanting them to take her away in the ambulance. They stuck her in the black body bag and covered her face, and I kept thinking she wouldn't be able to breathe. I didn't understand the concept of death. That's what the problem was and no one knew how to explain it to me. It really fucked me up, Vivi. It caused me to push away from people, especially women. I'm sorry." I scrub my face.

"For what?"

"Everything. Getting so drunk tonight. Being an ass to you all those times. For not being the man you want me to be."

"How can you know what kind of a man I want you to be? You've never asked me."

"Okay. I'm asking now."

She leans into me and kisses my cheek. "As much as I want to discuss this, we need to table this until the morning, when you have a clearer head. This is too important to talk about when your brain is fuzzy with alcohol."

"You're probably right. How come you're so smart?"

"I'm not. Look at all the time I wasted when I was pushing you away."

"Thank you for listening to me. I was afraid to tell you. I've only told about six people this story. Well, now seven."

"I Googled you. At the beginning. There wasn't anything about your mom."

"Granddad probably took care of that years ago."

"Prescott, I'll never ever breathe a word of this to anyone."

"I know. It's why I told you."

She gets up and I ask her where she's going. "To borrow a T-shirt. I can't sleep in this."

"Ah, all right. Hurry back."

All I know is everything feels right with the world as I close my eyes. That's true until I open them again to the blaring sun and a pounding hangover. Fucking bourbon.

CHAPTER 30

VIVI

Prescott fell asleep before I could make it back to bed. I lie here thinking about his tragic story. How awful to find your mother dead in a pool of blood. The terror of that alone, but then to not be able to express yourself about it for over a year? The puzzle pieces fall into place as I think on his behavior and the dominant part of his personality. His need for control isn't surprising after how utterly out of control he must've felt as a child. And now, the way he's extending himself, reaching out to me, makes my heart clench, because I can't begin to imagine how big of a leap this is for him.

In the morning, he sleeps soundly, allowing me to watch him unobserved. His face is relaxed and free of the usual lines that crease his forehead. He looks so innocent lying here, without a care in the world. I wonder if he's dreaming. I decide to get up and surprise him with a pancake breakfast. After I brush my teeth, I go to the kitchen where I find everything I need.

The refrigerator is stocked, thanks to his housekeeper. Gerard, his cook, has left dinner here, but not breakfast. Pulling out everything I need, I get the bacon started first. Then I brew some coffee. Prescott will need some juice, water, and ibuprofen, so I gather those together and leave them on his nightstand with a notecard. All it says is: *For you.*

Back to my pancakes, I whip up the batter and start cooking them in batches. They can keep warm in the warming drawer. The bacon is ready, so I pop it in there too, after stealing a piece. There's nothing tastier than crispy bacon.

All the pancakes are cooked and in the warmer, so I cut up some oranges to look pretty on the plates. Everything is ready, so all we need to do is serve it up. As I make sure all the counters are wiped off, my phone buzzes. It's Vince calling.

"Hey, Vince."

"I wanted to wish you a Merry Christmas. I'm headed out of town for the week to visit family and then I'll be back. Sorry we didn't catch up for lunch, but between studying, exams, and work, I didn't have a chance to break away. You doing okay?"

"Yeah, I'm better, actually. I, uh, landed an IT job at Whitworth."

"At Whitworth? Would that have anything to do with a certain guy you went to school with?"

I let out a happy giggle. "It might. I'll explain it all when I see you. Is Milli going with you?"

"She is. I'm introducing her to the family for the first time."

"Ahh. Good luck. I'm sure they'll love her. Have a great time and Merry Christmas. Call after the first. We'll get together then."

"Sure thing."

It was nice to hear Vince's voice. I hope his family likes his girlfriend since it sounds like they're pretty serious. I'm sipping my coffee and reading the news on my phone when I hear a loud groan.

"Uurrgghh. My head."

Laughing, I say, "That's what too much bourbon will do to you. Did you take the ibuprofen I left for you?"

"Yeah. Thank you."

He comes up to me and kisses me. "But it won't work fast enough."

"You need food. Hydration and replenishment."

He nods and sits next to me. I start to get up, but he stops me.

"Vivi, I just want to, uh, I ..."

"It's okay."

"No. I want to talk about what we talked about last night. My memory is fuzzy. Did I tell you?"

"About your mother?"

"Yeah." He looks almost scared.

"It's okay, Prescott. You told me everything. How you found her and didn't speak for over a year." I move to put my arms around him.

"And you're okay with this?"

"No, I'm not. It's awful you had to go through that. It's a terrible thing for anyone to endure, but for an eight-year-old— well, it's just horrific. I'm so sorry for you."

"I don't want your pity."

This is going to be a difficult thing, I realize.

"Do I look like I pity you? I empathize with you, but not pity you. My gosh, to go through that and then to live locked in silence, where you couldn't explain your feelings to anyone must've been torture."

"I don't really remember it."

"I can understand why you wanted to get drunk to tell me. But, I want you to understand something. I'm not the kind of person who'd ever use this type of information against you nor would I ever judge you for it."

"I never thought you would. I didn't tell you for a different reason."

I wait, but he says nothing.

Cupping his cheeks, I ask, "Because why?"

"It strips me of everything and leaves me vulnerable. I hate feeling like that."

Ah, this again.

"You're safe with me. I'm the Little Wolf, not the big bad one. I'm not going to hurt you."

His hands sink into my hair. "You're like a song. When I first saw you, I heard a few lines, but then each time, more notes were added until now I have a complex melody. And it gets better every day."

I think I like this guy standing in front of me. "I want to hear your song."

"I'm not sure how you can't. You're creating it." Then he kisses me and while he does, he stands and picks me up.

His mouth tastes like mint-flavored orange juice and I murmur against it, "I have pancakes."

"Will they keep?"

"Uh-huh."

"Good. Because I have something a little harder than pancakes. It's been extremely patient, but right now, it's dying to get to know you better. You okay with that?"

"It's about time. I was starting to think you were a monk or something."

"I've certainly been living the life of one ever since you entered the picture."

I have to admit, it makes me happy as hell to hear that.

When we get to the bedroom, he says, "Remind me to tell you how to work the blinds in here. When I woke up this morning, my corneas almost got singed."

He opens his eyes in such a comical fashion, they remind me of a cartoon. "It's because you were hungover."

"Vivi, I have room darkening shades in here. Look at all the glass. It's like we're right next to a solar flare."

While he's talking, he's pulling up the shirt I'm wearing. I have no bra on, only a thong. When he takes it off me, I stand in front of him basically naked and I get an instant case of nerves.

"In a million years, I never thought … oh, I fantasized, but never even came close to this." His throat bobs as he swallows. It must be a good thing. His hands reach for the hem of his shirt and he strips it off, baring a gorgeous torso. Muscles ripple with every move and I curl my fingers in, because they itch to touch him.

"Your arm?"

"Is fine. See?" I raise and lower. "The splint keeps it from moving the wrong way."

He hooks his thumbs in his boxers and slides them past his hips. I stare at his erection as it springs free. The long, thick, shaft begs to be touched, but my shyness keeps me from doing it. It's a pretty dick. Pink and lovely shaped, with a slight tilt to the left.

"Well? Does it pass inspection?" he asks, a playful note in his voice.

"It'll do, I suppose." I do my best to suppress my laugh.

"Since it's the only one I have, I hope so."

With an unexpected move, he tosses me on the bed and is between my thighs, pulling off my thong. He's smooth, experienced, unlike me, as a wave of shyness washes over me.

I cover my face with my arm and he says, "None of that. I want to see and hear you when you come."

A surge of bravery hits me. "How do you know I'll come?"

"Everyone has a unique talent. Your brain is yours. You're brilliant, Vivi. Mine is eating pussy. You'll be thanking me later."

His cocky smile disappears between my legs and less than a minute later, I'm convinced he's right. I hate to think how he became this experienced, so I refuse to let my mind go there. Instead, I focus on what his tongue and fingers are doing down below. And that is sending me into a world of happygasms. At one point I may have told him to insure his tongue for a billion dollars, because that thing knows how to please a woman. It swirls, vibrates, and I swear to God has a battery in it the way it tickles my clit. Add to that, his fingers press on my G-spot as if they were magnetized to it.

My legs drape over his shoulders as he tongues me over and

over, while his long fingers thrust inside of me. Then he suddenly flips me on my stomach and wedges a pillow under my hips. He still buries his tongue in my slit, licking and licking, driving me off the edge as his fingers thrust and one manages to slip inside my back door. This is a complete surprise to me and I jerk in response. His hand presses down on the small of my back, holding me steady while he slowly, slowly moves in and out. In a burst of pleasure, I cry out my orgasm.

Is this three or four now? And when will he stop? I don't care because I'm in this for the long haul.

When he finally surfaces for air, he declares I have the sweetest cunt in the world. That's a word I've never cared for, but when he says it, my *cunt* twitches for more of his filthy mouth.

"What time is it?" I ask.

"Um"—he looks at the nightstand—"eleven. Why?"

"Is it too early for a drink? I need alcohol after that."

"You'll really need it after I fuck that sass out of you."

"That wasn't sass. I've just never had a man's finger up my, you know."

"Ass. You can say ass, Vivi. And that's not all I'm going to put up there."

Jesus. I swallow.

Now I need a shot on top of that drink. "Yeah?"

He latches on to my nipple and bites it. I squeak. "Yeah," he says after letting go. This is going to be quite a day."

"Okay. It's a good thing we don't have plans."

Then his eyes widen in alarm. "Fuck. I almost forgot. We have the company Christmas party tonight!"

"We?"

"Yes. You're going as my date. You're an employee of Whitworth now, remember?"

Sitting up, straight as a board, I say, "Whoa, doggie. Don't you think it would look bad if I went? As your date, I mean?"

"Absolutely not. You're going, whether you want to or not."

He reaches over and pulls something out of his drawer. Then he sits back and rolls a condom on his dick. I'm in shock that he thinks this discussion is over.

"What time?"

He smiles wickedly. "Time to fuck this deliciously slick pussy." And he lifts my hips, puts his palms under my ass so he can grab my cheeks, and slides right on into home. The cliché is old but works for me, because it feels as though he belongs here. I stare at his corded abs, the way they ripple with each of his thrusts, and my belly tightens. His lids drop to half-mast as his thighs flex, but watching his mouth and the way his teeth bite into his lower lip is the kicker. One of his fingers reaches for my clit, rubbing it as the buildup begins again. The pressure is so tight I know it won't be long, and it makes me wonder how he'll be able to hold out. My hand reaches for my nipple and he groans as he watches me tug and pinch it.

He picks up his tempo, moving faster and harder, and the throbbing in my pussy, the ache that needs satisfying, grows. The buildup is at its peak and I'm going to come.

When I do, it's like the oxygen disappears. The pulsations go on and on until I want to scream for them to stop. So much, too much, almost.

He leans forward. "You may think that pussy is yours, but I have news for you. I own it now. It belongs to me. Every single bit of it."

He's right, so there's no point in arguing with him. He flips me back on my stomach, and, to my surprise, slips inside of me, fucking me again. Only this time, he lubes up his finger in my own wetness and pushes it in my backside. This is an altogether different sensation for me. It's more shocking than before, much fuller, but also pretty fucking extraordinary.

"Vivi, rub your clit. Get yourself off."

I'm not sure I need it, but I do anyway. Every time he moves his finger, I nearly orgasm, until finally, I do.

What the hell did he just do to me? The combination of the

finger thing and fucking was amazing. Then I realize I've been preoccupied with all my orgasms, but did he even come yet? How does he hold back?

He puts me on top and I'm straddling the pony.

"Ride me." He grabs the tops of my thighs with his large hands and spreads my pussy lips. With his thumb he plays with my now over-sensitive clit.

"Ahh," I cry out.

"Yeah, that's good. Put your hand on my chest for leverage."

Up and down, I ride him slow, and he meets me roughly with rocking hips. I reach behind me and grab his balls, then press the ridge behind them, massaging it.

He groans and tells me "more" and "harder." I keep it up until he grits out that he's going to bust it. With one arm thrown over his head, he surges into me, and his abs tighten as he climaxes. Then that arm comes up and grabs my hair as me jerks me forward for a brutal kiss. He ravages my mouth, sinking his teeth into my lip, not quite breaking the skin, but making it sting until I suck my breath in.

"Next time, I'm going to make you sweat for it," he says. He nuzzles my neck, licking it, and the scruff of his beard scrapes the tender skin there.

I've barely had time to recover from the gazillion orgasms I just had when he yanks me out of bed. "Let's shower. Then food."

"I'm starved and I know you must be."

"Yeah," I breathe. I follow him wobble-legged to the shower. "Where did you get all this energy?"

He waggles his brows. "Sex."

"Why don't I feel like that?"

"You will. You haven't been fucked by me enough."

He drags me into the shower, which turns into a soapy fuck-fest, and before I know it, he has me bending over to hunt for the soap, his little joke. He slides into me from behind while I hold on to the wall for support. But soon his arm comes around me, lifting me into an upright position, and he presses his entire body against mine. My chest and arms fall into the wall and the cool tile is a nice contrast to the heat of his body and his sex. His cock slides in and out, creating that perfect friction, exactly what I want and need. When I feel him reach down to rub my clit, it won't be long for me to push past that precipice. I'm raw and on fire between my legs. This man has had me more in the last hour than I've had sex in the last two years. It's not information I should shout off the rooftops, but then again, maybe it is. I clench my orgasm out around his cock as he says roughly, "I gotta pull out. I'm gonna come." Looking over my shoulder, I see his cock spurt onto my butt cheek.

His arm is against the wall, supporting his body, and he milks the last drop out with the other hand. At last he stands. "Sorry about that. I didn't have a condom on so ..."

"Uh, yeah. About that. Are you clean?"

"Yeah. I get tested every month, but I haven't been with anyone since I saw you in October. I was tested in November and was clear. I'm good. Still, don't want any pregnancies."

"I'm on the pill and I was tested at my last appointment about six months ago. My doctor in Virginia was a stickler for it. But I haven't been with anyone in two years."

"So, the big question is, do you still want me to wear condoms?"

"In order for me to answer that, I have one big question for you. Are we going to be exclusive?"

His mouth flops open and I have a true glimpse of a shocked Prescott.

"What the fuck, Vivi? What kind of a question is that?"

"A good one. I have to know before I commit to having sex with you without protection."

He rams his body up to mine and shoves me into the shower wall. "Then I guess I'm going to have to spell it out for you, because apparently I was wrong about your intelligence. I am head-over-heels, crazy in love with you. I have no intention of being with another woman, and if you so much as look at another man, I'll beat the living shit out of him." He grins and suddenly he looks like the Big Bad Wolf.

How did I miss all of this?

"Okay then."

"Okay then. That's it?"

I reach for his cheek, but he picks me up under my thighs, so I have no choice but to wrap my legs around him.

"I guess that leaves me with no other choice," he says.

"No other choice than what?"

"I'm going to have to fuck some sense into you."

I think he's too late, though, because he already fucked it *out* of me. I can't think straight anymore. Pretty soon, I'll be reduced to moron status, mumbling out incoherent responses to questions. Maybe my brain will return by the party tonight. If not, I'll be his idiot girlfriend, limping around because her pussy's been over-fucked.

CHAPTER 31

PRESCOTT

Fucking Vivi is everything I thought it'd be and more. The moves, the moans, the kisses, her incredible body, the way she looks at me when she comes, and that pussy of hers—that pussy is the sweetest thing I've ever had. But now, I'm pretty sure she can barely walk. I have to give her a break. She told me her thighs are already sore from spreading them wide for me. I've had her in the kitchen, living room, shower, bathtub, dining room table, and this is only the beginning.

We finally ate our pancakes, but that only turned into food porn, with her licking syrup off my mouth, and me eating pancakes off her nipples. That's how we ended up fucking on the kitchen counter.

Then she told me her pussy was getting sore, so I recommended a bath, which led to more fucking. Seeing her glistening sex as she was bent over the side of the tub with my cock moving in and out of it is more than any man could ask for. After that, we watched TV, and it didn't take long for me to rip off her shirt, get her completely naked, and have her sit on my face for a little ride. She loved it.

That's how she ended up on the dining room table, tied up and blindfolded.

"Tell me how you're feeling."

"Nice," she says.

"How's your pussy now?" My hand is between her legs, which are spread-eagled and tied to the table corners using my silk ties that I knotted together. I'm rubbing coconut oil on her, massaging her and teasing her, of course. She wriggles under my touch, but she moans out her response.

"Vivi, you haven't answered me."

"Soooo good."

I decide on another tactic. Untying her wrists and ankles, I slide her to the end of the table and retie her. Pulling her knees up, I use the chairs as anchors for them and her wrists too. Now she's fully exposed to me.

"So pink and shimmering." My fingers lightly touch her, tapping on her clit. She squirms, trying to inch closer, but I don't let her. This time, she's going to beg.

I drop my head and only touch the tip of my tongue to her clit, barely teasing the tiny nub. She hisses.

"Prescott, please."

I keep it up. Then I stop.

"No, please, more."

Instead, I go after her inner thighs, sucking and biting. She groans in earnest.

"I need to touch myself." She jerks on the ties, trying to get loose.

"Not gonna happen. Remember what I said? This is all mine."

I'm back to touching her clit with my tongue, but nothing else. I flick it super fast, but right before she comes, I stop. She whines in protest.

I take the coconut oil and let it run down her slit in a thin line, until it drips onto the table, forming a tiny puddle. Her breath comes fast now. My finger follows the trail until it hits her puckered hole, and then I slide in just a little and pull out. She cries out for more, so I comply. Once I'm in an inch or two, I move in and out, but just a little bit, until she's begging me to help her come. My dick is so fucking hard, I think I'll help her out.

I thrust inside her and she pants like she's running. "Yeah, there, hard."

My hand moves to her stomach to hold her steady because even though she's tied down, she's bucking like crazy. Then I use my thumb to add pressure to her clit. Ramming into her, it doesn't take but a few plunges to set her off. Her inner muscles clench rhythmically around my cock, causing me to shoot off into her. Her tight little pussy is fucking paradise to my dick. Leaning over, I take control of her sexy mouth. She tugs my lip with her teeth and I love how my Little Wolf is getting more spirited in our fucking. One of these days, her little claws will draw blood on my back, and that's fine with me.

When I untie her and take off the blindfold, she says, "That was fun. We'll do that again."

"Hey, Bossy Pants, I'm calling the shots here."

"Not always. You'll see." She smirks at me. "Now help me up so we can shower. Again."

Laughing, I say, "I've never bathed so much in my life."

She aims her finger at me. "It's all your fault. Pancakes and syrup and now coconut oil. We can't exactly sit on the furniture like this."

"It's worth it, though, right?"

By this time, she's untied, so she grabs onto me. "Nah, I didn't like it at all."

I slap her ass. "You need a spanking."

"I'm not into that."

"Have you ever been?"

"No."

"I think you might be, but on a different level than your regular old ass spanking."

She puts a hand in her hip. "What do you mean?"

"Have you ever had your clit spanked?"

Her eyes brighten and she's definitely intrigued. "No."

"You will one day. By me. And you'll love it."

By this time, we're in the bathroom. One thing turns to another, which involves lots of soap, and she's on her knees sucking my dick. I have to say she's not bad. With a few, "More lips," and "Watch your teeth," remarks, I'm tapping her head, giving her the signal and coming into her mouth like a champ.

"Damn, that was great."

"Thank you," she says with a satisfied grin.

As we dry off, she says, "Why bother with clothes?" It's true. Every time we get dressed, we only stay that way for five minutes or so. "But, Prescott, we need to go to my place soon so I get something to wear tonight."

"Why don't we do this? We get ready here, and then we go to your place and you get dressed there?"

That's our plan. The party starts at seven and it's in one of the company's many hotels. About five-thirty, we head over to Vivi's. I tease her on the way down to the car about the way she's walking, telling her she looks like she's been on a dude ranch for a week.

"I have and you're the dude," she comes back at me.

When we get to her place, Eric is there getting ready for the party. We ask him if he wants to come with us, but he declines because he's bringing a date.

Vivi asks, "Is it that one guy?"

"Which guy?" Eric asks.

"You know, the one who gave you"—she motions up and down her body—"that one night."

Eric's face goes up in flames.

"Ahh, one of those nights, huh?" I ask.

"Okay, shut it, you two."

"Well?" Vivi prods.

"I'm not saying," Eric answers.

"It is," Vivi declares, clapping her hands. "Oooh, I can't wait to see Mr. Hot Who Stole Your Sexy that night."

"He did not steal my sexy."

"He did too. You were all swoony that morning."

Eric jumps back. "Oh, like you were with Mr. Fancy Pants here?"

"Mr. Fancy Pants?" I ask. "I'm not Fancy Pants."

Both of them say, "Right."

Then Vivi adds, "Look at your clothes."

Glancing down, I look. I only wear tailor-made clothing. Yeah, okay, I get their point.

"See," Vivi says triumphantly.

"Well, you better get used to it, missy, because it won't be long before you're going to be *Mrs.* Fancy Pants."

Two sets of eyes are stuck on me like glue. I didn't mean to say that, it just sort of came out. I decide to go with it. "So own it." And I turn away. "Now, you'd better get dressed or we'll be late. And I can't be late being one of the principals of the company, and all, so get a move on, Little Wolf."

She scurries past Eric to her room. A few minutes later she comes out holding three dresses and asks which one. I pick a black one that's on the short and sexy side, yet it's simple, too, so it will highlight Vivi's beauty. When she returns dressed, she's striking. Then she asks if she should wear her hair up or down.

"Always down. Every time I look at your hair I want to run my fingers through it. If it's up, I'd want to tear it down."

"Then I guess I'm ready."

Eric tells us to have fun and we leave.

When we get in the car, Vivi breaks into a barrage of rambling words.

"Who will be there? What should I say about why I'm with you? What will they think? Maybe I shouldn't have come? They'll probably think I'm the company whore. Oh my God, I'm having a panic attack. I'm gonna be sick. Help me, Prescott."

Maybe teasing will help? "Calm it down there, Little Wolf.

299

My God, you're on the road to being a motor mouth and not making any sense. Where's that MIT brain of yours? You can fuck the paint off a fence. Trust me, you'll be fine at this party."

"What? How is that supposed to calm me down? Whatever you do, don't leave me for a second or I'll pee myself."

"It was a joke," I say. "An epic fail of one."

I have to find a way to get her to calm down. Maybe sincerity is best.

"Listen to me, Vivi. You're an accomplished woman. You're smart as a whip, the most beautiful woman I know, and you're clearly heads above most people. You're going to be fine. Believe in yourself for a change."

Granddad and Grand are arriving as we do and once we're inside where it's warm, I introduce Vivi to Grand. Then Grand surprises me by saying, "It's so lovely to see you again, dear. And you're looking so much better. What a beauty you are. Well, you were beautiful even with all those bruises but now, you're magnificent."

"Thank you, Sara, and it's a pleasure seeing you again, too."

"Wait, am I missing something here?"

"Prescott, did I not tell you I paid a visit to Vivi when she was staying with you after her unfortunate incident?"

"Grand! No, you did not, and, Vivi, neither did you."

Grand puts her arm around Vivi and laughs. "You know how us girls forget things like that."

"My ass, you do."

"Scotty, don't use such crass language around me," Grand scolds me.

"Yes, ma'am, but I wish you had told me of this visit."

Granddad steps in. "Son, you're wasting your time. This woman will do what she wants, when she wants, and will tell whom she wants. So my suggestion is to forget about it and move on. Besides, it looks like they got along just fine."

"Indeed, we did," Grand says. "If we hadn't, I would have told you about the visit and warned you to stay away from her.

Now can we move ourselves toward the party? I, for one, would absolutely adore a glass of champagne."

Grand takes Vivi by the arm and the two of them walk together to the ballroom where the party will be held. Their heads are bent together, so there's no telling what's being shared between them.

Granddad and I trail behind them like trained dogs.

"Is she always like this?" I ask.

"Your grandmother is."

Hmm. I never noticed this about her before.

The room is empty when we enter, save for the hotel employees and event planners. They're all rushing around handling last minute preparations. One of the Whitworth employees comes up to me to ask how everything looks. I let her know things are great and how pleased I am with everyone's hard work. She smiles her appreciation and rushes back to the staff to let them know. The food tables are filled and waiting to be uncovered for the guests.

We have approximately twenty minutes before everyone starts arriving. The bar is open and waiters walk around with trays of champagne glasses. Grand snags two for her and Vivi. They clink glasses and share a secret smile. I need to find out what that's all about, so I sidle up to them.

"So, ladies, how's it going?"

"Perfect," Vivi answers. "The room is gorgeous."

"Not as gorgeous as you." I kiss her cheek.

"You two are so cute together. I can't wait to see the great-grandchildren you'll give me," Grand says.

"Grand, don't you think that's a bit premature?"

"Not at all, Scotty. You're all over her like a blanket. I've never seen anything like it with you. I think it's fabulous."

This is awkward. "Thanks for your approval," I say. "But right now, before this party gets started, I'm going to steal my girl away for a minute."

I escort Vivi to a private corner and apologize for Grand's

forwardness. Then I ask her what she and Grand were discussing.

"Nothing. Just girl stuff."

"Why didn't you tell me she came to visit?"

"I forgot about it. It was when we had our falling out and other things took priority. She's quite the grand lady, though. And I'll say this. You are her number one priority."

"Yeah, I've always been her favorite. I guess after Mom died, she took it upon herself to fulfill that role, which included me never getting hurt again. Sometimes she goes a little overboard. She usually hates the girls I date, so consider yourself lucky."

"She did say I was the first one with a brain."

I throw back my head and laugh. "Leave it to her to say that. She always told me to look for someone with more than just a large chest." I nuzzle her neck for a second and then I add, "It's a good thing she doesn't know how much I love that tight pussy of yours."

"Yeah, well, let's keep that between us." Her hand moves to my cheek as she presses her lips to mine briefly.

"Mmm, is that cherry I taste?"

"Yep, sure is and maybe a little champagne too."

The room is beginning to fill with people, so I take her hand and ask, "Are you good now? You seem relaxed."

"I'm fine. Just don't stray too far."

"I'll never stray from you, Vivi. I promise." I bring her hand to my lips. "Like it or not, you're stuck with me."

"I like." She straightens my tie. "Have I told you how great you look tonight?"

"You just did and thank you."

"Hmmm."

"What?" I ask.

"Too bad we're not alone. I have this urge."

"Shut up. It doesn't look good to have a stiffie in front of all my employees, especially in these pants."

A tinkling laugh bubbles out of her. "Guess not. Okay, onward to the lions."

"Hey, you're a wolf. You can handle it."

"Right-O."

The night goes by well, as we have a few business announcements, but not many. Vivi chats a lot with Dan. We see Erik and his hot date, as Vivi calls him. But all the single women are eyeing Vivi and me. I knew it would happen, but it doesn't matter because they never stood a chance to begin with. Some of them look on in envy, and others whisper together. I wonder what they'll think when they see her in the building as an employee soon.

The band plays and strikes up a slow song. I drag Vivi out onto the floor, and even though she protests, I want her swaying in my arms, to the beat of the music. She looks up at me with gleaming eyes and her face radiates happiness.

"This is the best time I've had in ages," she admits. "I don't know why I was so nervous."

"After a few of my special twirls, you'll be so dizzy, you won't remember your name either."

"Mr. Fancy Feet too?"

"Not like Weston. But I can hold my own."

When the song ends, she says emphatically, "You really can dance. I'm so impressed."

"Told ya." I'm feeling rather proud of myself, until I hit a patch of spilled something or other on the floor and almost fall flat on my ass. My arms windmill for a second and Vivi has to save me.

"Was that one of your new moves, Prancer?"

"Ha-ha, no. But this is." I grab her, spin her around, then dip her, and slowly bring her up to a standing position.

The people surrounding us break into applause.

Vivi smiles a bit shyly, not caring to be the center of attention apparently. Then she holds on to my hand and asks if we can escape from here.

"I didn't mean to put you in an awkward position."

"No, it's not that. I have to use the restroom."

"And we need to eat," I add.

"Why don't you score us a table while I find the bathrooms, and then when I get back we can eat?"

Sounds great to me, so I watch her leave the room and as soon as she's gone, a group of women practically attack me. As soon as I get rid of them, another group takes its place. I'll never get us a seat at this rate. And where is Grand when I need her? One woman tries to drag me to the dance floor, while another tries to drag me to the bar.

I jerk my arms out of their hands, saying, "I'm sorry, but I'm not interested. I have a date tonight."

Dragging myself away, they follow me like gnats. I finally locate a table with two empty seats and grab them, but the vultures keep trying to sit at the empty one. "Didn't you hear what I said? This is saved for someone."

Grand shows up and swats them all away. "Will you women learn some manners and see when a man is clearly not interested in you?" She sits in the empty chair and becomes my hero.

"Jeez, I've never been so inundated before."

"You've never been so bold with a woman at a company event before. But, Prescott, you seem to be having a nice time with Vivienne. She's really a very lovely girl."

"She's very special to me, Grand."

"I can tell."

"Where is she?"

"The restroom. I wonder what's taking her so long."

"Women take longer than men. Be patient."

Grand must think I haven't spent much time around the opposite sex. I won't try to change her opinion. It's important to keep my reputation sparkly in her eyes.

"Prescott, I wasn't born yesterday. I know you've had your way with lots of women. This one is different and I don't need to explain myself. You already know that."

"How did you know what I was thinking?"

"I'm a woman. Women are smart. They think with their brains and not what's inside of their pants."

I don't know if I should be offended or not. This is my *grandmother* speaking to me like this.

"Get over it already. I have more stories than you can shake a stick at. I want you to listen to me, Prescott. You came to me for advice on Vivienne. You've never done that before. I knew then this girl meant more to you than any other. Seeing the two of you together confirms my suspicions. You're in love with her. So, take my advice on something. Don't wait too long to ask her to marry you. You've known her for years. Don't let this one slip away. The good ones aren't a dime a dozen and there aren't a million fish in the sea. Well, there are, but not many of them are worth a damn. When you find one like Vivienne, you grab her and run. Now that I've said my peace, I'm going to find your grandfather. He owes me a Samba, or something close." She sails away and the sea parts for the queen. She's exactly right and her words ring through my head. Vivi made me work for it, but damn, it was worth the wait.

CHAPTER 32

VIVI

My bladder's about to burst when I find the bathroom and make a run for it. Thank God there isn't a line like you usually find in the Women's Room. They are never big enough. Why can't the architects who design buildings, including the bathrooms, figure this out for once?

When I'm done, I stand at the sink washing my hands as a group of four women enter. They stare daggers at me and I wonder who they are. So I boldly ask them.

"Do I know you?"

"Don't think so," one of them says. But they don't move.

"Is there something you want?"

"You might say that. We want to know what you've done with Beckham to make him fall for you."

"What?" Did she seriously just ask me that? This is *crazy*.

"You heard us," one of them says. "We've done everything we know to grab his attention, to get him to notice us for a couple of years, and nothing. Now suddenly, here you are and bam, he's all over you like fudge on a sundae."

Shrugging, I say, "Guess he likes me." I smile and go to move past them, but one grabs my arm with the splint. Digging her fingers into it, she squeezes hard until it hurts. Snatching it away, I say, "Get your hands off me."

My voice is filled with fire and they notice it.

"Just what are you going to do about it? It's four against one."

I sneer. "Are you going to beat me up or something? What is this? Junior high? How old did you say you were?"

"We didn't," one snarls at me.

"No, you didn't have to. Seems to me you're about thirteen by the way you're acting. Oh." I click my fingers. "Now I know why Prescott didn't care too much for you. He likes his women to act a little more mature."

That was a mistake because one of them slaps me right across the face. But I'm not taken down so easily. "I wouldn't have done that if I were you," I say. Balling up my fist, I strike back without thinking, landing a decent jab on her cheek.

The only other times I've hit someone was when Joe Delvecchio attacked me. Maybe it taught me not to let myself be bullied anymore. She whines and starts yelling that I hit her. *No shit.*

"Of course I hit you, you whiny bitch. You slapped me first. Anybody else care to step in line?" Then I hear Prescott calling my name from beyond the door.

"In here. Come in and give me a hand with this pack of animals, will you?"

He runs inside and sees me surrounded by the herd of nastiness.

"What the hell's going on?" he yells.

"I'll be happy to explain." In the meantime, the other women are shouting that I'm a liar. My arm is already bruising where the one grabbed me, and my face has a palm imprint on it.

"Did you hit her?" he asks, pointing to the one I hit.

"Damn straight I did. And I threatened to punch the rest of them."

"My Little Wolf is fierce."

I hold up my fist to show him how much so. He covers it with his hand and then raises it to his mouth for a kiss. "Are you okay?" he asks.

"I'm fine."

One of the other women says, "She punched me first." The other three join in, claiming it's the truth.

Prescott gives me a look that conveys he knows they're lying. But now it's four against one. There's not a damn thing he can do.

Turning to the women, he says, "Get the hell out of here. Whatever it is you wanted from her, you can forget about it. And by the way, I'm officially off the market, if that wasn't obvious."

He looks at me and says loud and clear, "I'm yours, no one else's. Are you okay?"

"I think so, but is my face swollen?"

He takes my chin and tips it up toward the light.

"Nah, only a little pink. That pisses me off. I need their names."

"Eh, who cares?" I say.

"I do. They bullied you in the bathroom at a company event. Jesus. That sounds even crazier when I say it out loud."

"Let's go have fun and worry about it later."

He eventually agrees but wheedles a promise out of me. I'm to tell him if I recognize any of them when we get back there. I agree, but I tell him I'm positive they've already scooted out of here. They probably realized what they had done and how foolish it was.

The rest of the night is sort of spoiled, because he keeps asking me if I see them, making me continually search. I finally say, "You have to stop. I'm fine and it was only a speed bump. They were nasty women who got in my face and it's over."

"But—"

I put my hands on his cheeks. "No buts, babe. It's done. Don't ruin our night over it."

"You called me babe."

"Is there something else you'd prefer, because I can call you

Stud Monster if you'd like."

"Stud Monster?"

"Yeah, you know." I use my hands to show him. He laughs.

"It's kind of a brutish name, don't you think?"

"That was my intention. StudBubba then?"

"Um, that's the southern version. It sounds like a prison term."

"Exactly, and I'm your prisoner."

Then he pronounces it's time to leave, because if we don't, he might bend me over the appetizer table and make a terrible scene over the shrimp cocktail.

"We have to wait to leave at least until your grandparents do."

"Oh, hell no. Grand won't leave until two in the morning. I'm not waiting that long." He's adamant about it.

"Seriously?"

"She's quite the party animal."

"I can't leave without saying goodbye."

"Yes, you can. We'll call them tomorrow. Besides, we're going there for Christmas."

That's right. And I haven't bought anyone any gifts, because of my short funds. Shit!

"Okay, let's go."

By the time we get back to Prescott's, my thong is in two pieces and tucked into his suit coat pocket, like a silk scarf. It's a good thing they're pretty and lace. I didn't wear a bra because of the cut of the dress, so I have nothing else on other than my dress and shoes. When we get inside, he unzips me, drops the straps, and the dress slides off. I stand before him in black pumps.

"Hmm. What to do with this." He circles me like a panther, slow and steady, ready to claim its prey. My breath hitches in my throat as my belly tightens and an ache grows within my core. I already feel heavy and in need of a release. Soon. My hand moves between my thighs, and he stops it.

"Remember? Mine. Every single bit. Do not touch."

"I need —"

A deep chuckle rumbles out of him. "I know exactly what you need."

He takes my hand and walks me to the bedroom. Then he pushes me onto the bed. He takes off his tie and binds my wrists with it, asking if my arm is okay. It's fine, I tell him. All I'm interested in is him.

He strips and now we're two naked people needing each other. When I think he's going to fuck me, I'm wrong. He leaves. Then he comes back with another tie and wraps it around my head, using it as a blindfold. Good thing he has lots of ties. Now I'm in the dark, anticipating his next move.

He spreads my legs and tells me to keep them open wide. First I feel something cool, lube maybe? Then he rubs me all over, everywhere, in and out. His fingers massage me, coaxing me close to orgasm number one. Then he stops. He pinches my nipples, sucking hard, until I'm moaning — loud. Soon his mouth moves to my inner thighs, sucking and biting again. I'm already marked from earlier today, so he's only adding to the collection.

I'm not prepared at all for the first blow. He slaps my clit so hard it stings like fire. I don't know if he uses his hand or a belt, but I scream. Then he licks me and right before I come, he stops and repeats the entire process again. This time when he slaps me, he does it again and again until I come, screeching and suddenly it feels like I'm being iced, inside and out. Did he just shove an ice cube up my ass *and* pussy? I'm panting, trying to catch my breath, but I can't because he slams into me with his cock, tearing every last bit of oxygen out of me. My breathing is jagged as I grab onto nothing. My hands are tied, so I can't. I'm groaning in earnest now, so loud I can't hear anything but the sound of my own choppy breath. My pussy heats up from the friction and my clit feels raw until he flicks it hard and I cry out, not in pain but in pleasure. I'm getting ready to come again when he tells me not to.

"I have to."

"No." He stops, withholding it. Then he starts it all again, slowly building it up, until he slaps my clit hard, sending me off into waves of orgasmic pleasure. I'm so lost in the sensation, I don't even realize when he comes until he calls out my name. It brings me around and I feel his warmth explode inside of me. Then he pulls out and it's silent again.

I hear footsteps and then a warm cloth covering me, wiping me off. "Are you still comfortable?" he asks.

"Yeah."

"Good, because we've only just begun."

There's one thing I know for certain. This man likes to fuck, long and hard.

I'll need to get into shape just to keep up with him.

The room is silent for a while, until I hear footsteps again. I break out into goosebumps in anticipation. My heart beats a bit faster and my pulse races. He unties my hands and pulls me into an upright position. Then something is pressed to my lips and he says, "Drink." Cool water runs down my parched throat as I swallow. "More?" he asks. I nod and he gives me another long drink. I wasn't aware of how thirsty I was.

The glass is gone and replaced by his mouth. Warm lips tease mine, then travel over my mouth, tasting and exploring. He pushes his tongue through my lips and makes me forget everything else. If I weren't already sitting, my knees would buckle from the way he turns me into a boneless heap of flesh.

"Can you rest your weight on your arms?"

What? I'm trying to figure out his question when he flips me over and I'm on my hands and knees. "It wasn't a particularly difficult question."

"Oh, this."

"Yes. Lean forward on your arms and tell me if it's okay."

I try and my one arm causes me discomfort, so I tell him.

"Lie on your chest. Is that okay?"

"Yeah."

Suddenly, a huge mound of pillows is stuffed under my belly and hips until my butt is raised in the air and my thighs are spread wide. His mouth is on me once more, tongue drilling into me, making me squirm.

"Hold still," he says against me, and then he blows warm air on me. I'm still blindfolded, unsure of what's happening. But he stops and I hear something, though I'm unclear of what until something cool touches me and is inserted into my backside. I inch away, because it feels weird at first.

"Hold still. I'm stretching you."

"Stretching me?"

"Shh."

His finger moves around and I'm not quite sure what the hell he's doing but it feels better and better every second. He keeps playing back there and it's amazing. When he pulls out I beg for him not to, but he says, "Relax for me."

"Okay."

I feel something pressing against me. But this time it's not his finger. He inches in, stops, moves in a bit more, and stops again. Then he pushes through and at first there's a burn, then a flash of pain. But he's very still until everything passes in an instant. In the meantime, he's massaging my clit and I'm completely aroused by this.

"Vivi, how do you feel? Do you want me to stop?"

"N-no."

He begins to move faster, not much, just a little. Enough for me to feel the full impact of his erection. When he's seated all the way, he asks me again how I'm feeling and I tell him the truth. This is good. I feel stretched and full in a weird way, but it's good. Then he picks up a rhythm, not hard and fast like what he usually does, but super slow. His fingers find me again and massage my clit until I'm on the verge of having a mind-blowing climax.

"I'm going to come."

"That's the intention."

When I do, he moves just a fraction faster, holding my hips with both hands, fingers digging into my flesh. I wish I could see his face when he comes. But I can't. He groans out his own orgasm and as soon as his dick stops pulsating, he pulls out.

"I'll be right back after I get rid of this condom."

Condom? Maybe it's better for him that way? Or maybe less messy? I don't know. He returns and takes off my blindfold. He wears a sexy smile.

"Vivi, I thought your pussy was sweet, but damn if you don't have a sweet as hell ass too."

"Thank you, I think."

He half smiles, wipes me with a warm cloth, then tosses it on the floor. After he unties me, he wants to know if I'm thirsty.

"Yes, I'd love something to drink."

"Other than water?"

"No, water is fine."

He hands me a glass and I guzzle the thing down.

Then we're lying there, him holding me, when he asks, "Did you like it? And I want honesty."

"I did. It's not anything like I thought it would be."

He chuckles and his chest vibrates from it. "How did you think it would be?"

"Painful and … gross."

"It can hurt if not done properly." Then he laughs. "Gross, huh?"

"Ugh. I know." I put a pillow over my head. He rips it out of my hands.

"No hiding, Miss-I'll-Punch-Your-Face-In."

"Yeah, she was a bitch and deserved it. But butt love is a little weird."

Now he really lets out a booming laugh. "Butt love?"

"Well, yeah. That's a nice term for it. You were loving on my butt."

"True. And I'm in love with that butt of yours." He squeezes it for emphasis. "Would you be willing to do it again?"

"Sure, but I like it the other way, too."

"So do I. There isn't anything about you, Vivi, I don't love. Why do you think I was so relentless when I pursued you? Even when you just acted like you hated me."

Dropping my gaze to my fingers, I don't know what to say. "I never hated you, Prescott. Never. You were overbearing. Pushy. I didn't know how to take you. But hate is too strong a word. I feared how I'd react to you."

"Why? Why didn't you just go with it?"

Glancing up, I see him staring right at me. Our gazes connect. "Truth?"

He nods.

"I was so fragile. Still am. After Mom, and then the move here, I just couldn't chance getting hurt so soon after. I was afraid I'd fall for you. Back at Crestview, I had this … this thing for you. I used to fantasize that you were the guy who went after the fat girl."

"Shut up."

"It's true. I was overweight and extremely unhappy. The more unhappy I was, the more I ate. That whole vicious cycle thing. While all of you were off having a great time, having girlfriends and boyfriends, going to school dances and things, I was eating cookies and candy bars."

"I have a confession, too. I liked you back at Crestview. And more than just for my homework. But you were so shy. You never went to any school events. Or at least I never saw you at any." His hand brushes up and down my arm.

"I went, but hid. My mom dropped me off and picked me up, but I'd find a place to hide out until it was time to leave."

"Why?"

"Because I didn't want to be made fun of any more than I absolutely had to. You know, I had to go to school. There was no way to get out of that. But the school functions were optional. I wanted my mom to believe I was having fun. As soon as her car turned out of the parking lot, I'd run and hide."

"Where would you go?"

"Janitorial closets that were left unlocked, stairwells, bathrooms, there was always someplace."

He lifts up and braces himself on his elbow. His nostrils flare as he asks, "Stairwells? You hid in stairwells? You could've been … those are dangerous places."

"It was Crestview, remember?"

"What if those girls had found you? Did you ever think of that?"

Actually, I hadn't. "They would've done terrible things to me. Probably ripped off my clothes and made me walk home naked or something."

He lies back down and I put my head in his chest, making a circle with my finger.

He's silent for so long, I lift my head up to peek at him.

"I feel terrible for not doing anything," he says.

"You weren't even aware."

"But the administration knew, didn't they?"

"Yeah."

One corner of his mouth turns up.

"Why are you smiling?"

"Whitworth gives a lot of money to Crestview every year. I'm going to stop their flow. I believe the same principal is still there. When they reach out to me, I'm going to tell them I can't donate to schools that condone bullying."

"You'd do that?"

"Of course I would. My God, Vivi, you were treated terribly there and the only reason they did nothing was because those nasty girls had money. Well, I have more money, a lot more, and they're going to feel it where it counts."

Oh my God, this man. Was he always like this? How did it take me so long to realize it?

"I swear, Vivi, nobody will ever bully you again if I can help it."

His expression is so vicious, I'm almost afraid of him myself.

CHAPTER 33

PRESCOTT

MONDAY MORNING, THE FIRST THING I ASK LYNN TO DO IS notify Crestview that Whitworth is pulling all of its funding and grants in the future. This amounts to several million dollars annually. In fact, Whitworth is the biggest benefactor that Crestview has.

"Why are you doing this? Whitworth has donated money for years, ever since you went there, I believe," Lynn says.

"It's a long story, but the short of it is Vivi was bullied while she was a student there. The administration was fully aware of it and chose not to act."

"Well. That would cause me to pull my funding, too."

"When they call to talk to me, put them through if I'm here. I'll be glad to explain."

Then I fill her in on the bathroom incident.

"What the hell, Prescott?"

She asks who they were and I can't tell her, because I don't know, which is frustrating as hell.

"I can get you HR records of all females we employ between the ages of twenty-five and thirty. You can check out their pictures if you'd like."

"Was there an RSVP list for the party?" I ask.

She snaps her fingers. "Yes, there was. Let me check with our events department head and I'll get back to you."

Granddad drops by to tell me how much Grand likes Vivi and that they are looking forward to having us out on Christmas. That reminds me I need to shop for Vivi's present, which I haven't done yet.

I give Eric a call and check with him on a gift. He suggests jewelry, which was what I was thinking. But she needs a new coat. She's always freezing and hers is so thin. Maybe she'd accept one from me now.

Today isn't a good day to go shopping, because I have back-to-back meetings scheduled at work. But I decide that tomorrow, I'll go.

Lynn comes into my office around lunch with everything I need for my afternoon meetings. She tells me she has the RSVP list and has cross-referenced it with all single female employees between the ages of twenty-four and thirty. There were thirty-two who attended the party that night. This shouldn't take long.

"Your lunch is on the way, too."

"Thank you. Where would you like to go on vacation this year?"

"Antigua," she says.

"Just tell me the dates and pick the hotel. I'll get it scheduled for you."

"Thank you, Prescott."

"Thank you. For everything you do, Lynn. You're the best admin in the world. Oh, and get a decent replacement for you while you're gone. Preferably someone who doesn't want to date me, like that last girl you found."

"Oooh, I know. She lied and said she was married. I'll get you a middle-aged woman this year."

"Or a man even," I suggest.

"He may be gay. You never know."

"Yeah, true. I just want someone who will work and not try

to sneak in here and stare at me. I had to lock the door every time I came in here. It got so bad, I had Granddad call me on the way down and told him a secret knock. We had to change it every time so she wouldn't catch on."

Lynn laughs at me, because she finds it hilarious. It wasn't. The girl was creepy.

It doesn't take long to go through the names and HR files of the women, before I find the ones who attacked Vivi in the bathroom.

"Now what to do?"

"Fire them," she says.

"Can't do that. They claim Vivi struck first. Then I'd have to fire Vivi, too. Not to mention, it's four against one."

"Ouch. That's not good."

"No, but I won't condone bullying either. I may send out a company letter stating our policy on bullying and that it won't be tolerated at all. Maybe it will scare them."

"What does Vivi say?"

Rubbing my face, I groan. "She wants to drop it. Let it go."

"Then do it. She got the prize anyway."

"Not really. I did."

Lynn laughs. "Then you have your answer. The two of you should march on into the sunset, holding hands. Forget about them. You know who they are and be careful from now on."

"True, and they aren't in IT, so it's unlikely she'll cross paths with them. I'll tell her who they are just in case."

Lynn orders me to eat lunch and reminds me I don't have much time until my busy afternoon is upon me. The day flies by, as it usually does, when I barely have time to breathe. When I make it back to my office, it's already dark, but I have a few things to take care of before I leave. I text Vivi and ask her if she's interested in getting dinner. She hits me back telling me she's at work. Dammit, I keep forgetting she has that commitment to The Meeting Place.

Leaving work, I head home for a quick hour on the treadmill, and afterward I change and drop by to see my girl.

She's busy mixing up some kind of red drink, so when I take a seat in front of her at the bar, she doesn't notice. When she pours the drink and sticks an orange slice on the rim of the glass, she finally looks up right into my eyes.

"Hey, sexy bartender. Got a drink for a thirsty guy?"

"Sure do. What's your pleasure?"

"Can't say in public, but I'll take a Weller on the rocks, please."

"Coming right up."

The crowd isn't heavy, so she has time to talk. I tell her about finding out who the women are and that they don't work in IT, which pleases her. I also let her know my grandparents are excited about seeing us on Christmas.

"What can I bring?" she asks. "I'd like to take them a little something."

"Granddad loves scotch and ties. And Grand, maybe something girly. A handbag?"

"Jeez, I don't know her taste. Forget it, I'll come up with something."

"Men suck at this, don't they?"

"Yeah. I'll figure something out," she says.

I touch her wrist. "Are you going to tell me how the two of you became so chummy?"

She flaps her hand back and forth. "It was nothing really." Then she laughs. "She threatened that if I hurt you she'd destroy me. But I get it. You're her number one. She's awesome."

"Christ. I can't believe she did that."

"I can."

A couple drinks later, I tell Vivi the car will be waiting for her when she gets off work. But I ask her to stay with me. "In fact, I'd love it if you'd move in. Don't give me your answer, just think about it." I kiss her cheek and leave.

I'm asleep when she wakes me up, crawling into bed. I pull

her into the curve of my body, feeling her softness against me. Before I know what hit me, the room is lightening up from the rising sun.

Vivi sleeps soundly next to me and I don't want to disturb her. I have no idea what time it was when she got in. I sneak out of bed and take a shower. It's almost seven, so I leave her a note, telling her to call me when she wakes up. Then I'm off to work.

Lynn waits for me with coffee and breakfast, and notes that I look well rested. I am indeed.

"What's on the agenda today?"

"You have that meeting at nine with the investors on A Special Place, and then you're meeting with the resort group on the possibility of grabbing that property out in Tahoe."

"Excellent. What time?"

"That's at ten. Then afterward, you and Mr. Whitworth were going to look at that hotel in midtown."

"Right. Is the appointment set with their realtor?"

"It is. Mr. Whitworth has all the information."

"Thanks, Lynn. I'll get prepared then."

"Prescott, don't forget to go shopping for Christmas."

"I was doing that this afternoon. Wanna go with me?"

She checks her schedule and says she's able.

"I'll call you when Granddad and I are finished and we can meet some place."

The day runs smoother than expected. We end up making an offer on the resort in Tahoe, but passing on the hotel deal in midtown. Their financials are a disaster and the place is a shit hole. It would take too much to turn it around or even tear it down, but they won't budge on their price. So we walk.

Lynn is waiting for my call and I have her meet me at Saks. We arrive at approximately the same time. The first stop is the coat department.

"What do you think?" I ask. When I explain Vivi's coat situation, she agrees the two would be perfect. Then I ask for her help with Grand and she picks out a decent sweater. I have no fucking clue what a seventy something woman would wear, but this looks good, so I grab it.

"Shoes, boots, a handbag?" I ask.

"Eh, too personal. You need to know her taste. How about a fur coat? Does she have one?"

"Hell, I don't know. Probably."

"Get her another. Older people are always cold."

We go to the fur department and two sales people are more than eager to help us. Lynn picks out the size and then holds up three for me to choose from. I pick the sable one, which ends up being the most expensive. Who gives a fuck? Grand will like this.

The salesman starts running his mouth about how to care for it and store it and I cut him off. Don't have time for this crap.

"Just box it up and wrap it, please. If she doesn't take care of it properly, I'll buy her a new one next year."

"Y-yes, sir."

I turn back to Lynn. "Granddad?"

"Burberry. They are classic and I've noticed his coat has seen better days."

"He probably has twenty he won't wear," I say.

"Yeah, but the shabby one is a Burberry. Get him a new one of the same style."

"Damn, you're good."

She preens, but deserves the praise.

"Before we head over to the men's, what do you want? Pick out anything, Lynn, and I don't give a flying fuck about how much it costs. And don't argue with me."

She stares for a second, then heads to where the handbags are. I tell the fur guy I'll be back to pick up the box when we're done shopping here.

I catch up with Lynn and she's holding up two handbags. "One of these," she says. They're Gucci.

"Get them both. I don't care."

"You sure?" Her face is almost distorted by her scrunched up brows.

I give her one of my *you have got to be kidding* looks. It's not quite an eye roll, but almost.

"Okay." Then she claps her hands and I think she's going to jump up and click her heels in the air or something, but she doesn't. "Thank you. This is really sweet of you."

"What can I say? I'm a sweet guy."

"You're a great boss, but only because you're not drinking. It's Vivi, isn't it?"

"Yeah." In a word. I don't elaborate. I don't have to. She's smart enough to know.

We hit the men's department and she picks out the coat for Granddad and some other things, like a new sweater and some slippers. He loves slippers. Now we're done here.

We lug all that shit, with some help from a Saks employee, to the car, and then I ask her to go to Tiffany's with me.

"Hmm. What are you getting her?"

"Jewelry, of course."

"Not an engagement ring?"

"No."

She helps me pick out a diamond bracelet. I plan to replace the one she had to sell, but I'm trying to find the buyer first. I've been searching for him without her knowledge. In the meantime, I want her to have something really nice of her own.

While I'm there, I also pick up a necklace for her. I noticed the other night at the party she didn't wear any jewelry. I imagine it's because she doesn't own any. This is a timeless piece, something she can wear with anything. It's a series of flowers covered in diamonds. Lynn loves it, but I hope Vivi doesn't look up the price. She'll freak.

Once we're in the car headed back to Whitworth, I thank Lynn for all her help. "I owe you."

She pats my arm. "You paid me in Gucci bags. They're worth a month's rent."

"Still, you helped a lot. Let me buy you and your husband dinner. Wherever you want."

"We don't go out during the week."

"You know the deal. I'll have it delivered. Just text me what you want and I'll take care of it."

Lynn nods, saying, "Sure. Sounds great to me."

We drop her off and when I get the text, I order her dinner. Then I look around and am thankful the store wrapped all these gifts for me. I don't know how to wrap a present to save my life. When we get to my building, Kaz is on duty and helps me lug everything up to my apartment. I tip him and close the door behind him.

I hide Vivi's gifts in my safe that's located in the closet. She doesn't have the combination, so they'll be hidden from prying eyes, not that she'd search anyway.

About fifteen minutes later, I hear the front door opening and Vivi rushes in, holding out her arm. "Look!"

"No splint?" I ask.

"Yes! Only a brace for the next couple of weeks and I'll be done. And I have another surprise. I've been keeping it a secret, because I wanted to tell you when we had time to sit and talk, but I'm too excited to keep it to myself anymore."

She's smiling so broadly, I can't help but grin along with her. "What?"

"Let's sit. Do you have any wine chilled?"

"Always. Oh, and Gerard was here yesterday, so we have food for the week if you want." I go to the wine cooler and pull out a bottle of chardonnay. After I open it, I pour us both a glass.

"So?" I ask.

Her eyes sparkle as she tells me about the psychiatrist she's been seeing. She hasn't told me about it, because at first she didn't have a lot of faith that it would help. But now, after having several appointments, she's so relieved to be going.

"Oh my God, Prescott, this woman is amazing. She puts everything into perspective. My overeating when I was young.

How it ballooned when my dad died and how I masked those feelings with Mom. She's opening up so much stuff, making me really *think*, you know? And how I thought by staying at Crestview I was protecting Mom, but it was so stupid. I was hurting us both. Mom didn't get the best of me and I really got screwed out of my youth. But I don't resent it because it's all on me. And I own it."

Vivi is so animated as she continues to talk about the sessions she's had. She explains how the doctor tells her it's okay to be afraid, and how her therapy will include group sessions with other patients who have gone through similar experiences.

"I start those second week of the year. Apparently we share our experiences and learn from each other how to handle stressful situations that remind us of our attacks."

"Has anybody ever told you that you look like a ray of sunshine when you're happy?"

Her eyes widen at my question. "Wow, I wasn't aware of how poetic you could be."

"I wasn't either, actually."

We're suddenly kissing, like we can't get enough of each other, and maybe we can't. Is this too good to be true? Will it end abruptly, leaving me crippled and unable to function?

"What?"

She notices the change. "Nothing."

"Prescott, tell me."

"Is this real—you and me? It's so good, Vivi, it's scary."

"It's real. At least on my end it is."

"Mine, too. I just didn't know if you felt it, too."

Her throat bobs as she swallows. "I feel so much. Things I haven't felt before, didn't think were possible, and didn't think I ever would."

I pick up a chunk of her hair and rub it between my fingers. "It's hard to get through the day without calling or texting you every five minutes, just to see how you are. I feel like the biggest fucking pussy out there, but it's true."

"It's hard to sit here and not put my hands all over you."

Those are words I love to hear. So I ask, "What's stopping you?"

"I don't want to overstep—"

"Let me make something perfectly clear. There is no overstepping where you're concerned. Ever."

One second later, her hands are tearing off my shirt, only I'm wearing a tie and it's still knotted around my neck. It's so damn funny, seeing the frustrated expression on her face that I'm laughing as I brush her hands aside. Then I help her get me naked and then undress her too. I want to devour her skin, lick every inch of her until I've tasted it, then I want to eat her pussy and then fuck her until she's limp in my arms.

But first, she drops to her knees with a grin. When I see her gaze up at me, I say, "Put your mouth on my cock. Wrap your lips around me and suck."

Then I push back into her, slow, so she won't choke, but damn, I just want to go deep into her throat. Saliva drips out of the corners of her mouth, but she keeps taking me in. More and more with every thrust.

"So good. Yeah, suck hard, just like that." Tipping her head back, I tell her to relax, and I push in a little deeper. She hums and the vibrations are almost enough to make me come. She keeps it up exactly the way I love it and every muscle in my body is taut.

"I'm going to come, Vivi. Giving you a chance to let me pull out."

She sucks harder and hums more. That does it for me and I let loose in her mouth, pumping off my climax down her warm throat.

"Perfect. That's what you are. The perfect Little Wolf, even when you suck my dick."

"I thought the ending was a nice way to show my affection."

And it was. One of the best ways.

CHAPTER 34

VIVI

CHRISTMAS MORNING, I'M PRACTICALLY BURSTING WITH excitement to give Prescott his gift. It took me hours to decide, but in the end, I figured this was pretty ingenious. I invited his friends to spend New Year's with us. I took a chance and called Weston—whose number I got from Lynn—hoping he could help. He was more than happy to, along with his wife, Special. They called Harrison, who tried to get out of it saying something about one of his clients, but Weston told him he could break away for three days. So it's going to be the five of us, unless Harrison ends up bringing someone.

Then I asked Eric for a loan until my first paycheck, so I could buy Prescott some New York Ranger's tickets. He mentioned something about how much he loved hockey, so I thought taking him to a game would be cool.

Finally, I'm going to give him a personal Vivi massage. He'll get a little card, complete with any kind of massage he'd like, including the kinky type, if he chooses. I've purchased a red thong with white fur along the top and back, and a bra to match for the Christmas motif, along with some flavored oils. I'll look very festive when I give it to him. That should be lots of fun. The bad thing is we have to leave for his grandparents' early so he can't open that one until later.

As I'm thinking about this, we're sitting in bed when he gets up to bring me coffee. Only on the way back, he detours into his closet for a second and returns holding a couple of wrapped boxes in his hand. He hands me the coffee, sets the boxes on the bed, and darts back into the closet where he returns carrying two more giant boxes.

"Are we exchanging presents now?"

He wears a playful smile and nods his head vigorously, like a little kid would do.

"Oh, boo. Well, I'll open these, but for undisclosed reasons, I can only give you part of your gift today, and I'd like to give it to you later. The rest of it will come after Christmas."

He shrugs, saying, "That's fine. Go on, open one."

I set my coffee down and ask him which I should open first. He doesn't care, so I go for size.

"Is that an indication of something?" he asks.

"Yeah. You've spoiled me." I look pointedly where the subject of this conversation lies.

"You're a filthy Little Wolf."

I'm ripping into the thick wrapping paper as I comment back to him, "Only because you made me that way. I was as pure as the driven snow before you."

"That's probably true. But I love filthy Vivi. She's killer in bed and is amazing at sucking cock."

"Don't spread that around."

"Don't worry. I'm not a kiss and tell kind of guy. Besides, I own that, remember? Now open. The suspense is killing me."

I lift off the lid and there sits a gorgeous camel-colored coat. I lift it out and hold it up to me. It's soft, and the lining is slick and satiny. "This is gorgeous, Prescott. Thank you."

"You won't return this one, will you?"

I chuckle. "No. I'll definitely be keeping this."

"Damn good thing. Now I won't have to worry about you anymore, freezing that sweet little ass off. Okay, next box."

I smile, thinking about him worrying about me.

I open the next box and there sits the Canada goose coat. I immediately put it on. "I'm never taking this off."

"Oh, hell yes, you are. It would be way too hard to fuck with that thing on."

"Nah, look."

I stand up and do a demonstration of how we could make it work and he says, "Vivi, I'd have you sweating so much in that thing you'd have a heatstroke."

"Okay, you win."

"You have two more boxes."

"You've already given me too much."

He grabs my chin and kisses me. "You don't have a clue, Vivi Renard. I'd give you the fucking world, if you'd let me."

I grab his chin and kiss him back. "You don't know anything, Prescott Beckham. You already have."

"No, I haven't. It's only begun." Then he hands me another box. This one is considerably smaller. My fingers slide under the paper and unwrap it. When I pull it off, I see the blue Tiffany's box staring at me.

"What's in here?"

"You'll have to open it to find out."

And I do. It's a bracelet, a gorgeous diamond one. "Oh, Prescott. This is beautiful."

"Not even close to the one holding it."

I lean over to kiss him, then hold out my arm so he can put it on me. It's so pretty I can't stop admiring it. "Look at how it sparkles."

"Exactly like your eyes right now."

"You have to stop saying things like that. You'll give me a big head."

"Mmm, that's okay. You've given me big head a time or two so we're even."

"You're a real jokester." I elbow him in the ribs.

"One more—your last one."

I poke out my lip, not because it's my last present, but I feel inadequate with what I'm giving him.

"What? Did you want more?"

"No. I didn't get you enough."

"I didn't want you to get me anything. Having you here is more than enough for me." He pushes the box into my hands. "Go on."

When I open the thing, I find another blue Tiffany's box. He's out of his mind. But what I find inside confirms it.

"Oh my God, Prescott, what were you thinking?"

"That this would look lovely around your neck and this poor necklace needed an owner who'd make it look better. It was lonely in there, waiting for someone like you to wear it. So …" He spreads his hands wide and sits there like an eager boy waiting approval.

It's the most stunning piece of jewelry I've ever seen, even better than the things my dad gave my mom. Tears form in my eyes and I blink furiously, forcing them back. It doesn't work. I break down like a dork and cry helplessly in his arms.

"It is that bad?" he asks.

"No," I sniffle, "it's that good. It reminds me of my parents and the things Dad did for Mom. Thank you." I cling to Prescott like a big fat gooberhead, crying my eyes out. I'm sure he thinks he landed a whiny dweeb.

"Sorry I'm such a dork," I say after getting the tearfest under control.

"It's fine, and you're adorkable, so I don't mind."

"Adorkable? Thanks."

"That's being a dork in a very adorable manner."

"I sort of got that."

He wipes my face with his T-shirt. "Better now?"

I nod and he tells me to turn so he can put the necklace on.

"Okay, go look."

"Come with me." I grab his hand and he follows me into the bathroom. My hand reaches for the necklace, lightly fingering the diamonds. The piece of jewelry is a work of art with gems woven into each of the flowers, and I tell him.

"You make it perfect, Vivi. It was created for you."

I wrap my arms round his neck and look into his eyes. "I can't believe I wasted so much time avoiding you."

"Eh, we have a lot of make-up sex to do. It's going to be great."

"It already is."

Then he squeezes my ass. "I hate to break this to you, but we need to get a move on. Grand is eager to see us, though I think more so you."

We shower and dress, although we do take some time for a short shower fuck. We've decided it's impossible for us not to do that when we're in there together. While I'm finishing getting dressed, he calls for his car to be brought out. He's driving today since his driver has the day off.

"I've never even asked if you own a car," I say, on the way down in the elevator.

"I do, but I don't drive much in the city."

We walk out and there's a black fancy Mercedes waiting on us. It must be the top of the line because it has every bell and whistle imaginable. Not knowing a whole lot about cars, all I know is the dashboard looks like something you'd see on a space-ship. The seats are the most comfortable things ever that I could instantly take a nap if we were going on a road trip.

"Nice wheels," I casually mention.

"You want one?"

"One what?"

"A car like this?" he asks.

Is he crazy? "No! What would I do with it?"

"Drive it around."

"Where?"

He shrugs. "Let me know if you change your mind."

"You're a nut."

On the way out to his grandparents, it starts to snow. "Look, Prescott. It's snowing on Christmas Day."

"It's nice, yeah?"

"Super nice. I've never had a white Christmas before." I think about how Dad would promise one every year and then I'd wake up to nothing. He'd offer me a box of confectioner's sugar and tell me to sprinkle it on the grass. One year I tried it but ended up with a sticky mess. He laughed at me and I stuck my tongue out at him.

"What are you thinking about over there?"

I tell Prescott the story and he chuckles. "You would've needed a lot more than that little box."

"Yeah, well, I didn't know that."

By the time we get to the Whitworths', the ground is dusted in white powder. I'm way too excited for this little amount, but glad I'm wearing my new coat. Prescott helps me out of the car and we carry our gifts inside. When I asked him what he bought Grand, he wouldn't say. Whatever it is, it's in a gigantic box.

They greet us in the foyer with no amount of hugs to spare. Then we're ushered into a sitting room for warm cider, spiked coffee, or our beverage of choice. Soon, Prescott scurries me off for a tour of the large estate.

Room after room and my head swims. The upstairs is where all the bedrooms are located, six of them—each with their own elaborate bathroom—and then the main floor has a huge living area and several smaller sitting rooms, an office for Samuel, a sunroom, a massive kitchen, and dining room. It's simply an enormous mansion.

"Did you grow up in a house this large?" I ask.

"Yeah. It's not too far from here." His pupils shrink in size at my question.

"What is it?"

"Nothing. Just bad memories from last Christmas."

Taking hold of his hand, I say, "Sorry. I shouldn't have brought it up."

We walk back into the sitting room where the Whitworths wait for us.

"This Christmas will be much better than last, right?" Prescott says.

"Don't bring that up," Sara says.

"Son, have you given any thought to what you're going to do about the house?" Samuel asks.

"Yeah, I think I'll talk to him about it after the holidays."

I remain quiet during this, because it's not something I care to be involved in.

"How do you think he'll handle it?" Sara asks.

Prescott laughs bitterly. "Not too well." Then he glances at me and says, "My father won't be happy about the house he lives in. He still thinks it's his."

"Ouch."

"That about sums it up pretty accurately." Then he switches gears and suggests we exchange gifts. Sara thinks it's a great idea and so do I. Maybe it'll get his mind off his dad.

"Why don't you let Sara go first," I say.

"Great idea." He carries the boxes that are hers and hands her the small one first. It's the one from me. "These are from the two of us," he says.

She unwraps the first, and it's a blue printed silk scarf. The colors in it reminded me of her eyes. "Ooh, this is lovely. And you know, dear, scarves are an elderly woman's best friend." She holds it up to her neck to indicate why.

"That's not why I picked that one out for you. It reminded me of your eyes."

"Goodness, aren't you sweet," she says. She wraps it around her neck and says, "Yes, and see how it covers all the wrinkles?"

"You're crazy. It looks lovely on you," I say. And it does with her silvery white hair.

"Grand, open the next one. That great big one."

"I don't think I can lift it."

Prescott runs over to put it on her lap.

"Good Lord, what's in here? Bricks?"

"I hope not," he says.

She unwraps it and sees the Saks box. I wonder if he bought her a coat too.

When she pulls it out of the box, I nearly tumble out of my chair. It's a full-length, cream-colored fur coat.

"Well, my goodness, look at this, Sam. Prescott and Vivienne bought me a new fur coat."

Vivienne had nothing to do with that. That would cost me a year's salary. Well, maybe not, but damn.

Sara admires it and asks, "Is it mink?"

"Mink and sable, Grand."

"It's lovely. Thank you. I'll wear it often because you know how I absolutely freeze all the time."

"That's why we got it for you," Prescott says.

It is? Good to know.

She moves on to the last box, which turns out to be a sweater. What a letdown after the fur coat. Even I'm disappointed, and it's not my present.

Now it's Samuel's turn. I'm still stuck on the fur coat. I want to roll around on it. I wonder if she'd mind. Maybe I could borrow it for a day or something, just to sleep in.

I hand him the box I brought. It seems so insignificant now I'm almost ashamed to give it to him. But he smiles warmly and is so gracious as he accepts it.

When he opens it, Sara exclaims, "You must wear that when I wear my scarf, Samuel. It's so lovely."

It's a blue tie in a print that closely matches the scarf I gave her.

"Oh, it's wonderful, Vivi. Thank you. I have quite an addiction to ties."

"So I've heard. I'm glad you like it," I say.

Then he opens his gift from Prescott.

"Thank you, son. I needed a new coat. And Burberry is my favorite."

Must be the year of the coat. I wonder if Prescott needs another coat. He has that expensive cashmere dress coat. I used to envy him when he wore it into the coffee shop. Maybe he'd like another one.

"Isn't it, Vivi?"

"Sorry, what?"

"I was saying that Granddad's new coat looks very dapper on him."

"Oh, absolutely. You look like you stepped off the pages of a men's magazine."

He keeps on and on about his new slippers. He's really digging those. Does Prescott wear slippers or is that something older men prefer? I hate to say it, but I never paid attention. All I know is his feet are super sexy.

How do I know this? I've checked them out in the shower when I'm bent over holding my ankles as he's fucking me. Oh, shit. Why did I have to go there? Now I've done it. One thought and my sex has just fired up. Bam. Turn Vivi on, just like that. My clit nearly throbs and my pussy aches for his tongue and penis.

"Vivi? Did you hear Grand?"

"Oh, sorry." My face heats with the flush of desire and guilt for not paying attention to my surroundings and only my horniness. "What did you ask?"

"Grand wanted to know what I got you for Christmas."

"Oh!" An enormous grin takes over my expression and I show her my wrist, or more specifically, what's wrapped around it. "Prescott spoiled me. He was way too good to me this year."

Sara takes my arm to get a better look.

"It's quite beautiful, exactly like its new owner."

"Thank you, ma'am. What a kind thing to say."

"Vivi, did you wear the necklace?"

"Goodness, no. I'm afraid I'll lose it."

"That's what insurance is for," Prescott says. "Wear it."

"But it's so … diamondy."

His grandmother speaks up, "Tell me about it."

I describe it down to the last detail and she agrees it may be too fancy for everyday wear.

"Fine. But when you do wear it, I don't want you to be afraid of losing it."

That'll happen when pigs fly.

"Oh, but, Sara, he also got me the coat I wore today and a Canada goose coat, because I'm always cold, too."

"Wonderful. It's nice to know my grandson is so thoughtful."

"He's very thoughtful," I say, smiling at the subject of our discussion.

"Sam, get Vivienne her present," Sara says.

Sam hands me a small box. I'm pretty sure it's jewelry. I open it and inside is a gorgeous necklace, not a fancy one like Prescott bought me, but a simple chain and pendant. It appears to be silver, but knowing the Whitworths, I'd imagine it's platinum.

"How pretty. Thank you."

Prescott puts it on me and I move in front of a mirror to see how it looks. Then I run to hug each of them, because I didn't expect anything like this.

"It looks lovely on you, dear," Sara says.

Then they hand Prescott an envelope. I'm sure it's money or stocks or something. He sticks it in his pocket after he thanks them profusely and hugs both of them.

Not much later, the doorbell rings, and Sara claps her hands. "Oh, good, that will be Melinda and Robert. They're on time for a change."

Melinda is related to Prescott on Sara's side. Sara had a cousin who passed and it's her daughter. She usually comes for Christmas dinner every year. She was present for the debacle last year. Prescott is fond of Melinda and Robert. They're older, in their forties, and live farther out than here, so he doesn't see them often.

After all the introductions are made, we sit around and talk before an impressive dinner is served. Sara laughs when I compliment her on the wonderful meal. "Oh, darling, you must tell my lovely cook, Letty, who's been with us for years now. Bless her, she came in today because you really wouldn't want to eat my cooking."

Prescott laughs. "Oh, I don't know. Those hot dogs you made last year were pretty darn good." They fill me in on the meal they ate after his dad acted like an ass.

"Well, I love hot dogs."

Sara leans forward conspiratorially. "I do too, but don't tell anyone." Then she winks. I laugh at her.

"Grand can't cook, so don't ever let her try to fool you. One time she tried to make me a peanut butter and jelly sandwich. I almost choked to death," Prescott says.

"You too?" Melinda asks. "I thought I was gonna die. There was so much peanut butter on the thing it got jammed in my throat. I didn't know what to do."

"Exactly! I'd taken a huge bite and you know how peanut butter is. It was all gobbed up in my mouth, so I couldn't spit it out. A nightmare. Never again."

"Thank you. I did that intentionally so you two would never ask me to make a lunch for you again."

I'm sitting and observing the exchange. Sara is in heaven. She adores these two and loves to be the center of their attention.

"Prescott, I can't wait for you and Vivi to have kids. I'll make that child one, too."

Whoa. Again? She's sure set on us having children. Has Prescott shared something with her? My eyes dart to him and his are glued to me. A smile tugs at the corners of his mouth like he actually enjoys this idea. Maybe I do too, but I don't know if I can admit it quite yet.

After dinner, we all decide we're not quite ready for dessert, so we go and sit in the large living room where a huge fire is burning. The snow has continued to fall all day and by now there's a fair amount on the ground. I peek out the window and gaze at it longingly.

"Want to go out and play?" Prescott asks.

"I don't know. I don't really have any boots."

"Grand does. She'll let you borrow some."

When I'm appropriately dressed in Hunter Boots and a warm weatherproof jacket, Prescott and I go out for a romp in the snow. He takes me out back where the gardens are in the summer and we hold hands as he explains where Sara's different flowers are.

"In the winter she spends time in the city, but when the spring hits, you can find her right here, on her knees, digging in the dirt."

"Really?"

"Yes, and her flowers are unreal. I can't wait to show you. She'll have to tell you what she plants because I'm not good with flower names. But she sets it up so there's always something in bloom. You'll love it."

We're about to head back in when he bends down and throws snow in my face. It escalates into a war, but I'm no good at making snowballs, so I jump on him instead. We both fall to the ground, me on top, and it ends up in a kissing session.

"I like snowy Vivi."

"Mmm, so do I. This is fun."

"I'll have to take you ice skating," he says.

"I've never been. Is it fun?" I ask.

"Yeah, if you don't fall too much."

"Are you any good?"

He waggles his brows. "I can hold my own, though I'd never score a goal."

"Could you prevent me from falling?"

"Sure, if you don't do anything wild."

I brush his hair back. "No, just a plain old-fashioned fall."

"Hmm, maybe I want you to fall. Hard."

"What do you mean?"

"For me."

Grabbing his bottom lip with my teeth, I say, "Already have."

After I let it go, he says, "Good, because you know I've fallen for you, too. I'm so in love with you, Vivi Renard."

CHAPTER 35

PRESCOTT

I HADN'T PLANNED ON TELLING HER AGAIN, BUT IT WAS AS good a time as any. The smile I received in return was worth every word.

"I'm in love with you, too," she says. Then she gives me a loud smacking kiss and giggles like hell. It's the first time she's actually said the words and not just insinuated them, and I feel like I've been sucker-punched. It takes me a moment to recover.

"I think they heard that all the way inside."

"Great. That was my plan."

"I guess we should go back in."

Vivi gives me a huge smile. "Guess we should. I need to tell Sara I'm in love with her grandson."

"You do that." I can't wipe the smile off my face.

I help her up and brush the snow off her. Then we walk back holding hands. What a weird thing to do. I've always hated this kind of crap and now it's all I want to do.

We eat our desserts sitting around the fire and soon after, Melinda and Robert take off for home. We promise to get together soon.

Grand and Vivi sit close and chat. I hear something about

flowers. Vivi's probably asking about the gardens. Granddad and I discuss a little business and suddenly there's a loud commotion at the front door. I look up to see my father rushing into the room, shouting. What the hell is he doing here?

"Isn't this a cozy sight?" he snarls. "I know what you're up to. Isn't it enough that you kicked me out of the company? But now you're planning on kicking me out of my own home—the home I raised you in? The home your mother and I shared. Prescott, I don't know what's gotten into you, but is this a way to repay the man who raised you, who made all kinds of sacrifices for you?"

I sit, rigid as stone, mentally ticking off the things he just said to make sure I heard them correctly. Then I take a few deep breaths to get my thoughts lined up.

"You must be delusional," I begin. "First off, the house isn't yours and it never was. Second, you were kicked out of the company because of your own poor decision-making. Third, you do know what's gotten into me. It's that lying wife of yours. If you'd bother to fact check, you might figure a lot out. Why don't you start with the pool boy down in West Palm?" I shake my head in disgust. "And finally, these fine people in here raised me, not you. They're the ones who did the sacrificing, not you. I have nothing further to say to you. Leave now." By the end, my voice is booming.

He glares at me. "You're nothing but—"

"Yeah, I know. A disappointment. You want to know something? You're a bigger disappointment as a father and quite frankly you make me sick. You let my mother down. You verbally abused her. You knew she was depressed, you knew she needed help, and you did nothing, and for that I hold you personally responsible for her death. You knew you weren't my biological father and yet you did nothing. You sat there and watched her spiral toward her demise all because you wanted to benefit financially. Doesn't that make you a big man? Aren't you proud of yourself? I was going to wait until after the holidays to discuss this with you, but now that you're here, you should plan on vacating *my* house by next week. Now get out of here."

Evil spews from his eyes as he raises a fist. "You'll regret this one day. Mark my words."

"I seriously doubt it."

He storms out and I stare at the empty space in front of me. Then a vision fills that space. Vivi kneels before me. "Are you okay?"

I lift her off her knees and pull her into my arms. "I am now. Your face, your presence is what I need."

Her arms wind around me. "I'm yours. Always."

It's not really the place or time, but I don't give a damn. Grabbing her cheeks, I kiss her. Then I hear Granddad clear his throat and Vivi pulls away, nervous laughter bubbling out of her.

Grand claps her hands. "It's so nice to see such a happy ending to a bad interruption. But, Scotty, are you really going to force him to move out so soon? You know he can drag his feet if he wants to. You might be in for a battle."

"I do know, and I was talking off the top of my pissed-off head. I really don't care when he moves out. I'm selling the place anyway. I'd never live there with the memories I have."

Vivi squeezes my arm, giving me her support.

"He could claim squatter's rights or something equally ridiculous," Grand says.

I blow that one away. "He won't because I'd sue and he won't want his name dragged through the mud or the press."

Vivi sits up straight and makes a suggestion. "If you hate the house, why don't you make him an offer to buy it?"

That idea never crossed my mind. It could be an option if he'd talk to me about it. "That sounds good in theory. The only issue I see is he already considers the house his. But I'll try."

Granddad wants to know if I'm prepared to go to legal battle with him.

"If that's what it takes. I'm confident I can win."

He agrees.

Then Grand says, "Maybe I need to pay a call on Ms. Plastic Surgery."

Vivi busts out laughing. "What did you just say?"

"Have I not told you about her?" I ask.

"No, you've only told me about the Christmas dinner. Or at least that's all I recall."

Granddad launches into his version of her balloon lips and he embellishes it of course. "The thing is, she wasn't bad looking before, but you ought to see her now. It's downright scary. I told Sara after the last procedure she looked like a clown. And her bosoms look like they're aimed in the wrong direction."

"That's right, dear. The left veers left, and the right veers right. We don't know if it's because her surgeon was bad or she insisted on such large implants," Grand explains. But Vivi is giggling so hard she's bouncing all over my lap. The image Grand is describing is dead-on, though.

"Vivi, she's not exaggerating. You wouldn't believe her boobs. And she usually wears low cut tops, so you can't help but stare. But it's all for the wrong reasons. They're so abnormal looking."

Vivi finally takes a breath. "Oh my God. The part when you said how the right veers right totally got me."

"You need to come with me over there so you can see for yourself. You'll never be the same again. Isn't it true, Grand?"

"He's right. She could set her wineglass between them, walk around the block, and wouldn't spill a drop!" Grand says.

Vivi snorts so loud at that we all end up laughing.

After the topic of step-cunt's boobs die down, I decide we better get back to the city. It takes about a half hour to leave, with all the goodbyes, but we finally get on the road. Traffic is light this Christmas night, and Vivi watches the snow falling as we drive. Other than the Dad incident, I can say this has been my best Christmas ever.

When we get home, Vivi says she has a surprise for me. I'm to go into the bedroom and wait on the bed. About ten minutes later she comes in wearing a robe and hands me a little box.

344

"Merry Christmas."

I open the box and inside are two tickets to the Rangers game.

"This is fantastic. I love the Rangers."

"I remembered." She grins. "Oh, here."

She hands me an envelope. Inside is a card that says, "Welcome to Vivi's Massage Parlor, where she will fulfill any fantasy you may have." I look up and she's no longer wearing the robe. Instead, she has on a matching bra and thong. They're deep red, but they have bits of fur trim in sexy places. And damn, the woman is hot.

"Your wish, my command, sir."

Fuck me. My dick turned to stone the minute she got rid of the robe.

"Christ, Vivi, you're killing me."

"I don't plan on doing that. Only pleasing you. So why don't you take off your clothes."

"I have a better idea. Take them off me yourself. Start with my pants. I want you to unzip me with your teeth."

She grants me a naughty grin and unbuttons my fly, then bends down. Capturing the tab of my zipper, she puts it between her teeth and tugs. As soon as the thing hits bottom, my cock springs free. I want to shout, "Glory-fucking-hallelujah," but I groan instead because my cock is already in her mouth. She goes down on me like a fine-tuned machine, taking me deep and hard. I do my best to hold back, but it's impossible seeing her in that little Christmas getup.

"Fuck, Vivi, I'm coming." She looks up at me with my dick in her mouth, those lips tight around it, and sucks me dry. She licks her way to my mouth where she traps me in a searing kiss. Vivi's the first woman I could spend hours kissing. Her plump lips are so delicious, it's hard to stop once we start. I nip at them, sinking my teeth into her soft flesh. When she moans, it makes my limp dick come back to life.

She tugs my pants off then her mouth drops back down to

my balls where she licks and sucks. Nothing is left untouched. By the time she moves to my inner thighs, I'm hard as a rock again and writhing on the sheets. I've always known the inner thigh is an erogenous zone, but no one has ever done this to me. She moves to where my thighs join my pelvis and sucks and bites me there. I almost come unhinged. Her hand grabs my balls again and finds that spot, the ridge behind them, and presses down. This woman clearly controls me now. Her finger presses harder and slides around. Then her head dips back down and she licks me, tonguing and sucking my balls, circling and pressing that ridge, never touching my dick. I've never come this way before, but I think this is going to be a first. Her mouth is relentless until my back arches and I growl out an orgasm. My hand reaches for my dick, but her voice stops me.

"Mine." Her hand finishes off the job, pumping me, milking me dry. There wasn't much left in there, but now, I'm a limp soldier.

"Don't move."

"Couldn't if I tried." She leaves, only to return with a warm cloth to wipe me clean. Then she brings me some ice water.

"Mmm, that was … different," I say.

"You didn't like?"

"I loved it. I've never done that before."

"Good." She smiles. "Now roll on your stomach."

"Yes, ma'am."

After I flip over, I don't hear anything. But soon, she straddles me, and I hear the sound of a bottle opening. Then something drips on my back.

"Hmm. A massage." Her hands work the oil into my muscles and she rubs the kinks out of my shoulders and neck before moving down my back. She's not bad for someone who isn't a professional. She works her fingers into my muscles and it's so relaxing. Even my ass cheeks are getting their share.

When I feel her dripping oil into the crack of my ass, I have a feeling things are about to get kinky. And I'm right. Those fingers of hers are everywhere—on my balls and feeling my ass. When she slides a finger inside me, I lift up.

"You need to rub me off if you're going to do that."

"No, not if I want you to fuck me."

"Hmm. What happened to my wish and command?"

"You've already had two and I need at least one."

"I'll give you one." And in one smooth motion, I flip over and tell her to sit on my face. She complies.

But when she starts to suck my dick, there's just too much going on for her to continue. She stops and says, "I can't concentrate on this if you're doing that." She pulls away and tries to move forward so she can sit on my cock.

"Not yet," I say. I go back to licking and tasting her pussy. She seats herself on me and lets me have my turn. I tease her clit until she rides my tongue to her own ecstasy. Watching and tasting her gets my dick stirred to life again, so I have her straddle me next and ride me reverse pony style.

"Oh, what a great view. I love watching your ass when I fuck you. And I get to play with it too." I grab her bottle of oil and have my fun with it. From the sounds of things, she's enjoying the hell out of it. I can't see her face, but the way her hips are flexing makes me believe I'm hitting all her spots. Then her inner muscles clench my dick, and that sets me off again. She plops down, face forward, on my thighs, and lets out a long sigh.

"That was fun."

"I hate to tell you, but I think I ruined your little Christmas thong. The fur is a bit oily now."

She laughs. "I probably should've taken it off."

"Hell no. I'll buy you fifty more. It was too great to see you in it. I like the way that fur teases the top of your crack."

"That's why I bought it. Just for you."

I pull her on top of me and kiss her sexy mouth. "You have a mouth made for two things. Kissing and sucking my dick. Oh, and licking my balls. Where the hell did you learn that move you did?"

"You liked? I read about it online. It was on this blog I found."

Grabbing her ass, I tell her I loved it. Then I roll on top of her. "I love you, Vivi. I don't even know a way to tell you how much."

"You've shown me, which means more than words."

"I'm sorry you thought I was such a dickface at first."

"Me too. Look at all the time we wasted. But we're here now, so we need to forget about all that."

"I want to do something special, just the two of us, for New Year's. Maybe fly to the islands or something."

But she looks mortified at my suggestion.

"What is it? You don't like to fly?" I ask.

"No! That's not it at all. I, uh, it's just that I have a surprise for you that involves New Year's, so we can't go."

"Hmm. A surprise, huh? Okay, we can go another time."

"I have an idea. How about a shower? You and I are sufficiently oily enough to warrant one."

"Have you seen the bed? It looks like we swam in the stuff."

She takes a good look around and announces that we need to change the sheets. I have to agree with her. We put them in the washer before getting in the shower. As usual, the shower session turns into a sexcapade, where the hot water turns cold by the time we're done.

As we're getting out, I say, "Merry Christmas, Little Wolf."

"Merry Christmas to you, too."

CHAPTER 36

VIVI

IT'S TRICKY GETTING EVERYONE HERE FOR NEW YEAR'S without Prescott's knowledge. Weston handles most of it, but I drag Prescott out of the apartment that day, telling him I'm dying to see a movie. Of course it's a chick flick, one he has no interest in. Only I know he'll go, because at this point he'd walk on hot coals for me and I'd do the same for him. For example, for the week in January when Joe Delvecchio's trial will be, he said he'd clear his entire schedule just to be with me. It's not necessary because I'm stronger now than I've ever been. But it's nice knowing he's got my back.

We go to the movie and I have to pretend it's awesome, when it's awful. I hide my yawns and keep checking the time on my phone. Thankfully, we got popcorn, so at least I have that to enjoy. The timing is perfect, though. When the movie gets out, unless something happened, they should all be there, waiting on us when we get home.

On the way there, I suggest stopping at one of the liquor stores for some champagne. It's a decoy because I had the house-keeper load up when she did the weekly shopping earlier this week. We have tons of stuff for snacks too. Good thing Prescott doesn't pay attention to what's in his refrigerator.

We walk in the door and it's quiet, but I told them all to wait upstairs, and then to come down after we're home for a few minutes. We go into the kitchen to put the champagne up to chill and I ask him if he wants some water. As we're standing there, they all run down the steps, yelling "Happy New Year!"

Prescott nearly falls on the floor and I crack up.

"What the fuck? You almost gave me a heart attack!"

I bend over him since he's resting on his knees. "Merry late Christmas."

"This was your surprise?" he asks.

"Yeah. I wanted you to spend New Year's with all your friends, and me too."

He stands up and wraps his arms around me. "You're the best." Then he kisses me. They all clap.

Weston walks up first and we talk and then Harrison.

He starts with, "I can't believe you're the same Vivienne Renard."

"Yeah. No more fat girl, huh?"

"Damn. You sure got better while the rest of us suck."

"Hey, I don't think this guy does." I pull Prescott close to me. "He's pretty damn special in my eyes." Then everyone laughs.

Weston breaks in saying, "Speaking of Special." And he introduces me to his wife. We talk for a little while the men do their guy thing. I immediately like her. She's a no-nonsense kind of girl, but friendly to the point where I feel like I've known her forever.

"Prescott is something else. Remind me to tell you about the time I met him last New Year's Eve."

"I will."

The guys shout about something, and then they try to one up each other. Special shrugs when I look at her.

"Be prepared. The next couple of days will be like this. All I can say is I'm damn glad I'm not the only woman anymore."

"Harrison doesn't date?"

"Weston and I think he's seeing someone, only he's being totally tight-lipped about it."

"I see. Intriguing. Well, come on. Let's get some appetizers out. If they start drinking, we need food to soak up the alcohol."

The night goes on and everyone has a great time. Special and I let the guys catch up, but every now and then I catch Prescott eyeing me. He doesn't drink as much as the others and they comment on it. Then they say something else.

"Hey, Scotty, where's your bowl?" Harrison asks.

"In the bedroom, why?"

Harrison says, "Aren't you puffing on the weed anymore?"

"I haven't smoked much lately. Well, not since Vivi and I have been together."

"Well, fuck me. That's a first," Weston says.

So Prescott was a weed smoker. I'll be damned. I never knew. Not that it matters, but it does surprise me.

Special nudges me. "He must really care for you. He's completely different from the last time I saw him."

"You can say it's mutual."

She smiles broadly. "I'm so happy for you two. I hope it all works out."

"Thanks. That means a lot. I made him work for it, though."

The remainder of the night flies by in a blur and we ring in the New Year by watching the ball drop. The next morning everybody trickles into the kitchen, one by one, for coffee and juice. I volunteer to make breakfast, but Special steps up to help. She's the real cook in the house.

"I didn't invite you all up for you to cook. Now sit."

"Hey, it's what I do, Vivi."

The two of us put together a huge breakfast and the rest of the meals are eaten out. The group leaves the following morning and we promise to get together again real soon.

After they're gone, Prescott and I collapse onto the couch for a day of lazy TV.

"Best gift ever, Vivi. You don't know how much that meant, getting together with all of them at the same time. And you seemed to hit it off with Special."

"I really love her. She's awesome."

"You ought to meet her adopted son, Cody. He's a cutie."

"She told me stories about him and he sounds like a little charmer. I can't wait to go down to Atlanta and visit them."

We're lying on the couch where Prescott lifts up to one elbow. "I need to ask you something. I'm going to see my father about the house. It'll be very uncomfortable. Would you come with me? I totally get it if you don't want to."

"I'll be with you, one hundred percent. Just name the day."

"Tomorrow. I want to get this over with. I was going to do it this past week, but I didn't want to ruin our holidays."

The following afternoon, which is Sunday, we head out to Prescott's father's house around one. Prescott thought it would be best to take a couple of guys from the security team at Whitworth, just in case. This is more than a little scary for me. When I questioned him about it, he tried to allay my fears by explaining it was for witnesses in case his father tried to act out or do something crazy. But it sets me on edge, nonetheless. So here we are, headed out there, with two big burly guys in the front seat, as I clench Prescott's hand in the back.

"There's nothing to worry about, Vivi. Just think, you'll be getting a dose of the mega boobs too."

"You're not making me feel any better, you big goofball."

He throws his arm around me and pulls me into his side.

"You will. Have your camera ready for this train wreck."

Then I say, "Maybe you should call or give them a heads-up we're coming."

"That's the last thing I want to do. Catching him unprepared is for the best. Then he'll be defenseless."

"Was he always that mean?"

Prescott stares at the cars we speed past. "I was so busy acting out and trying to cause him as much trouble as I could, I honestly can't remember. He was always pissed at me, but I thought it was because of my shitty behavior. Now, after knowing what I know, maybe it wasn't. We probably just fed off each other. So toxic, you know? And then when I was a teenager —around fifteen, I think—I told him about why I didn't speak for all that time."

He talks about how he told his dad that he was afraid his mom couldn't breathe in the body bag and that she was suffocating, but no one could hear her. But his dad only looked at him and laughed. Basically let him know he was just a dumb kid.

I take his hand, only to show him how much I care. Any loving parent would've supported their son in that moment and not laughed at him.

"I'm sorry. It's too bad he couldn't see what beauty and love was in your heart."

Prescott is silent for the rest of the way to the house.

When we pull into the long drive, I admire the home when we finally make it there. It's a beautiful, sprawling brick mansion. Unlike the Whitworths', which is a white New England styled home, this one reminds me of something you'd see on a Virginia plantation. "This is really beautiful, Prescott."

"Yeah. Too bad my memories aren't."

I squeeze his hand.

"Ready?" he asks.

"Yep."

The four of us traipse to the front door and ring the bell. I'm shocked when the large-boobed woman answers. And nothing could've prepared me for those breasts. Sara was right about the misguided direction of each of them. They are the weirdest looking things ever. She wears a super low cut V-neck sweater that is way too tight for her. I almost feel like my eyes are spreading out, trying to focus. But the bad thing is I can't stop looking at them.

"Spectacular, aren't they?" she asks.

"Uh, well, they're really something, all right."

"You know, you could use some enhancing yourself." Our eyes are focused on each other's chests. If this were any other situation, it would be funny as hell.

Prescott nudges me as I yank myself out of the boobtrance I'm in. Holy hell.

"Jeanine, this is Vivienne. Is Dad home?" he asks brusquely.

She tips her head to look up at him and I finally get a good view of her face. Holy swollen lips. They look like two of those balloons the guy at the circus uses to twist up into wiener dogs.

What in the name of all fucks did his dad see in her?

She holds out her hand and says, "A pleasure." Her tone indicates the opposite along with her sneer. But I get the full shebang of her teeth with that sneer. They are so huge they look like dice. They have to be fake veneers. No one has teeth that big, not unless you're a horse. Is there anything real on this woman?

I do my best not to grimace as I take her hand and say, "Nice to meet you." This woman is a freak show. No one could've prepared me for this.

"Your dad is upstairs. I'll get him." She turns and walks up the massive staircase, sashaying her hips like we're at a striptease show.

When she's gone, Prescott lets out a chuckle. "Warned you, didn't I?"

"Not nearly enough preparation."

"Vivi, you have to get that look off your face. I almost cracked up when you saw her tits."

"Well, damn. Those things are an anomaly."

"In a word."

I peek at the security guys, and they stand there like statues. How do they manage it?

Miss Jug-A-Lug comes waltzing back down the steps and reports that Jeff will be down shortly. She aims her finger at Prescott. "You'd better not upset him. When he came back here on Christmas, I thought he was gonna have a heart attack. I was so worried about him."

"I'm sure." I'm surprised he doesn't add an eye roll. I have a hard time not doing it.

A few minutes later, Jeff appears. He's scowling. "What do you want?"

"I came to offer you a deal," Prescott says.

"What kind of a deal?"

"I'd like to sell this place to you for under market value. I had a soft appraisal done and ran some comps and you can have it for thirty percent less than what I can list it for. It's a damn good deal."

His dad laughs. "Is this a joke?"

"Not at all."

"Why would I want to buy this place when I can stay here without having to give you a penny?"

"I don't know why you believe that, but it's not true."

"I've consulted an attorney."

"So have I," Prescott says.

Jeff argues that he's set a precedent by living here all these years and that Samuel and Sara never forced him out. Prescott argues that they didn't because the two of them were on good terms. They go back and forth, and in the end, Prescott states that it will end up in court if he doesn't legally own the house.

"I'll push every button I have and with the fact that you are not even related to me, do you honestly think they'll award you this house?"

His father smiles smugly. "After I tell them how you've made multiple passes at my wife they will."

Now it gets interesting. I no longer observe Jeff, but switch my focus to Jeanine. She blinks rapidly, touches her nose a bunch, grabs her ear, and shifts from one foot to the other. Then she crosses her arms over her massive chest—no small feat indeed—and looks extremely uncomfortable. No doubt, she's covering up her lies.

"Go ahead. I'll subpoena the pool guys from West Palm. I have all their names and addresses. It won't work."

Now she's shrinking in her little spot where she stands. It's kind of hard to shrink balloon-sized lips and watermelon boobs, though.

"I never made a single pass at her and I don't give a fuck what she says." Prescott stands firm. "This offer is good for one week. If you don't take it by then, be prepared for an all-out legal battle. I won't lose. I. Never. Lose."

Then he grabs my hand and we head back out the door.

When we get outside, Jeff says, "I want a dollar figure on your offer."

"You'll have it tomorrow."

We climb into the car and drive off.

"He has to know she cheats. Her posture indicated she was a liar."

Prescott says, "He doesn't want to believe it. I think he likes the fact that she's young."

"But he's not that old. It's stupid on his part."

"To be honest, I really don't give a shit anymore. If he wants to spend his life with a woman like that, fine with me."

"Do you think he'll take your offer?"

"I do. He has the money. He's just cheap and trying to get around having to pay for it."

"Maybe if he cut back on Barbie's boobs, Ken would have a lot more money in his piggy bank."

He slaps his thigh and barks out a laugh. "I have to tell Grand that one. She never did care for Jeanine. I think the first time they met, Jeanine recommended her surgeon for Grand's crow's feet."

"Kind of like she did for enhancing my chest?"

"Yeah, and to that point, you'll never have anything done to your chest. It's perfect, just so we're clear."

"Thank you."

We drive back to the city and he tells the driver to drop us off at Rockefeller Plaza. I'm a little curious, but don't say so. When we arrive, we get out and the huge Christmas tree is still there.

"I meant to bring you here earlier, but time got away from me. I love it here," he says.

"It's so awesome." I crane my neck, up and up. The thing goes on forever. "Someday I want a tree of my own. I haven't had one in years."

"Next year, then. A large tree with lots of decorations. And you can fancy it up any way you like."

Taking the collar of his coat, I tug him close so I can give him a quick kiss. Afterward, he tells me to reach into his pocket for some gum. I dig inside and feel something in there. But it's not gum.

"What's that?"

"You'll have to pull it out to see."

When I do, I'm holding my mom's bracelet I sold a while back. I lift it up in front of my eyes in disbelief. "Where did you get this?"

"The strangest thing happened. I found it on the sidewalk the other day."

I smack his arm. "You did not."

Tucking a piece of my hair behind my ear, he tells me how he had an investigator looking for the buyer. He was able to track him through the website I sold it through. The man was pretty decent about it and negotiated a good price for him to buy it back.

I hug the piece of jewelry to my chest. "I don't believe you did this."

"I wanted you to have it. It holds sentimental value for you." And dang it, those silly tears start leaking from my stupid eyes.

His chest is the most convenient place to bury my face, so that's what I do. I talk gibberish until I stop crying, and then thank him profusely. "I promise to give you blow jobs forever for this."

"I'd rather fuck you, but blow jobs are good too." He laughs.

"How did I ever think you were an asshole?"

"Beats the hell out of me."

I look up into a face full of innocence. Then he gets that devilish look in his eye and I can't help but laugh at the big lug.

"Come on," he says.

"Where to?"

He doesn't answer, but ushers me into a cab and off we go. It takes us all the way down to Central Park where we get into a horse and carriage for a turn about the park.

"Aren't you the romantic?"

"I've got game, baby. But more importantly, I've got a woman."

"Yeah, you do."

"So, if you could take the ideal vacation, where would it be?" He wants to know.

"Oh, I don't know. The wine country in France?"

"Okay. Done. Let's go."

I look at him like he's insane. "Aren't you forgetting something?"

"Like what?"

"I have to start a new job tomorrow."

He waves his hand. "You're forgetting something. I own the company. You can take the time off."

"I won't be one of those employees."

He's so quiet, I think I've pissed him off for a second. Then he takes my hand and pulls it to his heart.

"Vivi, I love you. Beyond anything I ever imagined. Plain and simple. And I'm not a simple guy. In fact, I'm pretty fucking complex at times. But you manage to make life easy for me. Perspective, you know? What I'm hoping is that you'll be my perspective for life. Will you marry me?"

He reaches into his pocket and pulls out a ring. "I had this designed weeks ago. I've carried it around with me for the last week. Almost asked you on Christmas night. If you don't like it, we'll get you something else. The only thing that's important to me is your happiness."

I can't breathe.

Is it too soon?

I know I love him more than anything.

I think back to the time I wasted before and …

I blurt out, "Yes, I'll marry you. I don't care about the ring. It's you I want."

"But you haven't even looked at it."

When I do, I gasp. It's gorgeous. A large oval diamond, set in a flower, sort of like the necklace he gave me, but on a much simpler scale. In fact, you have to look closely to see that it actually is a flower. The petals are tiny yet they surround the diamond gracefully, creating an elegant setting. It almost looks like the diamond is blooming out of them.

"This is so beautiful, Prescott."

"I'm not sure if you remember, but I told you once you remind me so much of flowers—their soft petals, their perfect scents, yet strong enough to weather any storm. So I wanted you to have something to help you recall that whenever you looked at the ring."

"It's perfect. I love it."

He slips it on my finger and it fits.

"How did you know my size?"

"It was a shot in the dark of a guess."

I hold my hand out so we both can see.

Prescott takes it in his and tells me it's exactly the way he imagined it would look. Then he asks, "So when?"

"I don't have a date in mind. Do you?"

"I would like summer. And would you like to do it in Grand's gardens?"

"The question is would she?"

He laughs. "Are you kidding? She'd be in her element, showing both you and her flowers off."

"I guess we need to ask then."

A contrite expression flashes over him. "I kind of already did."

I laugh. "What do you mean by kind of?"

He rubs his chin and fesses up. "Okay. I full-out asked. I had to tell someone."

When we get home, they're the first ones we call. And Sara couldn't be more excited. Samuel is too, but Prescott is right. Sara is ready to parade me around in her gorgeous flower gardens.

"It has to be June or July. Around six or six-thirty. After the heat of the day. It'll be lovely," she says.

"Indeed it will," I agree.

Next we call Eric and he's so excited for us, but when I ask him to be my bridesmaid, you'd think I just handed him a million dollars.

"Oh my God. Yes, yes, yes. Wait! Does this mean I have to throw your bachelorette party?"

"Nah, I'm not having one of those. We'll just party at The Meeting Place."

"Okay, I'm all in. Wait. But I'm not wearing a dress."

"Why not?"

When there's no response, I'm afraid he hung up on me, so I call out his name.

"I'm here."

"Eric, I was only kidding."

"Yeah, I knew that."

He didn't. I gave him a small heart attack. Prescott is holding back a laugh and I'm having a tough time holding mine in.

"Viv, so I'm your man of honor?" Eric asks.

"Yep, you are."

Then we call Prescott's friends. We have them on speakerphone and Special yells out, "I knew it! I could tell something was up with you."

Prescott asks, "Me? How?"

"You were practically drooling over Vivi and wouldn't let her out of your sight. That's how."

"Yeah, dude, you were like her guard dog or something."

That makes me lift up and pay more attention to him.

"Really? He acts that way around me?" I ask.

"Good Lord, you'd better start paying attention more," Special answers.

We tell them the timeframe and they're super excited. Our final call is to Harrison.

"No surprise with the way you two were acting. You may as well just get it over with and elope."

"Nope. We're getting married in Grand's gardens this summer. And tell your parents because they'll be invited," Prescott says.

"Cool. I'll pass it along. And hey. Congrats, you two. I'm extremely happy for both of you. You guys are the perfect couple."

We thank him and hang up.

"That was fun."

"Yeah. But not as fun as this."

He pulls me to my feet and I have an idea of what he has in mind. I stop him and say, "I have to tell you, I can't wait until I'm Mrs. Beckham."

"I can't wait either."

He drags me into the bedroom, and his mouth crashes onto mine. At the same time, his hands part the opening of my shirt and tear it wide, popping every single button off. I gasp and he swallows it in his mouth as he yanks off my pants. Then he hoists me up and slams me against the nearest wall as he fumbles with his zipper.

"Can't wait. Sorry." His mouth devours mine again while his dick plunges into me. My fingers sink into his shoulder muscles as my heels find purchase on his ass. I meet his thrusts with my hips, using the wall as leverage, and look down to see his hard cock sliding in and out. It's hot, delicious, and sends more heat shooting through my veins.

Both of his hands are under my ass, but he moves one and pinches my nipple, playing with it. Then he crosses over to the other. Next he massages my clit and that's it for me. I'm off and running on the path to orgasmville. When I cry mine out, he follows, grinding his out against me. Then he drops his head into the crook of my neck, breathing hard.

"Love wall fucking you, Little Wolf. You sure know how to bring my dick to its knees in a hurry."

"Same for me."

He chuckles into my neck. "Didn't know you had a dick."

I pinch his nipple. "You know what I mean."

"Mmm. Yeah. I do know and love that I know. But know what else I love?"

"What?"

"Now no one ever gets to know what I know, because you're all mine and only mine. Forever."

CHAPTER 37

PRESCOTT—SIX MONTHS LATER

Large tents dot the vast grounds of my grandparents' estate. Grand's flowers are unreal this year. She had time to plan ahead for the wedding and planted varieties she'd never had before, expanding her ever-growing list of perennials and annuals. I'd never seen her so excited about the garden—and that was saying something. The caterers run all over the place, finalizing everything. The event planners are doing the same thing, coordinating with everyone.

Beneath one tent is a ten-piece band so we can dance the night away, along with a scattering of tables and a bar. The other tents will have food, tables, and more bars, including strawberries and our wedding cake. Vivi didn't want to go with the cupcake idea one of the planners suggested. She loves wedding cake, so we got the best of the best. We tasted them until we were blue in the face. The strawberries were my only requirement. I had to have them because they remind me of her luscious lips.

Weather-wise, the day turned out to be one for the picture books. The sky could not be any bluer or the temperature more ideal. It's almost four, so it's time for me to get ready.

Vivi is back in the master suite with Grand and Special. I think Special's grandmother may be back there too. I have no idea what Vivi's dress looks like. One time she told me it was covered in ruffles. I cringed. I fucking hate ruffles. Another time she said it had a high turtleneck with long sleeves. What the fuck? I don't even know what to think. I quit asking her.

I'm dressed and waiting with my guys when the wedding planner knocks on the door to take me downstairs. Vivi and I are meeting in one of the side gardens where it's private and away from all the activity. It'll be just the photographer, the wedding planner, and the two of us. When I arrive, the photographer tells me to face the other direction. Then I hear her call my name and when I turn, I'm speechless.

It's a damn good thing we did this first look because I almost fucking faint. If I had waited to see her to walk down the aisle, I would've looked like a super pussy.

She's the most beautiful woman in the world. Her dress is a creamy silk, but the top is lace and even though she looks naked, clearly she's not. When she stands before me, she winks, the little devil. She's going to get a good fucking tonight. It's the sexiest wedding gown I've ever seen.

"You're absolutely stunning … it's beyond my wildest dreams." I press my lips to hers. The whole time, the photographer is snapping away and I'm thrilled because this is a true photo op.

"You clean up pretty nicely yourself in your black tux."

We can only stare at each other because honestly she takes my breath away. For the first time, I truly know what that means. I take a moment to reflect back when she was attacked by Joe Delvecchio, then the subsequent trial, and his sentencing to twenty years in prison. She didn't cower in the courtroom or shrink from his venomous glare. In fact, she testified with strength and courage, and my pride in her grew exponentially. I'm not sure I could've done the same. This woman means more to me than my life.

Smiling, I ask, "So, I guess this means you're ready then? To become Mrs. Prescott Whitworth?"

"Yeah. And I'm glad you legally changed your name. Your grandparents are thrilled about that. And what better way for us to start out as a couple?"

The idea came to me shortly after Jeff accepted the offer I made for the house. Since there was never a relationship between us and never would be, it was crazy of me not to. So I submitted the paperwork. Then I wouldn't have to change it on our marriage license. My name change was made legal a month ago. I no longer have a middle name.

The wedding planner comes to tell us we need to get inside. "You don't want to be hanging out here when guests start to arrive."

We head indoors where all the guys, including Eric and Lucas, Special who is really pregnant and due in a couple of months, Cody, Special's grandmother, Grand, and Granddad are waiting. A tray of champagne is passed around and everyone except Special and Cody take a glass. A toast is raised to us and we sip our drinks.

"Are you nervous, Scotty?" Harrison asks.

"Not even close," I say.

"What about you, Vivi?" Eric asks.

"I'm only afraid I'll trip over these stupid feet of mine."

"Lucas," I say, "that's your job."

He gives me a thumbs-up.

The wedding planner comes in to let us know it's time. All the guests have been seated, and the guys need to take their places. I kiss my bride and leave, along with everyone else. Vivi, Lucas, and Eric hang back.

We walk in a line to the front, where the ceremony will take place, and I stand with my hand folded behind my back. Grand and Granddad sit smiling like they are the happiest people in the world. I almost wave at them, but catch myself at the last second.

Then Eric walks down the aisle. He looks so serious. I wish I could poke him and tell him to loosen up.

When the moment finally arrives, she walks down the aisle on Lucas's arm, carrying a bouquet of white roses. She remembered how I compared her to a rose that day and insisted she'd carry them today. Then I almost laugh at her ridiculous dress descriptions. Ruffles and a turtleneck. My Sexy Wolf. I can't wait to take that hot dress off her tonight to see what she has hiding beneath.

Uh, better not think of that right now, though.

The minister places our hands in each other's as he says our vows. We'd talked about writing our own, and went back and forth, but in the end decided to go with the traditional marriage vows. As soon as he says, "You may kiss the bride," I'm all over my wife, nearly picking her up off the ground to a round of applause. Then we turn to face our guests and the minister announces, "May I present to you, Mr. And Mrs. Prescott Whitworth?"

The clapping begins again with the music striking up. We march down the aisle and the party gets started. Vivi and I take the dance floor together and I do my best to show off, knowing I can't hold a candle to my buddy Weston. But Vivi loves it nevertheless. After the dance ends, Twinkle Toes himself steps forward and says, "Let me show the bride how it's done."

"Show-off."

I hand her over and damn, the man does have the moves. Vivi laughs and has a blast as he spins and dips her, and I've gotta say, I wish I had his finesse. When he's done, Eric steps up, then her friend Vince, and the line goes on. Finally I rescue my beauty and carry her off for a drink and some food. The night flies and at one point I'm standing with my bros when Weston raises his glass.

"You're not going to toast to my dick falling off, are you?" I ask. I do this because when he got married I gave the worst toast ever. It was to the tune of having so much sex his dick would fall off. I was hammered, what can I say?

"Oh, hell no. I wouldn't do that to you. I'm a little more poetic than you are, asshole."

"Thank God," I say.

"So raise your glasses, guys, and let's toast Scotty and Vivi. Dude, here's to a long, crazy, and mad life together. She fell in love with your madness. Don't ever try to be normal or change to fit in. She found your heart and loved the mad messy way it is. Whatever you do, don't try to fix it."

I clink my glass with theirs and realize he's right. I wasn't nor have I ever been normal and she never cared. She loved the raw and edgy person inside. I worried about it and made myself sick over it, but it never mattered because she loved me anyway.

"Hey, what's the cluster here?"

It's Vivi.

"Get over here." I pull her into my side. "My guys here were just toasting us." I glance at Weston and ask, "Wanna tell her what you toasted?"

He repeats it and she says, "It's so true." Then she stands on her toes to reach my lips. "Don't ever change. I'm in love with your madness, Scotty."

EPILOGUE

PRESCOTT

Three Months Later — Crestview Academy Ten-Year Reunion

"I can't believe you talked me into this," she says, tightening the strap of her sexy sandal.

"Why? You're going to kill it."

"I may kill them."

She turns around so I can zip up her dress. It's a sexy as fuck hot little black number that's simple yet elegant. When I'm done, I kiss her shoulder and spin her, getting the final view. The diamond necklace shimmers around her neck and the diamond stud earrings I gave her for a wedding gift reflect the lights, setting sparklers off all over the place. Diamonds really are a girl's best friend. I'll have to buy her some more since I adore seeing her in them. She doesn't give a shit about the things, but I do.

"You're going to blow everyone away with your beauty, Little W. You are extraordinary tonight. Every night. Morning. Day." I kiss her again. "Have I told you how damn happy I am that I went for coffee that day?"

She touches her finger to my lip. "Not today."

"Hmm. Too bad we have to meet everyone in the lobby." I pull the top of her dress down a little. "What I could do to those nipples."

"Stop it." She swats my hand away. "I don't want to walk around that party with a wet thong."

"You will. I've already decided on it." Holding out my hand, I say, "Let's go."

Everyone is already waiting. Special and Weston came for the night. Special's grandmother is babysitting their four-week-old daughter and both of them are a wreck over leaving little Sasha. We flew the Whitworth jet to Atlanta and picked them up before heading here. First thing in the morning we'll take them home. It's the only way we could get them to come and Vivi wouldn't go unless Special did.

"No way will I go to that thing," she said. "Those awful people." She shuddered.

"This could be your way of getting back at them ... of showing how you triumphed."

"I'll only go if Special goes."

Harrison and I had to practically kidnap both of the Wyndams. And Mimi, Special's grandmother, was never so happy in her life to be left alone with the baby.

"It's about time. Let's go," Weston says, walking outside, dragging Special behind him.

"What's your hurry?" I ask.

"The sooner this night is over, the sooner I can get home to our baby girl."

One look at Harrison and he and I both die laughing. We never thought our boy Weston would be so over the top about his kid.

"Slow down, I can't keep up with you in these heels," Special calls out.

"If we ever get pregnant, promise you won't get all nutty on me," Vivi says.

"Hey, no worries on that. I'm already crazy. Remember?"

"Right."

We climb into the giant van we hired for the night and are driven to Crestview. We have no idea why they decided to hold the reunion at the school, but whatever. When we get there, the place is lit up and it doesn't look like anything has changed since we graduated.

There's a table set up as we enter and we have to wear nametags. I write down Vivi's and my names and off we go.

The first person to approach us is our old principal. I smile because I know exactly what he wants.

"Prescott, it's great to see you. Could I have a private word with you, please?"

"I think anything you say can be said in front of my wife. You remember her, don't you? Vivienne Renard?"

I almost have to hand him his eyeballs back.

"Vivienne? Vivi Renard?"

"Hello."

He asks about the funding and I launch into the bullying, while Vivi observes with a smile. He's clearly out of his league. Then he tries to wiggle his way out of it.

Vivi steps in by saying, "You saw the way my locker was vandalized every day, yet you did nothing."

The principal squirms. "I didn't have a choice."

"You always have a choice," I say. "Nevertheless, I'm sure you understand why I can't support a school that condones and looks the other way where bullying is involved. Maybe this will be a lesson for you."

We walk away and run right into Felicia Cunningham.

"Prescott," she coos. "How wonderful to see you."

"Felicia. I think you remember my wife, Vivi Renard. Or Vivi Whitworth now."

"Ex-excuse me?"

"Hi Felatio, uh, Felicia. Hope you're well."

My cheek is raw from biting it at Vivi's name for her. And then Felicia can't speak. Before she utters a sound, we're making our way around the room.

"Nice. I liked that. Felatio."

"I honestly didn't mean to call her that. It slipped out." She laughs.

"Can I tell you something?"

"Sure."

"She tried to give me blowjobs all the time and I never let her."

Vivi stops and touches my elbow. "I'm glad you cleared that up for me." Then she kisses the corner of my mouth.

She takes my hand and we start walking again.

"I thought you should know."

She shakes her head and laughs. "At least you had discerning taste back then."

"I don't know about that. But she blew every guy and I think most of the teachers back then. She was actually pretty gross."

"Don't I know it. I caught her in the act a couple of times. That's where I got her name from."

The rest of the night we hang out with our friends, and most of the mean girls ogle Vivi. I'm sure they're envious because she's hands down the most gorgeous woman in the room.

Harrison comes stumbling over to the group and announces that Felicia wanted to know if he wanted a blowjob.

"She's still doing that?" Weston asks. "I guess some things never change."

"True, but others change for the better." I hold up my glass and say, "Here's to the better things in life. And may there be many more in our futures."

Later that night, when we're back in our hotel room, I look at my beautiful wife and say, "You've made me the happiest man alive. I thank God for that day I saw you and burned with a vivid desire. You made every single minute of chasing Vivi worth it."

She doesn't answer me with words, only with her hands, her mouth, and the rest of her body.

The End

Thank you for taking the time out of your busy life to read *Chasing Vivi*. I hope you enjoyed the book. If so, I would be extremely grateful if you would consider leaving a review wherever you purchased this book. Thank you very much!

*If you want to get the back story on Special and Weston, you might want to check out *A Special Obsession* if you haven't already done so.

A SNEAK PEEK FROM CRAVING MIDNIGHT

TO BE RELEASED 11/2017

*THIS IS RAW, UNEDITED, AND SUBJECT TO CHANGE

Chapter One
Harrison

As soon as the phone rings, I'm wide awake, pulled out of the coma-like sleep I was in.

"Kirkland," I answer, heading for the bathroom. Any time I get a call at 2 a.m., it means I'm going to work.

"Harrison, it's Wyatt. We have an issue."

"Who?"

"Midnight Drake."

Midnight Drake is the sultry actress who recently signed a multi-million dollar contract with Alta Pictures. "Didn't we get things ironed out for her recently?" I ask.

"Yeah. She was caught driving with an open container."

"Hmm. What is it this time?"

"Pack a bag, boss. You're flying to Manhattan. Wheels up in one hour."

"Fuck. That bad?" I ask around my toothbrush.

"Yep."

"Okay. I'll call you from the plane and you can debrief then."

In less than thirty minutes, I'm on my way to the airport, taking the backroads from my Malibu home. At this hour, traffic poses no problem. When I arrive, I drive straight to the entrance for private jets, and follow the road around, after going through the designated security checkpoints. I park, and my assistant is there, along with the pilot. Wyatt has assembled the team and they're boarding the jet as I do.

"Good morning everyone. Pete," I say, greeting our pilot. "Where's Tom?"

"He'll be here in a minute."

"Good. Do we have coffee yet?" I ask.

A flight attendant pops his head out from the back and says, "We will in a moment, along with some breakfast."

"Oh, hi Mike. Didn't see you back there."

"Morning, Mr. Kirkland."

Everyone takes a seat and I call Wyatt. "I want deets."

"Am I on speaker?"

"Yep."

And he begins, "Midnight Drake woke up in a hotel room about a little over an hour ago, naked, alone but with a shit ton of sex toys and three videos. Apparently while she was pumped full of heroin, a shit load of kinky fuckery went down, and the videos went flying over the internet. Her agent called and it is one freak show."

"Kinky fuckery, huh? Care to elaborate?" I ask.

"I'm hitting you with the videos now. But they include anal, butt plugs, whips, cuffs, flogging, a spreader bar, nipple clamps, labia clamps. Let's just say Midnight was on full display."

"Fuck."

"Exactly," Wyatt says. Alta is already saying they're dumping her.

"What is she saying?" I ask.

"She was drugged."

"Clearly."

"She says she remembers nothing."

"Did you watch the videos?"

"Yeah, and she's out of it. Unresponsive in the first one. Then the second she's a little bit there. The third, she's so fucked up she wouldn't care if someone cut off her head. I shit you not."

"Sounds like someone spiked her drink. Stupid or naive girl. Okay. Has our New York team found her bedmates? And have you pulled the videos?"

"Yes to the videos and working on the bedmates. Everything was sent from a cell phone."

"Track the fuckers. You know what to do. Where is Midnight now?"

"At the hotel with one of our team. She's totally freaked."

"Right. Wouldn't you be?"

Wyatt chuckles. "I'd be getting the fuck out of town."

Suddenly I'm pissed at those ass wipes. They're like those leeches or computer hackers, out to destroy lives, all for what? A good fuck? Or because they don't have anything better to do. "Wyatt, did they demand any money from her?"

"Not that I am aware."

"Let's find them and I don't care what it takes."

That gets the attention of everyone sitting close to me. Heads perk up, bodies stiffen, eyes open wider. They know when I'm pissed and mean business and this just hit me the wrong fucking way.

Pete pokes his head out of the cockpit and tells us we're ready to taxi. We should be cleared for takeoff momentarily, since it's now 3 a.m.

"Buckle up, Buttercups. We've got serious work ahead of us. You know I ask a lot of you and I'm sorry for the early hour, but I also compensate you well. You'll be given an extra bonus if we nail these fuckers. By the way, this one stays under the radar."

The jet taxis toward the runway and we're soon taking off

into the dark sky. It won't be long before we fly into the sun. The team starts making calls. I have one man in particular I want to contact so I make the call.

"Mr. Kirkland. Are you in New York already?"

"Not yet, Rashid, but I'm enroute. I need you to do something for me." I explain the situation and tell him exactly what I need.

"The videos I've already taken care of. They have been removed. But it may take a day for me to locate the phones."

The tension flows out of me somewhat. "Thanks, Rashid. I'm glad Wyatt got in touch with you. We'll be staying at The Plaza if you can't get in touch with me by phone."

"Certainly, Mr. Kirkland."

As soon at Pete says we've cleared ten thousand feet, Mike shows up with coffee and breakfast. Emily smiles her gratitude. So do I. She is a grouch when she's hungry and her brain is not worth a shit. Leland declines the food but asks Mike to come back in five with a coffee refill. I ask for an extra breakfast, while Misha, who appears meek, nods her thanks, but everyone knows she's the most vicious attorney in the country.

This is a top notch team on this jet. If we were to crash, the entire Hollywood entertainment industry would be in a fucking jam because there would be no one worth a shit to fix their fuck-ups. Usually I don't have these emotionally charged feelings, but Midnight Drake has had more than her share of hard knocks. In a way, she reminds me of my friends, Prescott and Weston. Every time she gets knocked to the ground, she pops back up with her fists raised and clenched, ready to fight whoever's trying to push her down. Whoever did this to her will pay. I'll see to it.

My phone beeps and I see it's a text from Wyatt. I open it up and it's all the videos. Holy mother fucker. These are worse than hardcore porn.

"Gather round kids. We are on DEFCON 1." Then I press play. The women are affected the worst. And these ladies are tough as nails. But I want them pissed as hell and the goal has been accomplished.

Misha nearly flies out of her seat and starts swearing. "Mother fuckers are going down. Harrison, I want to personally cut their balls off. Look at her. Just look at her. She's fucking unconscious. She doesn't even know where she is. That is disgusting."

Emily takes over where Misha leaves off. "They should be castrated. Anyone who does that to a woman doesn't have the right to a dick or balls. What slimy assholes. And how can that other woman participate? When can I get my hands on their dicks to personally rip them from their bodies."

"Okay, ladies, let's control ourselves here. We need our best brain-power and I won't have that if you're angry. Calm down."

After the smoke no longer billows out of their nostrils and they've settled back down, I explain what Rashad said. "You both know he's like a bloodhound when I put him on a task. He'll find their phones and when he does, we'll have one of the guys bring them in. We'll … handle them appropriately."

Misha's brow shoots up. "Handle them? I want them on the bottom of the East River."

"Misha, we're not in the business of killing people. You're losing sight of our purpose. We need to clean it up for Midnight and get things back on track. I need to find out what Midnight's contract states and if Alta can drop her. I thought we checked for that after her last little issue."

Her chest heaves with anger. But she nods and Emily says, "Yeah, our anger is making us forget that Midnight is our mission, not the dickfaces. We can worry about them later."

"Right. So, this is what we need. Emily, work on getting her into rehab. People are very forgiving about someone with a drug problem."

Emily's brow furrows. "But that's admitting she has one when she doesn't."

"Doesn't matter. Even though the videos were pulled, they

were on long enough for people to have screen shots of that shit. Their impressions are solid. We can say she doesn't have a problem until we're blue-faced, but they won't believe us and we need credibility. The best way to move forward is to ask forgiveness. But in the meantime, Misha, we will go after those men and get a confession. That way we get a double whammy and when Midnight gets out in thirty or sixty days, the public will be dying to see her. They will crawl all over her and want her as back just like they want icing on cake. If Alta drops her, they'll get down on their hands and knees, beg her to come back and we may even arrange for an increase in her contract fees. Oh, and Leland, get to work on her apology speech. Relate it somehow to her tragic childhood. Do we know anything about that? If not, dig up something. I don't care if it's about a cat that died and she never grieved appropriately. Make it heart wrenching and emotional as shit."

The team goes to work, while I do a little research on Midnight. She started out in the porn world, like some actors do, trying to get noticed. She got noticed all right. Long black hair with eyes to match, I wouldn't exactly call her a raving beauty. She is, however, unforgettable. There's something about her that screams sex. She's definitely not your average girl next door. Having been cast in the kind of rolls that not many mainstream female actors usually want, Midnight is willing to spread her wings and try anything. Apparently at one time, she also spread her thighs a little too much. That may be what's gotten her into trouble. But it seems like the girl can't get a break. Then I stumble upon something that makes me do a double take. Born in Phoenix, her birth name was Velvet Summers.

"You have got to be kidding me," I say out loud.

"What?" they all ask.

"Did you know Midnight's birth name was Velvet Summers?"

"Oh, yeah. Her porn flick name wasn't fake," Leland tells me.

"How did I not know this?"

Misha shrugs. "Don't know. We have a copy of of her birth certificate."

"Who the fuck names their kid Velvet Summers?" But after I say it, I think of my best friend, Weston's wife. Her name is Special. Who names a kid that?

"Yeah, people are weird," Emily says.

I keep reading and find some interesting facts. Midnight's mother was a dancer, and not the type you'd bring home to meet your mother. She ended up in foster care but then fell off the radar when she was seventeen. It looks like she never even finished high school. Maybe she really did have a tragic upbringing. Her mother died ten years ago, when she was only fourteen, so perhaps that's why the foster care. There's no mention of a father in the picture anywhere. The plot thickens even further.

Emily announces she's gotten Midnight into one of the premier rehab facilities in the country. Located in Arizona, it has a spa like atmosphere. She'll be secluded from the Hollywood gossip and the rest of the world for a minimum of thirty days.

"It's pricey, but worth it, I believe. The reviews are astounding," Emily says.

"Good. We'll drop her off on our flight back to LA," I say.

Misha announces our legal team in New York is ready for us and we will be having a press conference.

I have to laugh. "Maybe we need to discuss this with Midnight first."

"Oh, don't worry, boss. I'll get her on board. By the time I'm done with her, she'll be as eager to crush the balls of those men as I am."

What they don't know is I'm going to have first dibs at those mothers and by the time the girls have their chance, those shits won't have any more balls to crush. It's one thing to fuck with someone who can defend themselves but to go after a girl you've drugged and raped? That's inexcusable and I" make sure they pay for it.

A SNEAK PEEK FROM A SPECIAL OBSESSION

Prologue

Special

The text had me scrambling to get out to L.A. I wasn't sure what I'd find when I arrived, but she'd been my best friend since first grade, and we swore always to be there for each other, no matter what. I knew she'd been through every avenue to tame her addictions, but the demon of drug abuse invaded her soul like the devil it was. None of the interventions had worked, and two years ago when I finally walked away, I'd been determined to stay out of her messy life of addiction. It had broken my heart worse than anything, but it was tough love, or that's what they say.

Except life isn't always what it seems. The old saying about walk a mile in my shoes nailed me right in the gut when I was caught off guard by her call a few weeks ago.

"I'm in trouble, Spesh."

This was nothing new for Sasha. Drugs had caused her all kinds of trouble since we were teenaged girls.

"What kind?"

"The real bad kind." Her voice shook, and it scared me something fierce.

"Sasha, you talking the kind where you need to get help again? Like the hospital kind? Because you know I don't have much money to spare since I just opened the bar."

"I wish. I don't need your money. It's way worse than what you're thinking. I did something really stupid this time." She cleared her throat. Her voice had an edge to it I'd never heard before.

I scooted forward in my seat and asked, "What's going on?"

"I...I—" There was a loud banging in the background. "I gotta go."

"Sasha, wait." It was too late. She'd hung up on me. Sighing, I stared at my phone for a full minute before getting back to work, but I couldn't get her out of my mind. Something was up, and I questioned whether or not I should call her parents. Then I recalled what happened the last time I did. They told me never to mention her name again. Nix that idea. So I played the waiting game. One day turned into two, with at least a dozen of unanswered texts.

Finally after five days, she called again. "I don't know what to do."

"Sasha, I can't help you if you don't tell me what's going on."

"If I tell you, it could put you in a real bad place too."

What the hell does that mean? I took a frustrated breath. "Do you want me to come out there and bring you home?"

"I'm scared. I think I'm gonna die."

"Sash, don't say that."

"No, no, listen to me. I know you're probably thinking I'm overreacting, Spesh, but I swear I'm not. I need you to do something for me. There's this, this thing ... if something happens to me." Panic laced her voice.

"You're talking crazy now." I tried to calm her, but she kept insisting something terrible was going to happen. Only she wouldn't give me any information and then she hung up.

Another week passed before I got an emergency text.

I need you to come here. Please! There are some things you need to know. My apartment. As soon as you can. Hurry!

And that was it. I tried to call, but her phone went straight to voicemail. I almost called the police, but something warned me not to. That was how I found myself running through LAX toward the rental car buses. I had to get to my best friend—the girl who I'd known as long as I could remember—to see what had gone so terribly wrong.

When I finally parked in the lot of her apartment complex, I checked my phone. I wanted to make sure this was it. My GPS directed me here, and even though it didn't surprise me to see how seedy it was, I rubbed my arms as my skin itched with fear. My heart pounded out a rock-hard beat that traveled up to my cheekbones and almost made my teeth rattle. The sun had long since set, and it was more than a little creepy walking up the rusty metal steps leading to her second floor apartment. Wasn't she scared living here? I damn sure would be.

When I got to her door, I held up my fist to knock, but one touch pushed the door open. It was pitch-dark inside, so I reached in and felt the wall next to the door, hunting for a light switch. When I flipped it on, the sight froze me in fear. Her apartment had been completely trashed. I didn't get farther than the doorway, but everything in her tiny living area was in shambles. Broken pieces of furniture lay in scattered piles, and her couch had been ripped apart with the stuffing torn out. The scene was so frightening, I hightailed straight back to the car.

"Sasha, what in the hell did you do?" I murmured.

On a scale of zero to ten, my anxiety level was at one hundred.

About a couple of months back, Sasha had texted me a number to call in case anything happened to her. At the time, I thought she was overreacting; now I wasn't so sure. The person who answered gave me explicit instructions. I was supposed to go directly to this individual's home and not stop or speak to anyone. It was imperative I do exactly as she said. I was to monitor my rearview mirror to make sure no one was following me. If I thought I was being tailed, I was to continue driving until I reached a point of safety. When I finally made it to the destination safely, I could never have imagined in a million years what I was stepping into. Sasha could never have prepared me for this, for what awaited me, or for what I would gain in the process. I didn't know whether to scream or to jump for joy. But I did know one thing. My life would never be the same again.

Chapter One
Special

Three Years Later

Jeb leans over and asks, "Special, what are we gonna do about that one?" He gestures toward the corner booth, which holds the imposing figure of an extremely inebriated man. His head rests flat on the table, forehead planted firmly in place, and it's obvious he's not going anywhere, any time soon.

"Aw, fuck. Who kept serving him?" I ask.

"Josie. I think she was hoping … you know." He waggles his thick brows.

"Dammit. I'm gonna have a talk with her. She keeps *hoping* with every guy who walks in this bar. This isn't a damn whorehouse."

Jeb chuckles. "Yeah, you better talk to her real quick then, 'cause her attire has been leaning more toward hooker than wait-ress lately."

Running a hand over my sweaty hair, I shake my head in disgust. "The hell. I've been so busy, I honestly haven't noticed. That bad, huh?"

"Spesh, I don't know how she works in those damn shoes she wears. You'd think she was working the strip in Vegas."

"Oh, God." The groan I let out lasts for a minute. I'm frus-trated because it's difficult getting good help these days, and I'm working my ass off keeping this bar running. Not that I'm in financial trouble. It's the opposite. Business has been fantastic, and that's the problem. I need good, reliable staff, not the kind that are here to pick up men.

"Maybe you should cut back on the hours you serve food," Jeb suggests.

"You know that's where I make a ton. It's a cash cow. When the customers have too much to drink and need some food to soak up the alcohol, they turn to the late night menu."

"Yeah, but you're running yourself ragged."

"No, shit. That's because I can't seem to find solid help, besides you." I check the time; it's two forty-five in the morning. "Let me finish cleaning up back there," I gesture toward the kitchen, "and then maybe that dumbass will rouse enough so we can order him an Uber or something."

"All right. I'll get the bar taken care of."

When I'm done making the stainless steel in the kitchen gleam, I step back up front. Jeb is standing next to the booth where the dude is passed out.

"Any luck?" I ask, wiping my hands on my apron.

"Nope. But he's not your average poor motherfucker, I can tell you that much."

"What makes you say that?"

Jeb laughs. "Check out his watch."

A brief inspection gives me no hints. "Okay. What about it?"

"It's a Patek Philippe."

"Aside from the fact I can't pronounce it, what, is it like a Rolex or something?"

He laughs again. "Let's say you could probably buy a dozen Rolexes for what he paid for that one."

I shoot a look at Jeb. "And how would you know? You don't even wear a watch."

He shrugs. "I've always had a fascination for them, and the reason I don't wear one is because I can't afford the ones I want to own."

Jeb is older, maybe in his late forties, though I've never asked. When I opened this place a few years ago, he came looking for a job and said he would be my most loyal employee. He's been with me ever since and has lived up to his promise. I've learned a little about him, not a whole lot though, but maybe somewhere in his past he had money. He doesn't have much now, or at least I don't think he does. Jeb is a wealth of knowledge, from trivia to how to change the locks on the doors, and he looks out for me. I still can't believe my luck in finding him.

He interrupts my musing and says, "But that's not the only reason."

"What else?"

He holds something up between his fingers and thumb. "Well, holy cow. Now I do know what that is." It's a black American Express. Imprinted on it is Weston M.C. Wyndham, V. "Yeah, this dude is definitely Mr. Money Bags. Did you check out his name? So what's he doing in a place like this? Not that my place is a dive or anything." And it's not. But it's not what you'd call a high-class club, either.

"Who knows? Maybe he decided to check it out for something different."

"Okay, I'll give you that. But most people have a drink or two. They don't get completely plastered and pass out on the table."

"True. So, what should we do?"

"Did you check him for a wallet or a driver's license?"

"Yep, nothing except the AMEX, a key fob, and a big wad of cash," he says.

Releasing an exhausted sigh, I make a decision. "Take him to my place."

He shakes his head. "Spesh, you can't do that. He isn't a stray cat."

"Right, but I live the closest." In the building next door, in fact. "And what are our other options?"

"It's not safe," Jeb insists.

"Oh, like he's gonna attack me in this state?" I point at the heap of drunkenness.

Jeb chuckles. "Yeah, I guess when you put it like that."

"Besides, I have his black American Express and his watch as collateral. I do know how to take care of myself."

He eyes the guy for a minute. "Oh? How's that? Are you going to use your vast martial arts skills on him?"

"Okay. No use in being sarcastic. I'll pull out my biggest kitchen knife and threaten to kill him."

Jeb cocks his head. "Oh, really? What if he happens to turn that knife on you?"

I hadn't thought of that, but I'm not going to let Jeb know. "Come on. He's not a killer. He's a drunk."

"Just for the record, I'm not a big fan of this idea. Knowing you as I do, I won't talk you out of this though."

"Meh, he'll be fine on my couch."

"We could just leave him in here," Jeb says.

"Not a chance. With my luck, drunk dude will wake up and try to break himself out of here. Then I'll have that expense and mess on my hands."

"Make him pay."

"That's not the point. Who will I get to fix it on a Sunday?"

"Yeah, I didn't think of that. Your landlord would be mad as hell too. What if he wakes up and goes crazy on you in your apartment?"

"I'll lock myself in the bedroom and call 911. Come on. Help me drag his dead ass to my place. I'm tired and need some sleep."

"Okay, but if this goes badly, you call 911, you hear?"

"I'll do worse than that. I'll karate chop the motherfucker in his balls."

Jeb shakes his head. "Such a comedian."

Getting a tall—at least six feet—drunk, and very solid man out of the bar with hardly any help from him is not easy. He does walk, but his legs keep giving out and we have to poke and prod him like we're driving cattle. By the time we get him situated on my couch, I'm worn out.

"Jesus, that was the most difficult workout I've ever done." I wipe my sweaty brow with an arm.

"You and me both," Jeb says. "He has to weigh two twenty. Solid as a rock."

"Help me get his boots off and you can leave." We tug and tug until at last his stocking feet peek out at the end of his jeans. I wheeze from the effort. It's weird that he wears work boots, but I don't mention it to Jeb. "Thanks for the help. You need to get on home. I'll see you on Monday."

Jeb leaves with a warning in his eyes and I nod. "Don't worry. I'll lock my bedroom door and call 911 if I have to." I slide the deadbolt behind him and head to the shower. The bed is yelling my name. As soon as I finish, I throw a blanket on plastered Weston M.C. Wyndham, V, and head to bed. Since the bar is closed on Sunday, I usually sleep as late as I want. I don't move again until the sun is high in the sky and my room is bright.

ABOUT THE AUTHOR

A.M. Hargrove

One day, on her way home from work as a sales manager, USA Today bestselling author, A. M. Hargrove, realized her life was on fast forward and if she didn't do something soon, it would be too late to write that work of fiction she had been dreaming of her whole life. So she made a quick decision to quit her job and reinvented herself as a Naughty and Nice Romance Author.

Annie fancies herself all of the following: Reader, Writer, Dark Chocolate Lover, Ice Cream Worshipper, Coffee Drinker (swears the coffee, chocolate, and ice cream should be added as part of the USDA food groups), Lover of Grey Goose (and an extra dirty martini), #WalterThePuppy Lover, and if you're ever around her for more than five minutes, you'll find out she's a non-stop talker. Other than loving writing about romance, she loves hanging out with her family and binge watching TV with her husband. You can find out more about her books at http://www.amhargrove.com.

If you want to stay up to date, subscribe to my newsletter here. And don't worry about your inbox getting flooded. That won't happen. In fact, you might wonder where the hell she is.

STALK ANNIE

If you would like to hear more about what's going on in my world, please subscribe to my newsletter here
or join Hargrove's Hangout here
Please stalk me. I'll love you forever if you do. Seriously.

Website
Twitter
Facebook Page
Facebook
Goodreads
Pinterest
Instagram @amhargroveauthor
annie@amhargrove.com

For Other Books by A.M. Hargrove visit www.amhargrove.com

For The Love of English
A Special Obsession
Chasing Vivi
Craving Midnight (November 2017)

For The Love of My Sexy Geek (A Vault Novella
—October 2017)

The Wilde Players Dirty Romance Series:
Sidelined
Fastball
Hooked

A Beautiful Sin

The Cruel and Beautiful Series:
Cruel and Beautiful
A Mess of a Man
One Wrong Choice

The Edge Series:
Edge of Disaster
Shattered Edge
Kissing Fire

The Tragic Series:
Tragically Flawed, Tragic 1
Tragic Desires, Tragic 2

The Hart Brothers Series:
Freeing Her, Book 1
Freeing Him, Book 2
Kestrel, Book 3
The Fall and Rise of Kade Hart

Sabin, A Seven Novel

The Guardians of Vesturon Series

Made in the USA
Middletown, DE
18 July 2017